LAYOVER

R. A. SCHWARZ

Lisa — I love flying Alaska. Hope you enjoy the book a lot

Rob

Copyright © 2013 R.A. Schwarz
All rights reserved.

ISBN-10: 1482329190
ISBN-13: 9781482329193

For Carolyn   Always in bloom

Acknowledgements

Much thanks and appreciation to my writing cohorts who encouraged and assisted me throughout this novel: Irene Fernandes, Rev. Fred Jessett, Joyce Lindsey O'Keefe, Valerie Wilcox, Daphne Pilon, Barbara Ulrich, Jette Townsend, Ward Harris, Joe Julian, and Dee Barnes.

Special thanks to Julia M. Stroud, Ph.D., of Shrink Write.com for editing and valuable insight on all things human. Also to Rita Gardner for editing and her expertise on the English language.

I am indebted to flight attendant Dot Luthy for sharing her knowledge of autistic children and to Scott Gilstead and Ken Turpin, of United Airlines for flight times and in route planning.

And a huge thanks to the flight attendants at United Airlines whose support and good cheer carried me through. This story is about winners. This story is about you.

January 22, 1:45 a.m. PST

The Boeing 757 made a silky descent through 10,000 feet in the clear night sky. The cabin lights had been turned off for landing and, with idled-back engines and lack of perceptible motion, the 150 passengers were hypnotized into silence. Through the porthole of the darkened cabin at door three-left, moonlight spilled onto the two flight attendants buckled into their aft-facing jumpseat. Under the radiance, Mary Magdaleno's ebony skin glowed golden while Fox Revelstorm's sandy hair turned halo bright.

 Even though the jumpseat was sequestered in the galley away from the aisle, Mary kept her voice low as she ran her fingers over her flying partner's thigh. "You must be losing your touch, Fox. Not once on this trip did anyone stomp back here to complain of being insulted and demand your name, only to return and apologize for the outburst. And of course, had the poor victim of your verbal fencing been female, she would have left a cocktail napkin with her phone number scrawled across it."

The corners of Fox's mouth turned upward. Mary momentarily reflected on how his beguiling smile rendered any onlooker helpless—even Mary—while his words carved up his victims with the precision of Zorro's sword.

"You're right," he said. "I'm not only losing my touch, but my wit, my youth, and next, probably my hair."

The plane shuddered as the landing gear deployed, and the engines revved to life. Mary raised her voice, the hint of desperation harmonizing with the whine of the turbines. "Listen, I still think fifty is too young to retire. I mean, with only three months to go for you—you know how it is. With you not living around here anymore, I might not see you again. And even when you were living here, you weren't one to drop by."

He patted her knee with affection. "Twenty-eight years is enough. Just remember the good times. We had a lot of them together." He could not explain the electricity that crackled between them. When he had met her, more than twenty years ago, he was a year past being cast adrift from the college sweetheart he had planned to marry. Though he was smitten with Mary, she had met her future husband a month before. Over the years, they both had acknowledged their attraction, but he was not one to fool with another man's woman, and she was not one to cheat on her man. Flying together was bittersweet.

As the '57 dropped into a nose-up attitude for final approach, they pushed their heads back in the protective position against the headrest, and gripped the front edge of the leather seat. She placed her hand on his as they touched down, and the reversers screamed until the jet decelerated and turned onto the taxi way.

"I've never asked before," said Mary. "Where do you go these days?"

He flipped on the overhead light and turned to her. "Where there's no evidence of human beings."

She sighed. "Such a waste."

Fox shrugged.

"Everyone says it was because of Elaine," she went on, "but I haven't bought into that. I think it's something deeper, much deeper. Not that finding your wife in bed with her minister is a minor thing."

Fox laughed. "Mary, you were never one for sugarcoating."

"I'm serious. You must be carrying some huge burden. Why would someone with such a gift of oratory go off where there's no one to talk to? You might need someone sometime."

He shook his head. "I don't have a gift for oratory. I'm just willing to say what most people want to say, but won't. I've learned how to do it in a way that doesn't get my head shot off. What I desire is nothing complicated. I just want to quit the human race, but I'm not ready to die. And I'm not going to quit it forever."

They taxied through a cloud of kerosene vapor across runway 1-6 Left to the North Satellite of the Seattle-Tacoma International Airport. As they came to a halt, the seatbelt sign dinged off, and the purser gave the "prepare for arrival" command. They popped up, disarmed their doors, and stood in the galley as the cabin turned into a beehive of activity.

Mary thought she was acting a little melodramatic, but Fox Revelstorm had always stirred her mind and her body, and she knew her chances of ever seeing him again were small. As with all flight attendants, one might fly a month with someone, then not see them for another year. But there would always be another time, except for now. From her purse she fished out a business card she had produced on her computer. She pushed it into his hand. "Even though I'm in the flight attendant phone directory, I doubt you have one." She managed a small smile. "So, here's all my info, and even a picture so you won't forget the black girl with the blue eyes. Someday you're going to need someone, a friend, an ally, or maybe even—well, even *that*, too. I want it to be me."

Fox tilted his head, slipped the card into his pocket, and put his arms gently around her. He gathered her to him and placed his lips on hers, ending twenty-odd years of pent-up passion. A minute later they broke apart and found a teenage girl staring at them.

"I didn't know old people could kiss like that," she blurted out, then covered her mouth. "Is there anyone in those restrooms?"

"I'm sorry," said Mary, "we forgot to unlock them, and you'd be surprised what else people our age can do."

Mary and Fox stepped back and held each other's gaze. Finally Fox said, "I'm glad you met Ben before me. Otherwise, well, I don't know. Go back to Ben and Kylie, give them my best, and don't worry about me."

She hugged him one final time. "I will go back to Ben and Kylie and I will convey your greetings, but what I'd really like to do is go back about fifteen years to those Maui layovers. I never told you, but I'd follow you down to the beach at midnight and watch you swim naked in the ocean under the moonlight. I should have joined you."

"I would have loved that," he said in almost a whisper, "but it was best that you didn't."

The aisle had cleared, they gathered their bags, and Mary ruffled his hair. "I don't want to prolong this. I'm here for you. Don't make this the last time I ever see you." A tear slid down her cheek and she bolted up the aisle and into the jet bridge.

Fox hung his head, and breathed deeply. Despite her urging, he would not call her. He pulled out the handle of his Rollaboard and trudged up the ramp past the podium where the customer service agent stopped him and handed him a note.

See me in my office immediately for debriefing. Cory.

By the time Fox reached the deserted in-flight office, he figured he'd skip all the obvious questions, such as why are you in the office at two in the morning and why the fuck are you fucking with me?

He crossed the darkened room and followed the jagged light that bled from a single cubicle onto the floor. He slid his slender six-foot frame into a plastic chair on the other side of a small desk. A flat-topped head tilted back, creating a slight jiggle to its jowls, and in-flight supervisor Cory Gaston flashed him one of those cheesy "I've got you by the balls" looks. Gaston tapped a file folder with his pen. "Revelstorm, your day is just beginning. You're on a 2:45 a.m. charter to Quintana City."

"Quintana City? In Central America? Cory, what are you doing here in the middle of the night? Did wife number three throw you out again?"

Gaston's expression soured like week-old milk as Fox went on. "Sorry, I'm done. If the crew desk wanted to draft me, they would have called. I'm legal to make it about as far as Yakima."

"Oh, you're legal all right."

Fox stared at him.

Cory slid forward in his chair. "I guess you don't remember. You waived your check-in time. So, all that sitting around for seven hours of creeping delays doesn't count toward your duty time. As I've always said, it's all in the details."

"I didn't waive anything except good-bye," Fox said, while he observed the irony first-hand. He shook his head as he eyed two moldy buns with a piece of dead meat wedged between them, now probably teeming with bacterial life, the whole mess sitting atop of a foot-high stack of file folders.

"We're short a body," Cory continued. "It's a seventy-five-hour layover at an all-inclusive resort, right on the ocean."

"Go yourself, then. Maybe you can recruit another candidate to have an affair with."

Gaston shot up. "God damn you, Revelstorm. I could have had your ass fired ten times over, if it weren't for that hero shit, even though it's ancient history. No one talks to me like that."

"Except me," said Fox, in a weary voice.

Gaston slammed a meaty hand down on a thick file. "Three more complaint letters."

"And I bet there's six orchid letters to counter those. Come on Cory. I walked in here the other day and you're all over Jennifer Evans for too much toe cleavage. Do you know how much revenue that woman produces for this bucket-of-bolts airline? The business customers love her, and you're threatening her with a letter-of-charge over toe cleavage?"

Gaston exhaled and wiped the moisture off his reddening face. "Let's start over. Will you please just sit down and relax?"

Fox spread his arms and smiled. "I'm already sitting, and I'm quite relaxed. I might point out that you're the one standing and the color of your face reminds me of stewed beets, or maybe strangulation."

With a clenched jaw and practiced precision Gaston lowered his oversized rear end into his undersized chair. "I have a r-request of you. We have a charter scheduled to leave for Quintana City at 2:45. The charter will kick off daily service there from Seattle through L.A. However, this charter is a nonstop. It's a '57. We had it fully staffed with six. We're down to three. Five senior babes traded for this layover-in-paradise carpooled from the north. There's a police mess on I-5. They're not going to make it. One line-holder is here, we hijacked a reserve, who came in from Denver around eleven, and I rounded up a volunteer off the Dulles all-nighter. As if you didn't know, the FAA says we need one more to be able to go. Reserves are tapped. If you agree to do this, we can leave on time. And we need to leave on time. It messes up the package if we don't. Sales have been working hard to get this route back because we screwed it up in the past."

"That's a surprise," said Fox, drumming his fingers on Cory's desk.

The supervisor went on. "If you waive your check-in time you're legal by a minute. Now, I've pulled up your line.

You have two three-day trips left in the month. I'll make them disappear, and you'll get paid for them."

Fox shook his head. "The days of making deals are over."

"I can pull this off," Gaston insisted.

Fox knew Gaston would say anything to get him on the plane and afterward would swear that the conversation never took place. He stood up and went behind Cory's desk and tapped on his keyboard. A minute later the printer chirped into life and Fox tore off the paper and set it in front of him. "You sign this, and I'll go. It just states, that if somehow you don't make those trips go away, you will replace me yourself, and if necessary, pay me out of your own pocket, in cash."

"Shit, I'll probably get fired for this." Gaston frowned and scratched his name on the paper, and pushed it toward Fox. "Now, get going."

Fox was nearly through the door when Gaston called out, "Are you still retiring?"

"In three months, on my fiftieth."

"With any luck, I'll never see your sorry ass again."

Fox paused to call over his shoulder. "Why, Cory, on my retirement day I plan to march into your office, bend over, and drop my drawers, so you can officially kiss my sweet ass good-bye."

2:20 A.M. PST

Fox skirted his way through the dimly lit Jetway past the few remaining passengers not already boarded. He squeezed through the cabin door dragging his suitcase behind him. He turned left into the harsh bright light of the twenty-four-seat first class section to meet the purser. He hadn't taken the time to pull up a crew list, so he had no idea who to expect. A head popped out of the galley and Fox grinned, pleased to see an old friend, Mike Braun, toting a tray of pre-departure water and orange juice.

Mike laughed and tugged his free hand through his spiky dark hair. "This is getting better already. Step into my office," he said, pointing toward the galley. "You have the next six hours to explain to me how the hell you ended up on this boondoggle."

"Mikey, how are you, and how's the missus? Sorry, I forgot, you *are* the missus," said Fox clapping him on the back.

Mike flashed a rueful smile and shrugged. "Can you believe it? I've been monogamous for nearly five years. That might have to change on this layover. This body doesn't deserve monogamy, even if Richie does. Anyway, here's the story. Gaston pulled me off the DC trip. I thought, seventy-five hours on a beach, or eleven hours trying to sleep during the day at Dulles. I took purser sort of out of default. We're not quite full in the back. Flight time is 6:34. Captain is Betty Boop—not really, let's see," he said, and yanked the briefing sheet out of his pocket. "Betty Briggs, and Ron Johnson is the first officer, both L.A.-based. Betty says we're going around some weather. If it dissipates we might cut off some flight time.

"Who's our fourth person?" asked Fox, with a quick scan of the cabin.

"Rita Sanchez. She's working on a seat-duplication. You know her?"

"Spanish-language person? Funny and sassy?"

Mike nodded. "Yeah, except I flew with her a month ago. She was pretty subdued. Not like her at all. Anyway, lucky for us she saw this trip in open flying and picked it up. Christ, we're going to Central America. You'd think they would have *assigned* a language person." Mike waved his arms in surrender. "Don't get me started."

"Beverages and buy-on-board food in the back?" asked Fox.

Mike nodded his head and started to crack ice with a mallet. "Full dinner up front. Over six hours but it's only the a la carte stuff in the back. It makes you wonder. Anyway, I made you number four. Of course, you're senior, and if you want—"

"Number four is fine."

Mike grinned. "I wanted you near an oxygen bottle. You may need it after you meet your jumpseat mate. She could probably melt a Siberian Tootsie Roll."

Fox tilted his head. "What does that mean? How would you describe her?"

"I don't know—maybe a chiropractor's dream, because she wrecks necks. She's that attractive. I think she's only been in Seattle for a couple of weeks."

Fox exhaled and rubbed his eyes. "Is it you or the hour?"

"Both." Mike pointed to the closet. "May as well throw your bag in there, your overhead space is probably taken. Also, might be a little bumpy on climb-out so stay seated until Betty calls us, and about three-and-a-half out we're supposed to hit a pretty long stretch of turbulence, so be ready to sit. That should provide ample time for your thigh and your partner's thigh to become thoroughly acquainted," he said with a wink.

"That's what I love about you, Mike. As a purser you're always thinking of your crew, but if this woman is so hot, my thigh is the last thigh she'll want to get acquainted with."

Mike patted him on the back. "Give yourself some credit. Just do your usual bit of verbal bludgeoning and she may kiss you just to get you to shut up."

"Now, you're making sense," said Fox as he grabbed his small tote and made his way to the back of the plane through the thinning group of unseated passengers. He paused, yawning and flexing his shoulders, feeling the fatigue of being up all day. He had risen early in San Francisco, spent an hour in the weight room, another hour running along the bay, and had shown up around 2 p.m. at the airport for a leisurely lunch. After a series of weather incidents and mechanical problems, the scheduled 4:15 departure finally departed at 11:40. He was nearly to the back galley when a female voice behind him in the aisle stopped him.

"You, there, flight attendant."

Fox halted, spun on his heel like a dancer, faced the voice, and quickly appraised its owner.

She pointed to her bag that sat like an orphan in the aisle, an overstuffed Rollaboard. "Stow this and be careful with it, don't just slam it in there."

Fox rubbed his chin. She had obviously been planning for this trip. It was the dead of winter and she was already undressed for hot weather. Her skin was tanning-booth brown, bottle-blonde hair, body lean and buffed, and exposed abs, ripped. Her twenty-something angelic face belied the harshness of her voice.

In a gentle tone and with a smile on his face, Fox said, "So, you want your bag stowed. I suggest you begin to get a return on the money you spent for those enhanced eyelashes by batting them a few times. I'm sure that simple action will create an NFL-size pileup of eager he-men more than willing to convert your every whim into reality." That evoked a few snickers from nearby passengers. She reddened and narrowed her eyes.

"No one talks to me that way. I'm insulted."

Fox shrugged and widened his smile. "No, you're not insulted. You're just a little embarrassed for acting like the Queen of Sheba when you know better." Now the entire back half of the airplane was laughing. "I'm sorry," Fox continued, his voice light and bright, "but the company frowns upon us hefting bags. Bottom line is this: stow it yourself, get someone to do it for you, or take it to the door and we'll check it."

By now, two young men had hefted the bag with mock gentleness. One said to the other, "Remember, we're under orders to not just slam it in there," and they pushed it inch-by-inch into the compartment, gingerly shutting the door. Before returning to their seats, one formally bowed, the other curtsied, and the crowd clapped its approval.

"I'm going to write a letter and have you fired," she hissed.

"Good, if I'm fired we can spend more time together. I never said I didn't want to be your man, I just don't want to be your bag man."

She bulled her way across the legs of an elderly couple in the middle and aisle seats, not bothering to wait to let them get up, threw herself into the window seat, and stared straight ahead.

Fox snatched his tote bag and continued on to the galley amidst a smattering of applause.

. . .

When Fox boarded the airplane, flight attendant Antoinette Joséphine Sabatini was positioned in the extra space between the rows at the window exits, monitoring the passengers. In the middle of rearranging the contents of an overhead compartment, Joey turned to ask if she could place an elderly woman's bag upright, when Joey spotted Fox and froze, eyes wide.

"Can you what?" asked the lady already seated one row behind the exit.

Joey stepped back and bent over, gasping for air. She pulled a sickness bag out of the seat pocket and breathed into it a couple of times to catch her breath. "I'm sorry," she said, "I'm feeling a little faint. I think if someone can turn your bag up, this gentleman can stow his Rollaboard next to it."

"Honey," she said, putting her hand on Joey's wrist, "when I first laid eyes on you I thought I'd seen the second coming of Grace Kelly. But now, you look more like Casper the Ghost. Go take care of yourself."

Joey hurried to the restroom next to the aft galley, thinking of her great aunt's expressions of "nuttier than a fruit cake" and "loonier than Saturday morning cartoons." I really am nuts, she thought. Maybe I'm not totally crazy, only a little sick. But this was the moment she had been waiting for; this was the moment she had planned for. She eyed her complexion in the mirror, as her breathing slowed, rubbed some color back into her cheeks, and fluffed her shoulder-length blonde hair. Her apprehension remained acute, but she was determined to hide it from him.

As Joey stepped out of the restroom, she witnessed Queenie barking her demands to Fox and his performance.

Fox stepped into the galley and Joey took a deep breath, forcing a confident smile. "Your reputation may precede you," she said to him, "but the reality is right behind. I wonder if the second part of the equation will come down the way I hear it's supposed to—the part where she comes back to apologize and leaves you her phone number. I'm Joey," she said, extending her hand with a slight nervous shake.

Fox took it, as if to steady it, flashed her a weary smile, and nodded. "Fox Revelstorm. You know, Joey, I'm a freaking idiot. All I want is total anonymity. I spend my days off alone.

It would be so easy to sail under the radar with this job—" He stared at her, silent for a moment.

She cocked her head. "Are you all right? The legendary Fox Revelstorm at a loss for words?"

"Sorry," he said, his smile still intact. "You reminded me of someone I met long ago. Anyway, I'm the last guy who wants a reputation, but sometimes my mouth goes off before my brain is consulted," he said, checking his safety harness at the jumpseat.

"I've checked the equipment for both positions," she offered.

"Thanks," he said, inspecting the door pressure gauge with his flashlight. "I just got off the 57 domestic and I always have to figure out where all this over-water equipment is on the 57U. At least we'll have plenty of room on the jumpseat."

"I know what you mean. I came in from Denver sitting next to a girl so big that one of my cheeks was left hanging in the air." Joey pointed to the countertop. "My flight manual is still open. Coffee?"

He nodded. "Black."

She continued with some galley setup chores, all the while observing him complete his safety checks. She had heard he was about as cynical as one could get toward Consolidated Airlines, but, she noticed, not when it came to his safety check. On the other hand, she thought, he's been in a crash that killed twenty-one people.

Fifteen minutes later the 757 pushed back, and Fox and Joey settled side by side into their jumpseat.

"Mike said you're new to our base. Where did you come from, and why?" asked Fox.

"New York. Seattle doesn't open very often. I spent part of my childhood here. I heard the base was friendly and low-key."

"You realize you'll be an old lady before you get off reserve in Seattle."

"I know it's the most senior base—I just thought I'd give something new a try."

They leaned back as the jet started its takeoff roll. Joey closed her eyes for a moment to slow down her racing heart. *Why don't you just tell him? It's such a simple thing. Just ask him to put his arms around you, just as he did sixteen years ago. Now you're afraid. You're afraid it won't feel like it did back then. Of course it won't, but what if it does? That's even worse, because when he had his arms around you, you felt as if you were being cradled by the hands of God.*

3:00 A.M. PST

The jet streaked upward through the cloud layers, pitching and rocking in the light chop. Joey wondered what might be different the next time they climbed through 20,000 feet. After all, that was three days away. A lot could happen in three days.

They remained seated, waiting for Captain Betty's call, and Joey, still jittery, fought past her nerves to make conversation, thinking the mundane might make Fox seem more human. "So where do you live in Seattle?"

"I don't."

"Where then?"

"Around."

"Around where?" she persisted.

"What's with the twenty questions?"

"I might leave it at two questions if we could get past the first one."

"What if I said it was none of your business, where I live?" he asked through a smile and crinkly eyes.

"What if I said the reason everyone, including me, wants to know about you is because you don't want anyone to know about you?"

"I'd say you were probably right."

Joey loosened her shoulder harness. "I heard you don't own anything, that you cash your paycheck at a bank where you have a savings account with one dollar in it, and you just carry the money with you."

Fox reached into his pocket, yanked out a wad of bills, and tossed it in her lap.

"What's that?" she asked, with mock anger, "A proposition?"

He shook his head. "A down payment."

"For what?" she asked, handing the wad back.

"Your silence."

"But you haven't revealed anything, yet."

He turned to face her, once again drawn to her eyes sparkling like emeralds in the low light. He took in the smoothness of her skin and the symmetry of her face. "About every five years or so, I meet someone who affects me like a couple of milliliters of sodium pentothal." Almost unconsciously, with his index finger, he smoothed her hair back and ran it down the length of her cheek. "My pretty, freckled, young seatmate, when you get home you will probably plop down wherever it is you plop and ask yourself: Why the hell didn't I just sit on the jumpseat and keep my mouth shut, instead of encouraging a man old enough to be my father to blab away?"

"Maybe," she said, not believing a word of it and wondering if her cheek glowed where he had touched her.

• • •

Halfway through the initial beverage service in the economy section, the cabin hadn't lost many passengers to sleep. Most were watching *The Polar Express*, which provided jagged kaleidoscopic lighting, while others played video games, chitchatted, or read.

Subtly, Joey observed Fox's every movement and every snippet of dialogue, which is what you do, she thought, when you're obsessed. She initially wondered how someone like Fox could have ever been hired, if he wasn't a people person. From what she had heard, he had a reputation as being smart-mouthed, purposely engaging passengers to agitate and verbally spar with them. She saw and heard none of that. His demeanor was relaxed; he was polite, soft spoken, and friendly, especially with the seniors. He was a bundle of contradictions.

Fox leaned over and asked a rotund preteen kid playing a video game in an aisle seat if he'd like a beverage. Without looking up the boy replied, "It's about time. Pepsi, lots of ice, two straws and don't open the can."

Fox sighed, knelt down and in a soft voice replied, "When someone is serving you, you set down what you're doing, make eye contact, tell them what it is you want, and say 'please' and 'thank you.'" The kid banged the game down and glared at Fox, as did his father sitting next to him.

"The last time I checked, I was the parent," said the dad.

Fox nodded. "Part of parenting is teaching your child manners. So far, you've flunked that and nutrition," he replied, eyeing two seat-back pockets bulging with a large pizza box, two bags from Burger King, and a couple of empty Cinnabon holders lying on the dingy carpet partially in the aisle .

"That's enough. Give the kid his Pepsi and get out of my face."

"No problem," Fox replied, and placed the unopened Pepsi on the tray and began to fill a cup with ice.

"Harold," his wife barked out, "he's right. All this darn junk food. You two just keep stuffing yourselves like you want to end up as paté." She raised her head toward Fox. "Thank you, sir. Please give my son a cup of water and take away the Pepsi."

After setting the water on the boy's tray, Fox gazed across the cart. Joey was staring at him. "You need something?" asked Fox.

"Yeah, sorry," Joey blushed, fumbling through a cart drawer. "I was sort of lost for a moment. I need a vodka and two rums. The mini tray must be on your side." Fox handed her the three bottles and they continued to the rear.

Fifteen minutes later, after finishing the service and breaking down the beverage cart, Joey turned and, this time, caught Fox staring at her. *Returning the favor.* He didn't pretend he wasn't.

"Is something wrong? Is a foreign object hanging from my face?" she asked.

"No, ma'am. I was just sort of gawking. Well, not sort of, completely gawking."

"Why?"

"Because you're worth gawking at and I haven't gawked in a long time. I'm enjoying it."

Her face reddened.

"Look," he continued, "I'm not picturing you any other way than you are, and I'm thinking I may not be the first. I hope you don't mind."

"It depends on who's doing the gawking," she said, thinking she'd been the gawker ever since he walked on the plane. "Are you finished?"

"I don't think so. My eyes aren't as sharp as they used to be. They're telling me there may be something flawed in your makeup."

"Not likely—I don't use much," she said, her voice low and coy.

"I was talking about mental makeup."

"Of course you were. I suppose I should be honored for being called a nutcase by the great Fox Revelstorm." *And I am a nutcase.*

He smiled and shrugged his shoulders. "Flattered, not honored," he said moving toward the aisle. "I'm going to see how Mike and Rita are doing up front."

Fox strolled toward first class, mentally clubbing himself in the head with a baseball bat. *What in the hell do you think you're doing? You're coming on to her like you're a college kid. You're forty-nine years old and in the space of a couple of hours you've done something twice, that you've never done in twenty-seven years of flying—touched your jumpseat partner. What were you thinking, running your finger down her cheek?*

Shaking his head, he stopped to survey the first class cabin, standing just behind it.

But, what was she doing closing her eyes and moving her head toward me?

Rita Sanchez spun out of the first class galley, situated between the cockpit and row one, with a dinner tray in one hand and a basket of rolls in the other, heading for 6D, the last customer without a meal. Fox moved past her, plucking an empty wine glass from the waggling hand of a man in 4B, and gathered in two finished trays from a couple in 1A and B. Mike was setting bowls of ice cream on a three-tiered cart as Fox deposited the dirty trays into a battered tray cart.

"How's it going?" asked Fox.

Mike snorted. "Christ, you'd think it was three-thirty in the afternoon, instead of three-thirty in the morning. They're all awake. They're needy and whiney, but not a bad crowd, except for the Hitler-youth in 4B. If you have a chance, chop his balls off. He's running poor Rita ragged and, for some reason, she just takes it. Not like her at all."

"I've already had my one confrontation for the evening."

Mike yanked a couple of bowls of hot fudge out of the oven, yelped a little, and waved his fingers. "Yikes, that's hot! Maybe I can drop a load of this chocolate in his lap and scald his balls off."

Fox continued to pick up, ignoring the pointed finger from 4B, while studying him. In his late twenties or early thirties with short blonde hair and icy blue eyes, his body language told Fox that he was used to getting his way and to giving orders, probably brought up by a cowering nanny. When Fox reached his row, the man looked up and, through clenched teeth, said, "Where's my wine?"

Fox flashed him a benign smile. "I didn't know you brought any wine. How should I know where it is?"

"Listen smart—"

"Oh, I get it. You meant, where is *our* wine? It's in the galley. I'm guessing you'd like some more of *our* wine." Fox heard seats creaking and the muted squeak of leather as the passengers not watching the film craned their necks.

A row behind, Rita straightened up from pouring a cup of coffee, her eyes now suddenly bright and rolled her tongue around her lips in anticipation.

Out of the corner of his eye, Fox saw Mike emerge from the galley like he was Doc Holliday backing up Wyatt Earp at the O.K. Corral.

Fox continued in a flat tone, ignoring the passenger's clenched fists and bug eyes. "We respond really well to 'please, thank you, and patience.' We don't respond to pointed fingers and raised glasses."

"Nobody talks to me that way. I'll have your ass fired."

"It's a funny thing. That's the third time I've heard that tonight."

"Which part?" Mike chimed in.

"The 'nobody talks to me that way part'. The firing thing—only twice."

Now, headphones were coming off and chuckles were free flowing.

"Allow me to introduce you to Mr. Heinrich," said Mike.

Heinrich, stared at Mike, said, "Doesn't he know, the customer is always right?"

"So, Mr. Heinrich," said Fox, regaining Heinrich's attention, "you can be right, or you can drink *our* wine."

Heinrich snapped his head back to Mike.

Mike shrugged and opened his hands. "I pretty much have to go along with my flying partner."

Mike and Fox retreated to the galley. "Nice work," grinned Mike. "Balls removed with surgical precision."

A minute later Rita entered, dark eyes flashing and dancing, wearing a smile wide enough to hold the Rio Grande. "Do you, like, want to sleep with me tonight? It was so beautiful. I just stood there in front of Heinrich waiting—everyone was waiting—and finally the guy across the aisle, who I think may be his boss, said, 'Well, how bad do you want it? How bad do you want the wine? You heard the man, so do you want to sit on your sanctimonious ass and be right, or do you want to drink?' And everyone cracked up. Finally, he said it. It was like he was being tortured to say it. When he said 'please' everyone started to clap.. His face was redder than my lipstick. But, if looks could kill—"

"I'd be Swiss cheese," finished Fox.

"We heard the clapping," said Mike.

"I just hope we've heard the end of him," said Fox, and departed to the aft galley.

3:55 A.M. PST

As Fox made his way to first class, Joey Sabatini had leaned back against the counter in the aft galley. She rested on her elbows, wondering what had happened. For the last sixteen years she thought of Fox every day and admitted to herself that she had had no idea how she would react if she ever saw him. Since on reserve in Seattle, she could not control her schedule and, with Fox's records locked, she couldn't find out what and where he was flying. Just as she imagined, their encounter was totally random.

    When she was almost twelve, she flew from her mother's home in Seattle to live with her father in San Francisco. He was a single man, gentle, but a disciplinarian. Life with him was a boring prospect compared to her mother's mansion with its menagerie of singers, dancers, and thespians. Though Fox had sat and chatted with her on the flight, he had not given her advice. He had only asked if she thought her father loved her. She told him, "That's the only thing I'm sure of."

"So," he had said, "If I were you, I would give him a chance."

In that simple statement she felt as if she had somehow discerned Fox's essence. She remembered thinking, in her twelve-year-old fractured fantasy, that if she married, she would marry such a man. An hour later, Fox pulled her from the burning wreckage of the 737, protecting her body with his and holding her as they jumped on the slide. It had been ten seconds of perfection she'd been chasing ever since.

She knew she had deified him over the years and now, in the dim light of the galley, she understood that she had thought of him as a fatherly sage—a mentor or a guru—as he had seemed when she was a little girl. But something had happened. *I was expecting Obi-Wan Kenobi and instead I'm getting Han Solo. I'm coming on to him and he's responding. Oh my God, what's happening to me?*

When Fox returned to the aft galley a half hour after he'd left, Joey was perched on the jumpseat seat leafing through a stack of fashion blueprints. Fox pulled out a biography of Beethoven and leaned against the counter to read. They said little to each other over the next hour, except when Fox let her know that Mike had leftover steak in his oven.

"I think I'll go see if any vegetables came with the meat," she said, rising.

Fox nodded and she left. The movie finished, the stampede to the restrooms came and went. Most of the passengers closed their eyes, leaving nothing except shadows and strobes cast from a few reading lights, handheld video players, and the ever-present whoosh and hum of the metal tube slicing through the air.

Two lanky teenage girls appeared in front of Fox, faces screwed up, hands twitching, and feet moving in place.

He set down his book. "What is it, ladies....everything okay?"

"Um, we were wondering about the woman you're working with. Is she who we think she is? Is it really her? Her name badge says it's her."

Fox yawned, and set his reading glasses on the counter. "Who do *you* think she is?"

The older one thrust a magazine into his hand. "Her."

Fox glanced down at a glossy page and stared into the brilliant green eyes of Joey Sabatini modeling a black cocktail dress. He flipped through a five-page layout, while mentally flipping out. He let the magazine fold shut. *Vogue*. "Wow."

"Well?" she asked.

"Jeez, it sure as hell—I mean it looks like her. I only met her tonight. Have you seen other pictures of her?"

"Oh, yeah. She's sort of famous. Not like Kate Moss, but she's in all the fashion mags. That's why it's so strange to see her working on an airplane."

"Yeah. Wow. Um, she's taking a break, but when she gets back I'll send her over," he said, scratching his head.

"Do you think she'll get mad if we ask for her autograph?"

"I don't think so," he said, still trying to process his flying partner plastered across the pages of *Vogue* magazine.

"Twenty-nine A and B. Thank you, sir," said the younger one and they were off, leaving Fox as stupefied as they were excited.

"You look like you're in outer space." It was Queenie standing in front of him this time.

"I'm a little tired," he said, looking her over. He was surprised by her confident smile and relaxed demeanor.

"You had a little fun at my expense," she said, still smiling.

"I guess I did."

"But you tried to engage me; get me to laugh along."

Fox opened his hands. "That was the idea. Look, I'm really sorry. I should have just told you that if I got hurt stowing your bag the company would consider it my responsibility. That should have been the extent of the conversation."

She shook her head. "No, this is all on me. Thanks for putting me in my place, I deserved it. Celeste Starr," she said, extending her hand.

Fox took it, introduced himself, and let her go on. "It started with the Shuttle Express guy using his muddy foot to try to squeeze my bag into the back of his van. Then it was the Amazon with attitude holding me up in security and dumped the contents of my bag, then the bag itself, on the floor. Then I was subjected to a pat down," she said, tapping her flat stomach. "All that caused me to lose my first class seat and, on top of that, the customer service agent chastised me for being late—anyway, not only did I lose my first class seat, I lost my class. I treated you the way I was treated and I'm truly sorry. I want you to know I'm not a whiney helpless bitch on a rampage."

"Why do you want me to know?" asked Fox.

"Because you're right, I was embarrassed, and I'm still embarrassed. The other reason I want you to know is I figure I have a better chance of convincing you to let me buy you a drink in the next day or two. After all," she said with a shy grin, "you didn't say that you didn't want to be my man."

"I appreciate the apology and the offer, but I have to point out that I'm old enough to be your father," Fox replied, thinking her initial transparency was beginning to fill with substance.

She lightly pushed a blonde lock behind her ear. "Instead of watching the movie, I've been watching you. You don't seem the type to fish for compliments, and it's already been established that you're sharper than a scalpel. I figure I may have only one shot at this so, excuse me if I get too personal. But somehow you've become important to me. So, this is what I know: Your chest is bigger than your stomach, you're really nice to the passengers, and your flying partner," she waved her hand toward the front galley, "she looks at you like you're God. This is what I *think* I know. Your body is hard and your heart is soft. You're self-confident and unafraid, yet unimpressed with yourself. You escort little old ladies across the street, don't play video games, and, if we kissed, wouldn't try to give me a tonsillectomy with your tongue. Those qualities are attractive to me and rare. I don't *care* if you're old enough to be my father." She stepped closer. "So, how about that drink?"

"I'm going to be fifty in three months. What would we talk about?"

"I'm going to be thirty in two months. We could talk about art, we could talk about birds, or," she glanced at the spine of Fox's splayed paperback, "we could talk about Beethoven. Can you imagine being at the debut of his Fifth Symphony? It would have been like listening to Jimi Hendrix doing 'Purple Haze' for the first time."

Surprised, Fox studied her in the dim light, pleased that his initial impressions could be proved wrong. Suddenly her supple youth amplified the shabbiness of the airplane—foam molding half hanging from the ceiling, the battered and dented stainless steel that served as a countertop, the duct tape covering the clogged drain, and the stale odor emanating from the restrooms. The airline was in a state of decay, dying a slow death, and suddenly she was a beacon of life. He was tempted to grab hold of her. For an instant he wondered if it was more than a coincidence—his mind having been staggered by three women in a matter of hours—but he dismissed the notion and then dismissed Celeste Starr.

"I'm flattered at your interest in me, and I would be at any age, but I don't think it would be a good idea for us to meet. I like you too much already."

"I made the assumption you don't have a wife and three kids at home. Am I wrong?"

"No," Fox said, thinking her voice sounded like nectar, if nectar had a sound. "And, you?"

"Unattached. Can you elaborate upon your reluctance?"

He hesitated. "I'm sorry."

She nodded and slowly pulled something from the pocket of her shorts and, as if it were precious, gently pushed it into the palm of his hand. "Call me if you change your mind."

He glanced down to see a handwritten number on the back of a business card. "Where are you staying?" he asked.

"I own a home on the water. A cottage, really—with a studio. Think about it. I won't bite. At least, not at first."

4:45 A.M. PST

Alone, Fox leaned against the counter, carefully avoiding a jagged piece of protruding metal. He turned Celeste's card over to look at the photo of an Edenic painting. Fauna and flora glowed with lushness so bright it seemed to illuminate the dinginess of the galley, yet something dark and disturbing was also present. He studied the curly letters bisecting the mysterious view of paradise. *Celeste Starr Artist-Designer*

Slowly he pushed the card into his pants pocket and yawned again. On long, night flights most of the passengers slept, watched videos, others read. After using the restroom they might stretch their legs for a minute and engage the flight attendant in conversation before returning to their seats. But there were always one or two of the dreaded standers coming to the back galley to stretch their legs and to share their life stories. Usually, listening to a stander's monologue was like trying to follow a leaf in a hurricane or consuming a bottle of Excedrin PM. Like the passengers, the flight attendants had little space of their own. A couple of extra babbling bodies occupying it for long periods were an invasion. He was grateful for the solitude.

Fox took a couple of gulps from his water bottle. He plopped down on the jumpseat, his mind reoccupied with trying to digest the seemingly unbelievable fact that Joey was a fashion model working as a flight attendant. He wondered what the hell she was really doing. *Sort of like how everyone wonders what the hell I'm really doing.* He couldn't fathom it. Surely she made more in a few hours of modeling than she did in a month of flying max hours on reserve for Consolidated Airlines. FBI and CIA popped into his head. At the same time he noticed a shadow looming over him.

Fox raised his eyes to see Heinrich's blonde hair shining like a lightbulb. He slowly gathered his feet beneath him and covered his mouth as if to stifle a yawn. "Hello, Gustav, or do you prefer Gus?" he asked, as the jumpseat snapped shut into the wall.

"Mr. Heinrich to you," he said lurching a bit.

"Okay, Mr. Heinrich," Fox said, moving to the other side of the galley to fetch the coffeepot. "Care for a cup?" he asked as he poured one for himself.

Heinrich shook his head.

Fox noticed that, despite Heinrich's tailored gray slacks and light-blue designer sport shirt, a faint stench of nervous sweat emanated from his torso. He took a swallow of coffee, set down the cup, opened his arms, and flashed his best smile. "Apology accepted, Mr. Heinrich."

"I did not hear myself say anything, nor did I come back here to apologize," he said, his voice strangling the words.

Three passengers appeared, all eyes intent on the two restrooms, leaving an elderly red-headed woman to wait.

"Get you anything, madam?" Fox smiled.

"Call me Bess. *That's* the trouble," she said patting her stomach, "you keep offering water and I keep drinking it, and then I have to wake up my seat partners to get out so I can get rid of it. Next time I'll try for an aisle. Thanks for asking, but I've had enough." She glanced at Heinrich. "You don't look happy."

"This flight attendant does not understand the meaning of customer *service*."

She shook her head. "Could have fooled me. The two back here have been wonderful." She switched her gaze to Fox and raised her eyebrows as if to say, "What gives?"

"You know, Bess," said Fox, looking directly at Heinrich, "we sometimes have passengers who, no matter how much they get, it's never enough."

"I know exactly what you mean," she said, catching his drift, "and I just hate it when one selfish passenger takes up all the time of the flight attendants, treating them like they're his personal servants and the rest us have to wait to get any service. It's just rude, don't you think?" Directing her attention toward Heinrich, she continued. "On my last flight, the man next to me constantly rang the call button, demanding this, demanding that. He was about my age and when the other passengers would walk past my row they looked like they felt sorry for me, stuck with the idiot. I wanted to put a sign on my forehead that said, 'I'm not related to this bozo.'"

Heinrich grimaced and glared at her.

"Ah," grinned Fox, "sounds like an older version of Mr. Heinrich here. He has a first class seat, but mistakenly thought it was a throne."

A bead of sweat popped out of Heinrich's brow, and he tried to casually wipe it away.

The aft restroom door opened, allowing the escape of a plume of vintage blue-room odor, followed by a man barely squeezing himself through the door.

Bess grinned at Fox's comment, letting the air clear for a moment. But, as she was about to enter, she turned and pulled herself ramrod straight, as if to summon every ounce of moxie she possessed, and addressed Heinrich. "I bet you didn't care much for the comeuppance, young man. I saw how this gentleman handled a pushy blonde with the oversized suitcase and an ego to match. But whatever you got, it serves you right, because you should know better." She gave him one jerk of her head for emphasis and snapped the door shut.

Fox turned his attention back to Heinrich, who now looked like he was dressed in a straitjacket. Fox nodded his head and shrugged his shoulders. "That about sums it up, Mr. Heinrich."

Heinrich raised his hand and took a quick step forward. Fox calmly took a step back. Heinrich unclenched his fist and thrust it into his pocket. "I came back here to inform you there will be consequences for what you did."

"Oh, wonderful. You're actually going to pay me for the lesson. Fabulous. How much?"

"You don't quit, do you?"

"Well, the thing is, I live alone," said Fox, deliberately sounding inane, attempting to lighten the mood. After nearly thirty years of dealing with boors like Heinrich he had learned to repel their malice like water rolls off a duck's back, but Heinrich was a bit different. He had Fox's attention.

"You will not like these consequences, I can assure you," said Heinrich.

The smile vanished from Fox's face. "Would you care to restate that? Someone else might misconstrue that as a threat. I'm sure you had no such intention, since that could carry serious consequences."

"Are you threatening *me*?"

Fox ignored the question and leaned back against the counter. "So, why not tell me again why you came back here."

His ruddy face now drenched with sweat and turning even redder, Heinrich hesitated then carefully regurgitated the words like they were blocks of wood. "I'm informing you that I did not appreciate you using me as a prop to show off your unfunny comedy routine."

Fox nodded his head. "Fair enough. Message received. It won't happen again. Let's leave it at that."

A shadow seemed to momentarily engulf Heinrich's face then vanished through his pores. His hard stare turned into a knowing smirk and his taut body relaxed. He nodded his head. "Yes, you are right; we will leave it at that." He turned around and sauntered back up the aisle to first class as if he hadn't a care.

Fox shuddered. Experience told him that it was usually the wine talking, that Heinrich would take a little nap and wake up a new man. But somehow this was different. Heinrich was too focused and too deliberate. It was as if he had decided something, something that amused him. That thought chilled Fox, and he dumped his lukewarm coffee into the drain and refilled his cup.

He then rang Mike in the front galley and related the incident. Mike informed him that Gustav Heinrich had already drunk his last glass of wine.

After a brief conversation with a retired engineer who had been part of the original Boeing 757 design team, Fox made a swing through the dark cabin, doing nothing but answering "How much time is left?" "Three hours," was his reply. He returned to the galley and attempted to immerse himself in the Beethoven biography, but could not stop thinking about Heinrich. He had seen incidents where passengers lost their tempers, yelled and screamed, and calmed down. Heinrich hadn't done that. He had controlled his anger even after he seemed to cross the breaking point. *Anger and I go back a long way, and Heinrich's is the worst kind.*

He dimmed the light, mostly to obscure the stark shabbiness of the galley's décor, and took a seat. A minute later Rita Sanchez appeared in front of him and offered him a plate of chilled shrimp.

"Maybe later," he said. "Sit down, and talk to me. I need distracting."

"From what?"

"Your boyfriend in 4-Baker. He gives me a bad feeling."

"You, shaken up by a passenger?" asked Rita, with raised eyebrows.

"He doesn't fit the profile." He shook his head, frowning. "Anyway, enough of him. What about you? It has to be at least a year, maybe longer, since we flew together."

She sat down next to him, and pushed her long dark hair away from her face. "I was just thinking about that. We had a layover in San Antonio in the fall, so it was actually a little over two years ago. We did the Riverwalk, listened to a mariachi band, and had a couple of beers," she said.

Fox remembered how much he liked the sound of her voice, the richness in the way she rolled the vowels off her tongue. She leaned back and went on. "I asked you about your love life and you joked that you were down to one- or two-night affairs with married women and was I interested? In hindsight I should have accepted your offer, because at that very time my husband was beginning an affair with methamphetamine and his supplier."

"Whoa, that doesn't sound so good. I'm sort of afraid to ask what's happened since then. Don't you have a kid?"

Fox watched her head tilt as she emitted a little sigh. "A son. He's seven now."

"So, what *did* happen?"

She shrugged. "Nothing unusual. My ex blew through our savings, and ran up our credit cards to the max before I realized I was number three in his life, at best. I divorced him. He's in the East somewhere. He didn't even call last month to wish his son a happy birthday."

Rita shook her head, stood up, and rummaged for a tea bag. She plopped it in a Styrofoam cup and filled it with hot water from the spigot. Repeatedly dunking her teabag, she seemed mesmerized by the tea bag moving in and out of the cup, treating the bobbing bag as if it were a hypnotist's medallion.

Her husband's betrayal was nothing compared to her son's diagnosis of autism, which weighed on her heart like an anvil. Even though she was seeing a counselor, she had not told any of her flying partners. As she dunked she considered confiding in Fox.

Finished with the bag, she resettled herself next to him. She was about to blurt it out, but instead steered the conversation in a different direction. "It's not *that* dramatic," she said, raising the cup to her lips.

"What can I say? I just hope you're all right," said Fox.

She shrugged. "Yes, I'm fine, except for feeling like a statistical cliché. Another story of the single mom having to fly more because of salary cuts. It's not particularly unique."

In the dim light, he listened closely to the unhappiness in her voice. "I have a feeling you're past that and something else is wearing on you, besides flying a hundred hours a month."

She sipped her tea and took a deep breath. "I'll just spill it. I can do it in about three sentences. You can tell me what you think."

Fox nodded. "It's not like I'm pressed for time."

"So," she said, "what does a girl like me want? And what is about the hardest thing a girl like me can find? A good man. A man willing to take on my baggage, love me, and love my son like he was his own and give him, you know, the strong male presence thing. I found such a man. I've been seeing him for nine months. He's crazy about me. He's crazy about my kid. He wants to do Little League and all that stuff. Money-wise, he's loaded. He got into Google at the beginning and is still one of their top software designers. He wants to marry me and move us into his three million dollar home in Medina. He looks like a movie star, he's thoughtful and considerate. There's not a mean bone in his body. In short, he's perfect."

"I think that was twelve."

"Twelve what?"

"Twelve sentences, but then, who's counting?"

"Some wiseass, I think," she said, chuckling.

"Are you sure you want to know what I think. I'm not exactly Dear Abby."

"I should hope not, and I wouldn't have asked if I didn't want to hear it."

"Well," Fox replied, raising his eyebrows, "you told me he was perfect, but your voice told me he's not so perfect."

"No, he *is*. It's just that, well, emotionally he doesn't, um, thrill me. My heart doesn't flutter when I see him or think of him. There's no intensity."

Fox rubbed his chin. "Would you care to rephrase that statement?"

She took a deep breath and exhaled it. "Okay, in bed—"

"Ah, that kind of emotion. Now, we're getting somewhere. Sorry, go on."

"He's incredibly gentle and he knows what he's doing. But for me, there's no, um spontaneous combustion. I never feel like I can go crazy, you know, just sort of lose it. I'm just not getting the electricity. I feel like I might embarrass myself."

"Maybe you don't feel like you can spontaneously combust, because he hasn't spontaneously combusted himself with you," he replied.

"What are you saying?"

"How many times have you made love somewhere, other than in a bedroom and someplace other than in bed?" Fox asked.

"None."

"Okay, this is easy and because of your current financial status, I won't charge you. I might normally seek compensation in another way, but since I'm down to married women, that eliminates you as a candidate, so I guess this is a freebie."

"So, what's easy?" she asked, throwing up her hands.

"Finding out whether you should marry Mr. Perfect-not-so-perfect or you throw him back in the sea."

"How?"

"Simple. Get rid of your son for the night, invite Mr. Perfect over for dinner, and answer the door wearing only an apron. That should change the nature of his appetite. As far as electricity goes, your knees on the carpet in the living room should create plenty of that."

Rita rolled her eyes.

Fox shrugged. "You get my drift—I don't know. Maybe bring out a bowl of strawberries and whipped cream. Show him that sometimes it's more fun to have dessert first. Christen the kitchen table or something. I imagine that unless he's an alien, he'll spontaneously combust. When he does you will too, then you and your son can move into his mansion in Medina and live happily ever after."

Rita burst out laughing. "Where do you come up with this stuff?"

Fox grinned back. "I'm a multiple-time failure in love. Failure can be very educational. Listen," he said quietly, "It sounds like he *is* a great guy who's just a little overprotective, and treats you like a fragile piece of china. Just give him another side of you to fall in love with."

"You make it sound so easy."

"And fun." Fox made a circle with his thumb and index finger and put it in front of his eye like it was a monocle and scanned her up and down. "Ah yes, irrefutable evidence."

"Of what?"

"That you have the tools. So, use 'em."

Rita was grateful for the levity and the distraction. But she wondered why she hadn't told him that there would be no Little League, no Boy Scouts, and—as she had learned from her doctor only last week—no more children. She was afraid someday her perfect man would wake up and wonder why he had cast his lot with her, when he had wanted so much more.

6:30 A.M. PST

Fox wondered if Joey had been avoiding him, then dismissed the thought. Why would she? Nevertheless, she had spent nearly an hour in the forward galley chatting with Mike and Rita, before Rita had wandered aft. Twenty minutes later the captain called to warn of impending turbulence and to prepare to sit down. Joey finally returned and began to help him stow loose items—cups, water bottles, orange juice cartons, and half-filled cans of soda.

"Hey," said Fox, "I've got this covered. Before it gets rough, why don't you go see two girls in 29A and B? Take paper, something to write with, and don't worry about waking them." She started to question, but he shooed her away. "Get going: it could get bumpy any minute."

He allowed himself a moment to watch her step deliberately into the aisle, with a languid graceful glide, as if it were a fashion runway. He figured she was probably one of about ten women on the planet capable of making the Consolidated uniform gunnysack look decent.

Fox was strapped in when she returned, the plane already bobbing and weaving through the sky like a drunken sailor. Joey lurched toward the jumpseat. Fox grabbed her outstretched hand and hauled her down just as everything unsecured flew upward. He kept his hand on her knee as she scrambled into her harness.

Once belted in, she smiled at him. "Thanks, I think you would have had to scrape me off the ceiling. And I'm sorry for not letting you know."

"Know that you're a model?"

"Yes."

"You're not obl—"

"It's sort of awkward, because I feel like I'm calling attention to myself, but most of the time I let my flying partners know because usually one person on every flight tells me I look like me, just like those girls asked you. I mean, you had no idea, I'm assuming."

"You are correct."

"So, it's just being polite."

"So, obviously, you know the next question that's coming."

"Obviously. The 'what are you doing working as a flight attendant' question. And the answer is that I have my reasons."

"I might stop with the second question if I could get past the first," Fox mimicked her from their earlier conversation.

"I like it better when I'm asking the questions," she said as his body was thrown into hers.

"Fine. Ask away," he replied as she slammed into him.

"How did you end up doing this?" she asked.

"I was chasing love."

"Really?"

"Really."

"What kind?"

"The female kind, in the form of one Brenda Bethesda," he said his teeth rattling between words.

"Explain, please."

"I'll give you the really brief version and, depending upon how forthright you are, some more details later. I met her in college the middle of my junior year and she changed my life. Or, I should say she showed me how I could change my own life. She showed me how to let go of my anger, taught me how to deliver my message without malice, and taught me to let go of the past, at least as much as I can. She had taken a job with Consolidated and ended up in London. So, I joined up. Damn."

"What?"

"Some guy is up trying to make it back here," said Fox, eyeing the mirror in front of him which gave him a view of the aisle from their aft-facing jumpseat. Ten seconds later the man ended up in a heap next to them in the galley. "The Fasten Seatbelt sign is on," Fox, said, "and in case you haven't noticed, this plane has turned into a bucking bronco."

"I just woke up. I gotta go," he said, grabbing the counter and pulling himself up.

"Okay, I understand. Go into the restroom in front of us, but stay in there until we bang on the wall. You're safer in there."

Joey pinched his arm. "You were saying."

Fox exhaled and refocused. "Anyway, the London domicile wasn't open when I graduated from stew school. I ended up in New York. She got tired of the long-distance relationship. It took me a year to get based in London and, by that time, it was too late. She'd met a man she married and is still married to. I remember the last time I was with her. Maybe instinctively I knew it would be the last time because I savored every moment, and can feel it as if it happened yesterday. And, damn, I've been chasing that feeling of bliss, my arms around her, ever since, knowing it's never going to happen. I thought I had it back a time or two, but it was just a physical illusion. So, there you go."

Joey stared straight ahead as if she hadn't heard him.

"You okay?"

She didn't respond.

He gave her a little shake in addition to the moderate chop that still tossed them around.

"Sorry. I'm just a little light-headed," she mumbled.

They rode out the rest of the turbulence in silence, absorbed in their own thoughts. Fox's uneasiness multiplied as he wondered why he was preoccupied with Joey Sabatini. *Somehow you've put her off. Why do you care?*

Oh my God. The man I've been chasing all these years is crazier than I am. But through her hand she felt a sudden flash of perfect comfort, just for an instant. She looked down at the hand that he had grasped to pull her into the jumpseat, and it was the same hand that had pulled her out of the wreckage, all those years ago.

The turbulence abated, and with an hour-and-a-half left in the flight, once again Fox and Joey resumed their beverage cart duties, but there were few takers. When they finished Mike appeared with a half-full bag of trash and a crooked grin on his face.

"What did you do?" asked Fox. "Find yourself a date and you want early absolution?"

"Well, I *was* propositioned. Actually, all of us were."

"What are you talking about?" asked Fox.

"Jesus, Fox," said Mike, staring at him. "You should be nodding off by now, and you look wide-awake."

"It hasn't exactly been my average day. So, what's with the proposition?"

"Well, the guy in 4-Charlie? His name is Ramirez. He's some rich guy and he owns a bunch of land in Quintana. Tomorrow night he's having a huge bash and he wants us to help with the serving. He's a little vague on what exactly we're supposed to do. I guess dignitaries from a bunch of countries are attending and he thinks it would be quite a coup to have a crew of American flight attendants serving up the food. And here's the kicker: he'll pay us ten grand in American cash. If you're slow with the math, that's twenty-five hundred apiece. And I could use the dough. My house is bleeding me like a medieval doctor."

A ding-dong sounded, indicating a call from the cockpit. Mike answered the phone and a minute later set it down. "Betty needs a potty break."

"Do you need one of us behind the cockpit barrier? I think Rita may be chatting up some guy in the exit row," said Fox.

"No, Rita's in the galley. She can stand guard unless you want to hold her hand."

"Her hand wasn't what I was thinking of holding."

"Of course not," said Mike, striding into the aisle.

Joey peered up at Fox, her green eyes targeting him. "What do you think about Ramirez?" she asked, her voice quiet.

He shook his head. "No way. Heinrich is connected with him. At least that's what Rita said."

"I think she's right. I heard most of Ramirez' proposal. It's all of us or none of us," said Joey.

"It's not like I'm swimming in money, but I'd rather give Mike and Rita five thousand out of my own pocket. But what really bothers me is why would anyone, including Ramirez, pay that kind of money for a random, ordinary flight crew? It makes no sense. I'm sorry," said Fox, "I won't do it."

She rose. "I mostly agree. But it's hard to walk away from a windfall. I'll go tell them."

"No, I'll do it. I can be my own messenger."

"I'm going to have a talk with Ramirez," she said. "Rita told me that when everyone was laughing at Heinrich no one was more amused than Ramirez, which makes me think you're the one he really wants. But maybe I can convince him to take on the three of us, without you."

Joey was three steps up the aisle when she felt his arm on hers. They went back to the galley. "Look, I don't want you to go. I have a really bad feeling about this," he said.

"You don't understand. If Ramirez will take the three of us, I *have* to go. *They* need the money."

"Fuck. It's a mistake."

"We'll be fine. Heinrich has this vendetta with you. Not us. That's why Ramirez will go with the three of us. Once I make that clear, he won't want you two near each other. We're Americans," she added. "What are they going to do? Kidnap us?" She flashed him a smile and disappeared up the aisle.

Fox kicked the cart in front of him, the dread and adrenaline reminding him of the day he decided his foster father would die if the bastard ever laid a finger on his sister again.

11:15 A.M. CENTRAL STANDARD TIME

From the top of the hill, the hotel's red-tile roof projected bejeweled light into the surrounding flora. The four gaped through the smudged windows of their van. Even Joey, who was no stranger to exotic beaches and seaside resorts, blinked her tired eyes for a better focus. As they descended the switchback road, reddish-pink stucco cottages came into view, hovering above the ocean and glowing in the morning sun. Seabirds wheeled and cried and a faint saltiness emanated from the sea as they drew closer. One- and two-foot waves broke evenly on the white sand to frame the picture of paradise.

Five minutes later they stood under a porte cochère behind the battered Dodge waiting for the elderly driver to unload their bags. Joey seized the opportunity to study her flying partners for the first time in the light of day. Mike's cowlick-spiked hair and loose-jointedness gave him an impish look, a sort of dark Dennis the Menace. Rita undid her ponytail with languid grace, exemplifying the easy motion with which she moved. Joey turned to Fox, watching him rub his eyelid with his index finger, as if it would magnify his vision. She noticed a touch of gray at his temples and wondered which of his parents had possessed the youthful skin that belied his age.

Suddenly he turned to her, catching her stare.

"I was sort of gawking. Well, completely gawking," she said.

"Why are you gaping at a broken-down old man, when in any direction you can see Eden?" asked Mike.

"Contrast," she answered with a crooked smile, hooking her tote bag onto her Rollaboard.

They shuffled into the open-air lobby and returned morning greetings from the staff. After Mike had scribbled their company info on the sign-in sheet, he handed each of them an envelope with their key cards and announced he would be conducting a debriefing by the pool bar at 5 p.m., if anyone cared to join him. With contagious yawning they wound their way through a maze of gardens and bungalows until they reached the end of the asphalt path where they came upon two duplexes perched above the beach. Mike had seen to it that Joey and Fox occupied the same building.

Joey pushed open her door and went in to survey her surroundings. She came back for her bag, which Fox had just set down on the doorstep. She motioned to the wall. "Adjoining," she said.

"Have a nice rest," he said, retreating.

"What if I can't sleep?"

"I'll leave my adjoining door unlocked. You can come in and I'll tell you a bedtime story. And since I don't know any bedtime stories, I'll just ramble on, and pretty soon both of us will be asleep." With that, he ducked into his suite.

Despite her weariness and lack of rest Joey stepped onto her deck and plopped into a director's chair, staring at the waves. She found herself fantasizing about tiptoeing into Fox's suite as a kid in pajamas and having him hold her until she was either asleep or in heaven. The only problem, she thought, rising and snapping out of the reverie, is that you're not a kid anymore and you don't own a pair of pajamas.

Before climbing into bed, Fox showered for fifteen minutes, washing away the remnants of the long day and an unsettled mind. He had often thought of his life as a series of defining moments—mostly grisly events that had changed him—yet brought clarity and progress despite wholesale disaster. He shivered under the hot water. He didn't want another defining moment. He didn't *need* another defining moment, but wondered if another one was coming—as inevitable as the next wave breaking upon the sand below.

The crew met at five for drinks, which morphed into a sunset dinner with wine, witty conversation, and a frank question from Mike to Joey: "So, how much do you make modeling?"

"Way more than I deserve for what I do."

"Playing it coy, are we?" Mike grinned.

"I'm good at coy."

The banter carried on into the evening, filing off some of the sharp edges of Fox's unease. At nine-thirty he was back on his deck, staring at the ocean's phosphorescence below him, sleep merely an elusive tease. At precisely midnight he made his way to a secluded part of the beach, shucked his robe and trunks, and plunged into the sea. As always, the ocean felt like a giant womb, vast but personal, and he floated and swam in silence under the moon for nearly a half-hour before dragging himself back to his bed, now certain he could sleep in peace.

Instead, he dreamt he was back in the burning 737, flames shaped like fire-spitting dragon heads, billowing at him, while coils of smoke swirled around him, crushing his chest, muting his voice. He tried to scream out to the twelve-year-old boy staring at him from the other side of a pile of twisted metal and making no effort to crawl to safety.

His attention was diverted by a pair of green eyes, tractor beams that seemed to squelch the flames and dissipate the smoke while drawing him away from the boy. He discovered a young girl whose arm was pinned under a pile of carry-on luggage. In a blink he freed her, covered her body with his as they crawled to the exit, and held her in his lap as they jumped on the slide. Just as quickly, time decelerated and they inched their way downward in slow-motion for what felt like an eon. Finally at the bottom, they were hauled to their feet, and he felt her arms encircle him and her head sink into his chest. It comforted him for a moment. But with another blink he was back on the plane with the dragons and snakes, sure his body would explode from the heat and the pressure. He futilely implored the boy to squeeze his way through the tiny opening, but this time, there was no mistake—the ever so slight shake of his young head.

As always, that roar of silence awoke Fox. He rolled his drenched, naked body out of bed and into the shower. He jammed the handle to full cold.

During that late summer flight, fifteen years ago, he had chatted with the two unaccompanied minors. At the time, he thought it ironic both were on their way to new homes. Neither child was happy about it. Fox had sat down in the aisle seat with the middle seat empty between them and asked the boy if he was looking forward to living in California. The twelve-year-old hunched forward, folded his arms around his chest, and leaned into the window as if he were trying to disappear. He shook his head, jaw quivering. Because of Fox's own upbringing, a faint alarm went off in his head and he considered the possibility that the towheaded boy was facing sexual abuse. Fox's further gentle asking neither confirmed nor denied those suspicions. Finally Fox asked what he would like best about living with his aunt and uncle. The boy relaxed his taut body and almost smiled. They had an Irish setter named Fancy Feathers and all he wanted to do was run with her through the oak-lined meadow all day. Fox asked if he had a picture of Fancy. The boy nodded and struggled to squirm out of the backpack still attached to his left shoulder, to retrieve the photo. Fox reached over and slipped his hand under the strap. Fox felt the boy's body freeze, and the young voice say, "Please don't touch me," just as Fox's sister had said so many times until she was unable to discern affection from submission.

Fox withdrew his hand from the boy's shoulder, but not his concern. He had the address. He would follow up.

After the crash, he was sure the boy would have faced sexual abuse and his fury burned as hot as the fire that had consumed the boy. Fox was certain he had chosen to die in that airplane rather than face his uncle. Fox did not grieve idly.

His initial reaction was to kill this man; it was only a question of how and where. As the weeks passed, his explosive anger subsided into a controlled rage and, like the phantom he had been in his younger days, he invaded this man's house, sure he would discover evidence of a pedophile. But, after a thorough reconnaissance, he found nothing, only a husband and wife devastated by the loss of their nephew.

Who then, if anyone? He kept digging, spending his spare time invisibly surveying the seven-acre estate that sat on a knoll in Woodside, California. Finally his efforts paid off. He noticed that the gardener was always at the edge of the property near the road at 3:30 in the afternoon, the time when the school bus swung by and stopped, letting out several children. He began to tail the gardener, and gained access to his cottage. Fox found photographs of the nephew, as well as other boys. The photos were nothing incriminating, but Fox discovered a safe in a wall that he believed contained child pornography. He had no evidence. Nevertheless, he went on the offensive and sent a short note to the gardener:

Mr. Nelson, I know who you are and what you do to children. There is no place where you can hide from me. Try as you might, you will never see me, yet I will be watching. If you lay a finger on a child or have any sexual conversations or innuendos, I will render you unconscious. No, I will not kill you, but when you awake, the first thing you will see is a jar of liquid with your surgically removed testicles floating in it. You made Jonathon Wellington's life a living hell and, if you continue, I will see to it that hell seems like a vacation for you.

Fox periodically stalked him. It took nearly a year for Nelson to slip up. With an ultra-powerful zoom lens, Fox photographed him through the small rear window of Nelson's van, naked with a young boy. Anonymously, he sent photos and the license plate numbers to the police, hoping that there was sufficient evidence to search his bungalow. That started the downfall of Charles Nelson, as others came forward. He was later convicted of child rape and possession of child pornography, and sentenced to more than twenty years.

Fox told a woman about this—his brief onboard relationship with the boy, his outrage, and his plans. She was a surgeon willing to cut off Nelson's balls. She never received the chance.

Fox awoke at seven with an uneasiness he attributed, not to his recurring nightmare, but to his three flying partners' agreement to go to the Ramirez estate. As he made his way into the bathroom, he noticed his slightly bloodshot eyes in the mirror. He wondered if his misgivings also stemmed from his ridiculous flirtation with Joey Sabatini. *What kind of fool am I? The kind betrayed by a celibate body for almost a year.* His MO was to find a woman wanting precisely the same thing he did: splendid company, relaxing sex, a heartfelt hug in the morning, and a "Maybe we can do it again in a year or so" attitude. It was simple enough, yet extremely hard to come by.

While he waited for the faucet water to heat up for a shave, he was drawn to the brilliantly colored business card resting atop the marble counter. He fingered it and flipped it over in his palm. While the others were serving caviar and champagne at Ramirez's estate, perhaps he'd raise a glass with Celeste Starr. I deserve the distraction, he thought, and I suspect Celeste and I could amuse each other for a night and forget each other in the morning.

JANUARY 23, 8:00 A.M. CST

The first surprise of the day that Mike received was a call from one of Ramirez's people. Her accented English was singsongy and rapid. After her greeting and inquiries about the previous day, she merely said, "Please be ready at 11:30. We will pick you up."

"11:30? Mr. Ramirez said 2:30 to 3."

"Yes, that is when the guests will arrive. Please wear your uniforms."

"I'm sorry, I'm not sure about wearing our uniforms, since we're not representing Consolidated Airlines. And Mr. Ramirez said he would send someone to pick us up at around 2:30 to 3. Am I missing something here?"

"Yes, about one hundred sixty kilometers and nearly three hours of driving."

"What?"

"Yes, and since it will be late and the road can be treacherous at night, bring any personal items you need for an overnight stay."

Mike heard rapid-fire Spanish in the background.

"Will you be wearing your uniforms or not?"

"Yes," answered Mike, deciding on the spot, "but we won't be wearing our wings. What's your name?"

"Maria."

"Well, Maria, I'm not sure if this is going to work. I'm going to consult with the two ladies and have Rita, who speaks Spanish, call you back to make sure I didn't lose anything in the translation."

"As you wish, Mr. Braun, but, since you have already agreed to Mr. Ramirez's proposal, he will expect you to fulfill your commitment. Do you understand?"

Mike fingered the goose bumps on his forearm. "That commitment was based on being picked up at 2:30. He said his place was almost right next to the Paraiso."

"It is. He owns over two million hectares."

"We'll call you. The number, please."

Mike hung up, pulled open the slider, grateful for the sea breeze to cool his flushed face, and draped his body over the rail. He watched some kind of raptor repeatedly circle as he waited for a fish to rise too close to the rolling surface. Suddenly, with a screech it dove straight down, and after a few seconds of furious splashing the big bird flew off with a foot-long prize gripped between its talons.

"Oh man," Mike said aloud, "what in the hell are we getting ourselves into?"

But, he couldn't get past the money. Three thousand, three hundred dollars was almost what he made in a month of flying maximum hours. In one night. What could go wrong? And maybe, he thought, the high rollers might want similar types of services. After all, some sheik hired Linda Wilson to take care of his kids on his private 747, making a hundred grand and averaging about ten days' work per month.

Mike's little fantasy seemed to ease his distress and, when he phoned Rita, he kept his voice casual, not expressing any of the alarm he experienced in his conversation with Maria. He did, however, ask her to make the return call to confirm.

Fifteen minutes later, Rita, with excitement tingeing her voice, called back to say they were all set, that they were to be picked up in a Lexus hybrid. The drive would be spectacular, the accommodations as good as they were here and, of course, they would be paid in cash. She had already informed Joey. Joey was fine with it.

Mike hung up and sighed. He'd been deceptive with Rita, just as Ramirez had been with him. He had hidden his concerns from her and, he sighed again, he concluded that deception came easily to him, maybe *too* easily. He thought briefly of consulting with Fox, but decided against it—he already knew what Fox would say. He climbed into shorts he always kept in his bag and headed for the dining room, vowing that if he was indeed leading them into something unsavory he would surely lead them out of it.

Fox emerged from the shower, pulled on a pair of swim trunks and ambled out to his deck to survey the morning. He leaned out and peered past the divider. He could see Joey draped over the rail, her head tilted toward the ocean. Her blonde hair fanned by the breeze, tangled in a slow sensuous motion, beckoning to him. He allowed himself one moment of imagining his face buried in that hair, his lips on her neck. He stepped back, rubbed his chin, and finally acknowledged the truth: he liked her and was attracted to her. It was possible she was attracted to him. So, that's where he would stop it. She was an innocent. Perhaps every woman on the planet had a fatal flaw, a flaw which was never discovered—unless she was to join orbits with Fox Revelstorm. He was aware of the arrogance of thinking he possessed so much power, like a sports fan believing he could control the destiny of his team by watching or not watching the game. But how else could he explain it?

Celeste Starr was no innocent. He was sure of it. He sensed she had already dealt with her own tragedy and survived. He'd pose no danger to her.

Over the years Fox had learned that dwelling in the past was hazardous to his health. Self-pity gained nothing but more self-contempt, yet he experienced days when the only way to shed the past was to acknowledge it. He stifled the urge for a moment, and then gave in.

Fox had been divorced for ten years and, when not flying, had discovered an Eden-like existence—living in the remote wilderness of British Columbia monitoring the habitats, migration patterns, and the numbers of as many bird species as he could keep track of. He also studied the behaviors and ranges of the different felines roaming through the woodland. He did this using the skills he'd learned as a child, venturing forth almost invisibly.

The isolation and the absence of human noise were a tonic to him. As he became more and more invisible in the woods, he also disappeared from the outside world. He had practically managed to erase himself by owning nothing, possessing no credit cards, no phone, no Internet connections, and no computer except the one provided by British Columbia's Department of Wildlife.

He allowed one more thought of Joey, and for an instant experienced a yearning to wake up with the same person beside him, day after day. He mentally cuffed himself. Almost angry, his melancholy was particularly troublesome this morning. He had not wanted to travel this path, but finally, inevitably, he completed it.

Eleven-year-old Fox and his nine-year-old sister had spent a week with family friends at their summer cabin on the banks of a mountain lake in the Cascade Mountains. A middle aged acquaintance was also present. He'd frightened eleven-year-old Fox with his bulky size and leering eyes, and his continual touching made the boy uncomfortable. One afternoon, Fox had returned from a hike and discovered that rest of the kids and family— everyone, except this man, was out on the lake. He exposed himself, fully aroused, trying at first to entice Fox. When Fox did not respond, he became more aggressive. Fox shook his head, knowing the man could easily overpower him. He backed out the door, turned, and bolted. He ran—hot tar squished under his shoes and its smell nearly gagged him—nearly three miles down the road to the nearest phone at a general store beside the two-lane road.

"Fox, we're awfully tired," his mother had said. "Your father just drove all the way from Northern California. Can't we pick you up in the morning?"

"No, just come. Please come," he pleaded, choking the words, tears dripping off his chin.

"Tell me why."

"I can't, not here. I'm in a store. Just come for us. Please."

"Hold on." Fox could hear them talking in the background, his dad telling his mom that he was exhausted. She told him that she was tired, too, but she was worried and Fox's voice sounded funny. She would go. She *had* to go. They were her children.

"We're on our way. I'll bring Dad to keep me awake," she said.

But there was no one to keep him awake. They plowed through a guardrail and went over an embankment a mile from the turnoff.

Unseeing, Fox stared at the ocean. Finally he shuffled back into the bathroom, brushed his teeth for ten minutes, and then began to floss, fully aware of his obsession brought on by reliving it this particular morning.

Fox had returned through the deep woods but did not approach the cabin until everyone had returned. Two hours after Fox had called his mother, he stared across the dinner table at his sister stuffing her face with freshly caught rainbow trout dipped in drawn butter. Her cheeks puffed and glistened. Fox fought back his fear. The flaky grains of flesh seemed to find their way in between even the tiniest gaps in his teeth. His stomach roiled with the sickening odor of buttered fish and onions. He tried to act normal, which was nearly impossible since the man, upon his return from the store had cornered him again, and threatened to kill him and rape his sister if Fox said anything.

A State Patrol car roared up to the cabin. The trooper dashed from his cruiser. There'd been an accident. Mr. and Mrs. Revelstorm were dead. Fox ran outside and threw up. Everyone wondered why the couple was on their way to the cabin. Finally they got it out of Fox that he'd asked them to come because he didn't feel well. His sister rushed at him, yelling "You killed them, you killed them," pounding his face and chest with her fists, until blood gushed from his nose.

They pulled her away and the big man sauntered over, put his arm around Fox, and said, "Remember what I told you." Fox vomited again, and stumbled into the bathroom to rinse his face and mouth, but the grains of trout would not flush from his teeth. He found dental tape and like a zombie stood in front of the mirror flossing until his gums bled.

11:30 A.M. CST

The hulking black Lexus pulled under the porte cochère. Mike, Rita, and Joey rolled their bags behind the hybrid, and waited for the driver to pop out and load them. Instead, through the thick tinted glass, they witnessed one side of an animated phone conversation, at least if the flailing free hand of the driver was any indication. Finally, he snapped shut his cell phone and slammed it into the console. A small man emerged from the car. He was about forty and wore a black suit and crimson tie. His skin was nearly as red as his tie with beads of sweat that shined on his forehead. He pulled an already damp handkerchief out of his pocket and daubed his ruddy face.

"Good afternoon," he said, his accent sounding more southern US than Mexican. "My name is José. I will take you to Señor Ramirez. Please," he said, yanking open the rear passenger door and gesturing toward the opening. They climbed in and Joey noticed how cool the interior was and glanced at the dash. The climate control was set at sixty-eight. The rear door crunched shut. She said quietly, "I wonder why he's sweating? It's cool in here."

"It looks like he's nervous," said Mike.

"And that," said Rita, "makes me nervous."

"Last chance," said Mike as the driver's door opened. No one said anything as the SUV pulled away, but instead of turning right onto the main road and heading south, they turned left.

Mike leaned forward. "I thought Ramirez's place was south."

"I must go into the village for gasoline."

"Your tank is nearly three quarters full," said Mike craning his head to see the instrument panel.

"I never take the trip south without a full tank."

The first twenty minutes of the drive was like traveling through an arboretum. Cultivated vegetation, statues, and outcroppings were everywhere. The picturesque village of Carlotta gleamed with brightly painted stucco structures, red-tiled roofs, and swept cobblestone streets. He pulled into an old storefront with a fifties-vintage single gas pump.

To their surprise, the driver opened their door. "Please go in while I fill the tank."

"Go in where?"

"Inside. You are expected."

"You must be mistaken," said Mike, as they climbed out.

The man shook his head.

Mike glanced at Rita and she stepped forward, and unleashed a barrage of Spanish, in a tone of voice that was not complimentary. He yelled back, waving his hands. She glared at him, then turned back to Mike and Joey. "I asked him why he was sweating in a freezing car. I asked him why he hadn't already filled the gas tank, and finally I asked him about all the deception. I didn't get the answers I wanted. I don't like this. I say we walk back. I don't care how long it takes."

"What about our bags?" asked Joey.

"Let's grab them, and maybe we can flag down a cab or something," said Mike.

He had his hand on the tailgate handle when the driver said in a low even voice, "I wouldn't do that."

He pointed a small black pistol at Mike's stomach. Mike's first thought was to grab it and hit him over the head with it. He figured he had about a ninety-nine percent chance of snatching it away and rendering the audacious pip-squeak unconscious before he hit the ground. Instead, Mike heeded the one percent and stepped back.

"Just go inside for a few minutes," said José. "Then we'll be on our way. Everything is fine."

Mike said nothing, but backed away and motioned for Joey and Rita to join him.

"What are you doing?" asked Rita.

"Trying not to get our heads shot off. The son-of-a-bitch pulled a gun."

They entered through the creaking door of the small grocery store, which was jammed with canned goods and fresh produce. The smell of coffee and overripe fruit permeated the air. A girl of no more than twelve smiled and motioned them through another door to the back of the building. Inside, it seemed like a modern office with three computer monitors, printers, and a table full of other electronic equipment that the three could not identify. They were left alone for nearly a minute until a tiny woman with bright eyes and radiant skin seemed to materialize from the rear of the building. Her simple white cotton dress and lack of jewelry emphasized the depths of her pupils.

"Thank you for coming," she said.

"We had no choice. Our driver pulled a gun on me," said Mike thinking this woman could be Rita's mother or, even her sister.

She frowned and held her palms out in apology. "I am truly sorry. José has a flair for dramatics. I doubt the gun was even loaded. It probably isn't even real. In any case, no harm will come to you. I ask only for a few minutes of your time."

Rita, her brow furrowed, held her tongue.

"I will be brief," said the woman in perfect English. "My name is Esmerelda. I am a freedom fighter. As beautiful and peaceful as it is in countries such as our neighbor Costa Rica, it is as ugly and violent in Quintana. The government exploits the people and keeps them in poverty while they gain the riches of the nation. The government of Quintana is also in bed with the owner of nearly half the land. Your host, Mr. Ramirez," she continued, her voice taking on a venomous edge, "and for nearly two centuries his despotic family has ruled their holdings with a ruthless sense of justice."

Mike fidgeted while Esmerelda pointed to a monitor. "Observe what the people endure while the military lines its pockets with blood money." In ten minutes she rolled through nearly a hundred pictures of battered children slaving in mines and fields, the environment trashed, raw sewage running in the streets of villages, and stacks of bodies bulldozed into mass graves.

"Why are you showing us this?" asked Mike, horrified by the photos, but confused.

"You have an opportunity to do Quintana and mankind a great service, if," she said waggling her index finger, "you are willing."

"And what are we to do?" asked Rita.

"Let me pose a question," she said, moving a step closer to them, her neck craned to meet their eyes. Her voice was barely audible, but to Mike there was a formidable attitude behind her words. "If you had a chance to take out a despot, someone like Stalin after the war ended, would you do it? It's simple. The man carrying out the terror will be attending the party this evening. His name is Soriano. He is a general, also known as 'the Butcher.' We're not very original with our nicknames. But it is an accurate description. All those opposed to him, even military, are butchered. Kill him, and Ramirez, too, if you wish. But eliminating the Butcher could ignite the people who have been smothered by a terrorist regime."

"Is this some sort of sick joke?" asked Mike.

"No, and you can do this easily. I have a tasteless poison that you can slip into their drinks. It looks like a package of sugar. It does not act quickly—twenty-four to thirty-six hours. It will be diagnosed as a heart attack. Three packs will put a man down in an hour. The Butcher is a prime candidate anyway. You would be well away, and not connected."

"This is preposterous," said Mike. "There's absolutely no way we're getting involved in this."

"We are at war," she said, her voice still soft.

"*We* are not," Mike replied. "And why us? Why not another server?"

"You will be searched for weapons, but you will not be strip searched upon entering the compound. The other help is. You may say no, but we have to try. The poison comes in a regular sugar packet. I have three sets of three packets. Only one contains the poison in each set. If you all refill the general's glass, which will need refilling since he's a prodigious drinker, you will not know which one of you was responsible."

Rita and Mike stared at Esmerelda in disbelief. Joey stepped in front of them and calmly studied the older woman for a moment. "If what we see here is true, we can alert our government officials. Perhaps what Quintana needs is the worldwide spotlight. We can help with that. I can't speak for the others, but at this point I will not be a party to this," said Joey.

"Nor I," said Rita.

"I am outraged," said Mike. "We have no idea who you are and who has done what to whom. You're no better than the one you want us to kill. In fact," he continued, looking toward the others, "and I'm sure my partners are with me on this, we won't be attending Mr. Ramirez's party. And, finally, why would you trust us, anyway?"

She stifled a laugh and shook her head. "I don't need to trust you, and I'm not surprised you have declined our request but, for your own sakes, please attend. If you do not, you or perhaps your loved ones will be in danger. If Mr. Ramirez believes he has lost face, he will respond. His guests have been told to expect you, and if you don't arrive, he will have his vengeance, in some way or form. *Es verdad.*"

"He didn't seem like that type of guy to me," said Mike, shaking his head.

"You don't know him like I know him."

Rita stepped forward. "What exactly do you mean by vengeance?"

Esmerelda shrugged. "It could be anything: an accident here while swimming, cocaine found in your bag going back through customs. He can do anything he wants to do," she said, jerking her head toward Joey staring at her like she was a butterfly specimen.

Mike rubbed his chin and let out a breath. "Do you have more bags with poison?" he asked, holding out his hand.

She nodded. "Six."

"Then give them to me and get rid of the placebos. At least we'll have some sort of weapon."

3:30 P.M. CST

Fox had spent most of the morning absorbing the surrounding beauty—the sky and sea, lush plant life and colorful birds. He sat in the middle of a tropical garden with a see-through view to the sea. He closed his eyes and concentrated on the crashing waves and songbirds, until he at least felt neutral.

His discomfort was rooted in his flying partners' decision to attend the gala. Or more precisely, rooted in one Gustav Heinrich. At this point he could think of only one thing that could distract him from worrying until they returned safely: Celeste Starr. So, at noon he called her. He felt a touch awkward, but her voice was even more soothing than the sound of the ocean. She told him she'd pick him up at five.

He spent the next three hours hiking along the coastline, making forays into the dense jungle, to observe, marveling at the color and richness of the forest. When he returned at three, he opened his connecting door to find Joey's open with a note on the floor. *We had to leave early. It's a two-hour trip to the south. Don't wait up; we're spending the night there. Should be back around eleven tomorrow. Mi casa es su casa. There's a bottle of wine I've been lugging around for nearly a week on top of the dresser. Help yourself. Sweet dreams, Joey.*

"Damn," he said aloud, and closed the door.

Celeste Starr climbed out of a nondescript, late-model Toyota Camry wearing a knee-length, white cotton dress printed with red hibiscus flowers. She pushed back her hair and extended her hand. "I'm glad you called. I'm looking forward to spending time with you."

"As am I with you," he replied, lightly squeezing the tips of her fingers. He was already sidetracked and happy for it. As he slid into the car, he decided that on the plane, the first time he had spoken to her, he had sort of blindsided her. Why not again? He grinned and plowed ahead. "So what's with your name? Is it given? Or did it just fall out of the sky?"

She turned up the corners of her mouth. "My mother's name is Brenda—that's probably all you need to know. And I could ask the same of you."

"Actually, it was a cruel thing. My last name used to be Hound. But Fox Hound was too much. I had to change it."

"You mean like a baying-at-the-moon hound?"

"Is there any other type?"

"Maybe we'll find out, sometime later."

He laid his left hand on her shoulder for a second. "Thanks for the levity. I needed it."

"Thanks for the touch. I needed it," she replied.

They drove on in silence through lush green vegetation and small villages. She glanced at him. "You're trying to let go, but you can't."

He nodded. "It's my flying partners. They're off to some wealthy guy's manor to help serve an executive dinner. He's paying them ten grand. They need the money."

"So why are you worried about them?"

"Because of my big, smart-ass mouth. I made some young guy in first class look like the fool he is. He didn't like it. And he let me know he didn't like it. Turns out he's connected to the rich guy throwing the bash, and I've heard the rich guy owns half the country. It makes me wonder who these people are accountable to, that's all."

She ran her index finger over her lower lip. "Who's the rich guy?"

"Ramirez."

"You're right, Ramirez owns Imperio Dominio. It's almost like a principality. He probably doesn't answer to anyone. Is there something you want to do?" She paused, and tapped her cheeks with her fingertips, in thought. "It's a bit of a wild ride, but I can drive you there," she said turning her head to make eye contact.

"You would do that?"

"Yes, if that's what you want."

He shook his head. "I'd probably just inflame the situation."

"Are you sure?"

"I'm not, but I'm deciding not to go there."

"Then worry intensely about them for a minute and visualize the perfect ending—them having a wonderful time, returning with their pockets stuffed with cash—and then, let them go for the night."

Fox studied her profile with newfound respect. "You're wise. I'll try to let it go." He flashed a quick grin. "But, you have to help me."

The cracked asphalt lane wove through flora like a serpent, passing untamed jungle and, in other places, well-ordered gardens. At times it was like speeding through an animated tunnel, until the light steadily increased and suddenly a white cottage appeared against the deep blue of the sky.

She turned into a driveway and pulled into a garage. Fox climbed out, smoothed his golf shirt, and tucked it into his shorts. The same shorts he'd worn three nights ago in Phoenix, he remembered.

He walked slowly back down the lane to recapture what he had just seen, trying to comprehend the incongruities of what his eyes showed him and how it made him feel. Celeste followed, watching him. Finally he tried to verbalize it. "I guess, because you're an artist, I'm trying to think in artistic terms. But my thoughts are confused by what I've seen. It seems to me art tries to capture the essence of something real and dramatizes it, but here, visually experiencing this cottage and its surroundings, it's as if the real has been captured by the essence, making me feel like I'm standing in a painting. Does that make any sense?"

"Perfect sense. Leave it that way as long as you can—let the essence be the reality."

For the next half hour he followed her around the property and through the cottage, sipping on the glass of

Chardonnay she'd handed him, all the while captivated by a kaleidoscope of whirling colors and crosscurrent textures sourced from both nature and the creative hand of Celeste Starr. Finally, with newly filled glasses they stood in the ocean, gentle waves lapping against their calves, gazing back at the cottage, the gardens, and the jungle beyond. With her free hand Celeste gathered her billowing hair and held up her glass, clinking it against his. "I've shown you where I live and how I decorate my house." They both drank. "But, if you want to know me, I must show you my studio." She took a step closer to him, let her hair go, and stared directly into his eyes. "Do you want to know me?" she asked in a low, wine-scented voice. Before he could reply, she went on. "Let me rescind the question and make a statement. I *want* you to know me."

"Makes me wonder what's in the studio," he said, remembering how the painting on her card had affected him, but he kept his voice light. "The Garden of Eden? A House of Horrors? Shangri-la?"

She smiled, but Fox's vision flew past it, drawn into the blackest part of her eyes, until he saw himself reflected. She nodded. "Yes, all three are present, as well as the blood of my soul seeping, drop by drop, into my painter's palette. You'll see. Come with me." She took him by the hand.

2:40 P.M. CST

The big Hybrid bounded and pounded over a road alternately surfaced in dust, mud, bare rock, hard wash-boarded dirt, and occasional patches of smooth asphalt. Mike pictured his stomach hovering just a little above him, his heaving body catching it for moments on the way up and down. He wasn't queasy, but the emptiness in his midsection signified something more than physical discomfort. It was trepidation, he thought, probably no different from what he felt from spinning the roulette wheel. The excitement of what could be gained against the dread of what could be lost, when he couldn't afford to lose. Mike chose not remind himself he was a lousy gambler.

Instead he said, "This is like a typical descent into Denver."

"Except the descent into Denver doesn't last two hours," said Rita. She was sitting in the middle and glanced at Joey, crumpled against the door, her head rolling around, but cushioned by a folded sweater. "Incredible. She's been out almost the whole time. First, we're threatened and then our little meeting, and now, this cowboy ride into who-knows-where. How can she sleep? Anyway, I envy her."

"How much longer?" Mike asked the driver.

"You sound like a little kid," chided Rita. "You just asked him twenty minutes ago."

José turned his head slightly to reply, when his cell phone rang. He listened for less than a minute, grunted his understanding, and flipped off the phone. "Only fifteen minutes."

"I can't believe there's reception out here," said Mike.

"Yes," said José, "Good reception, bad roads."

Still close to the ocean they had ascended for many miles, cleared a summit, and began descending. Finally in the distance they could see what appeared to be a small village, its buildings clustered along the seashore. Back down to sea-level, but more than a mile from the village, Mike was startled when José swung the Lexus into a sharp left turn, and began traveling inland on a recently paved road.

Rita asked José in Spanish if Ramirez's compound was what they had seen earlier along the water in the distance.

"Si."

"Then where in the hell are we going?" she muttered in English.

"Ultimately, I don't know. I will drop you off shortly."

Austin Ramirez pushed his chair away from his desk, leaned back, removed his glasses, and rubbed his eyes. He had been pondering his mortality, resigned to the idea that if hell were part of the afterlife, he was probably headed there. Countless people had suffered for decisions he had made over the years, but they were never made in malice, he reminded himself. He had simply followed the family manifesto: preserve ownership of all the holdings, and preserve the land itself—however you must do it, for one day the land will pay you back.

Perhaps the hour was close at hand, yet the timing was delicate. At fifty he still possessed the energy and drive necessary, but his power of persuasion would ultimately determine his fate. He had never been so excited, or so scared. Just as with his father, and his grandfather before him, at times he had to walk with the devil in order to preserve the estate. He sighed and set his glasses on his desk. He knew the devil would prove to be a tough partner to get rid of, and he was dealing with more than one. He allowed himself a tiny smile. He was certain he possessed a conscience, if for no other reason than he was constantly in a wrestling match with it.

A rap on the door interrupted his thoughts. On his command it opened. He stood and, with a pen still in hand, used it to beckon forward the man standing on the other side of the room. "Sit," he ordered.

Without uttering a word, Gustav Heinrich sat in a straight-back leather chair facing the desk.

Ramirez remained on his feet, went around the desk, and stood directly over his nephew. "Thank you for coming by. This won't take long. You and I are at a crossroads. As I have told you before, you have done well and accomplished much for one still fairly young. However, and this I will not tell you again, your appetites and your temper will be your undoing if you do not control them. I will not be brought down with you. So let me make this crystal clear: Our flight attendants are arriving in fifteen minutes. As promised, tomorrow they will be delivered back to their hotel in one piece with their money in hand."

Heinrich breathed deeply and rolled his shoulders, his thick neck chaffed against his collar. "Accidents happen," he said, exhaling, the air whistling between his teeth.

Ramirez shook his head. "Not tonight. Undoubtedly you have some scheme in mind to hold them so your new friend Revelstorm will feel compelled to rescue them, but none of that is going to happen."

Unable to stand the menace above him, Heinrich pushed upward. Ramirez's firm hand on his shoulder held him down.

"Then why did you agree to my plan?" asked Heinrich, his voice low and raspy. "I have no other need of them. Our guests care nothing about an American flight crew. And you would let them walk out with ten thousand of our money? Why?"

Ramirez removed his hand and moved back behind his desk and sat down. "*My* money," he reminded Heinrich. "Ten thousand of *my* money. Big changes are coming and soon. We are at the point where we can actually get our business and the rest of this fourth-world country turned around—through legitimate means. If I had not agreed to your proposition then, as you asked, a team of your men would have, by now, extracted those American citizens and brought them to you, where they probably would have been raped, tortured, killed, and thrown into the ocean. No doubt you would have covered your tracks, but no doubt the US would do more than just poke into the affairs of this country, and since I own more than half of it..." He stopped for a moment, his eyes boring into Heinrich's. "So, our little group will return with a glowing experience of their time with us."

Silence ensued for a moment. "So be it, then," said Heinrich. "In that case, I have other plans. Please excuse me from this evening's festivities."

"No doubt to pay a visit to Mr. Revelstorm. I think not. Besides, the festivities have been cancelled. Instead, with the Americans as working crew, we're flying to Peru for an introductory meeting with Tunis, the jungle canopy ride maker. As you know, I have no interest in building such a thing, but I am interested in his construction methods. Since you have already met Tunis, it seems logical that you preside over the introductions. The general has also requested an audience with Tunis and will be accompanying us." Despite the distance between them Ramirez detected a flash from Heinrich's eyes and noticed the sweat gathering in the creases of his protégé's neck.

Ramirez stroked his mustache as an epiphany slapped him across the face. You've been in denial, he thought. *You cannot change him.* He exhaled and continued. "Gustav, you used to be much better at controlling your anger. As I stated, change is coming. The question is: Are you going to be part of it? You have eliminated the poaching, but now your job description must change or you're out."

The lines on Heinrich's forehead lengthened.

Ramirez pushed him harder, lowering his voice. "You should try sex with someone you actually like so you don't feel compelled to carve them up after the act. But, then again," he said holding out his hands, "you don't like anyone. What I'm wondering is, if you did have your way with our flight attendants, which one would you bed first? The beautiful and luscious Rita? The glamorous fashion model? Or, perhaps their leader, the one called Mike? Yes, I think Mike."

Heinrich bolted out of his chair, looming across the desk. He swung his fist toward Ramirez's head, but stopped it an inch from his uncle's chin. Ramirez had not flinched.

"Come now, Gustav," he said, "don't put on the outrage act with me. I *know* these things. In fact, I know everything." Ramirez dismissed him with the wave of his hand. "You stink when you're angry, and you're angry nearly all the time. Take a quick shower, change into a fresh suit, and put a smile on your face."

Heinrich turned toward the door, his body so constricted he almost had to use his hands to make his legs move.

Ramirez studied him as he crossed the room. In an instant he made his decision. Heinrich was a rabid pit bull, as likely to turn on his master as to defend him. It was time to put him down. "One more thing," Ramirez called after him, "I've changed my mind. Your evening is free."

The door banged shut and Ramirez returned to his chair, leaned back, and placed his feet upon his desk. The fact was: Ramirez *didn't* know everything, but the talk of torture, mutilation, and even cannibalism was probably true. *Yes, your purpose on this earth has come to an end. Therefore, so shall you. I gave you every opportunity to become a human being, but you had no interest, the same as your mother, who went to her grave believing I had fallen for her deception. How should I dispose of you? In the same manner as so many of your victims—bloodied, mangled messes pushed out of a helicopter at five hundred feet into shark-infested waters. I'd rather not. I'd rather let you hang yourself.*

Ramirez allowed a moment of regret to remember Heinrich as a twelve-year-old and the wild tapir he befriended. The female sniffed around on a regular basis and Gustav was able to scratch behind her ears. With her and most of the wildlife, he had a soft touch. But when Gustav saw two boys taunting her, he had to be restrained by two grown men.

Ramirez dropped his glasses on the desk, another epiphany crashing through his head. One of the boys involved drowned two months after the incident. At the time, Ramirez had thought nothing of it. The boy had been caught in a rip and could not pull free. But no one had seen him enter the water.

Ramirez shivered. He'd been blind to how early Heinrich's viciousness had started.

The Lexus droned on through the dense jungle, jagged shafts of sunlight strafing the interior of the SUV when the terrain suddenly opened wide. "Christ," said Mike. "An airstrip in the middle of nowhere. And the runway looks like it goes on forever."

More than a mile later they stopped in front of a modern two-story office building that stood next to a large hangar housing a plain, white-colored 737. A man wearing military fatigues with a rifle slung over his shoulder ran up and opened the door. "Follow me inside. You'll be briefed, secured, and soon we'll be on our way."

Mike was about to open his mouth when the soldier raised his hand. "I don't know anything, except that I'm to get you through our security and deliver you to the briefing room. The driver will take care of your bags. Please."

Mike shrugged, stepped out, helped Rita and Joey from the Lexus, then followed the soldier. Just inside the door they were lightly frisked by another security guard. They were led through a maze of corridors into a small room with temporary accordion walls, a round table, and four plastic chairs. "Wait here," he said and departed.

Five minutes later the door opened and Ramirez himself appeared with a smile and a firm handshake to all. "There's been a change of plans. We'll be leaving in an hour for a flight to a coastal city in Peru. You'll be our flight attendants serving snacks and drinks to a small group of business people. Once there you'll be on your own. We're scheduled to return at 8 a.m., so we'll need you on board at 7:15. You'll serve breakfast, then you'll be driven back to your hotel. The airplane is a Boeing 737-900, configured to the whim of its owner, a Saudi sheik, who loaned it to me. We're in the process of figuring out how to squeeze thirty percent more fuel efficiency out of the engines. We're ready for the next test. Hence the real reason for the flight." He waved his hand. "It is equipped with all the latest safety features; I'm sure you'll want to inspect it. I realize this is a different proposition than you thought you were getting into, so I hope four thousand a piece will mitigate the changes. Actually," he said with a half laugh, "this should be a much easier job. When we arrive, you will have whatever you wish from the bar and dining room. Questions?"

Mike flashed him his best aw-shucks smile. "Any chance of getting paid in advance?"

"Yes, of course." He reached into his inside jacket pocket and pulled out three envelopes.

"Hector Cato will be here in a minute to continue your briefing and provide you a tour of the plane," he said and departed.

They were silent for a few moments. Mike had folded the envelope in two and jammed it into his pocket. He ran his hand over the bulge. His inclination was to just go with the flow, but decided to ask what needed asking. "Ladies, does your intuition tell you anything about Ramirez? Any trip wires attached to the guy? To me, he seems trustworthy, but it might be the four grand in my pocket that's doing my thinking."

Rita nodded. "I think he's a little evasive, but I sense no deceit or any bad intentions. In fact, if anything, he seems protective of us."

"I agree with Rita, but are there any rules about this?" Joey asked. "Can we be fired for working on this plane?"

"No, I don't believe so and, besides, who's going to know?" said Mike.

Rita tossed her head. "The question is, who's *not* going to know, with the way your mouth runs on?"

Mike puckered his lips, thinking that *that* sounded more like the real Rita. "You're probably right, but it's common knowledge that on long layovers flight crews have flown to other cities, gone skydiving, or on cruises. I don't see this as being any different. It's not like we're working on a commercial airline."

"Then it's a go?" asked Joey.

"For once I agree with our fearless leader," said Rita, continuing to tease Mike.

Hector Cato wondered whether he was cursed from a previous lifetime or had he brought it on himself through naïve stupidity—believing he could work for Ramirez without getting mixed up in the internal political dealings of a wildly disparate organization.

Like his forefathers, Ramirez had cast his lot with the land, doing anything to keep it wild and pristine. And now the payoff was coming, for he was the champion of the environmentalists and every organization devoted to the preservation of habitat and species. Ten years ago, poachers were running rampant, bagging rare and exotic animals with impunity until Ramirez solved the problem and unleashed his nephew, the homicidal maniac. Now, there were no poachers left to torture and kill.

Cato had many problems, including raising his two young children with the help of his nearly blind grandmother. But he had another problem that was soon to come to a head. He would be forced to choose between Heinrich and Ramirez. If he chose wrong, he and his offspring were likely dead. Though he loathed Heinrich, he was not sure Ramirez could survive the brutality that always seemed to prevail in his tiny country. And any illusion he had about protecting his family was dashed when Heinrich had chased down an escaped poacher all the way to a small town outside of Osaka, Japan, leaving the man alive but with his knees and ankles smashed by a sledgehammer. The message was clear: You cannot hide from Gustav Heinrich.

Cato was a victim of his own attributes. He was educated, trustworthy, and believed in the environment, which had brought him to Ramirez in the first place. He was an ornithologist, trained at the University of Florida. He had acquired the ability to blend like a ghost into the jungle, a skill he had imparted to Heinrich and his band of psychopaths to capture the human prey. In short, Cato, without trying, had become the ear of Ramirez and Heinrich, as well as being their eyes. Each of the men believed Cato to be his most trusted confidant. He wasn't walking a thin line, he was treading a razor's edge. In a perfect world, he thought, one of Heinrich's victim's would somehow get hold of a knife or gun and kill him. But, the world was not perfect, not even close.

During these last few weeks even the most pleasant of thoughts, like the smile on his daughter's precious face, seemed to distort in his head, spiraling downward as he imagined her in harm's way. It was as if the lid to his tomb was nearly closed with only a single ray of light to give him hope.

Cato splashed cold water on his face, his bloodshot eyes staring back at him. He wondered how he could extract himself from the mess he was in. He'd seen Heinrich stomp out of Ramirez's office so enraged that the entire building seemed to take on his foul scent. He stretched the knotted muscles holding his wiry frame together, squared his shoulders, and patted his dark curly hair. "No problem," he said aloud, "all you need is a miracle." He was actually looking forward to spending a few minutes with the Americans. At least they wouldn't be totally crazy.

He pasted a smile on his face and entered the room, laid his eyes on Rita Sanchez, and nearly fell over. He gathered his wits, shook everyone's hand, and escorted them to the hangar. By the time they reached the airstairs, Hector was, at least temporarily, a changed man. In hardly more than an instant, his head had been turned upside down, the sordid contents emptied, and refilled to the brim with nothing but Rita, which to him seemed quite miraculous.

3:15 P.M. CST

For Mike and Joey, inspecting the private jetliner had been more like a tour of a luxury apartment capable of flight. Their young guide appeared tired, yet enthusiastic and professional. For Rita, it was more. It had started when she was standing next to Hector. He had just finished speaking. She took an innocuous breath of air that, instead of being quickly processed and expelled, dropped straight down, penetrating the deepest capillaries in her lungs, speeding the oxygen to her extremities. She took another and her body expanded further, spine straightening, torso opening, and chin rising. Now aware of the invisible cords that, her for the past year, had bound and constricted her body and her sense of capability she breathed deeply again. The cords had snapped like tired rubber bands.

On the other hand, the mental signals she picked up from Hector seemed like fractured mush. She wondered why.

She was confused, but believed her body knew exactly what it wanted. She thought of Fox's lecture on the nature of spontaneous combustion. *Damn, I'm about to go up in flames with a man who hasn't laid a finger on me.* She quickly compartmentalized it. *He seems a little nuts and I'm crazed. Perfect.*

They had entered through the aft left door. There was a jumpseat mounted to the wall on the right facing forward, just as in Consolidated 737's. Directly across, on the other side of the fuselage, was the right aft door and galley, which was nearly twice the size of any commercial galley and with the normal conveniences of any upscale kitchen. Forward of that were four conventional rows of three-by-three seating with a restroom on each side, and an open area designed for Muslim prayer. Then, moving forward and on the right, was a glassed-in office with normal electronics, and a bank of what looked like test instruments. Further forward on the right with a passageway on the left were three small bedrooms. Just behind the cockpit was the lounge and living and dining areas.

Hector left them for a moment while the pilots introduced themselves and gave the attendants another short briefing.

Cato returned and handed Mike a manual showing the location of all the safety equipment. Joey and Mike began their checks and, just out of earshot, Hector found Rita alone.

"Can I speak with you for a moment?"

Before he could say anything else, she asked, "Are you all right?"

"No, I'm not all right," he said, "and I haven't been for a while, and especially not for the last fifteen minutes. Look, I don't have any time right now, but since I met you, my head, for the first time in a long time, is filled with possibility instead of dread. When you return tomorrow, can I visit you at your hotel?"

Rita's mind seemed to evaporate as she stared at him.

He plowed on. "My wife disappeared four years ago. I haven't looked at a woman since, and felt like I never would. You hit me like a lightning bolt. I won't lie. I have two children, a girl, who is five, and a boy, who is eight and sort of lives in his own world. Can I see you, please?"

She didn't hear any of it, except *disappeared, a boy eight*, and *lives in his own world*. "Your wife disappeared?"

"Most likely murdered. She was a school teacher who taught kids about human rights and women's rights. Those in power frown upon such teachings." He paused for a moment. "I'd really like to see you when you get back. May I?"

"Yes," she heard herself say. He rewarded her with a pure, joyful smile.

"I need to grab the catering manifest to make sure everything is here. I'll be right back," he said.

Rita slowly walked forward as Joey hopped down from checking a beacon in an overhead compartment.

"You look sort of dazed," said Joey. "It's Hector, isn't it? He has no idea what Mike and I look like, because he never took his eyes off you. He's gorgeous."

"I'm not sure what happened, but I feel like an unrepentant Eve; I wolfed down the apple as an appetizer and I'm just getting started."

"Wow."

"Yeah, wow."

In the last year, Rita had agonized over decisions. She went back and forth, to and fro, listed positives and negatives, but in an instant she knew her relationship with Ted

Wright, was wrong. It was her fault. As soon as she returned home, it would be over. She owed him that much.

Hector floated back into his office, pulled up the catering manifest, and was about to yank it off his printer when Gustav Heinrich entered. Hector crinkled his nose. Heinrich looked awful, his eyes blurred and red, hair matted down with sweat. He smelled worse. Heinrich managed a slight upturn of his lips. He pointed to a small, paper grocery bag next to his shoes. "I would like you to do something for me."

"Sure."

"This sack contains a small cigar box. I want you to place it in the master bath in the compartment where the extra toilet tissue is stored. I would not look in the box if I were you."

"Yeah, sure," he said his mind still focused on Rita.

"Very well, then," said Heinrich.

At that moment it registered and Cato jumped up, his heart pumping wildly. "What did you ask of me?"

Heinrich repeated himself word for word.

Cato shook his head. "I can't do that."

Heinrich moved close and held his index finger in the middle of Cato's chest. "You will do exactly as I say."

Cato finally inhaled and let it out, his mind frantic, but knowing he must choose the right words. "This is not the way to get what you want. I will help you, but this is not the way to ensure your long-term success."

Heinrich stared right through him, his blue eyes pure ice. "Hector, have I made myself clear?"

"But, how can you expect—"

"By the way, how *are* little Angelina and José?" He raised his index finger again. "I'm sure they are well. I'm positive you want them to remain that way."

Hector stared. He was frozen and unable to blink.

"You are a valuable asset, Hector, but do not test my resolve."

Heinrich turned and strode out of the room, leaving Cato to choke and gag on the stench left behind. Hector collapsed in his chair, arms limp, while two visions played simultaneously in his head: a 737 exploding into a million pieces over the Pacific with a horrified Rita Sanchez plummeting to her death and his two children being raped and sodomized before his eyes, preceding his own slow execution. He didn't notice the tears streaming down until one reached his chin.

He pulled the manifest from the printer, staggered to his feet and took hold of the shopping bag, knowing with certainty as soon as he delivered the package he was dead. His heart would continue to beat, but his life was finished.

He went directly to the master bath and placed the small box behind a roll of tissue, praying that it did not contain what he thought it did. Then he managed to get Joey acquainted with the galley and checked that everything on the list was present, with a smoothness in his voice sourced only from the vision of his children alive and well.

He was nearly out the door when Rita's voice stopped him. He waited for her to approach, watched her face, mesmerized by her eyes, now aglitter, with complicity. She touched his hand. "Yes," she said, "please come to me when we return."

"I will," he said, and ran down the airstairs, and into his office. Burning up, he tore off his sport coat and shirt and flung them on the floor, panting. He was already in hell.

In a fog, Cato powered down his cell phone. For the next hour, he watched through the window in his office. Fuel pumped into the wing, a small amount of cargo was loaded in the belly, ten men and two women entered the cabin, and finally all doors closed and the airstairs backed away. All the while he had spun all manner of solutions through his head, but they were always short circuited with grotesque visions of his children. Donning his still-soaked shirt, he tossed his coat over his shoulder and trudged out to his car.

As the Toyota Prius hummed down the road, Cato heard the whine of the 737's turbines start to rotate. As always, he was about to give a clipped wave to the guardhouse, when a uniform jumped out in front of him.

Cato stopped. "What's up?"

"I don't know. I just got a call from the boss. He wants to see you."

"He's on the plane. Hasn't it left?"

"No. He said they're bringing back the airstairs."

Hector returned his car to the lot, straightened his tie, combed his hair, and ran up the stairs as soon as the door was opened by the ramp mechanic.

It was Ramirez greeting him at the door with a smile. "I'd already made up my mind. You're going to replace Gustav as my number two. I thought, why not start now? From now on, you're in on everything, and you don't know the half of what's about to happen." Ramirez paused. "Don't look so shocked. I should have done this a year ago. Come ahead; let's get this thing buttoned up and out of here."

"But my children—my boy, he depends on me."

"As we speak, I have someone on the way, someone who has dealt with troubled children. This will be a good experiment. It's only one night."

Hector continued his dumbfounded expression. He had told no one about his son.

He passed Rita and Joey standing next to their jumpseat, and made his way forward, plopped himself in a chair, and gulped down the glass of champagne that Mike offered. He closed his eyes and wondered what it was like to get blown out of the sky. He pictured his body on fire for a few seconds, then cool for eternity as it rested at the bottom of the ocean.

4:20 P.M. CST

Under the starkness of direct sunlight, Celeste appeared luminous, almost childish, despite the fact she was about to turn thirty. Yet, something emanated from her eyes that Fox couldn't quite grasp; it was a sadness, a world weariness, as if she were an old woman made young again by a magical spell.

They strode up the beach toward the cottage, snatching their sandals along the way, and then sat on a small bench to put them on.

Fox pointed to her empty glass that she had set next to her. "I need to fill that for you."

She turned to him and placed her fingers on his arm. "If you do, I won't be driving you back to the Paraiso tonight."

"Where will you be driving me, then?" He raised his eyebrows.

"Hopefully," she said, "insane."

They refilled their glasses, killed the bottle, and made their way to the studio. With a steady hand she inserted a key and unlocked the door. He followed her lead and set his glass on a small table just inside. She flipped a switch that triggered a maze of halogen lights. Fox was so dazzled that his breath seemed to explode from his lungs. His hands flew up to cover his face. A moment later he eased them down.

The building was much bigger than he had sensed. A high-roofed rectangle, its walls covered with huge canvases, most of them at least ten feet high and wide. Most were vibrant jungle scenes, yet a shadowed menace permeated the room. He was simultaneously captivated and repulsed.

He finally turned away and found her studying him.

"It's sort of overwhelming, isn't it?" she asked.

"That's an understatement," he said, trying to synthesize the light that leaped off the canvases with the perilous vortex that sucked it back into the shadows.

"Do you perceive great beauty?" she asked.

"Everywhere, aching beauty."

"But, it's quite uncomfortable?"

"Yes," said Fox, "I feel drawn in and repelled at the same time. It's a physical sensation," he said, trying to pull his eyes away once again.

She slid her hand under his elbow and pointed with the other hand to a door at the far end of the room. "This next experience will cause you even more discomfort, but it's necessary," she said her voice grave and formal. "This is sort of the moment of truth. Are you sure about this?"

"Are *you* sure?"

"Yes."

"Then, so am I."

She nodded. "Once you've entered I'll activate the lights. Remember, you are in no danger, you will merely be standing in the midst of a static work."

He looked at her, questioning.

"Trust me," she said.

When they reached the door Fox noticed it was part of a curved wall, suggesting that part of the room was round. He didn't hesitate and pushed it open. In the dim light he saw that indeed he had entered a circular enclosure and found his way to the middle, figuring the circular wall was five feet from him in any direction.

"I'm closing the door," she warned and backed out. A moment later Fox's entire body vibrated.

My God, this room is alive. Serpents appeared to writhe at his feet, their eyes locked on his. *Slither with me into the darkness or die a horrible death.*

Fox felt a slight breeze from above and listened to the rustling of branches. He raised his head and found a set of eyes in the face of a shadowed catlike beast ready to pounce, its lithe body partially hidden by broad leaves. Scanning further above, he found another pair of malevolent irises and a fanged open mouth. The dangling snake was the width of his leg. Sweat beaded on his forehead and he smelled rotting vegetation.

He gulped several deep breaths, knelt down and touched the jungle floor, and placed his hand directly on the visual rough scales of a slithering serpent. His brain argued that there was no movement as he ran his palm over the floor's smooth surface. He rose up in slow-motion and let in sink in without resistance. He concluded it was variable light and painted echoes of the serpents that created the motion.

Though the room had been cool when he entered, the blue sky spiking through openings in the jungle's canopy suggested heat and humidity. Beads of sweat became rivulets cascading down his face.

Finally, after turning in a slow circle, he calmed down enough to study the phenomena of her creation. He stayed inside for some time marveling at the detail and perspective. It was as if he were in a small opening in the jungle with peril everywhere, and yet there was a sense of distance, a suggestion of a horizon. Upon further study, he concluded that though the animals were incredibly realistic, they were painted much more dramatically than the real thing; every single set of eyes had a fearsome but unique human personality. He made his way to the door and pulled it open.

Celeste stood a few feet away, her arms down and fingers locked together. Her expression confounded him—eyes glistened with moisture, and her face emanated unabashed, almost childish gratefulness. Without thinking, he was beside her and slowly gathered her in, drawing her gently to him, her tears mingling with his own sweat.

She finally disengaged and backed away, smiling, and brushed a finger across her cheek. "Thank you," she said. "Welcome to my version of Disneyland. Did you enjoy the ride?"

They retreated to the main door, picking up their wine glasses on the way. His hand trembled. To keep from spilling the wine, he gulped it down. He flashed her a wry smile as she locked the door. "I know I need a shower," he said, "and I probably should be afraid to check the condition of my underwear."

Silently he followed her back into the cottage. She beckoned him into a small guest room. She pointed to the wall. It was a painting of a young girl standing in front of a palomino, a shy grin on her face.

"I painted that from a photo of myself taken when I was twelve. The painting was to be a birthday present for my husband. I had finished it five minutes before I received the news."

Fox rubbed his brow, and dropped his head for a moment, then found her eyes.

"They shot him," she said in a quiet monotone. "He was with a geologist taking core samples near an old bridge. He was a civil engineer who designed roads. The general's daughter is a runner and she ran past them, her entourage following behind. As she went by, a small wallet dropped out of her windbreaker. My husband fetched it and ran after her to return it. They shot him in the back. No warning, according to the geologist, who, not surprisingly, disappeared a day later.

"Of course, the one who shot him claimed he yelled out to my husband and was exonerated. What his family and I received was an official apology for the terrible accident. My husband was thirty. I was twenty-six."

Fox said nothing, but did not look away from her, though she seemed to look right through him.

"I was starting to make it in the art world painting English manors and Roman ruins with trees and flowers spilling out everywhere—places of great beauty, places that visually soothed the soul. I had commissions. My husband wanted to change the third-world country he was from, one road, one infrastructure at a time. Why he was murdered could have been simple overreaction, but I doubt it. His mother was, and still is, a leader in Quintana's political opposition."

Fox exhaled and rubbed his eyes, nearly overwhelmed. He had been right. She had her own tragedy. This is how she copes.

"How did you come to create what I just witnessed?" he asked.

"Technology-wise, with light refracting film loops overlapping static paintings. Almost any film run through my projector can be split and made into surround vision. Air is forced through special filters that can produce heat, cold, and odors to further enhance. With the help of my technical geek, it's the closest thing I know of to a 'holo-suite.'"

She drew her hand across her face. "I'm sorry. I've been rambling. None of that matters. Why I do it is what I want you to know. I've never told anyone. Somehow I believed you could understand."

"I want to understand," said Fox.

"A week after it happened, I stumbled into the jungle in a daze, and what you saw in the studio was how, in that moment, I saw Quintana. Evil," she said, her eyes now engaged with his. "After I painted my first piece from that experience, I recognized the power I possessed and what it meant. I think of it like this: The bullet that killed my husband also wounded my soul and the wound constantly drips blood, drop by drop, and when I feel like I'm suffocating, about to drown in it, I go into the studio and let it drain into my palette. Only when I feel like I'm about to succumb, can I paint that way."

She paused to let out a half laugh. "I, Celeste, possess the power to determine the general nature of a person, whether they're basically good or evil."

"How so?" asked Fox, aware that neither of them had moved since they entered the room.

"While most people may be awed by those pieces, they could never live with them on their walls. Men such as the general are drawn in. Unlike you, they are not repulsed. On the contrary, they revel in it. And they are my market, the despots of the world. They pay me exorbitant sums to see the visions of their mind's eye painted on canvas. I use their money to hasten their downfall. The general, also known as the Butcher, was my first customer."

Fox took in the defeat and the resolve on her face, then gazed at the self-portrait of the innocent Celeste Starr.

"So," she said, "I have not sold my soul to the devil, but I have made a deal with him. He will never possess my soul, but for now I ask him to leave it bleeding and, in return, I deliver to him souls he can claim for eternity. And that is the me I want you to know. My body desires to touch and be touched, but, if you're willing, I yearn for comfort—a lot of comforting, and I think I can find it in your arms. The reason I'm telling you this is because, I sensed during the flight, you need comforting as well. Was I right?"

Fox nodded.

"You can tell me as much or as little as you wish," she said. "The cloud has passed. No more dark talk."

"No more dark talk," he repeated and pulled her into his arms and gently held her head against his chest.

Fox rolled onto his back and watched the candlelight's shadow dance on the ceiling. He was surprised and in awe of the sexual chemistry that seemed to crackle like lightning between Celeste and him. But more than that, it was as she said. He provided comfort and drew it from her—as much as he wanted, and he was surprised at the depth of his emotional fulfillment. I'll be a better man tomorrow than I was today for having been here, he thought. He reached out and stroked her cheek, and she kissed his forehead and blew out the candles.

"Do I have permission to wake you up if I just want to hold you?" he asked.

"Yes, the blood of both our bleeding souls has comingled," she said with mock gravity.

"What does that mean?"

"It means my body is yours."

"Wow."

"Sweet dreams."

It seemed like seconds later that he felt her limbs entwined with his, her fingers caressing his face. "I'm sorry," she whispered, "I was afraid you were having a nightmare."

"I was dreaming," he said, slurring the words. He was going to explain but felt instantly aroused and they made love again, until they were spent, lying next to each other as the first streaks of light painted the ceiling.

"Care to talk about your dream?" she asked.

He rolled onto his side, facing her, his eyes playful. "It was about another woman."

"Yes, of course. How could it be anything but? You've conquered me; it's time to move on, if only in your dreams," she said, mimicking his smile.

"Seriously, a few years back I was in a plane crash. I have this recurring dream about it. But instead of that, I dreamed about a conversation I had with a young girl on the flight—she was by herself, and I ended up rescuing her. I can't figure out why I dreamed of her."

"Maybe your subconscious simply wondered what had happened to her and was triggered by your being in a strange place."

"I don't know. I keep looking at her, then her paperwork—it's just a piece of paper that has the names and addresses of the persons dropping off and picking up the unaccompanied—" He bolted up.

"What is it?" asked Celeste, rising almost as fast.

His mind's eye telescoped in on the paper work. *Child's name: Antoinette. Person at destination: Jeff Johansson. Person at departure...the paper began to blur in his head, then he made it out...Ashley-Lynn Sabatini.* "My God, it's her," he breathed.

"Who?" Celeste asked, sliding out of bed and standing in front of him.

"It's her! Joey, my flying partner. She was the little girl," said Fox, rubbing his chin in confusion.

"You mean the one who looks at you like you're God."

"She's the one I was working with," he said, rubbing his chin. "I wouldn't say God."

"I would. And now, maybe I know why. She's beautiful and looks vaguely familiar."

"That's the mystery, why is she working as a flight attendant?" asked Fox.

"Why shouldn't she be?" asked Celeste.

"Because she's a well-established fashion model. A couple of girls showed me her photos in a five-page spread in *Vogue*."

Celeste climbed on top of him, brushing her eyelashes over his lips, waiting a few seconds for him to sexually respond. "In most ways you're remarkably preserved, but perhaps your powers of observation have slipped a little."

"How so?"

She dragged her lashes across his mouth again. "The eyelashes you said were enhanced? All mine. And your partner Joey? I don't think it's much of a mystery," she said, reaching down and guiding him deep inside her. "I think she wants to get closer to God."

3:50 P.M. CST

The white jetliner hurtled down the runway, reached rotation speed, and soared into the blue sky to the south. As the plane gained altitude, some of the weight seemed to lift from Hector's head, allowing him at least a trickle of rational thought. He knew Heinrich well enough to believe that, if indeed there was a bomb on board, Heinrich would want the plane to explode over the ocean and go down in deep water. That meant Hector had a little time, at least. He also concluded that somehow the box must be revealed to the crew. He pondered the question: Was there a way to do it without implicating himself?

He sat behind the other nine passengers, who were intent on their reading materials. Despite the low-altitude chop, he rose without a sound and headed for the aft left restroom, the one he hoped the crew was most likely to use. He needed to get in and out without them seeing him, which was no problem so long as they were still in their jumpseats, the wall in front of them blocking their view.

Once inside, he silently locked the door. Turning around, he glanced in the mirror and recoiled. His skin was ghostlike and he dripped with sweat. Nevertheless, he yanked the roll of toilet tissue off its holder, reached down, and opened the compartment that held the used paper towels. He pulled the bin out, tossed the roll in, pushed the bin back into place, and closed the compartment door. He toweled off his face, took a deep breath, departed, and was back in his seat in less than two minutes.

The seatbelt sign dinged off and the captain made a quick announcement over the PA. "We're through this thin layer of bumps and it should be smooth from here on. As always, the cockpit door is open. Come and see us, if you've a mind to," he said, in his strong Aussie accent.

Hector eyed his watch. Another ten minutes had passed. Hearing footsteps behind him, he turned to see Joey making her way toward him. *Perfect*, he thought, but all she asked him was what he wanted to drink.

He began to sweat again as the flight attendants refilled glasses after a first round of beverages. *How long until I reveal?* For each passing second his heart seemed to beat twice, yet a minute felt like an hour. He glanced at his watch again. They'd been in the air for twenty-seven minutes. *Three more minutes is all I can wait.*

He was reaching for his seatbelt buckle when he felt her presence behind him. Joey knelt beside his chair and cocked her head with a self-deprecating smile. "I must be losing it. Before we took off I checked out everything: your extra equipment, lavatory smoke detectors, that sort of stuff. Anyway, I swear there was a full roll of toilet tissue in the aft left lav, but there's nothing there, and I couldn't find any extra."

"Not a problem," said Hector, as he attempted to smile back. "Master bath, compartment left of the sink."

After Joey pulled a roll of tissue from the cabinet, she almost had the door latched, when she decided it was worth another look. She wouldn't have given it a second thought, except that when she did her normal safety checks at work, in addition to checking the readiness of all of the safety equipment, she also checked the cubbyholes for items that didn't seem to belong. Like this one.

It was a cardboard cigar box. Upon closer inspection, using her flashlight, she deduced that the lid's lift-up seal had been broken and was attached, as it should be, only on the back side. Slowly, she lifted the lid, releasing a whiff of tobacco, and then pushed it all the way up to rest against the wall, expecting to find a box full of cigars. Instead, a surge of electricity coursed through her body.

"Oh my God," she breathed aloud. She took two steps back and inhaled deeply three times, willing her training to kick in. She took another deliberate look at the contents, then in a controlled rush, retreated to the lounge area to seek Mike. Not spotting him, she made her way back to the galley where Rita was pulling plastic off pre-plated shrimp cocktails.

"Rita," she said, placing her hand on Rita's shoulder. "This is going to be hard to believe, but I'm not joking. I found a suspect item in the master bath. I'm going to grab my phone and take a picture of it so the captain can relay the information more exactly."

"What? Are you serious? Are you saying that you might have discovered a bomb?" asked Rita.

Joey nodded.

"Okay," Rita exhaled, "I'm on my way. I'll guard the entrance." Once again Rita felt her stomach muscles flutter. Ten minutes ago, the cause of flutters had been visions of Hector Cato's naked ass, but now, she wasn't visualizing anything. She was responding as she was supposed to, her training taking charge.

"I'm right behind you," said Joey. She pulled her purse from the crew storage compartment and took one more deep breath before plunging her hand inside. *Joey, you are going to do whatever you need to do and you are going to do it right. You will concentrate on the task.,* It was a needless exhortation, for any fear she felt had already been swept away by the subconscious return to her moment of perfection, fifteen years before.

With steady fingers she pulled the phone out of her purse as well as a tailor's measuring tape, which she always carried. She strode forward with confidence and activated the phone. Rita stood in the doorway to the bathroom and stepped aside to allow Joey to enter.

Careful not to touch any surface, Joey snapped four pictures. She measured the components, wrote the numbers on a scrap of paper, and was on her way to the cockpit in less than three minutes. As soon as she departed, Rita stepped back in the doorway.

Mike was just turning aft out of the forward auxiliary galley with a bottle of wine when he spotted Joey coming toward him. The smile vanished from his face upon seeing the intensity on hers. "What is it?" he asked.

With a slight nod of her head, bidding him to follow her, she ducked into a sequestered space next to door 1-right. "I found a suspect item in the master bath. I think it contains all the components. I saw a timing device, battery, explosive, and what I think is the detonator. Am I missing anything?" she asked.

Mike shook his head.

Joey continued. "I measured and photographed it. Rita is standing guard. Please relieve her. She has a—"

"Holy shit," he said, setting down the bottle, his hand suddenly shaky. "I know. I'll get her as far away as possible. Update me when you're done with the captain."

Joey nodded, and departed, then entered the open cockpit. She closed the door. That action alone caused both pilots to crane their necks toward her.

Captain Bob Allenby was a sixty-three-year-old Aussie, who had been flying since he was a teenager. He was a fun-loving guy and he liked to hoist a few too many on occasion. But he was a nimble thinker and he knew the book inside and out, and used it.

"We have a situation," said Joey.

"Rico, fly the airplane," Allenby said, turning his body and full attention to her.

"I found a suspect item in the master bath, in a cabinet that holds extra rolls of toilet tissue," said Joey.

"Have you posted a guard?"

"Yes."

"Go on."

She described the device and pushed her cell phone and the notepaper with the dimensions toward him. "I have four pictures. It seems to me all components are present, as well as a timer that is active. I'm not positive, but I don't think there's a lift trigger underneath it."

"So we could possibly move it?"

"Yes, at Consolidated, the least-risk-bomb-location is always the furthest door from your seat, in this case, 2-right," she said, verbalizing the LRBL acronym so there was no confusion.

"Same here. Okay, this is how we'll proceed. Rico is going to get out our checklist and start descending the airplane, while I get through to dispatch, and ultimately the bomb guy at the FBI, the agency we use, and as Consolidated does, I assume. Obviously, if we can disarm it, that's our first choice. Second, and most likely choice, is building a bomb stack. Are you familiar?"

"Yes."

"Can you do it? I want both Rico and me in here."

"I'd feel more comfortable with my manual, but yes, I went to Recurrent Emergency Training two weeks ago. I can do it if we have the materials. What do you make of the timer?"

He studied the camera phone. "I'm not positive, but it looks to me like it's set to go thirty minutes from when you took the picture. We're at least forty minutes from anywhere we can land, so you need to work fast."

"I agree. First, I'll test for an anti-lift switch. If it slides under freely, I'll proceed," she said, deliberately stating the obvious.

"Get started. I'll give you a ding-dong when I get the bomb man on the horn. He might have questions. I'll make a quick PA announcement to let everyone know what we hope to accomplish. You, Mike, and Rita are in charge back there. That includes Ramirez. Do what you have to do. Questions?"

"Door open or closed?"

"Closed. I'm not worried about interference from any of these passengers, but if it goes off, that's one more thing between us and whatever is flying around."

Joey nodded and turned to go.

"Joey. Good work. I can assure you we know what the hell we're doing up here."

Joey emerged from the cockpit and sought out Mike, now on guard in the master bedroom.

"Captain is briefed. He's patching through to the FBI." She held up a plastic safety card. "I'm going to check for an anti-lift device," she said, sliding past him.

Millimeter by millimeter she pushed the card along the smooth tile under the cigar box, hoping her fingers were sensitive enough to notice even the faintest resistance, but she encountered none and completed the task. She left the card under the box. Her heart rate was somewhere between fast and racing, her forehead damp, but she was entirely composed as she faced Mike.

"It's clear. How do you want to proceed? I went to Recurrent Emergency Training a couple of weeks ago."

"It's been almost a year for me, so, you're in charge of assembly. Rita will assist you. I'll gather the materials. When you're ready to place the bomb, I'll bring it, and take over for Rita. In the meantime I'll get Hector to stand guard here. Are you okay with that?"

"Let's go."

"What do you want first?"

"Webbing material," answered Joey. "I think I saw a bag of headsets in the aft closet, which I can grab. You gather any available neckties and belts. Then, hardcase luggage. After that, wet blankets. And get enough thin plastic for two layers, for one under and one over the item. Forget that. I'll take care of the plastic," she said, remembering a stash of plastic trash bags in the galley. "Once you place it, I'll need soft luggage and seat cushions."

Mike nodded and was off. He strode into the lounge area just as the captain finished with the PA announcement. Allenby had explained that the crew would move the item and build a bomb stack in the rear of the aircraft at door 2-right. Detonation would be directed outward, causing the door, which is a natural breach in the fuselage, to bear the brunt of the explosion and minimize structural damage to the rest of the aircraft. All the passengers stood with their eyes wide and skin paled with fear. Except for Ramirez. He merely stroked his mustache, as if he were considering the crew's performance.

Ramirez eyed Mike and said, "Tell us how we can help."

"Thank you, all," said Mike. "First, I need belts and ties, and anything else that can be used for restraining webbing. Next, I need any hard case luggage, and don't take the time to go through it. Just bring it to me in the rear galley." He glanced down at the feet of a roundish middle-aged man dressed in a light gray suit, and spotted a hard-shelled suitcase. "Like that. It's exactly what we need. Bring it, please."

"No one touches my belongings and no one tells me what to do," he said, in lightly accented English, scowling.

Mike paused for a moment, Fox Revelstorm flashing through his head. He lowered his voice. "If you want to live, your best shot is with us, so you'll do exactly as we tell you."

"We will," said Ramirez, handing him his belt. "Please excuse General Soriano. He's used to giving orders, not taking them."

Mike quickly collected the other ties and belts from outstretched hands, thinking that making it to the ground in one piece was only the first of his challenges to stay alive. He'd just pissed off the Butcher. Nevertheless, failing to rein in his natural combativeness when confronted, he shot the general a hard look and said, "So, get used to taking orders, and bring your fucking suitcase to the aft galley."

He turned his head to Ramirez. "I need wet blankets. Soak them thoroughly. Use the large sink in the forward galley—maybe as many as twenty if you can find them, and after that I'll need the soft cushions from the seat bottoms in the aft three-by-three seats.

"As quickly as I can," Ramirez replied.

Mike started aft, then answered the dinging interphone. "Mike here."

"Mike? Bob. Who's going to move the package?"

"Me."

"There's nothing on the radar, but in another fifteen minutes we'll be down to about ten thousand feet. It could get choppy. So, it's your call—move it now while it's smooth or wait and risk a few bumps."

"We really have no exact idea when it will go, or, *if* it will go off, right?" asked Mike.

"Affirmative."

"I'll wait."

"Roger that."

Fuck, I don't need to be reeling around the cabin with a live bomb, but I also don't want it around my crew. Right now, Hector Cato is nearest to the bomb and he's more expendable.

Headset cords secured to safety handles on both sides of the door served as the anchors to the webbing, which would be sewn together in the center after the suspect bomb was placed into position. Joey and Rita were nearly halfway done with it when Mike entered the galley.

He placed belts and ties on the floor next to them. "The hard luggage should be right behind me."

"Good," said Joey. "As soon as it arrives, we'll stop the webbing and start building the stack. I'm going to need enough material to get to a height of about ten inches below the porthole. About three layers, I think, depending on width."

"That means about ten hard bags," said Mike. "I'm on it. Ramirez will bring you the blankets, and you have the plastic, right?"

"Yes," she said, taking hold of the first of the suitcases.

The interphone rang. Mike answered it, listened, and hung it up. "Joey, stay here. The bomb guy doesn't need to talk to you. Captain says to keep building; disarming is too risky."

Joey kept working without raising her head.

Mike moved forward passing a small group of passengers heading to the galley hefting suitcases. He counted only five hard pieces, general's not among them. He half-jogged back to the master bedroom. Hector Cato stood passively in the doorway, staring down at his shoes.

"Do they keep any spare luggage on the plane?" asked Mike.

Hector's head popped up, but his face remained blank.

"I need more hard-sided luggage."

Snapping out of it, Cato dropped to his knees. "Check under the beds in the other rooms. Here," he said, yanking one out by the handle, "I think there are three more."

"Pull them out, but don't let anybody get close to that cabinet. I'll be right back to get them. I'm going to check for more." But he found no more, and lassoing a helper on the way back, they gathered the four from the master suite and returned aft.

With the eye of a puzzle solver, Joey fitted those last pieces into place in quick order. "One more piece would make this more stable, but we have to keep going."

"Give me a half minute," said Mike.

He jogged back to the lounge and spotted the general's suitcase. It hadn't moved. He swept it up, at the same time pushing back the latches, until he felt the resistance of the locks. With one quick thrust, he broke through them, pulled the two sides apart, and shook the contents onto the floor. A meaty paw to his shoulder spun him around, but going with his momentum, Mike kept turning and slammed the suitcase into the general's ample stomach. Soriano stayed upright and sent a right hand toward Mike's jaw. Mike slipped it, tossed the suitcase aside, and stepped forward. He settled himself low under the general's extended body, and came up with his knee in the big man's crotch. Soriano started to slump forward, but with a powerful jab, Mike smashed the heel of his left hand into the general's forehead, reversing the forward momentum. Mike grabbed up the suitcase, and was away before the teetering general hit the floor with the back of his head.

Mike handed Joey the suitcase. "Anything else you need?"

"No, I'll have the first layer of blankets ready in less than five minutes. So, go retrieve the item. I'll be ready."

"Okay. Rita, go forward and gather all the passengers together in the lounge and keep them there—away from me. There's a guy up there I had to get tough with. I think I knocked him out. Check his condition. Once I—"

"What guy?" Rita interrupted.

"The Butcher."

"The Butcher?" Rita echoed. She ran a couple of fingers across her forehead "Great, gay blade cold cocks a third-world despot. That'll look good on your resume."

As he watched Joey continue to work, Mike refocused on Rita. "Once I deliver the package, I'll take over for you, so stay up forward."

Rita shook her head. "I can finish."

"It's a no-brainer, Rita. You're going forward, and staying forward," said Joey, ending the discussion.

Mike was already on his way to the cabinet when he felt the aircraft start to pitch. It was not violent, but he detected instability beneath him, as if the plane were riding on bubbles about to burst.

"Fuck," he said, aloud. "Hector, I'll take it from here. Rita should have everyone rounded up in the lounge area. I've checked my path to the galley and it's clear, so no one moves, until I'm finished."

"Do you want me to shadow you in case you start to fall?"

"Thanks, but no. You could end up landing on me."

Hector stuck a thumb up in understanding and left.

Mike's hands were sticky with sweat, so he washed and dried them. He had already decided that he would back straight out of the bathroom before turning. He checked the floor behind him to make sure it was clear, then moved forward.

When he lifted up the box, it seemed feather light, and for an instant he wondered if he was powered with nothing but adrenaline. As he backed out of the restroom, the plane pitched left, and his shoulder crashed into the door frame. But he held steady, got himself through, turned around, and moved aft. He set his feet wide apart, his butt low, and his elbows out, to act as bumpers if necessary. He held the box close to, but not touching his chest, ready to cradle it, if he went down.

The ride became rockier, but Mike kept steady. He fought the urge to rush, and made each step with as much precision and planning as he could, to make the next one as successful. After what seemed like an eternity to him, he finally set the box in its nest. He straightened and grabbed onto the galley countertop to quiet his shaking body and cramping legs. He noticed the ride had suddenly smoothed out and he shook his head. So far, timing had not been his forte on this trip.

Joey gave him about twenty seconds before she glanced up. "I'm ready for the next group of blankets," she said, gently placing a thin layer of plastic over the box.

Mike breathed deeply into his cupped hands. He felt his body relax and went to work next to her, first assembling the wet blankets and then the soft luggage and cushions. Five minutes later they tied the two sides of the webbing together.

"Nice work," he said.

"We better let the captain know we're ready."

"Let's get out of here. I'll call him from my jumpseat."

"We're ready to go up here," said Captain Allenby. "Altitude and speed are set, and the cabin's been depressurized. If the timer is correct we have about eight minutes. Take five and get everyone briefed and every loose item secured, then sit. Since you're down to one jumpseat, one of you can sit up here."

"I'll send Rita."

Mike assembled the passengers in the lounge. "In a minute we're going to put on our life-vests. Mr. Ramirez and Mr. Cato are our primary helpers. If we have to ditch the airplane, the first option is door 1-left. Second option is door 1-right. With seventeen of us total, we only need one raft. If Joey and I are incapacitated, get the door open. That action will deploy the slide and raft. Get everyone into the raft. At the door sill you'll see a quick disconnect handle. It's marked. Pull it. That will separate the raft from the aircraft. There's a knife in a pocket on top of the raft. Use it to cut the strap. Don't inflate your life vest until you're out of the plane. Get out quick. With no rear door we'll fill with water in a hurry.

Mike grabbed his life vest and held it in front of him. "Watch and listen to how we put on our vests. Then you do the same and be seated. Lean forward and stay low. Questions?"

Ramirez pointed to the general lying on his back. He resembled a small pitching mound. "What about him?"

"Rita says he's breathing and has a pulse. See if you can get him into a chair and get his vest around him, but, more important, get him belted in. I don't want him flying all over the cabin. Joey and I need to secure the forward galley and anything else that's not tied down. Can you handle it?"

"Yes," said Ramirez, "I can handle it."

Finally belted in, Mike glanced at his watch and listened to the familiar whoosh of the airplane, thinking it surreal with normalcy. But that was soon to change. He turned to Joey. "A minute to go. I guess we're going to find out just how good the FAA's ground simulation of the least-risk-location, works in the air."

"Why did you set your watch to a countdown mode? We only have an approximate time at best," said Joey.

"I don't know. I did it without thinking. Flair for the dramatic, maybe."

Joey raised an eyebrow. "You could probably give brushing your teeth a flare for the dramatic."

She took Mike's hand in hers. She felt him flinch as she gripped his hot sticky palm with her icy fingers. Mike turned his other wrist toward their faces and they watched as the countdown rushed into single digits.

4:20 P.M. CST

The beeping of his watch refocused Mike's glassed-over eyes. He jerked his hand across his body to silence the alarm. The hum, whoosh, and the low-altitude buffeting returned to his consciousness. The zero moment had come and gone, then another minute and another. He registered the lingering coolness of Joey's fingers wound in his and turned to her. To his surprise she looked as if she'd just left a spa—relaxed and refreshed.

"You're not afraid." he said.

"No, I'm not afraid. But," she smiled, "I am concerned."

Mike blurted out a nervous laugh, tossing his head backward into the leather headrest. "*Concerned?* That reminds me of my father on the day I told my parents I was gay. My mother says, 'Oh, honey, I'm so concerned.' My dad looked at her like he was going to kill her, after he was finished with me. He says, 'My only son tells us he's in love with another man and you're *concerned?*'. "I'm thinking, we're about to get blown out of the sky, and Joey is *concerned?* So, why aren't you afraid?"

She gazed at him for a moment and said in a soft voice, "Because the best thing that ever happened to me came out of the worst thing that ever happened to me."

The interphone chimed. Mike answered it. Captain Allenby said, "We're five minutes beyond the estimated time of detonation. Did either of you notice anything else about the package? Anything odd? I'm still patched through to the FBI."

Mike relayed the question and Joey shook her head.

"There was one thing," said Mike. "When I picked it up, I was trying to be as steady and deliberate as I could, but still, I nearly banged it off the ceiling in that little compartment. At first I attributed it to adrenaline, yet the whole way to the back, it just seemed featherweight. I thought those types of explosives carried a little weight."

"I'll get back to you in a minute," Allenby said, clicking off the interphone.

"So, how are things now with your father?" asked Joey.

"We're trying to figure out if this bomb is going to go off, and you're asking me about my relationship with my father?"

"Yes."

Mike rubbed his forehead and let out a little laugh. "You are one strange lady. Apparently, your picture is plastered all over the fashion magazines. Yet, you're flying on reserve for a washed-up airline, making a pittance, working the worst trips imaginable, and you won't say why. And now, when our lives can end any second, you look like you just finished a tray of tea and crumpets."

"I'll tell you why. But first, tell me how you get along with your father."

Mike sighed and nodded his head. "We get along fine. I'm sure he wishes I was married with three kids, but he finally understood that it wasn't what I wanted. It's not something I chose. It's terrible when you find out you're different. I did everything to fight it, because it's like being cursed. Finally, you accept yourself as you are and go about living. But that doesn't mean everyone will be happy about it."

Mike interrupted himself by again picking up the chiming handset. He listened for a moment, then turned to Joey. "He wants to confirm that you think there was a letter "O" on top of the explosive cylinder. He says that's what it looks like to him in the picture."

"Yes, that's what it looked like to me," she said.

Mike relayed the response and listened for another minute before hanging up. "They think it might be a fake. The explosives can be very light, but not weightless, and the letter "O" might be for "demo". Still, we're proceeding to Pais de Rosado, where they have a bomb squad. He wants us to stay seated, but first, I'm going to explain to Ramirez what's going on. And when I get back, I want to know what the hell you're doing here."

Joey barely moved her head in assent.

As Mike made his way into the lounge, he took in the group of twelve passengers, all quiet, most with their heads down, a few with lips moving. No doubt, he surmised, silently praying, trying to barter deals with God. If I survive I'll do, I'll be, I'll never again… Mike couldn't remember what he had been thinking as the clock wound down to zero, but he wasn't praying and he wasn't pitching deals. Since his first lover had been beaten to death by a gang of gay bashers fourteen years ago in Sydney, Australia, there was no one to bargain with, and no one to pray to.

But the senseless death had not been totally in vain. It brought his estranged father to his door in sympathy and finally acceptance. Mike remembered as a child starting a fight with another boy and being sent home from school. His father had told him: "You don't start fights; you finish them" and then offered to send him to martial arts school to learn self-defense and gain confidence. Mike declined.

The day his father had knocked on his door, he remembered the adage and vowed that he would never start a fight, but if he or anyone else were attacked, he would finish it. And before leaving, they embraced, and Mike thanked him for the years-old advice. The next day, when he went to enroll at the local dojo, he was informed that his father had been there the day before and had purchased a lifetime membership for him, if he wanted to enroll. Mike was twenty-one. By the time he was twenty-six, he was a lethal weapon.

He glanced at the general, his neck draped over the back of the sofa, snoring, as if taking a nap. Suddenly, Mike was angry—more at himself, than anyone.

Ramirez, by himself, was belted into a leather sofa that could hold three. Mike let out a deep breath and plopped down next to him.

"You don't look so good," said Ramirez. "And I was just starting to relax a little, since we're past the deadline."

"Actually, I have good news, maybe," he said fastening his belt. He noticed Ramirez was tense, but composed. A nod induced Mike to continue. "The bomb could be a fake. The explosives might just be empty tubes used for demonstration purposes. However, we're still proceeding to Pais de Rosado. The bomb squad will remove it and make the final analysis. I won't speculate as to why someone would plant a fake bomb on board, but it makes me wonder."

"I will speculate. Someone is making a statement. In any case, you and your crew were very impressive with the way you handled this whole situation, including the general. He's going to wake up like a mad hornet."

"Keep him away from me if you can, but remind him if you have to, that I could have killed him—easily. And probably should have."

Mike's head told him to shut up, but he lowered his voice and rambled on, as if the words had already been downloaded to his vocal cords. "My problem is that I can't get past being human. I should be elated that I might just survive this, but instead, I look at the piece of scum over there, and I get pissed off. By the way, your boy José, I have no idea who he's working for, but he took us on a detour to get a lecture from a lady. She wanted me to kill the general, and gave me poison to do it with. She said that if I were so inclined, to go ahead and knock you off, too. What she showed us wasn't pretty. So, while most of the time I'm a Boy Scout, I'm also a whore for money. As despicable as the general is, you're probably no better. But right now, I feel like I'm worse than anyone. I got my crew into this mess because I have a partner with health issues and a house I can't afford in the first place. Since I'm orally ejaculating like a teenager, I wonder what's in the contents of the mess that used to reside in the general's suitcase. What was he so keen on protecting? I'm thinking there's something there that can only benefit him, and no one else."

Ramirez narrowed his eyes. "Yes, I intend to inspect everything, now. And, I will find out exactly what has transpired today. Everything."

Ramirez opened his hands and flashed a small grin. "As to your diatribe, your description of the general and me is quite accurate. José is working both sides, though he doesn't know that I know, which is why he's constantly nervous. I suspect the woman who wanted us dead is the beautiful Esmerelda. I hope she will one day lead our country. And, I'd like to make you more of a whore for money."

Ramirez paused for a moment, slightly amused by the look of amazement on Mike's face, and then turned his head to the slumping general, and back to Mike. "During the flight from Seattle, while I was waiting near your galley for the restroom, I overheard you and Fox Revelstorm talking about his impending retirement. He had impressed me with his verbal wit and calm demeanor. Later, I paid him a visit in the rear galley and asked him if he would be interested in working for me. He told me, 'Thanks, but no thanks.' I extend the offer to you."

"What would I do?" asked Mike.

"I need leaders. You would lead."

"Lead who? Lead what?"

"There will be many opportunities."

"Have you ever seen *The Music Man*?"

Ramirez laughed out loud, discarding the somberness of an unexploded bomb. "So you think I'm Professor Harold Hill?"

Mike grinned back.

"Let me give you an example," said Ramirez. "I have met three times with a man named Hitesh Mehta. He builds eco-resorts that cater to tourists wanting to learn about a native culture rather than just escape their familiar surroundings. These lodges are designed to protect the natural environment and support the community. I need someone to coordinate all the pieces, to bring together architects, engineers, designers, environmental impact studies, and even seismologists. The experts are available. I need someone to pull them together: a leader. That's what I'm talking about."

"That's what you're talking about as we cruise back to land with a possible unexploded bomb perched next to the back door." Mike shook his head. "I just told you how I take care of my people."

"I've seen how you lead."

Mike shot him a wry smile and another shake of his head. "In case you haven't figured it out, I'm gay. Would that make a difference?" he asked, straightening his back.

"No, it wouldn't," replied Ramirez, his body relaxed.

"You think I'm capable of doing something like you just described, based on observing me for a few hours?" Mike asked, rising.

"If you assured me your personal life was stable and you promised your best effort, I'd take a chance on you."

"I appreciate the vote of confidence. If we get out of this in one piece, we can talk later. I feel more comfortable in my jumpseat, where I belong."

"And I," said Ramirez, rising with Mike, "intend to find out what the general is hiding."

Mike buckled himself back in next to Joey with a miffed expression on his face. "Sorry. How long was I gone?"

"A little under three minutes."

He glanced at his watch. "Seemed like three hours. I don't know what to think about Ramirez. I dumped Esmerelda's flattering opinion of him over his head. He immediately agreed with the assessment, which sort of shocked me. Then, he told me he wants to make her president of the country. How weird is that? I mean it's not like the president and the speaker of the house taking a few verbal shots at each other. She wanted Ramirez dead."

Joey thought for a moment. "Ramirez seems like a basically good man who has to make tough decisions. Somewhat like you."

"Okay, how *not* like me?"

"You don't hurt other people when you make tough decisions."

Mike raised an eyebrow. "That remains to be seen. How do you know all of this?"

"I don't. Idle speculation."

"Touchdown is supposed to be at fifteen after the hour. That means nine more minutes. They'll go a lot faster if you tell me what your story is."

"All right," she said, her voice neutral. "At Recurrent Emergency Training, you've seen the video and pictures of the 737 crash in San Fran in the mid-nineties."

"Yeah, the landing gear collapsed."

"I was in it, almost twelve-years-old. Fox Revelstorm pulled me out of that burning airplane. It changed me—so much more for the better, but I can't let go of the feeling of, for lack of a better word, perfection, when he had his arms around me. That's why I'm here."

"You're kidding!" Mike stared at her and then ran his fingers through his coarse hair. "What is he supposed to do? Does he know?"

She shook her head. "I don't think he's figured it out and I have no idea what I want from him. I expected the unexpected and, so far, what's happened, is um, expectedly unexpected."

"I don't get it."

She rubbed her chin. "I think I projected him as a wise old sage, and maybe when I got up the nerve, I'd just ask him for a hug to see if I felt anything like before. Instead, I've been sitting here trying to deny it, but can't. I'm physically attracted to him and I think he is to me."

"Whoa, the guy's in great shape, but he's almost fifty. What are you? Twenty-four or five?"

"Almost twenty-seven."

"You don't have a boyfriend?"

"No."

"When's the last time you did?"

"Never." She paused. "Let me qualify that. I've dated some men that I'm quite fond of, but nothing serious. I've never fallen in love."

"You're closer to thirty than twenty, and not once have you gone ballistic over some guy?"

"Not once."

"That's hard to believe. I mean it's crazy."

Joey shrugged. "What you really mean is that Joey is crazy. Now you know my story."

Mike shook his head. "I don't think so. There's way more to this. So what are you going to do when—and if—we get back to the hotel? Go through the adjoining door and climb into bed with him?"

"I'm considering it, but his bed might be empty."

"What are you talking about?"

They both paused, feeling the floor vibrate from heavy footsteps. Ramirez appeared, his face slightly flushed and he pointed to the cockpit door. "I'll go over it later, but I believe the general is behind this whole thing in order to get us to land in Pais de Rosada. It's a tiny country run by a military as ruthless as ours. After I explain to Allenby what I've found out, I'm sure he'll agree that touching down there might be more dangerous than the threat of the bomb."

4:25 P.M. CST

During the last twenty minutes of descent, Hector Cato had made peace with himself and his existence, even if it were to be short-lived. He had also decided upon his course of action. He stopped perspiring. His body, which had been coiled with tension, began to unwind.

He was seated to the right and behind Ramirez, while the general slumped in his chair to Ramirez's left. As soon as he and Mike ended their conversation, Ramirez was up, rifling through the contents of the general's suitcase. Hector stood up to offer assistance, but Ramirez waved him into the space Mike had just vacated. He held up several CDs and DVDs. "I need to check out these in the office. If he starts to stir, ring your call button as a signal," he whispered.

Five minutes later, Ramirez returned the discs to the pile and sifted through the rest of the mess. He scanned papers and documents, then rearranged the contents exactly as he had found them. He tossed a large plastic garbage bag at the general's feet. With a small smile on his face, he pulled out a tiny Dictaphone from his pocket and pushed the record button, leaving it hidden in his palm. With his other hand, he took hold of the general's shoulder, and shook it several times. At the general's first response Ramirez resettled himself next to Hector. The plane was on final approach.

The general's eyes fluttered, his head flopped back and forth, fingers clawed at his nose and eyes, and after a minute, his pupils finally focused.

"Welcome back, general," said Ramirez.

"What, what happened?"

"You were knocked out by Mike Braun, the purser."

Soriano rubbed his temple and said nothing, still trying to piece it all together. The sharp jolt of the landing gear deploying seemed to shake him into full consciousness, and suddenly he sat up and peered out the window. "This is not Pais de Rosada," he shouted.

"No, general, it's not."

"But they're expecting—"

His eyes widened at his blunder and then, like a little kid, he puckered his lips and covered his mouth with his hand.

The touchdown had been a grease job. Captain Allenby didn't want to cause any kind of bump—just in case. The plane slowed, but continued to taxi to the end of the runway where two fire trucks, a hazmat vehicle, airstairs, and two vans awaited.

During the taxi, the passengers listened to Mike's short PA reiteration of what he had told them on the descent—they were landing at Ramirez's strip. They would not blow the slides, unless there was an emergency, but they were to deplane, as soon as the stairs were in place.

After the bomb stack had been dismantled and the nature of the bomb discerned, all luggage would be brought to the main office. Hector was surprised that there was no mention of questioning or detention. As they shuffled across the tarmac to the waiting vans, Ramirez had merely promised to get to the bottom of the incident. The passengers all climbed into one van, including the still dazed general and an aide lugging the contents of the general's suitcase stuffed in the garbage bag. The crew, Ramirez, and Hector climbed into the other. Hector sat next to Rita and, without hesitation, covered her hand with his. He felt her squeeze back. He acknowledged the possibility that it could be the first and last time. But for now, he was totally relaxed. As soon as the plane was on the ground, he had called his grandmother and she assured him that the children were fine, except for their usual fussing about washing their hands before supper. He exhaled in relief.

When they reached the office area, he led Rita, who couldn't stop smiling, and Mike, who couldn't stop chattering, and a strangely somber Joey, back to their briefing room. He promised to return when he found out what was to happen for the rest of the evening. He hurried into the restroom in his office, toweled himself clean, brushed his teeth, and combed his hair. He wanted to get it over with, but wondered if he'd have to wait before catching Ramirez alone. Nervous energy he had jettisoned during the descent reignited throughout his body, and he left his office feeling like a walking dial tone. But, Ramirez's door was open. He was alone and had just set his phone down. Hector took a breath and rapped lightly on the door.

"It's confirmed," Ramirez said, looking up and motioning him in. "It was a fake."

Hector closed the door and approached the desk. "Sir, I know you're working hard to figure this out, but may I have a few uninterrupted minutes of your time?"

"For what purpose?" asked Ramirez.

"On the tarmac, you said you promised to get to the bottom of this incident."

"Yes, and I will."

"I'm here to tell you, *I* am the bottom of this incident."

Ramirez leaned forward in his chair. "You?"

"Yes, me. I placed the package on the plane. I didn't know what it was, but I suspected it was a bomb. I had no idea it was a fake."

Ramirez said nothing for nearly a minute, rose, came around the desk, and stood facing Hector. "So, when we initially pushed back, you expected us to die?"

"I didn't know for sure, but, yes, that's what I expected."

"Explain yourself. Tell me what happened."

"About an hour before departure, while I was running off the galley manifest, Heinrich appeared in my office with a bag and a box inside. He told me where to place it. When I told him I couldn't, he made it clear to me that my children would suffer if I didn't."

"You were willing to trade the lives of seventeen for the lives of two?"

Hector's voice remained steady. "I would have sacrificed the lives of my children, but I was willing to trade seventeen lives not to have them raped and tortured, before they died. I would make the same choice again."

"How could you allow them to be in such jeopardy?"

Cato flexed his hands, still at his sides. "A monumental lapse in judgment. But it's more complicated than that. It was a symptom of a general meltdown on my part."

"Be more specific," ordered Ramirez, with a low, hard voice.

Cato took a deep breath and exhaled, some of the rigidity escaping his body. "Lately, I have been thinking reactively and negatively. I thought, where could I send them? Who did I still know in America? Who could I turn to? I kept reaching dead ends. I was paralyzed with fear. So, I did nothing else, except sweat."

Ramirez eased back around his desk and sat. He motioned Hector to do the same. "What else?"

"Surely it's obvious that in the near future you and Heinrich cannot and will not coexist. Like a fool, I tried to figure out who would win," said Hector.

For the first time, Ramirez's face lost its neutrality and he stared at Hector in more apparent disbelief than when Cato told him he had placed the bomb on board.

"I never doubted your strength, but I have seen Heinrich's brutality," Hector went on. "Like I said, my thinking has been negative; the future seemed black."

The little composure that Ramirez had lost was quickly regained, and his voice took on an even harder edge. "Your weakness disappoints me, Hector. All you had to do was to ask me. Your children would be safe in Los Angeles, right now. Perhaps I am the fool. It never occurred to me to question your loyalty. So, why the confession? You might have been able to slide through this without me finding out."

"I doubt it, but you're right. Weak is the way to describe me. No more. I'd rather die than keep living the way I've been living. I know you may eliminate me and, if so, I am content with that. But, I know you would never harm my children. At this point, that's all I care about."

Ramirez leaned back in his chair, a look of consternation on his face. "If I allow you to continue, will you pledge your full support to me, and do whatever I tell you?"

"Yes, in that, nothing will change."

"Until this moment, you have been my employee. You are more now. If necessary, I expect you to lay down your life to save mine. Will you?"

Hector wiped his brow. "Yes."

"Good," replied Ramirez. Abruptly he rose. Cato mirrored him. Ramirez yanked open his right desk drawer, removed a revolver, placed it on the desk, and pushed it across to Cato.

"Pick it up, turn to the left, and put the barrel to the right side of your head. Then, pull the trigger."

In a split second it occurred to Hector that Ramirez's instructions were more practical than dramatic: his splattered brains would end up on the floor, not all over Ramirez's desk. Hector's fingers hovered for only an instant before gripping the gun with his right hand. In an unhurried but steady motion, he placed the gun above his ear and, hesitating only a second, squeezed the trigger.

The resonating click sounded like an explosion to Hector, but before his body had a chance to sag, Ramirez's voice brought him back to attention, like the lash of a whip.

"Pull it again."

This time Hector did hesitate, his other hand unconsciously touching the place where a cross used to hang from his neck. A cross he had thrown into the ocean, along with his religion.

"Now," barked Ramirez.

Once again, the gun clicked and Hector, still holding it against his skull, turned his head to find Ramirez's eyes.

"That's enough," Ramirez said, reaching out his hand.

Trying not to shake, Hector slid his hand down on the barrel, and extended the butt end. Ramirez took it and placed it back in the drawer.

Cato felt his knees weaken, but he managed to stay on his feet.

"Go pull yourself together, but do it fast. I want you back in here in fifteen minutes, composed, and clearheaded. We have business to discuss, and little time to do it."

"Yes, sir."

Ramirez flashed him a hint of a smile. "Don't call me, sir. This isn't the army. With your help and any luck, in a couple of days this country won't have an army."

Cato departed, but halfway through the door he spun around. "Does the gun have—"

Ramirez shook his head. "You'll never know."

Showered, shaved, and dressed in fresh clothes, once again Hector sat across from Ramirez, waiting for him to end a phone conversation. As soon as the headset was cradled Ramirez started in. "A sizable stash of cocaine and heroin was found in the cargo hold. That fact, combined with what I learned from the contents of the general's bag, leads me to believe that we were to land at Pais de Rosada, where I would be held for transporting drugs. The general, being cozy to their military, would broker a deal for my freedom in exchange for a chunk of my holdings and a barrel of cash. I will have confirmation later. Obviously the general and Gustav were together on this, but their plan has blown up in their faces. So, what do you think Heinrich will do?"

Hector rubbed his chin. "What did you find in the general's suitcase?"

"In due time. Answer my question."

"The general and the army will protect Heinrich. But he's not the type to wait it out. Just because he failed today—I don't think he'll stop. Except for a trifling amount of protection, you've never been security conscious. That should change. I've seen this coming. Heinrich has turned his cards over and tossed them aside. I would say it's imperative that you neutralize Heinrich before he gets to you. If I didn't make myself clear enough, Gustav will attempt to kill you."

Ramirez drummed his fingers on the desk, and nodded. "Unfortunately it has come down to this. We are in agreement."

"What would you like me to do?" asked Hector.

"Accompany the flight attendants to my estate. I have already arranged extra security for the outer perimeters. Set them up in the guest wing. Dinner will be served on the terrace. You are the host. Show them a good time. When you have finished, spend the night or have José drive you home, but before you leave, you must be honest with them."

Hector nodded his head. "I'm dreading it, but I'll tell them the truth."

"As for your children," continued Ramirez, "I have dispatched four men to protect them. Tomorrow morning at eleven, the plane leaves for Los Angeles. Your grandmother and the children will be on board. I have just finished the arrangements. After they are gone, I expect you to turn your full attention to locating Heinrich and figuring out a way, as you say, to eliminate him. I'm putting this on you because, other than his own sick underlings, you know how he thinks better than anyone—even me. Any resources you need, including firepower and muscle, are at your disposal, but ideally you will make him disappear just as he made his victims disappear: without a trace."

Ramirez rose to dismiss him. "Check in with me tomorrow, say around noon. I will be spending the morning alone—with a lady."

5:30 P.M. CST

Hector sat rigid in a beach chair facing the ocean. The half-dozen buildings of Ramirez's compound were perched behind him. The sky was taking on a burnt orange hue. An epic sunset seemed inevitable, yet he was scarcely aware of anything or anyone, except Rita. He had run every possible scenario through his head a thousand times, but his brain kept defaulting back to the same one: Rita gapes at him in utter disbelief, sinks to her knees, and retches up the bitter bile of betrayal, as he pleads and begs for forgiveness and understanding. The first part of the scenario was probable. The last part was unacceptable. He would tell it straight, as he had with Ramirez. No pleading for anything.

He glanced at his watch. Not even an hour since he had confessed to Ramirez. Rita wanted to walk in the sand with him. While he waited for her, the surf, mimicking his heart, pounded.

Quietly, she appeared in front of him wearing a white two-piece swimsuit and a wide smile, clutching a towel bag he recognized from the room. He stared at her for a moment, then embarrassed, he dropped his eyes.

"Are you impressed?" she asked. "I want you to be."

"Very," he said, rising. "You must work out a lot."

"Not so much," she said, with a wry smile. "Anxiety is an excellent catalyst for weight control. Let's walk."

He was tempted to ask about her anxiety, but decided to plow ahead. "Before we do, I have something to tell you," he said, standing up. "You might want to be close to your room."

Rita dropped the bag in the sand and stood with her arms at her sides and waited, the outline of her body silhouetted against the reddening horizon.

Keeping his voice even, he said, "I was the one who placed the device on board. I never opened the box because I didn't have the courage to do so. I suspected it was a bomb, one that would go off. I thought I was sending all of you to a horrid death."

Their eyes remained locked. Hector forced himself to continue. "After I boarded the plane, I devised a way for you or Joey to discover the box's location."

Inexplicably Rita did not cry, scream, retch, or even react. She continued to study him as if to ascertain the nature of his core being. Hector felt his insides knot and resolved to let her have anything she wanted.

"I'm so sorry," he said.

"I know that. I think I know most all of it."

"Rita, I don't believe you understand. I betrayed you, and everyone." He rubbed his eyes and stared at the sand.

Rita shook her head and took his hand. "No one knows betrayal better than I do. Let's walk," she repeated, more forcefully.

They moved along the water's edge, waves breaking over their ankles, sand squishing up between their toes. Finally she stopped and once again faced him. "I appreciate your forthrightness. Yet, I expected no less from you. That's why we are here, together. When we first boarded the plane and when you left to retrieve the galley manifest, there was joy between us. When you returned, you tried to maintain it, but failed. You were somber. It had occurred to me that you had just found out that someone close to you had died. I almost asked. An hour ago, in the briefing room, I asked Joey if she had noticed any change in you when you reboarded the aircraft. I was so blown away by my initial reaction to you, I didn't trust my own perceptions. She looked at me for a moment and said, 'Hector placed the device on the airplane. I know because I saw the toilet tissue in the spool right before I sat in my jumpseat.'"

Rita stopped for a moment, and opened her hands before continuing. "It gets down to this: for once I have listened to my heart. My heart tells me you are a compassionate soul with great integrity. Joey and I asked each other: How could he do such a thing? We decided that you had no choice. Something dear to you was threatened. We're guessing it was your children. If it was, I understand."

Hector blinked. "You didn't even question my motives or my loyalties?"

Rita shook her head. "No, I didn't. I told you. For once, I let my heart guide me."

"Yes, Heinrich threatened me in my office. He is a killer. But he does not kill quickly or cleanly. He tortures. He would not hesitate to torture my children to get his way."

"Have you told Ramirez?"

"Yes."

"You need not speak of it again." Rita nodded her understanding. "I will tell Joey and Mike. I know Joey harbors no ill will toward you, and I believe Mike will feel the same. I think you should get your children and yourself away from here, until Heinrich is stopped."

Hector stepped forward and buried his head in her neck. When he finally pulled back, he shook his head.

"My attraction to you is more than my heart can hold. I'd say anything to get you to like me, but I won't. The truth is, I totally screwed up. I knew this was coming and did nothing to protect my children. I could have killed you all. Protection has been arranged for them. They leave for Los Angeles in the morning, but I will stay. I've cast my lot with Ramirez. I owe him. You're right, Heinrich must be stopped. I am the one to do it."

Rita shivered as the sun began to slip under the horizon.

Mike leaned on the rail of the terrace, his eyes glued on Hector and Rita. He glanced back over his shoulder at Joey sitting with her hands in her lap and staring into an untouched glass of white wine. The liquid was rapidly taking on the pinkish hue of the sunset.

"They look sort of intense," said Mike.

"What?"

"Elephants can fly."

"How high?"

"So, you *are* paying attention," he said, and ambled back to the small table and settled himself next to her. "It's not like we haven't had a weird day, but you look way more distressed now, than when you were building the bomb stack."

"What were you saying about Rita and Hector?"

"They looked sort of intense."

"Having to explain why you brought a bomb on board might have something to do with it."

"What? What are you talking about?" he asked, thinking that the roar of the waves had impeded his hearing.

"I'm sure Hector placed the box on the plane."

"Hector? You're kidding."

Joey shook her head. "Why?" asked Mike.

She opened her hands. "I imagine he was threatened. Rita and I were watching him. Given what happened, it all adds up."

Mike whistled through his teeth. "No wonder you look glum."

"Hector has nothing to do with it. If he needs forgiving, I've already forgiven him. You might think about how you feel toward him."

Mike sat quiet for a moment and reflected on Hector Cato. Not able to conjure any animosity, Mike let him go. "So, why the long face?" he asked "It's a beautiful sunset, we're alive, and four thousand dollars richer."

Joey reached for her glass and finally took a swallow of wine. "You're right. This is so unlike me. I'm always happy because I can shed negative emotions as easily as a golden retriever sheds hair. But I'm having trouble shaking these ridiculous thoughts."

"What thoughts?"

She blurted out a half laugh. "I thought I was immune to these stupid mood swings." She sighed. "I'm pretty sure Fox is spending the night with Celeste Starr. I like Celeste Starr. I can tell she's smart and sincere, not to mention beautiful. But, I'm afraid Fox will like her better than me. I think she's prettier than I am. She's probably a better lover than I am. I'm not even sure whether I want Fox to like me in a romantic way. I'm not sure whether I want to be his lover, and I'm afraid he won't want to be *my* lover. And, I wouldn't be thinking of any of this if he weren't spending the night with Celeste Starr. It makes no sense."

Mike stared at her, not bothering to hide his amusement. He smiled, then reached over and lightly tapped her arm with the tips of his fingers. "I don't know where you've been lately, but welcome back to the human race, sweetheart."

January 24, 6:30 a.m. CST

Rita and Hector poured their limp bodies into canvas chairs parked on the beach. Above, pink and amber streaks of light slowly blotted out what was left of the fading stars. Last evening, Hector had left the flight attendants to dine while he returned to his apartment on the outskirts of Quintana City to prepare his children and their grandmother for their journey to Los Angeles. He had returned to Rita's room just past midnight. After a six-hour session of getting physically acquainted, they staggered to the sea. Hector, in shorts, pulled a T-shirt over his head. Rita wore a sundress with a towel hanging over her bare shoulders. The temperature was in the mid-sixties and rising. A bowl of fruit sat on the sand between them. Rita popped a handful of grapes into her mouth. Munching them couldn't disguise the smirk on her face.

"What?" Hector asked, with a yawn.

"I know every mark on your body."

"So?" he said, perking up. "I know that my tongue in your ear drives you nuts."

"Your tongue anywhere, drives me nuts. So, how did you get the scar on your right cheek?"

He flashed a pained expression. "What scar?" he asked, running his fingers down his smooth face.

"Not that cheek."

"Oh."

"Well?" she persisted.

He shook his head. "I vowed to myself from the moment I saw you, that I'd never lie to you. But now, I'm sorely tempted."

"The truth can set you free," she said, jerking her head up at the whoosh of an egret's wings, as it took flight.

"So can a well-crafted fabrication. But I'm too tired to think of one."

Rita kept staring.

"You're not going to let this go, are you?"

"No."

"Okay," he sighed. "I was a teenager. It was a class project. I was profiling a macaw family and I had put off filming one more shot that I needed from atop the clay lick. It's the place where they flock to every morning for nourishment. It got down to the last day. I had to get there by eight in the morning, but the night before we had torrential rains. The river was too fast to ford at the normal place so I had to go way upstream to cross, and then cut my way back through the bush."

"You mean jungle?"

"Dense jungle. So, I hacked my way along, not really worried about anything except army ants. But, when I was a little kid, I had come face-to-face with a green snake hanging from a tree branch. It must have been in the back of my mind. Anyway, after about an hour of slicing and dicing, my right arm gave out. I switched to the left, and kept going, then in a flash, I saw something green behind me, and it brushed my rear. I flinched, then flailed at it, and ended up slicing the hell out of my ass. That's it."

"Did you get the snake?" she asked.

He shook his head. "No snake. It was probably a baby Festive parrot that fell out of his nest. He was lying on his back trying to stand. He stared up at me as if to say, 'Gee, aren't I supposed to fly?' With a finger, I helped him get on his feet. The parents were screeching like there were a hundred of them, and I could feel blood running down my leg into my boots."

"It must have hurt."

"Physically, some. But, mentally, even though there was no one around, I felt like an idiot—probably knowing then that someday, I'd have to spill this stupid story."

"It's not common knowledge?"

"No, and I'd like to keep it that way."

"Did you get the footage?"

"Yeah, I got it."

Rita leaned across and administered a quick kiss to his forehead.

"All better now," he said.

She grinned, shaking her head. "What is it about the people here? At the Paraiso everyone speaks really good English, but with a definite Hispanic accent. Here, everyone sounds like they're American, like you."

"And *you*," echoed Hector.

"That's because my father is from Mexico and my mother is from central Washington State. Dad spoke Spanish to me and Mom spoke English to me."

"And my father is from California and my mother was from here. So far, you've mostly met people from Ramirez's organization. Many, including my own children, are citizens of the US as well as Quintana. Ramirez's mother is from Texas and his father met his mother at the University of Texas. Take a guess at what his first name is."

Rita paused for a moment. "Isn't the U. of Texas in Austin?"

"Yes, and that's his name."

"Interesting. So, how long have Austin Ramirez and his ancestors been here?" she asked, reaching for an orange.

"Since 1815, I've been told. Most of what I know I learned from Ramirez's father, Rafael. He was sort of a father figure to me because my dad was gone a lot. He passed away a year ago. I miss him. Anyway, Ramirez is a direct descendant of an American from New York, named Wilson. He was a man of science and an inventor. Invention has been a theme in the family nearly every generation. Proceeds from a metallurgical process gave Wilson the time and means to seek out answers to questions and to put his theories to the test. And then, he found this place to do it."

"What questions, and what theories?" asked Rita.

"Questions like, were sanitation and sickness related? If people survived a serious disease like smallpox, why didn't they get it again, when each year they come down with the common cold? Was there any relationship between the domestication of animals and human illness? He spent one spring in a remote Asian village where human waste was buried and everyone bathed every day. They scrubbed their teeth with a rough cloth and used strands of hair to floss. Most of the elderly still had all their teeth. The people were the healthiest he had seen and, of course, they smelled better. He sought a place where he could adapt that lifestyle, set up his shop, and continue to investigate the unseen world through his microscope."

"Did they originally settle right here?"

"No, farther south. There was a residence and a laboratory. It burned to the ground in 1937 with Ramirez's grandmother trapped inside. The grandfather could not bring himself to rebuild it. They moved the compound to this location. However, when Ramirez's older brother Ramón married in 1976, his new wife had it rebuilt."

Rita stood and stretched her arms high above her head. "Since Ramirez is not a Wilson, then—"

"About four generations in, Wilson had two daughters and no sons. The eldest moved to New York, the youngest stayed and upheld the family manifesto. She married a fellow ornithologist, named Francisco Ramirez."

"I see, so, Ramirez's father passed away a year ago. What about his mother?" she asked, reseating herself.

"Doing fine at seventy-five."

"Where is Ramón now?"

"In heaven I hope, because his time on earth, as far as I know was pure hell."

The sun burst above trees behind them and Rita watched Hector's face with an almost adolescent fascination, and wondered why he had such an effect on her.

"How was his life hell?" she asked.

"I don't know the half of it, but he had malaria as a child and was in a car wreck at twenty, the result of which was constant pain. He became addicted to painkillers and everything else, including gambling. He died in 1982 at the age of thirty from a blocked bowel. According to people who knew Greta, his wife was a monster and she raised a monster. The monster's name is Gustav Heinrich, and he still mostly lives in the fortress his mother rebuilt."

"I hope I never see him again."

"And I hope I can get him to leave."

That statement silenced Rita. Hector started to trace the line of her jaw with the tip of his finger. He brightened his tone. "Speaking of houses, I want to show you one of the original lodges. We can leave early and then rendezvous about halfway up the road with José, who will be transporting Joey and Mike."

"Okay, but how was she a monster?"

"Originally from Austria, she was said to be the daughter of some SS officer loose in Paraguay. She was like an Amazon—blonde and beautiful—but into the Aryan superiority thing. She made her own son work in the mines as a child to toughen him. If he didn't produce more than the other boys, he was beaten. When he grew strong enough, he fought back, somehow bonding with Otto, the behemoth overseer of his beatings. As he grew older, he began to assist Otto in the brutality, which, of course, is exactly what she wanted, or so I'm told.

"Meanwhile, in a moment of lucidity, finally understanding Greta's true nature and intentions, Ramón handed over nearly everything he had to Austin so he wouldn't lose it at the tables, or to his wife. One day, when I was nine, a couple of months after Ramón had died, I was helping Ramirez's father tend his garden. He told me in no uncertain words to stay away from Greta, that she was evil. I asked why Austin permitted her to stay. He didn't know, but suspected it was a deathbed promise to his brother to look after them, to try to set Heinrich right, and to give him a stake in the business."

"Why doesn't the army just take Ramirez's land?"

"Castro syndrome. Ramirez and the generals have one commonality. They both want Ramirez's estate devoid of people. For Ramirez, preservation of the land. For the army, so they can keep the dissidents where they can see and find them, and to prevent some leader from doing what Castro did: take over a country with a pittance of men."

"One last question—for now, that is," said Rita. "Why is his last name Heinrich?"

"Because, it was her last name."

Hector and Rita turned off the main north-south road and started inland, gaining altitude. The Prius was nearly cresting a rise when Hector spotted a blue fender in his rearview mirror, another Toyota accelerating rapidly.

"Get down," he said. "I don't want them to see you. I think this may be someone from Heinrich's posse."

Rita casually dropped her head into his lap, looked up, and said, "So, what you're saying is that someone might want to force you off the road for a conversation or send our car into a river or off a cliff?"

"You make it sound like fun. Listen, I want you to count to ten, then sit and re-buckle."

"What are you going to do?" she asked, latching her belt.

"This." He bounded into a sharp turn, came out of it, and stood on the brakes, decelerating to twenty miles an hour. He yanked the wheel dead left into the bush. Rita instinctively put her hand in front of her face, but the foliage seemed to part, and then they were through it into an opening.

"Whoa," she yelped, "I feel like I just entered the bat cave."

Hector stopped and rolled down the window. A couple of moments later they heard the whoosh of the passing car. "There's about twenty of these little hiding places throughout the estate. They were built in the forties to help stop the poaching. It's the same idea as cops hiding to catch speeders. The natural growth sits on submerged hinged concrete boxes. It's directed slightly inward. The weight of the car pushed the foliage upright. The same thing will happen when we go back through."

"Wouldn't whoever was following you, know about this, too?"

"No. Only Ramirez, me, and now you. However, I imagine those in his inner circle must be aware of their existence, but not the locations. I know that Heinrich and even Ramirez's brother have never been privy to these hiding places."

Back on the road, they proceeded another mile then veered off onto a dirt spur, which led to others and weaved their way inland. They emerged from the foliage onto a bluff, the sun behind them. They gazed down at the stately lodge. "My God, it looks like a miniature English manor house," said Rita.

"Yes. It's called Heritage House. It's sort of out of place, but they wanted to pay homage to their ancestry. It was completed in 1880. No one knows for sure but it probably had the first flush toilet in Central America. Internally it's been constantly updated for electricity and plumbing, but the exterior, including the slate roof from Wales, pretty much stands the way it was originally."

They entered through a modest wooden door, and she was hit with the sweet aroma of aged lumber. The first level was one large room with a massive fireplace, kitchen, and huge windows on either side that opened to a view of a ten-acre pond fifty yards down a grassy shallow incline. At the east end of the pond stood a blind, with a thatched roof and retractable walls of fine mesh that glinted in the sun.

The kitchen was modern and she could hear the slight hum of the refrigerator. "Where does the electricity come from?" she asked.

"At first, like most remote places, it was from diesel generators. Then about thirty years ago, we switched to solar, which we have continually updated. Next year, we're going to experiment with geothermal."

"What kind of wood is in here?" she asked, following him up a staircase.

"The steps we're climbing are oak from California. The beams overhead are Douglas fir from the Pacific Northwest. Most of the paneling is pine from North Carolina. The inlay work and the built-in library shelves are native, beech and gum."

"Who uses this place?"

"It's rented out a lot. Two newlywed guides from Peru just spent a week here. Since it's only two bedrooms, it's mostly for couples. Ramirez rewards his people by giving them a night or two when it's empty."

He led her into the master bedroom. She stopped and gazed at the monstrous four-treed bed. "Do people actually sleep in that thing? It's huge!"

"Make love there, too."

She raised an eyebrow. "So, this is your real motive—to bring me up here, just to pull my panties down one last time."

"One *more* time," he corrected her.

She shook her head. "Well, I can't let you do that."

"No?" he asked. Her faint grin seemed to indicate amusement. "No?" he repeated.

"No."

Hector crinkled an eye.

Rita puffed out her cheek with her tongue for a moment and finally she said, "You see, I can't let you pull them down, because I didn't bother to put any on."

They lunged for each other. In full grope, spinning toward the mattress, Hector managed to switch on the ceiling fan—to high.

Twenty minutes later they descended to the main floor. Out through French doors, they followed a path in the tall grass that led to the pond. A variety of birds skittered on the surface, creating little ripples that eventually found their way to shore. Rita placed her hand on his elbow. "I've been putting off asking, but what happens now?"

Hector glanced at his watch. "If we're lucky, nothing. I show you around here for the next hour, take you to the meeting point, and hook you up with the others. I go back to the strip, and settle my kids on the airplane to L.A."

"What if we're not lucky?"

"I'll give you a scenario."

"I'm familiar with those. We use them all the time in training. Only we never know which one is coming."

Hector nodded. "Welcome to my life." He inclined his head in the direction from which they had come. "There's a cottage somewhat like this where Heinrich sometimes likes to hang out. When I told you to duck down, I suspected it was one of his men, Vincent or Juan, going to encourage me to continue down the road to have a little chat with Herr Heinrich. Whoever it was should be arriving there just about now. This means I'll probably receive a call soon, asking me to join him."

"You're *not* going to meet with him, are you?"

"I have to at some point. I might be able to get him to pack and leave, permanently."

"You said the guy is a monster and, from what I've seen, I believe you. You need to stay away from him."

"He can find me, probably easier than I can find him. I'd rather talk to him before things start to heat up."

"Are you nuts? What do you want?" she asked, holding out her hands. "The mercury to shoot out the top of the thermometer?" She didn't bother to keep the irritation out of her voice. She wondered if this was what the families of military personnel felt like when their loved ones were shipped off to a war zone. They felt sadness and fear, but plenty of anger, too, because the god damn United States military is *voluntary. And so is this stupid spat in this crazy land.* She wanted to hit Hector over the head, knock him out, truss him up, and drag him onto the Consolidated plane. She turned away and allowed her rational mind to remind her of things like patriotism and helping those in need, as well as the fact that this was Hector's world, and his livelihood. *Screw that.* Why couldn't Ramirez face off with the monster himself, instead of sending an underling to do it? Instead, she commented, "Your mind is made up, isn't it?" Not waiting for a reply, she jogged back toward the lodge.

Hector paused and watched a caiman glide through the water, with only his bony eyes visible. He went through it again in his head, asking himself if his reasoning were flawed. "Fuck it," he muttered, and trudged up the hill after her.

He found her in the great room, raven hair tied back at the nape of her neck, right hand clutching an unsheathed ancient sword that had been mounted above the fireplace.

She approached him and with deliberation placed her right foot forward, opposite his. She moved her left foot behind, jutting it out and back, slightly more than ninety degrees, heel in line with the heel of her front foot. She bent at the knees and raised the blade, in the classic en garde position. With a mere flick of the wrist, the tip sliced the air in a figure-eight. "I feel better," she said. "We now have a weapon." In an instant she hopped forward and thrust the blade past his wide-eyed expression. "Potentially quite lethal, I might add."

8:30 A.M. CST

Back at the same table where Joey had voiced frustrations the night before, Mike drum-rolled the tips of his fingers on the glass table in rhythm with the crashing waves. Once again, he peeked at his watch. Joey was thirty minutes overdue for their breakfast rendezvous. He didn't know her well enough to determine if she were a late person, or if something was wrong. Two years ago on a layover, a flying partner had failed to show up in the hotel lobby for the crew's pickup. It was because she was still lying in bed, dead of a brain aneurism. His stomach grumbled, and he decided it wasn't from the half grapefruit he had eaten. His gurgling gut also told him Joey was neither habitually tardy, nor inconsiderate.

    He rose, tossed his napkin on the table, and made his way to the rail of the deck where he scanned the beach in either direction. Empty. He hurried back to his room and rapped on their adjoining door. He called her name. He heard nothing in response and no sounds from the shower. He pushed the door open and peered in.

"Joey!" he shouted, startled. She was on her back, eyes closed, hair spread out over the pillow. He rushed to her. "Are you all right?" He leaned over and put his ear to her lips. She wasn't breathing. His index and middle finger probed her neck for a pulse. He found none. He yanked the blanket off her, slid his arms under her back and legs, and lifted. He set her naked body on the floor. On his knees beside her, he pushed her forehead back ensuring her airway was clear and, with his other hand, pinched her nostrils closed. He blew two long breaths into her, making sure he could see her chest rise. He intertwined his fingers and placed the heel of his left hand on her sternum to begin CPR compressions.

He heard a soft voice say, "Mike, what are you doing?" It seemed to emanate from her, though her lips barely moved and her eyes were still closed.

"Joey?"

The green eyes fluttered open. "Yes?"

Mike rocked back on his haunches with his mouth open, *his* heart beating wildly. Joey rolled her legs under and pushed up to sit on the edge of the bed.

Mike looked up at her. "I swear to God you weren't breathing, and you had no pulse, plus I was shouting at you."

"Sometimes I sleep *really* soundly and my heart beats *really* slowly," she said, not lying, but not exactly telling the truth, either.

Mike shook his head. "I wasn't gentle getting you on the floor. You look dazed," he said, and rose to his feet. He pulled the sheet up to cover her. "I'm going to find out about getting a doctor over here. You might have had some sort of heart attack."

She jerked her body up and the sheet slipped off and fluttered to the floor. She pirouetted on the toes of her right foot. "See? I'm fine. Thank you for your concern and I don't doubt you thought you were doing the right thing. I'm sorry for scaring you."

"You're damned right you scared me. I still think—"

"No," she said, and strode toward the bathroom with some deliberation in her step. Before she closed the door she turned to face him, "I'll join you in twenty minutes." She cocked her head and flashed him a half smile. "If I'm not out in thirty, come back in and get me." She shut the door and sat heavily on the edge of the bathtub, her head swimming. *Oh my God, you nearly killed yourself.*

Mike stood for a moment and rubbed his forehead, the image of Joey standing in the doorway a moment ago still fresh in his mind. She seemed about as self-conscious of her naked body as a toddler. Yet, it was the image of her body that he couldn't get out of his head. It had seemed luminous, like she was an angel backlit in a Cecil B. DeMille epic. *She was gone.* He retreated to his room and cranked on the water and set it to cool, for the day's second shower.

Twenty minutes later Mike emerged onto the sundeck somewhat surprised that Joey was already present. She sat in a deck chair with a mug poised in her left hand. A teapot rested on the glass table in front of her. She scribbled in a notebook with her right. Mike plopped down across from her. She looked up and smiled. "Another day in paradise," she said.

"I want to know what happened in there," said Mike.

"You already know."

"So, that's the way you're going to play it?"

Joey stared right back at him and nodded.

"Okay, I'm scanning in every direction, and I see only peace and beauty. No drama. I hope it stays that way. Do you keep a journal?" asked Mike.

"No, but I write things down when they make an impression on me."

"What kind of things?"

"Drama."

Mike laughed. "Care to expound?"

"I thought you were sick of drama."

"I guess I'm like a *National Enquirer* reader. I'm into drama as long as it's somebody else's drama, and I'm not involved."

"I was having an intense dream when you woke me. I'm writing about it before I forget it. Someday it might mean something."

"Want to tell me about it?" he asked. "That way it will have two memories."

She lowered her cup and flashed an impish smile. "Not a chance."

• • •

After Mike left, Joey picked up her notebook and continued to write. *It was a vivid dream in the present time, sharp in color and texture. There was with no blurring edges and no mistaking who said what, except at the end when it got a little fuzzy. It was mostly Lulu Looper talking, her voice squeaky and scratchy, like chalk scratching an Einstein equation across a blackboard. I sat, like a stoic, on the couch in my mother's great room. I was distracted only by tree shadows dancing on the paneled wall, when Lulu entered. I offered my congratulations on her recent success: star roles in two successful comedies and recently hosting* Saturday Night Live.

"Do you remember Bob?" she asked, sitting down next to me.

"The dead cat you had and hadn't known when he was alive?" I answered. "Yes, when I was a little girl you told me of having daily conversations with him."

"I still do, and that's why I'm here. Sometimes he tells me things about other people, mostly people I care about. Then, I have to decide if I want to tell them what Bob had told me. Do you want to know what he said? I think you'll want to know because Bob says you're sort of obsessed with wanting to know. So that makes me think I should tell you."

"Then please tell me."

She nodded as if I had made the right choice. "It's about the plane crash. You wanting to know what happened to you. Bob says you were touched."

I peered at her. She went on. "You may have heard of this. When good people are about to die horrible deaths they are raised up just before the moment. You were exposed to the light for only an instant, but it was enough to slightly touch your soul."

"I don't understand."

"The fuel in the right wing was supposed to explode, and you with it."

"Why didn't it explode?" I asked.

"The temperature of the existing fire came within one one-hundredth of a degree hot enough to cause the explosion, but stopped heating."

"How?"

"Bob says occasionally the will of a mere mortal can be strong enough to overcome the laws of physics. That's all he said on that aspect of what happened to you."

"My will to live altered the outcome of the fire?"

"He didn't say which mortal stopped the explosion."

I glanced around the room and felt a sense of comfort in my surroundings, but the main source of contentment emanated from Lulu herself. She was thirty-six and still seemed childlike, yet I sensed peace and confidence in her that was similar to my own sense of ease following the accident. "Tell me about being touched," I said.

"Bob says it's like a tattoo—you can't get rid of it. It becomes a part of every thought and, for the most part, it's a good thing. He calls it ethereal Prozac, for it calms silly fears. When you were in high school you didn't care if you knew the right people or wore the right clothes."

"You're right. I didn't."

"See? That was good," she said.

"But?"

"Okay, I'll tell you. Bob says people who are touched have a tremendous longing and aching for the lost moment of perfection. They chase it like you have chased Fox Revelstorm. Oh, and I must tell you, he is only a man, an untouched man."

"So, it's a futile chase?"

"I didn't say that, and neither did Bob." Lulu stood and petted my hair. "You should do what I did," said Lulu.

"What did you do?"

"For me, the acting was always easy. I'd say to the director, just tell me what you want and I can give it to you. It was the living in real life that I couldn't get right. I thought I was stupid. I didn't know who I was or what I really wanted. Bob suggested that I go to a place where I felt comfortable and loved, and have a serious conversation with myself. So, I came here. Bob helped me ask the questions. I found out that I'm an immensely talented imitator driven by the child who lost her father at the age of nine, and what I want is my father. He was my world, but until I die, I can never have him back. Knowing this changed everything. I fired my agent and my publicist. I asked myself who I wanted to work with and I auditioned. I've nailed every part I really wanted. I do everything for myself now. I talk to Bob every day, and I long for my father every day. If I'm on the stage, I picture him in the audience clapping for me. You need to sit down and ask yourself who you are, what you really want, and what you are willing to do to get what you want."

"I think I need Bob," I said, as Lulu dissolved into the paneling.

Joey bit the end of her pen, struggling to remember the last residue of her dream. *Suddenly it was later in the day, for the light had shifted and the green of the stained glass was darkening the wood. I thought: now is the time to have the conversation. A voice in my head said, yes.*

I felt a stirring in my body and a shadow emerged from my chest. I glanced up and gaped. Across from me, sat another me. "Ask away," said the other me, "and I will answer."

"Okay, who am I?"

"Oh, come now," the other me chided, "you know exactly who you are and what you are. Solid, and with the gift Fox gave you, even more solid."

"So, it was Fox?"

"No, Fox is only a man but, a man remarkable enough to stop the plane from exploding."

"Fox was the mere mortal?"

"Yes. Let's not waste time. Get to the point."

"What is it that I want?"

"Excellent, we're getting to the crux of things. You want more of what you felt when Fox's arms were around you, hurtling down the slide."

"Can I have it?" I asked.

"Yes, but the price may be rather expensive."

"I just want it for another moment."

"Why settle for a moment when you can have it for eternity?" the other me asked, her voice suddenly seductive. "Very well, lean back and focus on the light shining through the green glass. Slow your breathing, feel your heart pump, and let it slow as well…"

I stared at the green light and slowed my breathing. The light turned golden and nirvana washed over me. I felt the sense of weightless perfection I'd been yearning for all these years. The other me climbed back inside my body and repeated "Why settle for a moment when you can have this bliss for eternity?" I reveled in it and didn't want to leave, but I sensed a longing pulling me back in the opposite direction—to the surface. I would return, but I would wait until I was down to the one last heartbeat, that could create another. From far off, as if in a forest, the fluttering of leaves served a warning of an impending blast of air. I felt the gust rise in power, knowing soon *it would rush over me. I felt my chest rise in anticipation of the last heart beat followed by another. I opened my eyes.*

Joey straightened in her chair, and stretched her back. She took another sip of tea. It was cold. What did her dream mean? What had happened to her?

So, what does it all mean? Could I do this again? Could I do it any time I wanted to? Does this mean I don't need Fox? I think the experience was similar, but not the same as with Fox.

She discarded her pen and rested her chin on folded hands. After a few minutes of further reflection she decided that she wanted him and was determined to ask him to hold her.

11 A.M. CST

The morning after his night with Celeste, Fox dropped his tote bag on the coffee table in his room, pushed his way through the slider, and sank into the canvas deck chair. With glassy eyes he stared at the pristine blue rollers obliterating themselves into white foam as they crashed onto the sand. His thoughts seemed to mirror the waves. How could he feel so good, so alive, so energized from his time with Celeste, yet feel so unsettled? Of course, it was Joey. He decided to focus a while longer on Celeste.

He was amazed at her strength, something that seemed neither masculine nor feminine, but drawn from deep within her. He could imagine spending hours, days, and even years with her for one simple reason: she did not need saving. And if she did, she would save herself. She had admitted her vulnerabilities, shown him the child in her, and wept when he held and petted her, yet this only made her seem stronger.

In a moment of clarity he understood that Elaine, his ex-wife, was simply a parasite in need of a perpetual savior. She needed a fresh host into which she could inject her life-sucking melodrama. He had not seen her in almost ten years and had not spoken to her in five, but because of last night, the last mooring line had been severed. His sister was the same as his ex. He would always support her, but he was through saving her. *In fact, I'm out of the savior business.*

He thought of his old high school football coach, who had successfully channeled Fox's anger into the uniform of a ferocious middle linebacker. The coach had told the team that in some ways life was incredibly complicated, yet one part was easy. Align yourself with winners and stay away from losers. Listen to your gut. It *knows* who is who.

Celeste Starr was a winner. Mary Magdaleno was a winner. Ex-wife Elaine Blue was a loser adept at climbing onto the backs of winners until they were ridden into the ground and either tossed her off, as Fox had, or succumbed.

Giving way to the inevitable, he stood and stretched, and conjured his last moments with Celeste. They had barely spoken in the car, each content and wearing a smile. When they arrived back at the Paraiso, she turned to him before he opened the door.

"Learn what you need to learn and, if you can, come back to me," she said, and flashed a broad smile. "Or, if you don't, come back anyway. I want to see you—I don't care where. In fact, I can picture us wandering around the wilds of British Columbia like Adam and Eve."

"I hope we're wandering with DEET slathered all over our bodies," he laughed, climbing out.

"DEET, lotion, butter, cream. It's all good," she said.

He leaned his head in the window. "Yes, it is."

Last night, despite bonding with Celeste, Fox had still worried about Heinrich and the rest of the crew, so he had made a call back to a Seattle friend working on the ramp for Consolidated. Fox's black bag, stored in his friend's locker, would be entrusted to the purser on the night flight and arrive in the morning. He didn't know if he would need it, but felt better having it available. On the way back to the Paraiso, Celeste had brought him by the airport.

What Fox needed to learn was the answer to the riddle of one Joey Sabatini. He didn't think it arrogant to believe he was her motivation for joining Consolidated Airlines. He scratched his head. She seemed like a winner. At this point in her life she didn't seem to need saving—he was sure of it. And he was sure he had no intention of trying to save her.

Yet, minutes later, he inexplicably found himself standing in her unit. He studied a shaft of light that bisected her sofa, listened to the hum of the mini-bar, and tried to soak up her essence, as if she had left a shadow of herself behind.

He made his way to her bedroom and found the bed linens partially pulled down and thrown over to the side, accenting the invitation. On the pillow lay a folder with a small sticky note attached. *Fox, If you're in here, it means you know. And you're wondering why. I wish I could just tell you, but I don't know exactly why. Read this if you want. See you soon. Joey.*

Fox sat gingerly on the edge of the mattress. He opened the folder as if it were a Dead Sea scroll, and started to read.

LAYOVER

When I was a girl of ten, I lived in a mansion with my mother, and an assortment of thespians, singers, and dancers. Among them was a talented actress named Lulu Looper who, despite her pixyish demeanor, possessed the ability to conjure tears of laughter or yank the collective heart out of an otherwise bored audience. Yet, without a script, she possessed about as much grasp of the English language as Elmer Fudd.

However, one bright morning I heard her naturally squeaky voice echo off the polished fir panels in the great room, pontificating on the virtues of walking backward to tone her calf muscles, but remembering to do it on her tiptoes so as not to trip over the cracks in the sidewalk. When I asked her to whom she was speaking, since she was alone, she cocked her head, bit her lip for a moment, and then admitted to having daily conversations with a dead cat named Bob, whom she had not known when he was alive. But, in the next breath, Lulu assured me that she was okay, because, as she said, if a person knows they're sort of nuts, it means they're not really crazy. *I considered that statement for a moment and then cast it aside, for I knew I was easily the sanest person in the household.*

Eleven years later, when I officially became an adult, I considered her premise again and concluded that even if she were right, the knowing does not make the craziness any easier, nor is it a comfort.

My obsession is nothing complicated. When I was almost twelve, a man put his arms around me, and that action has colored my existence ever since. That he pulled me from a burning jetliner may have something to do with it. For over fifteen years, I've wondered whether my affliction is a result of nothing more than a frightened kid's reaction to near death, my peculiar upbringing, or perhaps divine intervention.

Though I possess a diversity of interests and plenty of normalcy, my life has been a methodical zigzaggy path back to him. Ninety-nine percent of my mind tells me that when and if this man puts his arms around me again, nothing will happen. But I will not listen—the one percent guides me and, as I write this, I have finally plotted our courses to intersect. And when we do, if he chooses to put his arms around me—either to protect me or because he cares for me—I shall either be cured of my affliction or I will be whistling hello to a cow as we jump over the moon.

Suddenly tired, but totally engaged Fox's head sank to the pillow. He pulled his feet up, lay on his side facing the wall and continued.

When I was almost twelve years old I was sent south to live with my father, a prospect I did not welcome, for he was disciplined and a disciplinarian. In comparison, life with my mother was like living in a human menagerie of quirky characters coming and going, preening and performing, whether actually rehearsing lines or engaging in their own personal drama. Opening my eyes in the morning was like the curtain rising...

A ringing in his ear and a prickling on the back of his neck worked their way into Fox's consciousness followed by an all-out buzzing in his brain. He tore his eyes from the page, jerked his head back around, and looked up. Joey stared down at him, her green eyes drawing him to her.

He sat up. "I didn't hear you come in."

"For a moment I thought you were asleep,"

"No way," he said shaking his head.

"How far did you get?" she asked.

Fox laughed, finally easing some of the tension. "Far enough to know that you're probably certifiable."

"As in crazy? There's no 'probably' about it. Just like there's no probably that you spent the night with Celeste Starr."

He blinked again. "And?"

"Ramirez changed our agenda. There was some drama. When it was over in the late afternoon, we finally made it to Ramirez's compound and ate dinner overlooking the ocean in a truly majestic place. We were served, not serving. But I felt flustered and emotional. I think I was experiencing something I've never experienced before: something called jealousy—an absolute waste."

Fox said nothing, distracted by the silkiness of her voice as she went on. "Near the end of our flight from Seattle, Celeste approached me, telling me she had invited you. She wanted to know if she should withdraw the invitation. That's when I lied. I said no. She asked me if I was sure, since she thought I looked at you as if you were some kind of deity. I laughed it off. I told another lie—that I'd only met you that night."

"Why are you telling me this?"

"So that I can admit to someone what a terrible liar I am, what it cost me, and that I'm through lying."

"Do you want to tell me about this drama you mentioned?"

"No."

Fox felt his body tremble. "What do you want me to do?" he asked.

"You know what I want you to do."

"Say it," he said studying her, his mind trekking a long journey of intuitive speculation in a matter of seconds. By admitting the truth, she could hold nothing back from him. She was fully clothed yet he had never seen someone so exposed, so naked, in front of him. *This is the moment of truth for her. Yet, she expects only what she will receive and if she were to receive nothing, she would absolve him. What will happen*, he wondered? *If she's deeply affected, is it me or is it solely something manifested within her? Or is it no different from lovers blasting into infinity, fueled by the blending of their bodies and souls?*

She dropped her voice even lower. "Move over a little, onto your side, and when I lie down in front of you put your arms around me and pretend that you care for me, as if I were precious."

Fox pushed himself further across the bed and rolled onto his side facing her. "I don't have to pretend, you *are* precious."

She hesitated, their eyes still riveted to each other.

"Come here," he ordered in a soft voice. "I will not make light of this, but you need to understand: I'm only a man, full of flaws, gray hair, and probably a few burrs."

She sat and gently rolled her body into his, her back into his chest, finally resting her head in the crook of his neck.

He didn't know what she wanted, but whatever it was, he was sure he wanted her to have it. That much he knew. His arms went round her, pulling her into him and for a moment he felt their bodies meld, somehow noticing the suppleness of her skin even through the cotton. He thought to ask her if he was holding her the way she wanted to be held. But his mind seemed to disengage and time ceased to exist as he slid into sleep.

• • •

The man pushing the housekeeping cart pulled his cap down low to obscure his face. He cast his eyes sideways, and grunted a return greeting to another room attendant passing him on the walkway. He stopped in front of room K-2 and draped two bath towels over his forearm concealing the long switchblade knife clutched in his fingers. He rapped on the door with his left hand, verbally announced his presence, and pressed the tab releasing the knife blade. He waited. Nothing.

Gustav Heinrich knocked again to no answer, glanced around, and, seeing no one, placed his ear to the door. He heard nothing. He had seen Revelstorm enter an hour ago, and had been able to keep his eyes on the entrance for most, but not all of that time. It was possible Revelstorm had departed unseen, yet it was also possible he was sleeping or taking a shower—an even better prospect than stabbing him in the doorway with a quick upward thrust and quietly closing the door.

Heinrich had salivated over the prospect of dismembering Revelstorm piece by piece; his mind's eye relishing the slow removal the bastard's impertinent tongue. But, with contingency plans already in motion and the airplane diversion botched, he no longer possessed the time for a proper maiming. To Heinrich's outrage, Revelstorm remained a distraction that must be eliminated, before he could proceed with a clear head.

He slid the electronic key card into the slot, pushed open the door, slipped through, and closed the door without a sound. His eyes swept the interior of the front room. Finding it empty, he moved forward. Heinrich noticed Fox's adjoining door slightly ajar. He ignored it and completed a quick but thorough reconnaissance of the bathroom and bedroom before returning to the adjoining doors. He pulled Fox's in, then inch-by-inch pushed Joey's door outward. As soon as he moved inside and bent his head toward the ocean he saw a tangle of legs through the door in the bedroom. He raised the knife and crept forward in silence.

・・・

As Joey snuggled into Fox's body she was aware of nothing more than a neutral sensation of having someone she liked and was attracted to hold her. Pleasant, but hardly remarkable. But, flawed or not flawed, and even with burrs, his body was a comfort, and she was in no hurry to detach from him. After a little while, she felt his warm breath on her neck becoming hotter, much hotter. She wondered if he were asleep, but did not ask. She grew aware that this air was penetrating her being, filling her with a strange sensation, as if the heat would cause her cells to eventually ignite and burst.

She resisted, afraid to lose control. Then she did lose control and broke loose, soaring into a bright light with her eyes closed. It felt like she was falling in a dream and she was unsettled. Unlike her dreams, she did not land and kept accelerating. But she now felt safe. She opened her eyes and saw nothing she could discern, only the sensation of speed, as if she were sucked inside the white light of a comet's tail.

Sometime later her awareness extended outside the light to a great shadow, which drew her toward the edge of consciousness where a nebulous evil lurked. It beckoned her, arrogant with the promise of a fascinating perversion: witnessing her own demise. In an instant, she knew she was in great danger. She banished the very notion of fear, then moved back into the center of the arc, becoming the light, knowing that if she burned intensely enough, she could repel the darkness and its bidding.

• • •

When Heinrich peered into the bedroom and saw Joey's face he froze as if she were a chunk of Kryptonite and he were Superman. On the flight Joey had given him the creeps, for she was the only woman, other than his mother, that he couldn't conjure images of himself engaging in violent sex with. He had stared at Rita and Joey together in casual conversation, easily imagining the vicious fantasy with Rita: her screams of pain and horror as he carved her up. He had tried to imagine the same interlude with Joey, but could not. He tried other visions of brutality with her, but that morphed into a waking nightmare, where he could only watch her laugh at his shriveled penis.

Without a sound, he drew in a breath and expelled. *These are two people asleep on a bed.* Two people you hate, he reminded himself, and pushed the point of the knife to within an inch of Fox's neck. *Kill him, you idiot. Kill the fucking condescending smart-ass.* It was as if his arm was held in a vice and he could not move it forward. *Slit his throat. Cut his head off. Make her drink his blood.* The knife drew closer, but did not penetrate. On the verge of a meltdown, he stepped back and almost gagged. He sweated freely and wondered if he was in the twilight zone. He swung the knife back and forth, underhanded in an arc, to prove to himself that he could do it. He calculated the distance he'd need to plunge it fully into Joey's belly and twice mimicked the move like he was standing over a golf ball and taking a couple of practice swings.

The chaos in his mind was deafening, but he knew he still hadn't made a noise. He moved into position and with acute deliberation shifted the knife back, paused, and with every muscle fiber in his arm fully flexed, thrust it forward.

To his utter amazement, those same flexed muscles involuntarily contracted halfway to his goal and, once again, stopped the knife a millimeter from her blouse.

He staggered back, stunned, and not caring if he woke them. In a fog, he retreated the way he had come in, barely aware of where he was until he made it outside. He stumbled unseen out of the resort's compound to his secluded van and then ripped off the stolen uniform, as if it were responsible for his failure, and climbed into his own clothes. He took several deep breaths. Aloud, he gave himself a pep talk. He reminded himself of his power and that soon there would not be a person in the country to defy him… *If there aren't any more fuck ups.*

The pause in the oratory was a mistake. The silence causing him to wonder what had happened to him. *I kill people whenever it suits me. I like killing people. Why this?* It only led him to another horrifying vision of asking Joey forgiveness for attempting to kill her, her smiling, patting his head, and then telling him "You are forgiven."

"I don't want your fucking forgiveness," he seethed, pounding his fist on the dashboard, finally able to conjure one further image: his ordering his most efficient and vicious underling, Vargas, to kill them. He said it out loud three times to make sure he was capable of giving the command.

11:30 A.M. CST

The voice on the phone was gentle and not authoritative, but so persistent. *Please, it is of the utmost importance.* He would come alone—discreetly.

The thin man, dressed in overalls and a speckled painter's hat, climbed out of his van and stretched for a moment before reaching into the passenger's seat to extract a palette of color samples and a cardboard tube. He made his way to the front door of the cottage and paused, briefly enchanted by the mid-morning sun dancing off the white foam of the breakers against the deep blue of sea and sky. He refocused and knocked lightly on the door.

Celeste Starr had been home only a few minutes after dropping Fox off at the Paraiso. She answered the rapping and motioned the man inside, eyeing him with a practiced wariness that did not emanate from her core, but something she wore like a garment, a cumbersome one at that. In fact, her intuition was to like this man despite the bitter rancor her mother-in-law held for him.

For a moment loyalty and intuition clashed, keeping her silent until she said, "It was you who sent the money after my husband's death was declared an accident." She was referring to a sizable cashier's check from an American bank with a note: *The State did wrong by your husband. This is to partially atone for his loss.*

"Yes," he said, removing his hat, and smoothing back his thick graying hair. "Do you mind if I step out of this outfit? It's a little tight."

She nodded, noticing his slim profile and thinking it didn't look tight at all. "As far as the check goes, thank you. The money was put to good use."

"No doubt to expedite my demise," Austin Ramirez said with a smile. "Did you enjoy your evening with Fox Revelstorm?"

She couldn't help but laugh out loud. "It doesn't surprise me you knew he was here. You have your spies or perhaps they're my spies on your payroll. I never see them. I never asked for them. I don't pay them. At first I resented the idea of someone always watching, but now it's a comfort. I don't know whether they know it's you or not."

Ramirez shrugged. "Your spies, my spies, it makes no difference to me. Both have the same objective—your protection."

He had set down the palette and tube while he removed his outer garment. He stood before her in light gray slacks and an open-necked cotton shirt.

"Suppose I believe you," she said. "Why are you so keen on my protection?"

They were still just inside the door. She wore shorts and a tank top, her thumb and index finger resting on her chin. He clutched the folded overalls.

She motioned him into her small living room and directed him to the sofa as she settled herself into an overstuffed chair and pulled her bare feet up and under. She hoped her mind would follow her body's relaxed manner.

"It's obvious I would want to protect the one who will someday possess everything that I possess," said Ramirez. "Hopefully later, much later, but there's a distinct possibility it could be very soon."

Celeste's casual repose disappeared as she sat up, her back now ramrod straight. "What did you say?"

Ramirez turned the palms of his hands upright. "Your friend Fox, unwittingly acting as the catalyst, has started what I hope will be a bloodless change of government in our country."

She shook her head as if to clear it. "Fox? How?"

Ramirez told her of Fox's verbal undressing of Heinrich in front of the laughing first class passengers. "Heinrich was so enraged by Fox's stunt with the wine that I believe he planned to kill Fox. I intervened. I forced his hand. I also believe Gustav Heinrich and the general will solidify their power and attempt to confiscate my holdings. My death could enable that process considerably. In that event, there are certain things and people you must know in order to stop those two and complete the governmental changeover."

Celeste stared at him. "Mr. Ramirez, if your objective is to shock and befuddle me, you have fully succeeded. Could you clarify yourself?" she asked.

He nodded, decided to plunge ahead, and felt a little wicked for it. She'd soon catch up. "My aspirations are modest: merely a change of government," he shrugged. "In forty-eight hours, if all goes as planned, the general will be behind bars to stand trial for covering up the murder of your husband and for heading up one of the largest rings of child pornographers in the world. If he's still alive, Heinrich will be charged with the attempted sabotage of a jetliner. The army will begin to unload its arsenal and transition into a citizen-friendly police force. The puppet president will resign and appoint an interim president. Political parties will surface and campaign." He paused. "This will be a difficult and dangerous undertaking, but with luck it can happen. Within a year an election will be held."

There was almost a minute of silence between them. Celeste blinked her eyes. "And you, no doubt will be the one appointed and elected."

He shook his head. "Never."

"Then who?"

"Esmerelda."

Celeste bolted up. "My mother-in-law? She despises you!" Catching a glimpse of herself in the hall mirror, Celeste wondered how she'd managed to look both mortified and thrilled.

"There are times when individuals must put aside personal differences. I hope that she will forgive me. But no matter, I will do everything I can to put her in power for the transition. She has the best chance of making it work. In fact, the sooner we can get every qualified woman involved, the better. The women of my country not only carry their own weight, but the deadweight of most of the male population."

"If you manage to put her into power, the first thing she'll do is come after you, perhaps even to seize your land. She hates you almost as much she hates the general."

Ramirez smiled. "I believe I can convince her that the country is better off with me continuing to own and manage the estate. What about you? How do you feel about me?" he asked in a blunt voice.

She sank back into the chair to consider her response. "My husband admired you, which drove his mother crazy. It seems as if it's something personal with her," she said, her voice trailing off. She remembered how Ramirez had been repulsed by the idea of hanging one of her jungle scenes in his home, thus passing her "art" test. She threw up her hands. "I have been taught that you are a cruel and greedy despot, but I'm disinclined to believe it."

"Very well, I will take that as a vote of confidence."

"What is it you really want?" she asked.

Ramirez stood and ambled over to the wall as if he were a tourist in a park, admiring the self-portrait Celeste had shown Fox the night before. He turned to her. "For me, personally, three things. First, I would like to be a jungle guide, like I was as a teenager."

Celeste stared at him.

Ramirez continued. "In five years, I hope to see the army totally transitioned and military money flowing directly into education and healthcare. In ten years, I hope to see our literacy rate on a par with our northern neighbors. In twenty years, I hope the world recognizes our country as the greenest on the planet, a Mecca for innovations that protect the environment, and has one of the largest natural habitats left on earth. People from everywhere can visit, learn, and marvel at the wonder of this place.

"But, more important, starting with the day Esmerelda is sworn in, anyone can say anything, and every woman can walk down the street without fear of being raped or kidnapped. In other words, we will become civilized. That is the gist of it."

Celeste felt a trickle of sweat slide between her breasts. "What are the other two things you want?"

"What?"

"You said for you personally you wanted three things. What are the other two?"

Ramirez was bemused but not surprised that she had not even asked him about being his beneficiary, which was one of the main reasons he had chosen her. He turned sideways and pointed to the painting. "I'd like you to paint something that is joyous and beautiful, without the evil."

"I don't know if I can."

"Perhaps not now, but someday."

"Yes, maybe someday when my soul has healed. I would do that for you."

"Perhaps Fox Revelstorm has helped with that healing process?"

"Perhaps you are wiser than I thought, or your spies have cameras in my house."

He shook his head. "For the most part, I wish to protect your privacy, not invade it."

She arched an eyebrow. "For the most part?"

His voice rang soft and neutral but his tone was not apologetic. "I felt it necessary to invade your past and I did. There are startling facts you will soon be privy to. It was necessary to fill in a few blanks. I sought a confirmation of what I had learned and what had led me to pick you as my beneficiary. I even spoke with your parents while I was in Seattle," he said.

"My parents? About me?"

"Yes, about you and about them, as well."

"And they cooperated?"

"Yes, they did," he said.

"I don't get it. Doesn't Heinrich automatically—"

"Most people think our land is like a kingdom, ownership passed through right-of-birth. It is property like any other property and in my will, you are listed as beneficiary, that is, if you accept the responsibility and the manifesto."

Celeste pushed a strand of hair behind her ear and scratched the side of her head. She thought of Alice tumbling down the rabbit hole.

"And what exactly is the manifesto?" she asked, feeling a touch queasy.

"It's more complicated, but I will give you the bottom line. The land is preserved, at any cost," he said, his voice dry and terse.

"At *any* cost?"

"Yes," he nodded his head, "and at times the price has been quite steep."

Celeste stood up and gazed out the window at the sea, almost on the verge of nausea. Ramirez was asking her to step into the future, to shed her grief. She wished they could talk outside. The walls of her cottage kept echoing her confusion. She stared at the horizon. For the first time in four years she wondered what lay beyond. She sighed and relented, knowing she must endure the discomfort of discarding her old skin for a new one. Fox had started the process, and soon she would adapt and evolve. Whether she joined Ramirez or not, she would not be the same person tomorrow as she was yesterday.

"Surely you must have someone groomed to take your place, someone well acquainted with your holdings, someone who thinks as you do."

"Of course, I have such people, people I trust to put the good of the estate first. My companies will run smoothly in my absence, but the people in my inner circle all agreed that in the long run you are the best choice."

"I still don't understand. Why me?" she asked, returning to her chair.

He waited until she appeared comfortable. "Okay, I'll begin with the finite—your credentials of two undergraduate degrees—in business and art from the University of Washington—and an MBA from the University of Chicago. All accomplished by the age of twenty-five.

"Then heading a private organization that raised money from large corporations. That money was then used to broker deals and land swaps for preservation and protection of large tracts destined for oblivion."

He paused for a moment, then tapped the coffee table with his index finger "All of that is important, but it's the infinite combination that puts you at the top. You have the ears of CEO's and government officials. You can talk to anyone, and you have. Yet, above all, you are a true artiste, with each side of your brain fully engaged with the other. And, I need not remind you how you are connected with the people of Quintana. Your husband was becoming known in his own right, not just as the son of his mother. The overwhelming numbers at the funeral came not to just honor his life, but to share their sympathy and grief with you, for you. When you stood and spoke, thanking them for coming, thanking them for standing up for your husband, they were moved."

"That's because I was moved," she murmured. "I thought there would be maybe a hundred."

"There were more than two thousand," said Ramirez nodding his head. "You are charismatic. Young and old are drawn to you."

She smiled. "Thank you for the kind words. Rather inflated."

"I wouldn't say inflationary. That's how I think of you."

She laughed. "Talk about inflation. Ask Fox about the first time he laid eyes on me. He thought there was nothing but helium in my head. He made some reference to the cabin ceiling needing padding. That's how impressed he was."

Ramirez returned the chuckle. "Yes, but in the end, it worked out rather well, I imagine," he said.

"Yes, it has," she said, and fell silent.

Ramirez made no attempt to interrupt her thoughts. Finally, she raised her head. "If I agree, what am I to do?"

"You will become me, like I became my father. I have far exceeded my father's accomplishments. I picked you because I believe you can far exceed mine. Provided I live, your involvement can be gradual, but in the end it will be you bringing about the changes I have put forth."

"I still don't understand your vision of me, but what is it that you want me to know should something happen?" She rubbed her eyes. "I'm sorry, I've been rude. Would you care for anything?"

Ramirez laughed again, and Celeste thought he sounded warm and unforced.

"A glass of water would be nice," he said.

She rose, went into the kitchen, and then returned with a glass. As she handed Ramirez his drink, she smiled and reflected upon the irony of it all.

"You're amused with something," he said. "Would you share it?"

Her smile widened. "I just imagined myself telling Esmerelda. Yes, not only am I throwing in with Austin Ramirez, in fact I will *become* Austin Ramirez. How do you think it will go over with my mother-in-law?"

"Since I just flew over the top of it, Mount Saint Helens comes to mind."

"Or, Vesuvius," she said reseating herself, and nodding for him to continue.

"Any questions, for now?" he asked

She hesitated for a moment. "Am I wrong in thinking, that since the beginning, a direct descendant has ruled the estate?"

"I don't like the word *rule*, but, yes."

"So I would be the first outside the family to—"

"I'm not dead yet and, with time, perhaps you will become family."

He had not meant to reveal his third personal aspiration.

Celeste blinked, thinking his definition of family must mean his business associates. Or, did it?

Ramirez stood and turned his back to her for a moment, then faced her. "Circumstances have forced my hand. Do you accept the manifesto? Are you in? Saying no doesn't necessarily mean I will change my will, but knowing you are with me would be a great relief."

Celeste hesitated, wondering if she was really up to it, if Ramirez had her under some kind of spell. But she felt herself rise and held out her hand. "I'm in," she said, and they shook hands.

Ramirez motioned her back into the chair. He sat facing her and leaned forward. "Two things, in addition to knowing you are the beneficiary. First, I have an advisory of two people. I rely on these people. One has been with me since my grandfather died and the other for the last ten years. They are invaluable assets, but it will be up to you to decide whether to retain or dismiss them."

Ramirez took a deep breath and then exhaled. "I am sorry to throw so much at you in so little time, but there is no other way. It cannot wait. In addition to the regulations that come with the land there will be a ceremony in which you will swear to uphold a tradition that has been ongoing for nearly two hundred years. The size of the estate is a little over five million acres. An indigenous population occupies approximately eight thousand acres of interior land and has since long before my ancestors arrived. Except for those people, the remainder of the land has been virtually deserted. The population was probably decimated by smallpox and the rest, believing that gasses escaping the earth were killing them, left."

Celeste stood up and paced the room while trying to make sense of it all. Ramirez said nothing. Finally she stopped and faced him. "So you're saying that when your ancestors came, they believed there was no one else living within the five million acres? And, that right now, an indigenous population exists that is totally isolated?"

"Yes."

"Unbelievable."

Ramirez barely nodded his head. "It is a heavy responsibility. Perhaps you are now beginning to understand the weight of my world and how much I believe in you to someday, carry that weight."

She stared at him.

"You are starting to comprehend. If you feel like it, we could sit, and I will give you an overview."

Celeste nodded.

While she settled herself again Ramirez retreated to the kitchen and returned to her with a glass of water and a wry smile. "Your voice sounded parched."

"I'm surprised I can even talk."

Ramirez sat down and leaned forward. "Our goal is a continuation of zero contact. Only five people in the world at one time can know about this. This maximum number was decided upon to ensure security, but also continuity. So far, it has worked precisely as it was meant to work. Right now there are only three of us. You are the fourth. My advisors travel with me quite a lot, hence the rather urgent need for another. We have a system of long-distance monitoring we employ—we will advise you of that later—but only three words are used: safe, threatened, and compromised. In my life there have been two threats and one compromise."

"Only three people know about this, and now me? Oh my God," she muttered covering her face with her hand as if the implication had slapped her across the cheek. She lifted her head. "There's no going back, is there?"

Ramirez shook his head. "There's no going back. You are committed. You are also anxious, overwhelmed, and probably dumbfounded. Anyone would be, at least anyone who's human."

Celeste exhaled. "What made you so certain I won't blab it to one person or the entire world?"

"Without anyone knowing it at the time, you managed to get the CEO of Weyerhaeuser, the governor, the head of the Department of Forestry, and the president of the Sierra Club into the same room at the same time and hammered out a deal. That does not happen if you have loose lips."

She eyed him. "Is there anything you don't know about me? I mean, do you know my favorite color?"

"No, but I think I'd like to," he replied with upturned lips.

She returned his smile, continuing to warm to him. "So, what happened with the threats?"

"They were aborted with no harm to anyone."

"What about the compromise?"

"An outsider had captured a native in the Forbidden Zone and was attempting to walk out with him. Luckily, the native had been alone. They were both eliminated."

"Who ordered it?"

"It was observed by my father and carried out by my father. He did not mention it to the others."

"But, he told you."

"Yes, at certain points in his life he revealed things he thought important. He told me that piece of information two weeks before he died." He eyed her. "Are you still proficient with a gun?"

Again Celeste was caught off guard.

Ramirez smiled. "Your father told me that he was a skeet shooter, and you had become quite proficient at target shooting. As I have told you, I have never had to deal with a compromise, so the chance of it happening to you is minute. However, I will leave with you a special phone and a decoder." He went on to explain the basics of how the alert system worked.

"This is getting surreal," said Celeste. "If I had to eliminate someone, I could be arrested and sent to jail?"

"Yes. That possibility exists." He chuckled and rose. "I think that's enough for today. I will leave you to digest what you have learned." After Celeste stood he handed her a single sheet of paper. "This is the structure of my holdings and the key people in my organization. I suggest that you start to meet them as soon as you are ready. They will make you feel welcome." He began to slip on his overalls.

They stood inside the door again, Ramirez in his costume.

"Digest?" She patted her stomach. "I feel like an anaconda that just swallowed a horse." She pointed at the tube. "What is that?"

"A present for you. In there you will find the drawings and blueprints of a true visionary. I hope someday they become reality. Of course, they were done by your husband. It is the complete original set."

Celeste had to support herself against the wall. "*The lost drawings?*"

"Yes, all of them."

She choked up, sobbed, and suddenly threw her arms around him. "This means everything to me!"

Ramirez stiffened with surprise then returned the embrace with a paternal squeeze.

"Oh, one last thing," he said reaching through his overalls into the pocket of his slacks and producing a small, yellow envelope. "After my audience with your parents was finished, your father asked if I would wait while he prepared a note for you. I have no idea what it is—an endorsement, an indictment, or perhaps news of the family dog." He pushed it into her hand and was out the door.

She watched Ramirez climb into the van and slowly drive away, thinking that she did not want him to die. That she and whoever else was left to tangle with the general and the psychopath would not be strong enough. Perhaps Ramirez was ruthless, but he and his ancestors had come to this place in Central America and protected the land with ferocity. The result: he still controls five million pristine acres, not for him, but for the people of the world.

She slit open the envelope and pulled out a card. Folded inside was a small sheet of paper, a photocopy of the original. It was in her handwriting, the handwriting of a nine-year-old.

I'm going to be a great artist. I want to paint beautiful things and I want to save all of the beautiful places in this world, and I want to be important and help all the people. On the outside of the card was a crude watercolor rendition of a forest in the Northwest painted by her youthful hand. The inside was blank except for what her father had written: *Dreams come true. I trust this man. Dad.*

No, she didn't want Ramirez to die.

12:30 P.M. CST

Fox's eyes fluttered open, but he saw nothing, his face obscured by a tangle of Joey's blonde hair. He gently pulled away, drawn by a faint, but familiar odor. He crinkled his nose. A swarm of bees shot up his spine. Heinrich. He scanned quickly, but saw and heard nothing. Joey stirred and he disengaged his arms and stroked the side of her cheek for a moment as if to ease her return back from the unconscious journey. Then rising up, he checked the rest of the suite, and thirty seconds later he was back, sitting next to her on the bed.

She half rose, then turned on her side facing him, her eyes slightly unfocused.

"Did anything happen?" he asked.

She waited before answering, as if to assimilate the words for what she had experienced. "I think so. Of course it was nothing like when I was a girl yet, just as amazing."

Fox squinted at her. "Are you all right?" he asked, touching her arm.

He waited while she gathered her thoughts. She rubbed her eyes. "I don't know. I remember feeling safe and, um, secure, but then everything changed. I felt danger—evil hovering over us and I had to dash my fear and climb into the brightest of lights to repel it. And I did. It mocked me—invited me to witness my own death, but I didn't give in." She watched his face for a reaction. "You're keeping something from me," she said.

"No, I'm sort of processing what you just told me with what I sense, and it doesn't *make* sense unless we end up with one very preposterous notion."

She eyed him and sat up, now focused. "What?" she asked.

He shook his head. "My brain is scrambled and I'm at a loss for words. Let me try to process this again." He studied the floor and noticed a couple of drops of moisture glittering on the hardwood. He slid off the mattress, dropped on all fours, and sniffed the drops. He lifted his head and looked straight into the bright green eyes of Joey, also on all fours, staring down at him from the edge of the bed.

"It could get interesting if I were down there or you were up here," she said.

"Yeah," he said, rising. She sank back on her haunches and waited.

Fox rubbed his chin, distracted, wondering why she was wearing her uniform and why he hadn't noticed before. He refocused his thoughts. "I know this sounds crazy, but I think Heinrich paid us a visit while we were asleep."

"Whoa. Really?"

"I could smell him when I woke, and I just confirmed it. It seems to me that if he just wanted to scare us and let us know that he could get to us any time he wanted to, he would have left a more obvious calling card than his own stink. It's sort of like bad breath; whoever has it is the last to know. Which leads me to only one conclusion: he came to do us harm and for some reason, he didn't. I don't believe in magic. But after you told me what you did, I can't totally discount the idea you might have somehow stopped him. Or he stopped himself because of you. Obviously, I don't know Heinrich well, but I know him enough to believe he would kill and maim, and probably has. I don't know which is freakier, the idea that someone came in here to kill us or that you had something to do with stopping him."

She nodded.

Fox stared into space for a moment before turning back to her. "What are you?" he demanded.

"I've been asking myself that for nearly sixteen years. One thing is for sure: I'm deeply affected by a certain man."

"I don't know about that."

She shrugged, set her feet on the floor, and rose up into his space. "So, what now?"

"Now I tell you thank you, for maybe saving my life."

"And?"

"This," he said, pulling her gently to him, kissing her, and feeling her kiss back with a hunger.

They broke for a moment. "Was that a thank you? Was that a kiss of gratitude?" she asked.

He shook his head. "I think I've wanted to kiss you from the moment I first saw you. But getting older is like being a teenager. You try not to dwell on anything that's out of your league. And rejection at my age is even more unthinkable. I had a hard time believing you wouldn't cringe at the thought of kissing me, let alone the act. So, how did I do? I don't see you spinning cartwheels across the room."

"Maybe because I spun them so fast you couldn't see me."

He smiled, and turned away. "I'll leave you to change." He shook his head as he went through the adjoining door. He couldn't figure it out. He'd kissed three different women in forty-eight hours. Was his testosterone raging with one last gasp before he keeled over? He wanted to turn around and rip the clothes from Joey's body, and he half believed she wanted him to do it. Perhaps solitude wasn't all it was cracked up to be. It's just that for him it worked far better than any other arrangement. Possibilities began to seep into his mind, and he did little to stop them.

• • •

He closed Joey's door and stepped into his own room. It was like falling into a vacuum. His space became a void. His left hand was clenched in a fist and his right hand was involuntarily shaking. During the last ten years Fox had orchestrated his life with the rigidity of a baton, operating within the confines of the solitary British Columbia wilderness and the interiors of Consolidated Airlines metal tubes, venturing out only occasionally to observe and verify that the world was going mad.

He tried to breathe deeply but only rasped as if trapped in a sealed mine shaft, and wondered if there was no escape. His own perfect world seemed destined to blow to bits. He wanted to curse her, but could not. He could not remember such an intense primal longing and it had happened almost instantaneously. Or had it happened long ago? *Is it her or is it me?*

He tried to block the insistent image but all he could see were her glittering green eyes, penetrating the thick smoke in the burning plane, impelling him to her. Through the smoke he found her face again, only now she was a grown woman. But the result was the same.

He could not resist her pull. He took three quick strides, threw his forearm into her door banging it open so hard, it bounced off the wall and back into his arm. He smashed it open again. Joey stood in the doorway of the bedroom in her bra and panties, arms at her sides. Her head rose slowly, revealing her eyes and a slight, luminous smile on her face. Three more strides and he crushed her to him, his momentum crashing them onto the bed. He could feel her legs wrap around his waist as her back hit the mattress. He buried his lips in the nape of her neck, left hand around her back. "My God," he breathed, "I think I'm insane. I felt like I spent an eternity in that room without air."

"Yes, three or four minutes can seem like an eternity. I think I lived for an eternity in the four or five seconds we were in the plane's slide."

Fox gulped a breath of air, now aware that almost his entire weight was resting on Joey's chest, as she exhaled a little cough. He raised himself up, back from wherever he'd been, now fully conscious, wondering how it all happened. "I'm sorry," he said, trying to push further up and away.

"No," she said and pulled him back, kissing him with urgency. She freed her right hand and moved it toward his groin.

"You don't understand," he said, "this may not be good. I sort of hashed it out in there. I don't know why or how, but I don't just want to make love to you. I think I want to consume you."

"I guess that I've always wanted to be with you, but I didn't know what that meant. I don't know why or how, but yes, please consume me, and…"

"What?"

"Hurry."

They were stopped by a rap on the door.

12:35 P.M. CST

Ramirez left Celeste believing that it had gone about as well as it could go, except for the verbal blunder about her becoming family. He had surprised himself with this Freudian slip. It was as if his libido or his romantic inclinations, hidden even from himself, had surfaced like a chunk of Styrofoam suddenly freed from a watery grave. He admitted he wanted a child. Until that moment however, he hadn't known Celeste Starr was a candidate to be its mother. He shook his head.

He had felt a schoolboy's embarrassment as the words had slipped out. With comfort and ease, Ramirez met regularly with people such as Gates, Buffett, leaders of the green movement, including the ingenious Scandinavians. He asked for help, advice, and money. He usually got it. He didn't slip up, and with these people he wouldn't ask for more than he could put to use. They trusted him.

And now, as he drove through the jungle, he was afraid she would think an ulterior motive had been leaked, that he was trying to buy her. He shuddered. He truly wanted her for exactly the reasons he had put forth, yet somehow his emotions had sabotaged his purpose.

"*Enough,*" he said aloud and moved his attentions to the next crisis.

From the time Ramirez had discovered what was hiding in the general's suitcase, it was clear to him that the key to eliminating Soriano was self-incrimination. Ramirez had thought of making copies of what he had viewed, but decided not to, lest he be accused of possession or pandering to it. He had also thought of holding Soriano on the plane for the authorities, but the general simply held too much power. He'd never be prosecuted. The solution was that he must be exposed in a manner so that even those profiting from him and privy to his sordid nature, would shun him like an ancient leper, lest they, too, would become lepers through association. To wait patiently for Soriano to hang himself without assistance was a possibility, but in Ramirez's mind the stars had aligned. Now was not the time for hesitation.

He pushed the buttons for the driver and passenger windows to retract. The spiced scent of the jungle blew through and eased his mind. It was a particular stretch of highway he always enjoyed, a windy path through dense foliage next to the ocean. Ahead was a turnout with a view of the sea. He pulled over to hash it out one more time. He was ten miles north of the Paraiso, his next destination.

Ramirez rubbed his chin in reflection. For the last five years General Soriano's top underling had been Colonel Miguel Gota. Gota was growing tired of the downward trend of military brutality aimed toward any who would question their ways and means. Yet as long as their power was not threatened, the military rulers did little to stop the general lawlessness that prevailed in the streets.

Gota was a good Catholic and a family man. Like most men, he dallied from time to time, only because it was expected of him. His pleas to protect women and children had changed nothing. Gota had complained that Quintana was becoming more dangerous for women than South Africa. Two weeks ago one of his daughter's favorite teachers had been found in a ditch raped, and her throat slit from ear to ear. Gota was ready for change and Ramirez believed he could rally him to his side, especially after Gota came to understand the depth of Soriano's depravity.

Furthermore, taking down the general in another manner, such as an assassination attempt, could backfire by galvanizing an increasingly apathetic army into action. Let sleeping dogs lie, Ramirez thought.

So, what he needed was a sting, an impersonation of someone who moved in the shadows, someone who could make Soriano salivate, someone capable of taking it to the next level, someone who could line the general's already overstuffed pockets with even more tainted money. Ramirez had made enquiries to the FBI and other law agencies asking for a lure. In the shadowed world of child pornography cross-referencing revealed one common name: Wesley Thorpe, a ghostlike Canadian from Vancouver, a Caucasian believed to be forty-seven years old and perhaps the mastermind behind the world's largest distribution system. Six months ago it came to Ramirez's attention that Soriano had sought out this man.

Who can be briefed quickly, think on his feet, and not be intimidated? Who could play the part of Wesley Thorpe? And, in only a few hours, make Soriano believe he's meeting with the real Wesley Thorp? A London group specializing in just this kind of operation had volunteered to do it, but they wanted at least two months to put it together. Ramirez had barely two days. When he queried the group he didn't elaborate on the fact that he had more on his agenda than just taking down a slimy child porn king. Toppling his government—well, he didn't mention it.

Ten minutes after Heinrich pulled his van out of the trees next to the Paraiso, Ramirez pulled into the same spot and climbed out of his overalls. He walked slowly to the service entrance gathering his thoughts, then burst onto the property in full stride, as if he owned the place. He forced himself to move with confidence, smiling at everyone he passed.

This was the first of several critical steps. He had made big pitches before: procuring a half-million inoculations from the Gates Foundation and convincing Alcoa to build the greenest recycling plant in the southern hemisphere. But as he stood in front of Fox Revelstorm's door, he had never been more nervous. Without Revelstorm he couldn't pull it off, and Revelstorm would have to be perfect. And, if he wasn't perfect, he'd probably end up dead. *Would* you *do it, if you were him?* Not a fucking chance, he thought and rapped on the door.

8:45 A.M. CST EARLIER THAT DAY

At the same moment Mike blew a breath into Joey's lungs, Hector's clanging cell phone interrupted his dropped-jaw look at Rita and her sword. He stepped outside through the French doors, and turned his head into the quickening breeze. Overhead, a neotropic cormorant wobbled its way toward the pond's rippling surface, barking like a distressed sea lion, as it planted itself in the lilies with a splash. The comedic sight relaxed Hector. He let his phone ring five times before answering.

"Cato here."

"Good morning, Hector. This is Heinrich. A conversation is in order. We need to talk."

"About what?"

"The future."

"Go ahead."

"We must converse in person so there is no misunderstanding."

"Just like there was no misunderstanding with the package. Let me guess. Your connection is not so good."

"Precisely. Come down to the cottage at Jenny's Blind."

"If you want to meet, I'll see you at Juanita's. One of the visiting guides thought he spotted a scarlet macaw. I'm going to check it out."

"Are you there now?"

"No, but I will be in forty minutes." There was a pause on the other end. Hector could almost hear Heinrich's brain turning over. Hector had never before spoken to him like this. He had always been accommodating and deferential. No more.

Finally Heinrich said, "I will see you there."

Hector snapped his phone shut. Rita had followed him outdoors with the blade still in her hand. "It was Heinrich. We need to move fast. If he's where I think he is, he can make it in forty minutes. We can make it in twenty," he said, locking the French doors.

"Why not here? What's better about Juanita's, whatever that is?"

"It's an elevated blind on the Rio Ondulado. On the opposite bank, one hundred and fifty yards away, is one of the most active clay licks in the entire estate. Lots of parrots and macaws. There's a good chance a guided group or two will be there. This is the right time of day for it."

"That makes sense."

"Every once in a while it just slips out," he said, waving her through the front door.

"What slips out?"

"Something sensible."

They drove in silence for the first ten minutes. Rita had questions, but she held her tongue. It was a tongue, she noticed, that had become increasingly pert over the last thirty-six hours. It's a good thing, she thought, *because it's the real me.* Fox had peeled off the plastic wrap that had effectively kept her sealed, allowing Hector's persona to penetrate and stimulate her inner core. If Hector proved to be nothing more than catching a lightning bolt for an instant, he had at least provided her the impetus to regain her passion for directing her own life, instead of leaning on someone she did not love just for security. She remembered her father telling her, "Rita, there is no such thing as security. You live life without a net."

Hector interrupted her thoughts. "You know how to use that thing?" he asked pointing to the ancient blade.

"It's been a while, but I think I can hold my own."

"Are you experienced?"

"I was in a fencing club throughout high school and college. I switched to an actual sword swashbuckler and worked a show in Las Vegas at the Excalibur Hotel. For almost two years, I, the damsel, fought off the bad guys for eight shows a week."

He laughed. "Lying next to you in the middle of the night, I was thinking that you could carve me up. But I was thinking in verbal terms. I guess I need to amend that to literal terms."

"Absolutely. But, did we ever just lie on the bed next to each other?"

"Of course," he answered.

"Yeah, I suppose when one of us had to roll off so the one underneath could catch a breath."

"That's what I'm talking about."

They pulled off the road into a small parking area, the ground covered with a layer of bark mulch. It was deserted.

"Damn. No one here, but that could change anytime," said Hector, grabbing his binoculars. "It's about a half mile to the blind, a ten-minute walk."

Rita noticed the increased avian racket as they made their way along a winding path. Thick green foliage high on either side still blocked most of the sun. Gusts of wind harmonized with the birds. Five minutes in, Hector lagged behind for a step or two, then caught up to her, his eyes ablaze.

"What?" she asked.

"It's not every day you see a girl in a short, tight sundress sporting a sword, but no panties. It's quite stimulating."

"How much time do we have?" she asked.

"Enough for liftoff, but not enough to float down and regain any sanity." He paused. "Speaking of sanity, I thought I had this figured out. Not quite. The very first thing is your safety. Unless I'm about to die, stay out of sight and don't engage. I don't want him to even know you are or were here. I've assumed he's coming alone. That's probably wrong, which means you need to go back to the parking lot. There's enough cover to stay hidden and still determine how many men are with him."

Hector glanced at his watch again. He changed his mind to send her back immediately. "We're almost to the blind. It's worth the chance. I want to show you where I'll be and a place for you to hide so you're close enough to hear us without showing yourself. Let's hurry."

They broke through the tree line and into the open on the edge of a flood plain. The distant river looked like a mere trickle. If it were the rainy season, they were likely standing near its edge. To the right was the blind, about eighty feet long, the floor was built fifteen feet in the air, for better viewing and against threats of flooding. To the left stood a grove of gum trees that jutted out, almost perpendicular to the water's path. In the past few years the channel had darted in, allowing the trees to establish themselves.

"I'll be standing in front of those trees. There's a little trail that runs behind them. You should be able to get close. You can find it by ducking in here," he said, pointing to a vine. "The only critters around right now that can hurt you are ground insects and scorpions. Keep checking your shoes."

"What if Heinrich sends one of his men to do the same thing?"

"I don't think he knows what's behind the trees. If he does, he'll know that I do, too. Plus, I'll be watching. He should be here in five to ten minutes. So, you need to go. Listen for him and listen for the car, in case he gets here quicker. You might have to jump into the bush."

They flung their arms around each other, squeezed for a moment, and then she was gone at a brisk clip down the trail to the parking lot.

It's good to be alive. You just have to make sure you and your man stay that way.

She was hidden by a thicket when Heinrich pulled in. Two men got out of the car—Heinrich and a V-shaped giant with shoulder-length blonde hair topped by a blue bandanna.

Both wore loose-fitting light-cotton safari shirts and pants. Rita wondered if the behemoth was a refugee from the NFL or the World Wrestling Federation.

"Excellent, Emile," said Heinrich, surveying the lot. His tight jaw softened as his lips turned up. "A private conversation is best."

Rita crept closer to better hear their faint voices faint.

"Can you convince him?" asked the man named Emile, stifling a yawn. His high-pitched, almost feminine voice contrasted with his girth.

"Cato has proven to be quite pliable. Don't underestimate my powers of persuasion. Hang back. I won't need you, but stay within the range of my voice."

Emile smiled. "I assume you will either return with a partner or return alone."

Heinrich faced him. "You are incorrect, my friend. Cato will definitely return with me, either on his feet as my loyal aide or over my shoulder as fish food."

Rita tightened her grip on the sword.

9:25 A.M. CST

Hector waited to see Heinrich's shadow, before raising his binoculars.

"Have you spotted the scarlet?" asked Heinrich, sidling up next to him a few moments later.

Hector lowered the glasses and made a quick appraisal. Heinrich appeared calm and his shirt was dry. "Not yet," he said, raising them again, "and it looks like it's going to be awhile."

"Why?"

Hector pointed to the horizon on the right above the river. "I think it's Arnold and Jenna." A second later a loud and reedy two-note blast erupted from the sky, echoed by two descending notes. A crescendo of cawing ensued as hundreds of macaws vacated the clay lick just as the duet of horned screamers touched down.

"How can you be sure it's them? I thought they stayed in the south."

"They usually do, but Arnold has an uncommon, long white horn and at low altitudes always looks like he's about to auger in."

"Maybe they have lost their way. Perhaps they have forgotten where they belong."

Hector shook his head. "I think they know exactly where they are and where they want to be. And they'll know precisely when it's time to leave."

"Perhaps," repeated Heinrich with a shrug, "but we will never know."

"If not from the screamers, you could learn a lot from the parrots and macaws," said Hector, pulling the binoculars away from his eyes.

"Me? Me, *personally*?"

"Yes, the parrots give way to the macaws and the macaws give way to the screamers. They know when it's time to leave. There are governments who would hire you to do what you do and look the other way, just as Ramirez has done. There's an elephant crisis in the Congo Basin. The Chinese are driving the price of ivory through the stratosphere. You'd be going up against militias."

Heinrich opened his mouth, but stopped.

Hector nodded his head and went on. "You know what I'm saying? License to kill. Hell, those governments would probably pay you a bounty for every poacher you wasted. But, here, your work has been completed. You keep on doing what you're doing and eventually you'll be arrested either to rot in jail for life or to fry in a chair."

A bead of sweat finally leaked out of Heinrich's forehead and more of his eyeballs showed.

Hector kept going. "Changes are coming. The general is going down."

"No, Ramirez is going down, and out."

"You're aligned with a moronic buffoon. Do you think that plan with the airplane had a chance? Did you know a flight attendant knocked the Butcher out with one punch? By the way, the heroin and cocaine you planted in the plane's belly? Destroyed. About three million dollars up in smoke, right? Three million isn't exactly chump change for the general."

Heinrich's jaw dropped in disbelief. "That was—"

"Supposed to be off-loaded by Juan Gordon. It was. Gordon took it straight to Ramirez. He works for him, always has. Not for you, not for the general."

Hector caught the first waft of Heinrich's stench. He had Heinrich's attention all right, but not in a good way.

Rita's knees ached from crouching. Heinrich and Emile had started to the blind together, but a minute later Emile returned and opened the trunk. The open lid blocked her view, but she could hear the sound of clicking metal. Finally, it was slammed shut and Emile took off in a slow amble, apparently in no hurry to catch up with his boss. A pistol hung loose in his right hand, as if he were carrying a fly rod to his favorite fishing hole.

By the time she emerged onto the main path, he was too far ahead of her. She had to scramble through the bush without making a racket. She tried to imagine herself as a cat, moving close behind him without him noticing. She hoped he wouldn't see the blade behind her back. At that moment she heard the screamers' booming approach and the ensuing wall of sound. Rita hurried, under the cover of the noise, through trees and vines to a place ahead of Emile. She found her spot, and tried to catch her breath, without giving herself away.

She rolled three scenarios through her head as to how he would react, thinking she had covered herself. When he was two paces past her, she stepped out. "Emile, I want that gun. I prefer not to have to take your hand off to get it, but I will if I have to. Just drop it."

Emile stopped and turned his head a degree or two. "I would be happy to comply if your face is as beguiling as your voice."

This was not one of the three scenarios. Her words mimicked her thoughts. "You're a thug. Where do you come up with 'beguiling'?"

"A thug, true enough, but a well-schooled and well-read thug. In fact, I possess a PhD in Thuggery."

Rita almost missed the subtle movement of Emile's left foot. "Don't turn around. Just drop the gun."

"Then, dear highwaywoman, I believe we are at an impasse." In an instant, he lashed out with his left leg and dropped down. He turned counterclockwise, swinging his gun under and around his right shoulder. But, Rita's sword caught him flush in the back of the calf, then between his thumb and forefinger. The gun skidded onto the dust. Emile merely yelped as he hit the ground. Lying in the dirt, he stared up at her. He then lunged for the gun with his left hand. She sliced his forearm. While holding the sword's tip to the base of his throat, she knelt and retrieved the pistol with her left hand.

With deliberation, but showing no more than a casual interest in his wounds, Emile rolled into a sitting position, and looked up again. He studied her face and shook his head.

"I really wish you had let me look at you. I'm not enamored with the idea of handing over my gun to a stranger. However, to a beauty such as you, I would have complied. You'll notice that I didn't turn off the safety. But tell me, fair lady, are you thinking of killing Heinrich? If so, will you merely shoot him with my gun or perchance will you run him through as if he were the evil Sheriff of Nottingham and you Maid Marion rescuing dear Robin Hood?"

Rita just stared at him, his blood seeping into the ground, and shook her head in disbelief.

Emile continued. "It's not that I'm expectant one way or the other. But, it is rather exciting and intriguing. Here I find myself, a three hundred-pound man of great speed, power, and skill, suddenly disabled by a woman weighing perhaps one hundred and ten. It's quite extraordinary and, I'm curious, do you think you can bring down a man skilled with blades, who thinks of me as ordinary?"

"One-oh-five, and not if he's smarter than you are."

Emile dismissed that notion with the wave of his left hand, flinging drops of blood as he did so. "It's extremely difficult for me to question my innate intelligence, even though I'm sitting here sliced up like a Sunday roast. Because, I ask myself, have I suffered at the hands of another thug or a poacher? No, I've been carved up by a sex-oozing señorita wearing nothing but a sundress and wielding some sort of ancient blade. It just doesn't happen very often," he said, with a self-deprecating smile. He tried to get up, but sank back down.

Rita felt a giggle coming on. He was right. It was absurd. *The whole past twenty-four hours have been absurd.* "Let me spell this out," she said. "You might be able to drag yourself back to your car. But, your Achilles is probably severed, your thumb will most likely have to come off, and, in case you haven't noticed, blood is shooting out of your arm like a broken hydrant. You better hope someone comes along who can take you to a hospital and you better pray that Heinrich behaves himself. You can scream if you want to, but you're not close enough for him to hear you. Nevertheless, if I detect a sound from you, I'll return and, before I'm through with you, I'll make you look like a soaker hose. If I were you, I'd conserve my energy, and put a compress over that arm."

Emile shrugged and waved her off. She trotted up the trail, gun in her left hand and the blade in her right. She turned into the bush where Hector had told her to and moved into position behind the trees.

Hector turned away from Heinrich, knowing he would want to continue the conversation face-to-face, and forcing Heinrich's back against the blanket of green. A strong gust of wind coursed through the treetops followed by disgruntled chirps and squawks.

"Hector, I don't care for your tone of voice," Heinrich said, swinging around. "If I didn't know you better, I might think you were threatening me."

"I'm just stating the facts. Leave while you can or you'll regret it."

"You amuse me. You think I would actually leave here when I am on the brink of owning half this country and answering to no one? I came here in good faith to offer you a chance to reap the benefits of my new regime. Once I get control of the estate, I will require someone with your knowledge and capabilities. We have worked most efficiently and amicably together in the past. You will be well compensated, *very* well compensated. Are you with me?"

"No."

"That is your final answer?"

"Correct."

"Then I will have to dispose of you," Heinrich said matter-of-factly, as if Hector were a pesky house fly.

"I don't think so," said Hector.

"You believe you will actually survive more than a minute?"

"I'm very quick, Gustav."

"So am I," he said and yanked a gleaming knife from under his shirt.

Hector jumped away from the bush, which created more space between them.

"I will enjoy gutting you," said Heinrich, closing the gap. He held the knife out. "This blade is strong and sharp. In through your navel and, with one upward thrust, I shred your guts, shatter your sternum, and split your heart."

A female voice said, "Not today, you don't."

Heinrich whirled. A light glinted and the buttons on his shirt fell like heavy raindrops, kicking up dust as they hit the ground. Rita emerged from the foliage with her blade resting heavy and flat on Heinrich's forearm. Hector fell in next to her. Heinrich dropped his arm straight down trying to clear himself, but was rewarded only with a deep slice across the wrist. His knife fell to the ground. Now, she had the point of her rapier in his stomach, her face knotted in anger. "Should I do to you what you wanted to do to Hector? I have a vivid picture in my mind of you holding your intestines in your hands. Now, back up."

Heinrich stood his ground, face reddening. "You don't have the courage to spill my guts, you little bitch." In an instant the sword flashed. Seconds later Heinrich's shirt was in tatters and turning red, his chest riddled with flesh wounds.

"Back up," she repeated, her eyes becoming slits. Hector stood right next to her.

Enraged, Heinrich retreated, inspecting himself. "Emile!" he bellowed, "Come here and shoot these two."

"Don't expect Emile or his gun," she said, and whipped her left hand from behind her back to show him.

Heinrich made a gurgling noise and dove for his knife. He got his hand around it and managed a feeble toss in her direction before he fell back against a tree. Hector started to retrieve the blade. Rita shook her head, handing him the pistol. She switched the sword to her left hand. With her back to Heinrich, Rita knelt and retrieved the blade. "Your problem is you throw like a girl." Quickly, she raised her right arm and, pivoting on her bent left leg, turned and hurled the knife. It embedded in the tree, quivering an inch above Heinrich's head. "But, not like this girl. Don't even think of rescuing your precious knife. It's buried like Excalibur and you're no Arthur. Nevertheless, if you raise a hand, it's coming off."

Hector and Rita backed out of earshot from Heinrich. She looked at Hector and grinned. In a low voice she said, "We have the bastard. Let's deliver him to Ramirez, and that's the end of Gustav Heinrich." Hector rubbed his forehead and pursed his lips. "What's the matter with you?" she asked.

She noticed Heinrich attempting to rise. "Don't even think about getting up," she yelled. Heinrich slumped back against the tree.

"Nothing," answered Hector, "thanks to your handiwork. But, we can't take him with us."

She glared at him about to explode. "Are you crazy?"

He hesitated, smiling, before he answered. "Probably."

"What's so funny?"

"Well, I'm hoping to somehow spend a lot of days with you, like thousands of them, and I'm wondering if you'll be able to get through even one of them without asking me if I'm crazy or nuts."

"Well, what if I can't?" She cocked her head to one side and frowned.

"I can live with it," he said. "Besides, I ask myself that question about once an hour. I know it sounds a little weird, but first and foremost, I don't like our chances of bringing Heinrich in and us staying in one piece. And second, there's really no place to bring him to where we can be sure there's enough motive and firepower to hold him."

Rita lowered her voice again. "We have a gun and a blade."

"It doesn't improve our odds that much."

She was about to respond, but instead inhaled and recalibrated her senses. The steady breeze wasn't strong enough to mask Heinrich's smell or the metallic scent of fresh blood. She glanced over her shoulder and noticed a mass of blue and red, as the macaws squawked their way back to the lick. Heinrich was sprawled against a gum tree, chuckling, as if privy to an inside joke. Hector looked focused and calm. She touched his forearm with her index finger. "What now?" she asked.

"We take his cell phone and leave. I'll explain later."

Carefully erasing any irritation from her voice she asked, "Could you give me the really short version, now?"

Hector nodded. "We're about twelve hours too early. By the end of the day, if Ramirez is successful, a warrant will be issued for Heinrich's arrest. I'm choosing not to run into the cage of an agitated jaguar. I've seen what can happen."

He approached Heinrich. "Your cell phone, please."

"You'll have to retrieve it."

"I thought as much. Rita, the tip of the sword at the base of his throat, unless you can think of a better place. Apply pressure." He pushed the gun into her left hand. "I'm going to reach into his right pocket and retrieve the phone. If he moves a hand or leg, finish him. He might try and grab me and pull me across his body. Use the sword, the gun is a last resort. I don't want to die in the arms of Gustav Heinrich with a bullet in my back."

Heinrich shrugged. "As you wish, I will give it to you." Deliberately he pulled it out and tossed it in Hector's direction. "You are going to lose because you are weak. Your only chance is to kill me now. I do what is necessary. When you are staring up at me without hope, you will regret your sense of morality."

Hector stared at him. "No, Gustav," he said, his voice barely audible, "you will die from an overdose of arrogance, like your mother, and if you move from this spot in the next half hour, you will die a minute later."

They found Emile, a benign look on his face, leaning against the car in the shade, as if he hung out every day with a bandanna tied around his arm and parts of a torn shirt wrapped around his thumb and leg.

He smiled. "I heard no gunshot, so Maid Marion here must have smote him with her sabre. Are we quite done with the bastard?"

"Who *is* this guy? Hulk Hogan's brother?" asked Rita. "And it's a rapier, probably late eighteenth century."

"Hulk Hogan? Oh, please. Hogan is a mere pip-squeak and, my God, he's bald. But never fear, I, Emile can recover from such an insult. I can tell by now that Herr Heinrich lives and will soon amble down the trail."

"You guessed it," said Hector. "What are you doing here?"

"Bad luck. I ran into Heinrich at the gas tank. He said, 'Let's go for a ride.' And so, here I am."

"Rita, as you know, this is Emile. He's like I was until yesterday—trying to figure out who's going to win and not committing until he has to commit."

"I almost had to commit about twenty minutes ago," said Emile.

"Yes?"

"Yes, as you know I volunteered to help clear out the poachers. I had no problem with Heinrich killing them because they deserved to die. But, you don't deserve a common cold, let alone a knife buried in your gut."

"What? You were on the way up the trail to help Hector?" asked Rita.

"Until some maniacal woman wielding a sword waylaid me. Excuse me, a rapier. Actually, I retract the maniacal part. Hector, your lover is quite clever, as well as dangerous." He paused as they stared at him. "Oh come now, you two are quite obvious. As I was saying, she described my wounds in the most horrific manner, hoping I'd be paralyzed by fear.

Achilles severed. She cut right next to it. Thumb nearly gone. I have a deep wound, but she missed the bone. However, as promised, she nicked my vein quite convincingly. Made an unsightly mess."

"Does he always talk like he's making a speech?" asked Rita.

Hector grinned. "Always."

"Well, for what it's worth, I'm sorry I injured you," Rita said to him.

"Apology accepted. You might ease up a touch on Hector. It's very difficult to worship a man, make love to him, and kill him, all at the same time. However, your anger only makes your face more beautiful."

"What the—" Rita sputtered.

Emile raised his wrapped hand. "My guess is that you got the drop on Heinrich and you can't understand or believe that you let the Hun go when you had him down and seemingly defenseless. I would have chosen exactly as Hector did. Heinrich is extremely dangerous in confined areas, like automobiles. He can cause chaos in an instant. Your biggest problem is finding someone willing and capable of holding him. He has a transmitter beneath his skin so he can be tracked by his core group of twelve. They call themselves the bloodhounds and think they're brilliant. They're fools, but they are well equipped. They all have transmitters and communicators. I have sometimes worked the GPS board. My point is, right now, you'd need to get Heinrich over the border into a Costa Rican jail before any of his hounds could get to you. It's unlikely."

"So you work the board," said Hector.

"I used to because they needed someone to coordinate everyone's position and they knew I had no interest in their extracurricular activities."

"In case you haven't figured it out, I'm with Ramirez. You could possibly be a help with that board," said Hector.

"Possibly."

"At some point you have to choose," Hector prodded him.

"I will not oppose Ramirez. And if it gets to the point where my weight could topple Heinrich, I'll step on him. Fair enough?"

"Fair enough."

"You have his phone?" asked Emile.

"Yes."

"If it rings, do not answer it."

"Right. Heinrich's going to want to know why you didn't call anyone," said Hector.

"How could I call when Rita took my cell from me?" he said, handing his phone to her with a glint in his eye.

She banged the palm of her hand against her head a couple of times and grinned. "How could I be so stupid?"

"Swashbucklers swashbuckle. They can't be expected to deal with such trivia."

Rita yanked open the driver's door, reached in, and popped the hood latch. Then she scrambled around to the front, raised the hood, and glanced at the exposed engine. She tore out the wire connecting the distributor to the coil and held it up. "Maybe not," she said. "But, I can learn."

4:15 P.M. CST

Under a gray-blue sky that produced only a waft of wind, Fox stepped out of a fifteen-year-old diesel taxi in Quintana City and smoothed his freshly tailored gray suit jacket. He noticed it was a bit hotter here than by the ocean, perhaps around eighty. He squelched the urge to touch both his ears that held the small voice transmitters deep in his canals. Ramirez's men were sitting in a van somewhere prepared to receive and record the ensuing conversation. Though his ears were obstructed, Fox's hearing was barely compromised. He only hoped he didn't detect a nearly inaudible beep indicating the device had failed, which would further complicate his mission. The devices had not been field tested.

He sniffed the air. It reminded him of Taipei and Seoul—thick with particulates spewed from a menagerie of old diesels and two-cycle vehicles careening through crumbling streets and alleys along with the ever-present lingering stench of sewage. He stood across from the single oasis in the dull brown-and-gray of Quintana City, Central Park, three blocks long and a block wide. He adjusted his fedora to a lower angle, and pushed the dark glasses up past the bridge of his nose. He opened a rose-covered gate and entered the nearly deserted park. It was off-limits to the citizenry except on special occasions, when they were then required to show their enthusiasm for military parades.

Inside, he made his way through one of four openings in a circular laurel hedge that surrounded the main fountain and waited. A man approached through another opening, his uniform sporting more color than Fox had seen since entering the city's outskirts.

For a brief moment Fox pictured an alternative existence on the beach—a cold beer an arm's length away and Joey's legs resting on his. He refocused. From his sister's experience, Fox knew firsthand about adults sexually abusing children. But he knew nothing of the business of child pornography. He had been smitten with acting in high school; the chance to be someone other than himself had provided a strong appeal. He had been quite good. But here and now, he had a hard time believing the general would think he was Wesley Thorp. Ramirez had told him, "Become Wesley Thorpe and Soriano will believe, because he desperately wants in. And Wesley Thorp is the pinnacle of this business."

On the airplane ride from Seattle, Fox had assessed Ramirez in a brief conversation. He concluded the man was tough, but not anything like Heinrich. Fox detected no malice on the part of Ramirez. What Fox hadn't accounted for was while he had sized up Ramirez, Ramirez had conducted his own surveillance on the flight attendant.

Fox agreed to play the part, not because of Ramirez's pitch because there had been no pitch. Ramirez had said nothing as to why Fox should do this. He did not attempt to tell him how his efforts could positively affect many people. Nor did he offer monetary compensation. Ramirez merely laid out the plan and asked him whether he was in or out. Fox had been an all-state point guard in high school. Somehow Ramirez had discerned that Fox was the type of guy who wanted the ball when the game was on the line, was willing to take the last shot, and then was willing to live or die with the consequences.

Two aides flanked the general's rotund figure. Neither Soriano nor Fox offered a hand. As one of the aides moved toward him Fox raised his arms. "My apologies," said the general.

"None required, I expected no less," he said, handing over his hastily assembled Canadian passport. The aide did a thorough job, even checking under collars and lapels for evidence of a wire, and examining the document as if he were a customs official. He returned the passport and nodded to the general, who dismissed them both.

"Shall we walk?" asked the general, pointing to a serpentine path dissecting the length of the park with an eight-foot laurel hedge on either side. They could not be seen unless a helicopter hovered above. Crunching gravel underfoot the general said, "Thank you for responding to my earlier introduction. What do you propose?"

Fox took a few more steps before answering. "There is no question that Quintana is on the map as far as the legitimate sex industry goes. It is my understanding that you wish to expand your business in a way that aligns with my specialty."

"Yes."

"The problem I have is maintaining a steady flow of product. Operations exist and then dissolve; they come and go. It's not lost on me that since you are basically the law, the law would not interfere with that steady supply."

Fox stopped to inspect an orange tree, allowing him a moment to check out his surroundings. The one thing Ramirez could not provide was a guarantee that Heinrich would not be with the general. At the moment, no one knew where Heinrich was, but Ramirez's people had no recent sightings of him in Quintana City.

When they moved forward again, Fox continued, "I propose you put together a portfolio of six or seven twenty-minute shorts, the usual array of combinations. No toddlers. The Russians are very adept at getting ten- to thirteen-year-olds to show great enthusiasm. That's the ticket. It sells quite well. I leave the rough stuff to the legit adult Internet sites." Fox remained deliberately silent for a few paces before dropping the bait he hoped the general could not resist. "And I don't sell rape, although I know of those who would pay dearly for it."

The General stopped. "How dearly?"

"Very. This interests you?"

Fox noticed the general's cheeks flushing just a bit.

"Life is cheap here. I could find candidates. What are we talking about?"

"I know of a man who paid well over six figures for a fifteen-minute tape of an eight-year-old."

The General lost any pretense of subtlety. He cleared his voice and thrust out his jaw, temporarily reducing his number of chins. "Some more details, please."

On the move again, they slowed and lingered less than a block from the end of the path. "You complete the portfolio and call me at this secure number," said Fox, handing him a small folded piece of paper. "I'll send a runner for all the material. It must be professional and in high-definition. You will hand over everything. You will not make copies, eh? If you do, they will get out, just as your initial attempts got out and went nowhere. I will know about it and that will end any business association between us. I distribute only discs that cannot be easily copied. While I can manage a large volume, I don't want the market flooded. There's something to be said for the De Beers method."

Fox glanced briefly over his shoulder, thinking he might have seen a flash of blonde.

"What about payment?" asked the general.

"Electronic—to a numbered account. We use a bank on Grand Cayman. You can choose, as long as you meet our specifications. I was going to deposit a nominal amount, say fifty thousand, just to let you know I'm serious. However, if you like, I could provide you with a name instead, should you think you'd like to pursue this other sideline on your own. At least initially, I could broker that for you. Which would you prefer?"

The general didn't hesitate. "The name, please."

"As you wish. You'll have it shortly. However, I must warn you. If you give me the material as I described it and in the manner I asked to receive it, I can insulate you. This other thing, actual rape, I provide the name and nothing else. Is that understood, general?"

"The name will provide me with those who will pay?"

"The name is capable of connecting you. Whether the name does or does not is out of my control."

"Very well," replied Soriano, "give me the name. It will take me in the direction I want to go." He flashed a half salute, turned and retraced his steps.

Stifling the urge to sprint, Fox emerged onto the street in a languid manner. The taxi waited a half block ahead of where they were supposed to rendezvous, but Fox checked the cab number to confirm it. He ducked in, about to breathe a sigh of relief. Instead, in the rearview mirror he spotted the pale blue eyes of Gustav Heinrich.

"What's your name?" asked Heinrich, as he mashed the taxi into gear.

Fox dropped his chin. "Who wants to know?"

"You first."

"Thorp, Wes Thorp."

"Well, Mr. Thorpe, excuse me, but I must take up just a bit more of your time. Once or twice around the block and I'll reunite you with your driver who was so kind as to let me borrow his vehicle for a few minutes. You see, I'm a partner of the general's and I didn't hear of this meeting. What did it concern?"

"We only made contact two hours ago."

"And?"

"And, what?" Fox pursed his lips slightly to flatten the vowels and disguise his voice to sound Canadian. "I'm sorry, but put yourself in my position. I don't know you. If you are partners with the general, I'm sure he'll fill you in. I don't go blabbing my business or the general's to every cabdriver in the city. Make that *any* cabdriver anywhere."

"I'm not a cabdriver."

"Then what the fuck are you driving one for?" Fox lowered the "u" just a tad and was quite pleased with the subtle change in his voice, until he thought, with horror, his material sounded a bit too much like Fox Revelstorm's.

Fox watched Heinrich grimace and expected a gun in his face any moment. Instead Heinrich shrugged his shoulders. "Very good, Mr. Thorpe. You're right. I've been out of contact all day. And, if you had told me anything, I most certainly would have asked the general in what manner he wanted you eliminated. Your driver waits up ahead."

Heinrich pulled up to the curb, yanked up the brake stick, and climbed out. The Fiat's rear window was so low that Heinrich only made a passing sweep with his eyes. "I'm sure we'll be in touch, Mr. Thorpe."

Fox did not reply. An instant later his shirt was soaked.

5:45 P.M. CST

The four flight attendants sat at a bar situated in the middle of the Paraiso's swimming pool. Joey stared at the sun's last tendrils of orange and pink until the fiery ball slid beneath the horizon. She disengaged and dragged her attention back along the ocean's glittery surface, across white sand, through the light filtering palms, and into the bobbing surface of the pool. She listened with rapt attention and casual detachment to Rita and Hector's encounter with Heinrich and Emile. Joey smiled as she watched her flying partner describe in understated detail how she had disarmed the two men with the old rapier. Forty hours ago on the plane, it seemed as if Rita could barely generate enough strength to make it through the night. Now, it seemed as if she could power an entire city.

Joey glanced at each of her flying partners and, now, friends. There was much to admire, and each had demonstrated unique abilities. She was sure they also possessed doubts and secrets, such as she did. But her personal secrets seemed beyond even her own comprehension. She thought of herself as arrogant or insane, possibly even both. Nevertheless, she now believed she possessed the ability to stop her heart from beating. She marveled and shivered at the thought that with her mental telepathy she had prevented a man from killing her—and probably Fox.

After Rita finished her story, the crew downed what was left in their beer glasses, waded over to the steps, and climbed out of the water. Mike nodded to everyone. "I think we've had enough excitement. Why don't we change into dry clothes and meet back here in about fifteen minutes, to have a little conversation. The gist of it will be how to avoid any more such…um, excitement."

"I concur with our leader," said Fox, raising a hand.

Joey almost giggled. It seemed as if her friends were masters of understatement. Earlier, she had listened as Ramirez had pitched Fox to play the part of Wesley Thorp. No impassioned speeches and no fist pounding. Fox merely stood, shrugged, and said, "Let's get started." And then there was Fox's story of his meeting with the general he described as a walk through the park. Mike dismissed cold cocking the general with, "I needed his bag and didn't have time to argue." Just now, Rita had tried to blow through her story as if the sole reason for telling it was that Heinrich had one more reason to be mad at the crew. The only time she became truly animated was when Hector's name came up. Joey could almost feel heat waves emanate from her.

What about you? You came within a split second of doing yourself in, forcing your flying partner into nearly full-on CPR, and you completely blew him off. On the other hand, what could I say? That I was playing a game of chicken and didn't care if I lost?

They ambled along the path under light provided by hissing tiki torches. When they reached their building Fox asked Joey, "May I escort you back for our little meeting? There's something I need to discuss with you before we see the others."

Ten minutes later, changed into shorts and a T-shirt, Fox knocked on their adjoining door. She opened it and he started to speak. She interrupted by wrapping her hand around the back of his neck and pulling him to her. They kissed for over a minute before finally breaking, slightly out-of-breath and a bit disheveled. "Wow," breathed Fox. "Why did you do that?"

"To see if you liked it," she answered.

"To see if *I* liked it?"

"Yeah, I kind of need to know."

"Why?" he asked, pulling her a little closer.

"I've always been pretty reserved. With you, I don't feel reserved and I don't want to feel reserved. I want to feel like Rita feels. I've never felt that way before."

"Let's see, feel, feels, felt. That about covers it. So how exactly does Rita feel?"

"Crazy and invincible."

"And you don't?"

"I have the invincible part down. The crazy part is up to you."

"Maybe we can make a deal. I've been dealing with the crazy part for nearly fifty years, but I don't have the invincible part down at all. In fact, that's why you surprised me. My head's been in survival mode. And that's what I wanted to talk about for a minute," he said, stroking her neck with the tip of his index finger.

"Okay," she nodded.

"Mike, Rita, and I have each crossed Heinrich's demented line. But, they don't know *you* did anything to him."

She cocked her head. "What did I do to him?"

"I think he came to kill us. He didn't. I can't believe I'm saying it, but I'm sure you're the reason why he didn't."

"So am I."

"There's no need to tell the others, but I believe your action more than any of the other slights will motivate him to, shall we say, exact his revenge."

"You call getting carved up by Rita's sword a *slight*?"

"Of course he'd like to butcher her, but getting busted up in a fight is probably standard procedure for him. He has scars all over his arms. You're different. You're in his head, you're female, and you controlled his actions. I can picture him standing over us not being able to plunge the knife into our flesh. I'm no psychologist but I don't think he will accept that failure."

Joey sighed. "Probably not."

"Anyway, I'd like to move to another place, but they're not going to understand why, and we can't explain that Heinrich has already been here. So, I'm going to insist we have protection. I think I can get it from Ramirez. Ramirez figures he'll have a warrant for Heinrich's arrest," he glanced at his watch, "about now. He thinks that will keep Heinrich on the run and in the jungle. But, as brilliant as I believe Ramirez to be, he's juggling about five razor-sharp chainsaws in the air. We're not his top priority, but I think I can convince him to give us what we need."

"You would know," she said.

"There's one more thing," said Fox, staring at her. "Mike told me you gave him a scare this morning. But he left it up to you to tell me or not tell me. All he said was that if we were sharing a bed, to be aware of how deep you sleep. Care to expound on that?"

She knew this was coming but somehow it had sneaked up on her. Her immediate reaction was to follow the pattern of her flying partners and play it down, as she had with Mike. She had often fantasized about finding someone with whom she could be intimate—stripped naked, physically and mentally, and never holding back. She pushed a strand of hair away from her cheek and plunged ahead.

"I had this intense dream. I was once again seeking the feeling I had when you held me as we hurtled down the slide. And, I found it, and it was as good as it was then. I had to make a choice: to return, or to stay in the bliss for eternity. It was close, very close. I chose to return but I waited until I was down to my last heartbeat. That came at the exact moment that Mike blew air into my lungs. He said that I wasn't breathing and that he couldn't find a pulse. He was about to pound on my chest when I asked him what he was doing."

"Jesus Christ!" said Fox, eyes wide. "I don't know whether to squeeze the daylights out of you or beat your ass."

"Why not both?" she deadpanned. "But the thing is," she continued, in earnest, "I believe I can make it happen again—anytime I want." She held her hands apart. "Now you know everything I know about Joey Sabatini."

Fox tried to keep his expression neutral as he wondered if what she was telling him was actually possible. He scratched his head. Finally she broke the silence. "So, did you like kissing me?"

"Yes, but I'd better make sure," he said, gathering her to him.

Ten minutes behind schedule and halfway to the pool, Joey stopped. "Do you believe what I told you about being able to stop my heart?" she asked.

"I don't know what to believe. I guess I believe that you believe. But, do you know what I think?"

"What?"

"That, metaphorically, you smoked the biggest, purest bowl of crack cocaine and got away with it. I wouldn't go there again, ever, until you're ready to go away—forever."

When they reached the pool area there was no sign of Rita or Mike. Joey felt a prickly sensation on her arms, which led to concern about them. She barely listened to Fox's phone conversation with Ramirez while her eyes scanned the pool area. She exhaled with relief as she spotted Mike and Rita thread their way through the sprawl of tables and lounges. They slumped into their chairs. Joey sensed the ominous again. Rita's puffy dark eyes conveyed anything but invincibility. With a trembling hand Rita set a manila envelope on the table as if it were a bottle of nitroglycerin. Mike plopped down another folder, pulled an eight-by-ten photo out of it, and crumpled into his chair. They waited in silence for Fox to end his conversation.

He did, a minute later. "Ramirez is sending four men," said Fox. "That should be enough to protect us."

"Maybe," said Rita, the light missing from her eyes, "but who will protect my son Eduardo and my sister who is caring for him?" She pushed the envelope across the table.

"And what is Richie supposed to do?" asked Mike, shaking his head.

7:15 P.M. CST

Fox studied the photos, but waited a moment more to compose himself before he raised his head. He could not allow himself to deflate. He could not, even for a minute, wallow in the horror of what he saw in front of him. He pointed to a nearby table. "We need more light." They reseated themselves and Fox turned his gaze into the dark, past the flickering tiki torches to the waves in the distance aglow with phosphorescence. He turned back to Mike. "Given the circumstances—"

"Right now, I feel like I've been run over by a semi," Mike said, who rose like an old man from his chair. "Give us any leadership and insight you can." He trudged off toward the bar.

Fox knew their shock and weakening resolve was only natural, yet it must be temporary. Given what he saw in front of him, there was only one solution. He studied a photo printed on high gloss paper. It was a head shot of Mike's partner, Richie, standing in front of a Boeing engineering building in south Seattle. He set it back down on the table as Mike returned with four small glasses of tequila gripped in his fingers. Mike placed one in front of each of them.

"This was taken by a SLR equipped with a powerful telescopic lens," said Fox. "Range is probably around three hundred to five hundred yards. I'm not an expert on guns, but no rifle scope that I know of also acts as a camera which means the crosshairs have been superimposed. But the message is clear: what can be shot with a camera can be shot with a rifle. Mike, when does Richie usually arrive at work?"

"Around 9:30."

"Timeline wise, it makes sense. It would have given Heinrich a little over two hours to make his way from the clay lick, connect with his man in Seattle, and for the contact to take the shot, unless Richie went in on Sunday."

"Richie never goes in on Sunday. What does this maniac want? I mean if Heinrich can do this, surely he could get my cell number and call me with the threat."

Fox sat back in his chair. "Yes, but there's an old axiom in writing. Maybe it applies to threats—don't tell, *show*. Heinrich wants to inflict pain and anguish. And it starts in the mind. He's figuratively stuck a knife in our guts and he's going to twist it awhile."

Rita listened with her head bowed and her hands covering her face. It was as if a boa constrictor was squeezing the life out of her. Joey arose, stood behind Rita and rubbed her neck, then bent over and whispered in her ear, "Stand and breathe deep." Rita dropped her hands, and pushed herself up, slowly inhaled as if the air were an elixir, and finally raised her head. "There, that's better. I should have killed him when I had the chance. I won't make that mistake again." She sat down but kept breathing slowly.

Mike looked as if he wanted to smash something as he eyed the tequila. Instead, in a steady voice he said, "Suggestions?"

"I want to back up a little bit," said Fox. He reexamined a photo of seven-year-old Eduardo bundled up in his winter coat during recess next to a playground slide. "It's very difficult to tell if this was taken with the same camera that shot Richie. Eduardo has his hood on, but none of the other five children are wearing anything to cover their heads. The light is so flat, that I can't tell the time of day, or if it's raining. Definitely no rain when Richie was shot."

"Could you use another word besides *shot*?" asked Mike.

Fox nodded and continued. "Rita, what are the possible recess times and what about Eduardo's hood?

"It varies by the day and the activities, so, it's hard to say. He loves his hood in almost any weather. His school is in Renton. If it were mid-morning I suppose someone could make it from Richie's office to the school in a half hour to forty-five minutes. So it could be the same photographer."

"But now, as we speak, Richie should be at home in West Seattle and Eduardo should be at your sister's in, what, Bellevue?"

"Somerset. Her name is Sonya."

"One person couldn't keep an eye on both of them. Neither of you have called, correct?"

"I had the number dialed. I wanted to hear his voice, but I didn't know what I would say," mumbled Rita.

"We decided that cooler heads should prevail until we calmed down," said Mike.

Fox paused for a moment, threaded his fingers together, and then pulled them apart. "Okay, this is how I see it: We must get Richie, Eduardo, and any other local relatives off Heinrich's radar. This won't entirely stop the possibility of other threats, but I have an idea I believe will work. And getting them to safety will at least buy us time."

"Time to do what?" asked Mike.

"Counterattack and eliminate the threat—one way or the other. Agreed?" asked Fox.

No one said anything. "Rita, what do you want to do?" Fox went on. "What's your gut instinct?"

"To get home as soon as I can on any airplane leaving, so I can protect my son," said Rita.

Fox put his hand on hers. "I'm not trying to mess with your head, but what *is* it that you really want, right now?"

Fresh tears spurted. "Oh God, you're right, it won't help. I just want to hold him and tell him he'll be all right. It's so hard. He's different. I'm away so much. He—"

Mike exhaled, nodded his head, and touched her forearm. "Listen, Rita. I know he's challenged. I know it's hard."

"You do? How?"

"You told me. Six months ago. On a Narita trip. You complained that you'd barely slept the week before. You, Tom Martin, and Katie Smith came to my room for the usual 'debriefing.' You drank way more than I ever saw you drink. You said it was so you could sleep. You staggered up to leave and crumpled to the floor. You broke down, but I think it was good. Between sobs we found out what you're going through. Then you passed out. We put you to bed. The next day you seemed fine. You didn't mention anything and neither did we." Mike placed his hand on hers. "I'm sorry if I breeched your confidence, but the three of us who were there have told people, people who care about you. I was going to tell Joey and Fox. It's obvious this burden is crushing you. I was going to talk to you about it sometime on this layover, but crazy things began to happen."

Rita covered her face with both hands and sobbed. "I'm sorry," she sniffed. "I have to find some middle ground, some sanity. I'm out-of-my-mind with Hector; I felt like a god when I engaged Heinrich. Now look at me."

Joey rose and grasped Rita's elbow. "Let's take a short walk." Rita used the table to pull herself up. With Joey's arm around her waist they made their way to the beach. Nearing the breaking waves, Joey shed her sandals and motioned for Rita to kick off hers. She walked straight into the ocean. When a wave broke over their shorts, Joey kept going, Rita in tow. When the water was belt high Joey stopped, disengaged her arm and made a diving motion with her hands. They both dove into the wall of an oncoming breaker.

The shock of the cool water startled Rita, and a moment later she felt the wave try to toss her further under. Her instincts took over. She kicked her legs and pulled with her arms and surfaced. She gathered her bearings and turned around, faced the shore, and trod through the water with ease. She thought about the phenomena of buoyancy—at the fact that if she stayed on top of the ocean, she was indeed quite buoyant. She watched Joey stroke toward shore, gather her feet under her, and stride out of the surf with aplomb, as if she swam everyday fully clothed. Rita shook her head as if to clear it, and followed. With lighter steps they returned to find Mike and Fox still in their chairs engaged in quiet conversation.

Rita stood over them dripping and shivering and finally nodded her head. "Fox is right; the best thing we can do is to eliminate the threat for good. Otherwise, when will it ever stop? I remember flying the troops to Kuwait last year. I asked this guy who was about to begin his third tour of duty if he was ever afraid. He said yes, he was *always* afraid. But fear can be a friend or it can get you killed. He said he uses his fear to heighten situational awareness, instead of inducing paralysis, which is where I've been since I saw the photos."

"Me, too," said Mike, who bolted out of his chair, "but no more."

"No more," the others echoed.

8:15 P.M. CST

A half hour later, with Joey and Rita showered and in fresh clothes, the crew raised their glasses and downed their tequilas with a toast to downing Gustav Heinrich—all the way down, if necessary. Fox looked at each one of them. "I'm thinking this up as I go along, so I'm going to run the basics of the first operation past you. Let me know if I'm not making sense. For the sake of speed, I'm going to assume certain things and err on the side of caution."

"What kind of assumptions?" asked Joey, breaking her silence.

Fox looked around. The pool area was nearly deserted, and he could hear the din from the dining room gaining volume. He turned to Joey. "That they, *they* being Heinrich and his operatives, have tapped the phones—ours here and Mike's and Rita's at home, cell and landlines. However, I'm going to take a chance and commandeer an empty suite here and make two calls to put the plan into action. So, the first time that Richie and Sonya will know anything about this is when Mary Magdaleno raps on their back door or window and flashes her Consolidated badge. I also assume Heinrich has someone watching both houses from the street. Mary is going to need to approach the backs of the houses. She'll need to park two or three blocks away and weave her way through side lots and backyards. I'll need both of you to suggest a route for her to avoid detection. Are you with me so far? Is making contact from the back of the house doable?"

Both Rita and Mike nodded, but to Fox they both looked a bit bewildered. Nevertheless, he plowed ahead.

"Okay, first critical question: Have Richie or Sonya had a DUI in the last ten years? The reason I'm asking is that if they have, they can't get into Canada right away. That's where I'm sending them."

They both shook their heads.

"Passports?" asked Fox.

"Yes," said Mike.

"Sonya has hers. But Eduardo's is at my house," said Rita, "I have a copy of it with me."

"Then, we're in business. I can fax the copy to Mary as well as a note from you giving her permission to take Eduardo across."

Fox opened his palms. "The idea is this: Mary is going to pick them up, take them to the waterfront on Mercer Island, and hand them over to my friends. They will take at least two boat rides and end up in a floatplane flying to Bliss, British Columbia. This will include vehicle changes. If Mary can grab them undetected, none of it will matter. But if she is spotted, we'll have three more chances to shake them."

"What about Mary? What if she's seen? Then she'll be dragged into this mess," said Rita.

"Mary will drive my car, which is registered to my ex-wife's maiden name at an address that doesn't exist. Once she reaches the residence on the island, she will go through a gate at the top of a long driveway. It winds down to a house that can't be seen from the street. She will drop off the passengers and proceed along a hidden lane, then pull under a tree and switch cars. She will exit two blocks east and north from where she entered."

"How do you know she'll do it?" asked Mike.

"Because, if I asked someone else to do it, she'd probably kill me. We go back a long way. Now, my first call is to a man who will arrange the details. My second call is to Mary. Mike, while I'm making those calls, talk to Ramirez with this phone," he said, handing over a cell phone Ramirez had given to him. "Brief him and ask what he knows. When Mike's finished, Rita, do the same with Hector. Let's get started. With luck they could be safe in three to four hours. Objections, ideas, comments? Anyone?"

"How the hell are you going to pull this off?" asked Mike.

"By calling in a ton of favors."

"I can hardly wait for part two," said Mike, rising.

"You're going to have to. Like I told you, I'm making this up second by second."

• • •

By 5:45 in the afternoon Austin Ramirez had listened to the playback of Fox's conversation with the general.

Revelstorm had done his job to perfection but the general's distinctive voice was muddied, leaving a doubt as to who was really speaking. Nevertheless, he slipped the CD into his briefcase and eased out of the van. A garbled voice was better than no voice.

Ramirez glanced at his watch as he climbed out of his car parked in front of the small store in Carlotta, the same one the crew had visited the day before. It was almost 6:45. He was certain he would be subject to venom, claws, and explosions. But he would weather it. Esmerelda was the right choice.

He swung open the door and a bell rang. A child's voice greeted him. "Hello, is that you, Alexis? Is your aunt here?" asked Ramirez. The girl had been stocking shelves and danced around the corner, then froze with her eyes wide. "Don't worry," he smiled, "go back to what you were doing, I'll locate your aunt myself."

He found Esmerelda sitting at a desk in the cluttered back room, her back to him, long hair gleaming, and her diminutive back as expressive as a conductor as she typed with a fury on a laptop, the keys spattering like gunfire. *Angry gunfire*, he thought. He glanced about and noticed the electronics and a few pictures, he figured he was in the same place as the flight crew had been. "Good evening, my dear."

The typing ceased. Dark eyes ablaze, she turned to him and rose, her lean body nearly rigid. "I forbade you to ever come here and you agreed! How dare you barge into my house? If I had a gun close by, I'd shoot you."

In three quick strides he closed the distance between them as he reached under his jacket for his pistol. He held it out. "Go ahead," he said, and thrust the butt end into her hand, "but before you pull the trigger, just answer one question. Do you want to be the president starting tomorrow or the next day?"

"The president of what? The Chamber of Commerce?"

"No, the president of the country. Our country."

"You mean *my* country? You have your own country."

In a heartbeat all of the tension drained out of him. He smiled, taking her in. He hadn't seen her up close in over ten years. He was surprised that with only one close look, she still stirred him.

She pointed the gun at him for a moment, then set it on the desk and crossed her arms. "I would like to shoot you, but I can't gun down a man who's obviously insane."

"Perhaps," he said, "but no more insane than kidnapping an American flight crew and asking them to murder someone they don't know or never heard of."

She spit out a breath. "That was hardly a kidnapping."

"The police would think differently. I persuaded the crew not to report the crime."

"I committed no crime."

"Shall we talk to the police about it, or should we talk about the future of *our* country?"

"I should also shoot you for endearing yourself to my son. I had to listen to him go on about you for so many years. Or, did you break into his life because you thought he might be *our* son?"

"At the very beginning I took an interest in him, not because of the remote possibility he was my son, but because of the certainty he was your son. It was the only way to stay connected, somehow, with you."

"You never tested him or tried to find out?"

"No, it would have made no difference."

The color in her cheeks deepened. In her youth she had been quick to anger, but he never minded because he thought it made her look even more alluring. He had usually laughed, which made her even madder.

She took a step and whirled back around. Ramirez held his hand up. "Please?" He steered her back to the present and told her of his plans. She scoffed. "You think Gota can convince the other generals to stand down? You think he can get the president to resign and appoint me? No way."

"The Butcher will fire himself. The army is apathetic. They know there's a better way. You are the one for the interim. The only person the people of all the factions trust. Especially the women. And it's the women we need the most right now."

"Like lost little boys, who need their mothers to make everything better?" She half smiled.

"Do not make light of it. If you want to think of it that way, I won't disagree."

"You speak of trust. How can I trust you after what you did?"

"That was a long time ago," he sighed. "Let it go. I'm not the enemy."

"Let it go?" she almost hissed. "You betrayed me in the worst way."

"Yes."

"You did not care."

"My heart was broken into a thousand pieces."

"I begged you to tell me why. I would accept anything, any explanation. But, you would not. What was I to think? What am I to think now?"

"Think of your country."

"You have aged well," she said. "You have forged your empire with the help of the despots. And now, you need me to keep them from overrunning you. Is that it?"

"The first part of what you said is true. The second part is not true."

She lowered her head for a moment, then raised it. "If you wish me to proceed, you will tell me why you did what you did."

"No."

The blow to his cheek by her open hand sounded like the crack of a whip. Ramirez did not flinch and he stifled an urge to touch his face. The door to the room opened and a frightened Alexis peered in. Esmerelda dismissed her with a subtle wave of her hand and turned her attention back to him. Her voice trembled. "The truth is that I cannot effectively lead and be in your presence, as I'm sure will be the case. I must have some kind of closure. Maybe you're right, maybe *I* am the one who is insane. But, I can never let it go unless I know why. I had access to your soul and your heart. I did not notice that it contained the seeds of cruelty. I gave you all of me. And you took it all, and I'm left with a carcass."

Ramirez stared at her, noticing his own tired eyes reflected in the moisture of hers and in an instant, relented. Keeping his voice barely above a whisper, he began. "It was your father. He was worse than the general. He systematically destroyed people. He wrecked lives for pleasure. You know what his nickname was?"

Esmerelda shook her head.

"Slim Dandy. Because he made fat wallets slim and dressed like a fop." She started to interrupt. Ramirez held up his hand. "If you don't want the truth, I'll stop here. No interruptions until I'm finished."

She nodded.

"You remember how unstable Ramon was. He was another one who couldn't stay out of your father's casino. I finally convinced him the tables were rigged, so he tried his hand at poker. He was no match against professionals. However, a few months before you and I were to marry, our family got Ramon sober and his head clear. He turned all of his holdings over to me, in return for taking care of Frau Heinrich and Gustav. A couple of years before, the government had tried to implement this crazy tax code that forced my father to put other parcels of our family's estate in Ramon's and my name. When the government abandoned the change we put everything back, or at least we thought we did."

Ramirez had been pacing the room and, suddenly aware of it, stopped in front of her. "Back to Ramon and poker. With his head on fairly straight, he jumped into a high-stakes game, one he was winning. In the end, it came down to him and Slim. Your father raised him more than he had. Ramon, in essence, raised your father around a million dollars, for he threw in the deed to the most crucial piece of land we owned, to see the bet. Ramon told me later he didn't even know he still had it until the day before and thought the parcel was nearly worthless.

"Of course, Ramon lost and signed over the deed. He had laid down a full house, but your father produced four aces. Witnesses told me he had cheated. I confronted him. He said, 'So what? Prove it.' He didn't stop there. He told me he would sign the deed back over to me if I terminated our marriage plans. And I could never tell you why or how. If I did tell you, someone would wind up dead. That scared me but I felt I could defend myself and the rest of my family. It was like he was reading my mind. I'll never forget his ear to ear grin, and then the laugh. 'No Austin,' he said, 'not you, but that whore of a daughter of mine. You say anything and I will have her killed and it will be on you.'"

Esmerelda clamped her eyes shut and violently shook her head.

Ramirez continued. "I said to him, 'You would never harm your own daughter.' He replied, 'Her mother was a whore; anyone could be her father. I asked Esmerelda but one thing, to stay away from you. She laughed at me. So, my boy, in the blink of an eye, I will have her put down.'"

Esmerelda couldn't contain herself. "We could have gone away somewhere. You could have protected me. You threw me over for a piece of land?"

"Yes, but not any piece of land."

"Where is it?" she demanded.

"South central."

"Next to the Forbidden Zone?"

"It's part of the zone. I'm going to tell you something that presently four people in the world know about. There are indigenous people living on that land, as far as we know, the same way as they have for at least eight hundred years. I'm sorry, but I'd make the same choice again."

Her tears gushed hot and free-flowing. He gently put his arms around her, not knowing how she would react. Her body collapsed into his. "I knew my father hated your father," she said, her words muffled against his shirt, "and I knew he was shady. He had forbidden me to see you, which I ignored, but he told me two weeks before the wedding that I would deeply regret my decision to even associate with you." She pushed Ramirez away hard and held him at arm's length. "Swear on the names of your ancestors that you are telling the truth, that he threatened to kill me and he called me a whore."

He looked straight into her eyes. "May the land I have spent my entire life preserving be struck from me if I am lying. I have told you the truth."

"Then," she said, "My father did kill me."

JANUARY 24, 5:55 P.M. PST

Bellevue, Washington

Mary Magdaleno had spent the last two-and-a-half days sprawled in the overstuffed chair in her library, staring out at the treetops and the blue-gray lake shimmering 1,200 feet below. At night the lake took on an amber glow from the millions of lights that streamed out of Bellevue and Redmond. Mary wondered if some other poor wretch under one of those lights stared out at *her* window and gazed toward Mary and the glow of radio towers perched on the summit of Cougar Mountain.

That she had come home from her six-hour delayed flight to a darkened house was not unusual. After all, it had been a little after three in the morning, but she was shocked to find an empty home and a note from Ben sprawled on the kitchen counter like a discarded grocery list. Ben had written that he was through with their marriage and would call in a couple of days to sort out the details. He wasn't having an affair, according to the note, nor had he even once been with someone else. But he was suffocating and not sure if he loved her anymore. And he was no longer sure if she loved him. He wanted the freedom to do anything with anyone, blah, blah, blah.

Her favorite mug sat on the end table next to her chair, filled with tepid Earl Grey tea. A pan of tomato rice soup sat cool and untouched on her stove. Her creature comforts were no comfort at all.

She had moved from disbelief, to anger, to emptiness, and back to disbelief, but came to the conclusion that she loved Ben, though she couldn't remember the last time she had told him that. Her emptiness mirrored the house. Daughter Kylie was in the middle of her junior year at Western Washington University in Bellingham. Snow White, her beloved seventy-five pound Samoyed lap dog and personal down comforter had been gone nearly two years. Mary had wanted a replacement, but Ben wanted to wait so they could travel to places like Peru and New Zealand. With the exception of a weekend at Ocean Shores, two hours away, they had been nowhere.

Although certain that she had seen Fox Revelstorm for the final time and had left him with more than the usual melancholy, idle ponderings, and what ifs, she had also felt giddy entering her dark house. From her long, deep kiss with Fox, she felt like a school girl. The taste of him that still lingered on her lips was wonderfully wicked and delicious. She possessed not an ounce of guilt and had even considered bragging about it to Ben, but of course that—and the likelihood of another kiss—would never happen. The giddiness was gone in an instant. She had never imagined not being married to Ben.

Her head was heavy with useless circular thoughts. She had dozed off until awakened by rainfall, just as the afternoon light began to fade and the blue surface of Lake Sammamish had bled out into gray. Just before nightfall the drops grew heavy and luminous white. Somehow she thought the raindrops looked like pregnant nuns—faith falling from the sky, splattered and dead on the ground.

She jumped at the sound of the phone, anxious and fearful, sure it was Ben finally calling her. She didn't bother to check the caller ID and nearly dropped the receiver when she heard Fox's voice. He made it clear from the start he didn't have time for chitchat. He told her the situation, asked her if she were willing to do the job, and pointed out that despite safeguards there was the possibility of serious danger.

Through all of that, she had been able to listen, yet she pictured herself hurtling down an elevator shaft, the sound of Fox's voice providing a glimpse of light that steadily increased until she saw a rope and grabbed it. She leapt at the chance to get outside of the shaft, outside of herself. She put him on speakerphone, sat at her computer and typed in all the names, numbers, landmarks, and directions. Then she repeated everything back to him.

She had not intended to tell Fox about Ben's note. But in the end Fox thanked her and told her to give his regards to Ben, and it spilled out. After a moment's hesitation he responded, his voice as soothing as a spoonful of honey coating a sore throat, as he told her that Ben would come to his senses.

By the time she hung up the rain had turned to snow. She glanced out the front window to the steep driveway below. It wasn't sticking—yet.

She called her contact, Broderick Smith, and gave him a rough timetable. She and Fox had concluded it would take three-plus hours to switch cars, gather the passengers, and make it to the Mercer Island drop-off point. She confirmed the gate code with him and promised to let him know when she was on her way to the island.

She climbed into a pair of jeans, and allowed herself the tiniest of smiles, for the jeans were a touch loose. She took a moment to study her image in the mirror. She had always kept herself trim and fit and, despite being forty-five, her ebony face was virtually unlined. Yet, somehow for Ben, it wasn't enough. Doomed marriages, she thought, were the ultimate appetite suppressant. She'd only eaten one bowl of cereal since she'd been home. She dragged a comb through her hair, while her stomach grumbled. Her head felt like it would float away if it wasn't attached to her neck. Five minutes later she had finished wolfing down a piece of wheat bread slathered with peanut butter. It would have to do.

In the mudroom next to the garage she gathered a pair of hiking boots with Yaktrax attached to their soles, the equivalent of chains for boots, plus gloves, hat, and a parka. She threw them in the back of her Land Rover and was gone. Although the 1,000-foot concrete driveway was still clear, snow was sticking like glue to the two-lane road that would lead her off the mountain. She skirted a flat part and went easily around a ninety-degree turn, then slowed before reaching a long, steep stretch. Ahead and down the hill she could see a shine rising from the asphalt. She knew what that meant and yanked the transmission into compound low, dialed down the gearshift to first gear, and descended the hill without touching the brake pedal.

Headlights zoomed into her rearview mirror, then veered into her side mirror as a small pickup truck zipped around her. But when he attempted to get back to his side, he went into a slow one-eighty, stopping sideways, blocking the road just in front of her. She spun her wheel hard-right and slid the SUV into the entrance of the Morningstar subdivision. The Land Rover bounded up over the curb of the center median garden and crunched down a row of snow-laden winter cabbage, before returning to the pavement. She was able to make an easy U-turn around the median, but the old battered Toyota Tacoma pickup still blocked her way, engine revving, but tires spinning futilely, sounding like out-of-tune sopranos.

She was out of the Land Rover in an instant, jogging carefully and motioning for the driver to roll down his window. Finally he did. She wanted to yell at him, but kept her voice level. "Listen, I've lived up here for twenty years. You're thinking that all you need is about five feet and you can get yourself pointed downhill again. Forget it. Your tires are bald and you have no weight in the rear. She peered into the cab. "Put it in reverse, pop the clutch, and back down to the entrance of Lemon Lane," she said, and pointed down the road. "Try not to use the brakes, and if you do, tap them. If you slide, don't stand on them, let off."

"But the entrance to Lemon Lane is on a blind curve," said the twenty-something, his unkempt dark hair spilling out of a knit hat. "Maybe you could jump onto the back bumper for extra weight."

"Get out of the car," Mary demanded. "I don't have time for this shit."

"Are you crazy?"

"Yes, I am. Get out. I'm going to back this piece of junk down the hill for you. If I hit anything, I'll pay for it. Now, get out and start walking."

It took her two minutes to go a hundred feet. The kid waited for her. She jumped out. "Slow down, and get some new tires or you're going to need all that tape and spackle in your cab to patch yourself up."

He shot her a lopsided grin. "Hey, I'm sorry. How about if I let you go by, since I held you up? That way in case I—"

"Thank you, that would be most appreciated," she interrupted, and flashed him a quick smile. She plowed her way back up the hill, wishing she was wearing her other boots with the Yaktrax.

By the time she reached the lower part of Forest Drive, some eight hundred feet down in elevation, she had made up her mind. On a wide part of the white road she pulled off and dialed Broderick. "Can you move the operation up an hour? Maybe even more?"

"Why?"

"The snow is sticking. It's slippery, and I doubt Fox's twelve-year-old Nissan Sentra has all-wheel-drive. I have a Range Rover with compound low. I'm going to need it to get to these people."

"It isn't safe for you to use your own car," he reminded her.

"It's the only way I can get them to you in one piece."

"It's no problem on our end. Everyone is waiting and ready."

"What about the plane? Can it takeoff and land in this stuff?"

"Yes, and so far, down here on the water, it's raining. No snow."

"Okay, my first pick-up is only about ten minutes away. I'll call when I leave West Seattle."

"Okay, copy that. Be careful."

"It's my middle name," she said, and snapped the phone shut.

Mary started up Highland Drive, gaining altitude again, and used the windshield wipers to clear the ever fluffier snowflakes. She parked a block below and two blocks short of Sonya's house, glanced again at her instructions, then raised her head and spotted her landmarks. The rear hatch open, she changed boots, donned her hat and parka, and slipped her hand into her jeans pocket one more time, feeling for her ID card, and then pulled on her gloves and started to move. It took her about five minutes to make it to the stairway that led up to the back deck of the house. As promised, right at the top of the stairs was a kitchen window. A tangle of dark hair was bent over the sink, soapy hands scrubbing a pan.

With her left hand holding the Consolidated ID against the glass, Mary rapped softly on the window pane. Sonya didn't respond. Mary knocked a little harder. Sonya's head jerked up and with a wild look in her eye, dropped the skillet in the sink and recoiled from the splash. Mary tapped the ID again and pointed to the door.

With a wary look Sonya left the kitchen and opened the slider a few inches.

"I'm sorry I scared you. My name is Mary. I'm a flight attendant with Consolidated and a friend of Rita's."

"We have a front—"

"I know you have a front door. I came to the back because you are in danger. This is going to be really hard to believe, but it's no joke."

Finally beckoned inside, Mary left her boots, came in, sat down, and explained the situation to a stunned Sonya.

"This is what Rita wants me to do?"

"Yes, I was told to take you and Eduardo, no matter what. Even if you're kicking and—well, kicking is okay, but no screaming."

Sonya shook her head and ran a hand through her thick hair. "What on earth did Rita do to get a guy pissed off enough to threaten her son?"

"It's not just her; it's the whole crew he's pissed off at, but apparently she *did* carve the guy up with some kind of sword."

Sonya rolled her eyes. "Enough said. I'll wake Eduardo from his nap. Sometimes he makes loud noises. While I gather our things you can talk to him—quietly though. Waking him and quick changes are hard for him."

Mary didn't know much about autism, but as Eduardo stumbled into the family room with his head down, dragging a blanket, she thought he looked like any other sleepy-eyed seven-year-old. When he looked up and saw her, he cocked his head, smiled wide, and ran to her with his arm raised. Mary knelt down and winked at him. She made no attempt to stop him from running his still warm hand all over her face.

"Hello Eduardo. My name is Mary. You know what?"

Sonya returned to the room. "He may like you and he may want to touch your face."

"He already has. Why is that?"

"I don't know, but every time he meets a new black person, that's what he's done."

Though Eduardo remained mostly quiet and wouldn't meet her eyes, she knew she had his attention and spoke very slowly, remembering something about autistic kids not being able to process sounds at a normal speed. "How about a fun adventure? *Really* fun," said Mary. "The bad guys are out there and we're going to get away from them. I'll take you and your aunt to a place on the water. Then," said Mary, holding up two fingers, "you get to go on two boat rides. And last, you'll fly on an airplane that takes off and lands on the water. You'll love it. We're leaving through the back door and we need to be extra quiet so no one knows we left. Okay?"

He responded by rubbing her face again then ran off toward his bedroom.

Fifteen minutes later Eduardo re-emerged wearing winter clothes and Sonya behind him toting a duffel bag. "This should hold us for a few days," she said, her fingers creeping along the wall, feeling for the light switch.

"Just leave it," said Mary. "Once you're away it won't matter, but for right now we need the status quo."

Sonya nodded.

"Your husband is out of town, correct?"

"New York."

"Passport?"

"I have it."

"Stay close and follow me. It gets a little dark in places, but the snow lights up everything. If you slip, go ahead and grab hold of me. I have good traction. But most of the way I managed to find patches of grass to step on. If we can avoid leaving tracks, all the better."

It seemed to Mary it took about a half hour to reach the car when in reality it took seven minutes. Eduardo didn't make a sound until they were halfway down the hill. Mary got the Land Rover turned around and, once again, she used the low end of her transmission to inch down the hill.

Eduardo and Sonya sat in back, the boy straining against his seat making loud one- syllable squawks. When they reached Interstate 90 Sonya asked Mary, "Do you know anything about where we're going? This Bliss, British Columbia?"

"A little. It's about a hundred miles north of Vancouver in the mouth of Desolation Sound, which is a beautiful place for summer cruising."

Eduardo wiggled his fingers in front of his eyes and repeated, "A little, a little, a little."

Mary continued. "It's a small community on the water, several little coves and inlets—maybe ten or twelve houses—owned by some moneyed folks. But, not moneyed in a bad way. Fox, the flight attendant who put this together, knows most of them. He sort of looks out for their places during the winter and does things for them. He says they're really good people."

"They must be, to be doing this for us at the drop of a hat."

"My thoughts exactly. I don't know where you'll be staying, but it will be cold and beautiful, and you'll be safe."

"When we get there, I can worry about Rita," said Sonya.

At sea level the interstate was clear of snow, but as soon as they crossed over the Spokane Street Bridge into West Seattle Mary could see that the main drag leading up the hill was white, with plenty of red taillights visible indicating heavy and slow moving traffic. Instead of tackling the incline, she wheeled right to stay close to the water where the streets were clear. She found a place to pull over and punched Richie's address into the GPS. It pulled up the route Fox had detailed and she asked for an alternate. She'd have to keep an eye on the display, to watch for Holden Street, which was where she was supposed to park. It was a roundabout route but eventually she reached the destination and pulled over in the designated spot.

Mary glanced over her shoulder at Sonya. "When I get out, sit in the driver's seat. I'll leave the key in the ignition. If anything doesn't look or feel right, go, just go, and call me. I'll have my phone on vibrate. Okay? I don't know how long this is going to take. Put Eduardo in the front seat, if it's better for him to be next to you."

"We'll be fine," said Sonya, glancing at her still restless nephew. Mary nodded and started her upward trek. Sonya popped outside then slid into the driver's seat. She reached back and gave Eduardo her own set of keys. He flipped through them methodically, one by one, quickly rubbing his index finger over the rough edges and now totally occupied.

Once again Mary climbed, and hugged a tall, ancient, and rotting fence. Because of its lean, it created a pathway free of snow. Then she turned left and traversed the inside of another fence, then right, again up the hill, on the lee side of a laurel hedge leading to Richie and Mike's backyard. She came up even with the rear of the house and darted left across the empty space visible from the street. She stopped at the corner of the mid-fifties rambler and looked back. Her tracks were easy to see. She spied a tall Japanese maple and what was left of its withered leaves and skinny branches supporting fingerlings of delicately balanced snowflakes. She grasped the trunk with both hands and shook it. A white mist settled on the ground, covering her footprints.

She took a deep breath of cold air and wondered if she could get past the next problem as easily, for she could clearly hear every note of some symphonic piece blasting from inside the house through her thick knit hat covering her ears. Under the eaves she made her way to the elevated back door, treading on the rotted remnants of summer annuals. The door opened onto a cast concrete porch three feet high. Feet still planted in the garden, she reached up and knocked on the battered wooden door. As she feared, Richie didn't answer it. She banged as loud as she dared. Still no Richie. She resigned herself to wait until the classical movement ended, and prayed it didn't last another twenty minutes.

She only had to wait ten. When the music stopped she banged hard on the door fearing she might have only one chance. She was right. The music started again, and she leaned back against the house rubbing her forehead, wondering if perhaps curtains were open somewhere across the back. She noticed a movement to her right and the door moved inward a few inches. "Wait!" Mary rasped, as Richie had started to shut it.

He pulled it in and the light spilled out and so did Richie, who ducked slightly to get his head under the door frame. He wore sweats and a black T-shirt. He ran his long slender fingers through a blondish mop of hair. "What do we have here?" he asked, peering down at her.

Mary flashed her Consolidated badge while listening to a car door slam and an engine start. "I'm a flight attendant. You're in danger because of what's happening to Mike's crew in Central America. You're coming with me out this door. Grab your passport and belongings for a couple of days."

"I'm not going anywhere."

"It's what Mike wants you to do."

"Why didn't he call, then?"

"Your phone may be tapped." She held up a hand. "Wait one second. I have to check this out." She darted around the porch, back under the eaves and peeked around the far corner of the house. A gray Mercedes S-type sedan, illuminated under a streetlight crept toward them, tires crunching the glowing snow. A man strode next it, keeping pace, dressed in an overcoat and a tam hat, left hand gloved, right buried in his coat pocket like he was holding something. Something like a gun.

She ran back to Richie, now standing on the porch, slippers buried in snow. "You have one minute. Winter clothes and your passport."

Richie stroked his upper lip with his thumb and forefinger. "This is crazy."

"I know. But please go now and leave everything that won't burn down the house exactly the way it is."

"Okay," he nodded.

As ordered, he returned in less than a minute, slipped out, and locked the door.

"Follow me, try to step where I step," ordered Mary.

They were halfway down the hill when they heard the voice shout, "I think I see something or someone moving. Next street down is Holden. Go! I'll stay on foot."

"As fast as you can without falling," whispered Mary, bolting ahead. She made it to the Land Rover, caught Sonya's attention, and waved her out of the driver's seat. Behind her, she watched Richie stumble down the hill. He groped the rickety fence for balance until finally he slid into the SUV, stopping himself from going down by grabbing the passenger door handle. In a second he was in and Mary had the car moving.

"I need a steep hill," said Mary.

"Up or down?" asked Richie.

Mary stifled her exasperation. "Up."

"Second right, but it's *really* steep, and long," he said, reaching for his seatbelt.

"Good."

Mary made the ninety degree turn at twenty-five miles an hour, and drifted left almost into the sidewalk before the tires bit. She tromped on the gas and they shot and sluiced their way upward, wheels alternately spinning and grabbing, jerking them all over the road. Eduardo giggled like he was at an amusement park, and rocked back and forth.

"Look for a gray Mercedes that I'm hoping won't have all-wheel-drive," said Mary.

"Nothing yet," answered Sonya, craning her head.

Just as they crested the hill, Sonya spotted two beams of light far below, then the gleam of gray under a streetlight. "I just got a glance as we hit the summit. I think he went clear over the sidewalk, but I'm not sure."

"Do you think he got a decent look at us?"

"I doubt it because it would have been the same for him as it was for me, just an instant. Judging from by the way he came around the corner it looked like he was out of control, so his concentration might have been elsewhere."

Mary glanced at Richie. "We're going to Mercer Island. Give me the fastest way. We could have been spotted by that guy who yelled. So, I'm betting that I have a better vehicle and that I'm a better driver than anything and anyone coming after us."

Twenty-five minutes later they were through the gate winding their way down to the water. "Jesus Christ," said Richie, "I never realized how many gray Mercedes sedans are out there. Every time I saw one it was like sticking my finger into a light socket."

Mary flashed an exhausted smile. "I know what you mean."

As soon as she stopped the Land Rover under a palatial porte cochère, a man and woman in parkas ran out to open the car's doors.

Mary shook Broderick's hand, a little startled by his youth. If he was forty it was barely, and the woman looked even younger. "Any trouble?" he asked.

"We may have been spotted, but I think we got away."

He nodded. "We'll stay with the plan, and make all the switches and progressions. My wife Carol will accompany you," Broderick said to Richie and Sonya. "Are you ready? Do you have everything?"

They nodded. "Whatever else you need we either have it at the house or we can get it."

He turned back to Mary. "You're welcome to any vehicle I have for as long as you need it, including the BMW SUV," he said, pointing to the garage.

"No, thanks. I feel more confident in this and it will be parked in the employee lot at the airport, which is secure."

"As you wish. Thanks for getting them here safely."

"She was magnificent," said Sonya, with a heartfelt hug of Mary.

"Thanks for not letting me say no," said Richie, with a grin.

They started down the foot path to the dock. "Wait," said Mary. "How do you know Fox?"

Broderick turned around. "He's a strange guy. Charming, witty, but he's also shy. He likes to be by himself. For the last eight or nine years he's looked after our place up there. And most of the others, as well. He's always doing little repairs, and making sure the house is ready when we arrive, usually with a fresh salmon in the refrigerator. We try to pay him, but he won't take a dime. He's like the Godfather. He just says that someday he may need a favor. Well, he finally asked. We're all tripping over each other to do it."

As they had descended the hills of West Seattle, the snow had turned to rain, and now, the rain had turned to a mist. Mary watched the Bayliner slip away from its mooring and disappear into the night. Disappearing suddenly seemed appetizing.

Again, Mary concentrated and gripped the steering wheel with both hands, continually checking her mirrors for any sign of a tail. When she reached the employee parking lot at SeaTac Airport, she slumped back into her seat as if her body had turned to Jell-O. It was all she could do to climb out of the car and stagger to the employee bus stop. Though her body was limp, her mind began to ramp up. The image of Fox Revelstorm blotted out everything else. She told herself she had no choice. She might have been spotted. She must leave. She would go to Fox.

Mary boarded the half-empty plane bound for Quintana, with a stop in L.A., squinted under the harsh light and greeted an old friend, Karen Adams. Karen eyed her. "You're going to Central America with only a tote? You didn't check a bag, did you? There's plenty of room."

Mary shook her head. "It's complicated."

"Oh, well. All I know is that you have nothing, so when you get there, you'll have to shop for everything. Perfect."

Mary managed a slight smile and made her way toward the rear of the 737, and slid into a window seat in an empty row. As the plane bolted into the air she allowed herself to sink back and close her eyes.

She was now hurtling her way to Fox at 500 miles an hour. First she pictured him hugging her, his arms tight around her and squeezing ever so gently. This led to a lush kiss, deep and lengthy, and when they broke, they stood in the ocean, waves washing over their legs and the red sun still warm on her shoulders. As the darkness settled in they stripped out of their suits and swam. Yes, Fox would comfort her, and make her feel like she used to feel: needed and desired.

She felt a tap on her shoulder, opened her eyes and looked up at Karen.

"We're on final, honey. You had yourself a nice nap."

Mary nodded and moved her seatback into the upright position. After the plane touched down and stopped decelerating, out of habit, she flipped on her cell phone. Two voice messages: the first one from Fox. *Mary, thanks to you, everyone is safe and secure. They arrived at midnight. I was told you may have been spotted, but from a source we learned that all they knew was that you were in a white SUV. You're in no danger. Go home and make it work. I'll talk to you when this is all over.*

She exhaled with relief, but felt a different discomfort. *Now what?*

She pushed the button for the second message. *Mary, I can't believe what I did. I am so sorry. It's one in the morning. I'm home waiting for you. I spent two miserable nights away. I'm never leaving again. I don't know what happened. I just went temporarily insane. You are the most precious thing on earth to me. None of this is your fault. It's mine. Please come back. I promise to get myself together. I promise. I love you.*

Mary could hardly breathe and wondered if she had ever cried so hard. She finally composed herself and made it to the front door, the last passenger remaining. Karen looked at her in alarm. "Are you okay?"

"Yes, but I'm changing plans."

"You're not going? You're not staying on?"

"No, I'm not needed there, but I *am* needed at home."

8:45 P.M. CST

Fox dropped the phone into its cradle and unconsciously touched his left ear. It was still hot, having been singed by Mary's sad news. He sat alone in a partially cleaned suite obtained for thirty minutes in exchange for fifty U.S. dollars. He gazed through the open slider to the placid sea below. It moved with serenity and order; small phosphorescent rollers broke evenly on the sand with precision timing. A beautiful illusion, he thought, for beneath the surface, the ocean roiled with the haphazard rhythm of chaos and death. *Poor Mary. What the hell was Ben thinking?* He exhaled deeply, but did not allow himself the indulgence of more sympathy or contemplation.

He snatched up the receiver and punched in Celeste Starr's number. He was a touch nervous but squelched any awkward small talk by telling her straight out that his night spent with her had been the best in a long time. "We have a situation," he said, coming to the point.

"Does it have to do with Ramirez wanting to topple the government in the next couple of days?" Celeste asked, half joking.

"Yes, we're assisting, still pulling a plan together."

"Are you sure you want to get mixed up in this?"

Fox relaxed, instantly soothed by the sound of her voice. He eased back into the sofa and plopped the heels of his bare feet onto the coffee table. "At this point, we don't have a choice. It's in our best interest to engage. We've been in Heinrich's crosshairs since before we arrived." He sank back further into the upholstery, thinking for a moment that it felt good and natural to talk to her as a confidant. "You know about what happened on Ramirez's plane?"

"The gist, not the details."

"I'll save those for later. Right now, the upshot is that I'm not sure which part of the general's skull hurts the most; his forehead where Mike unleashed the blow that knocked him out, the back of his fat noggin on which he landed, or the lobe where he thinks of his three million bucks, up in smoke. And, within a couple of hours he'll discover he wasn't chatting up Wesley Thorp, the child-porn baron I claimed to be. He'll also discover his hard pitch to produce and sell films of child rape was secretly recorded for his countrymen to hear.

"As for Heinrich, he's also had a tough couple of days. It started with me embarrassing poor Gustav on the plane. Then Ramirez fired him. Rita used his body for sword practice, and don't ask me to explain this, but while Joey and I slept, he paid us a visit." Fox heard a small exhale, and understood how that sounded, but he plunged on. "I think he came to kill us, but couldn't because of Joey. Joey thinks she stopped him with her mind. So, tell me, do you think those two are a little upset?"

"In every way possible," she answered with a light voice, then more serious, "What about this mind control thing and Joey?"

Fox sat up straight. "I told you not to ask, but—"

"Did she use it on you? You didn't waste much time, did you?" she said.

Fox hesitated.

Celeste remained silent.

"I gave her only what she wanted," he finally said.

"Which was?"

"As we suspected, she believes that my pulling her out of the plane changed her life. She said that when I had my arms around her she experienced perfection, like she was in heaven. Her desire to have me hold her again is what drove her to me. So, with both of us fully clothed, I put my arms around her and held her, and we fell asleep."

"Is there something else she wants?" Celeste asked.

"What do *you* think?"

After another moment of silence she said, "I think I should stop the interrogation. At this point, no matter what you do, you're welcome in my house."

A trickle of frustration, spawned from hearing the word interrogation, pulsed through Fox then dissipated, along with the cockeyed notion that he could conduct a thirty-second business conversation with Celeste after sleeping with her the night before. Instead he gave way to a vivid recollection of his body entangled in her lush, lank legs. Then inexplicably, he remembered his face buried in the nape of Joey's neck and feeling the supple contour of her form through her clothes.

"Fox, are you there? What are you doing? Comparing me to Joey?"

He decided to be honest and leaned back into the sofa. "I wouldn't exactly call it comparison. What are you wearing?"

"Nothing," she replied.

"Nothing?"

"I just got out of a hot shower and I'm lying on the bed with my arms and legs out, so I won't sweat while I'm cooling down."

"You're lying," said Fox, feeling a bead of his own appear on his forehead.

"Yes, of course I am. I already told you," said Celeste.

"What if you're not telling the truth?" he asked, standing up.

"Well, what if I'm not?"

"Then—continue to do it," he said relaxing his fingers, which held the receiver in a death grip.

"My motives are not hidden."

"Apparently, neither are your attributes, which I'm visualizing in my mind in high-definition."

"LCD or plasma?"

Fox smiled, rubbed his eyes and eased her image from his head, and pondered what was right. "You're not out of line at all to ask about Joey and me. No one is more baffled than I am, except maybe Joey. Look, you said I was welcome any time. Could that include the rest of the crew? We're up to our necks in this mess and diving deeper. The three of them are headed for Esmerelda's but if that doesn't work out, at some point we may need a refuge. You mentioned having people you never see look after you."

"That's what I'm told… Maybe more so, now that I'm aligned with Ramirez."

"I know about his offer. So, you've given him an answer?"

"I'm in. And your crew is welcome here any time—day or night—right now, if need be."

"Thanks, it's a relief to know we have options," he said.

"One more thing before you hang up. Have you heard about the jaguar that killed Heinrich's mother?" she asked.

"Not really. Rita said something about it."

"Well, about five years ago Hector Cato found this female kitten with half its ear torn off. After she was sewn up, Greta Heinrich insisted on keeping her despite Ramirez's policy against harboring wild animals. Of course, the cute kitten Greta named Ursula grew into a big cat, one that did not take kindly to enclosures or training. One day, her trainer had had enough and fled the exercise area, claiming Ursula was too dangerous and not trainable. Greta grabbed his whip and lashed him a few times, screaming at him, yelling that *she* would show *him* how to handle the unruly beast."

"Did you see this?" asked Fox.

"No, not in person, but the trainer did. He told me. Anyway, Ursula sat calm on the far side of the enclosure, about fifteen feet away. Greta stepped inside and latched the door closed. As she started to raise her whip arm, Ursula leapt, took Greta down and bit off half her face. It took two days for her to die. Ramirez immediately had Ursula taken back into the jungle and released before Heinrich could kill her. She hadn't been seen since, and it was assumed she didn't make it in the wild. Yesterday, she was spotted by Jorge, one of Ramirez's men."

"Alive?"

"Yes, in an area frequented by Heinrich. Luckily Jorge had a tranquilizer gun, another man with him, and a pick-up truck. He shot her, and they removed her right away. Of course, they ran some tests on her and found out she's nursing. So, as soon as she's ready, probably sometime early in the morning she'll be released, Heinrich or no Heinrich. So, she's here now, resting peacefully in a temporary enclosure. Even a little doped up, she looks magnificent."

"She's at your place?"

"Yes, right here, with a new name, Janelle. I'm telling you all this because I'm going to paint her—in a good way. No darkness. It's because of you I think I can do this and that maybe my soul has stopped dripping blood into my paints. You helped me heal and if the painting radiates her true beauty, it's yours."

"I predict a wonder to behold, and I would be honored to accept it. That is, if I can keep the general and Gustav from doing to me what Ursula did to Frau Heinrich."

"Yes, be careful. Don't underestimate Heinrich, like Greta underestimated Ursula. Despite his emotional instability, Heinrich is intelligent and cunning, with plenty of resources. But there's one more thing, and it's important. When they delivered Ursula, they gave me several DVDs of Ursula's training sessions. The first one I popped in was the last one recorded, when Greta was killed. It went down exactly like the trainer said it did, but there's much more to it. It's very powerful and shocking. It might help you," she said.

"What's your point?" asked Fox.

"I'm no psychologist, but his seeing this film could break Heinrich. What I'm saying is that I might be able to cook something up in the round room, or what I call the enclave. I can make him feel like he's there, eavesdropping on his mother."

"I don't know how this will play out," said Fox, "but go ahead and start cooking. It's another option."

Fox hung up and sat still. He willed his mind to do the same, but failed. If Fox's self-image was about anything, it was about containment and discipline, paring expectations to the minimum, snipping off buds of desire before they fully bloomed, thus leaving no chance to witness their inevitable wilt and decay. But he was also about the truth and the truth, just revealed to him, was that when it came to Celeste and Joey, he had totally lost containment and any illusion that he could regain it. The truth was laced with exhilaration and horror: he wanted them both.

In a minute he would emerge and rendezvous with the crew, find out what Rita had learned from Hector, circle back with Ramirez, finalize the plan, and act. He would remain rational and composed but wondered how he would see through whatever gushed in his head, blotting out everything that wasn't Joey and Celeste.

Even though he felt like a befuddled and besotted fool, he left his self-conscious embarrassment in the room. *The reality is that I could be dead by dawn. The reality is that whatever feelings both of them have for me could be dead as well.*

8:35 P.M. CST

In the dim light of an otherwise empty café situated in the outskirts of Quintana City, Colonel Miguel Gota and Attorney General Antwain Fuqua lit fresh cigars. Ramirez briefed them on the recent events, including Esmerelda's willingness to accept the presidency. Following the update, Gota and Fuqua leaned forward to listen with rapt attention to the recording between Fox and the general. They replayed it a second time and followed along with a printed transcription. Fuqua peered into his empty coffee cup. In response to the slight nod of Gota's head, his dark-haired niece, who ran the lunch-only cafe, appeared with a pot and refilled their cups, then disappeared.

Gota's wan body, thinning gray hair, harsh voice, and terse language contrasted with the robust Fuqua's stocky build, overabundant mane, and physical exuberance. Gota wiped down his reading glasses with a tiny cloth and blew smoke up to the blackened ceiling, then turned to Ramirez. "I have been skeptical, Austin. I have questioned your motives and your methods for years. I have also questioned whether the country would be better served with a woman president, no matter how strong she is, and a sharply reduced military. But, I have also listened carefully to you, and to this recording. Your man was impressive. It's hard to believe he is only a flight attendant," he said, waving his hand through the smoke. "No matter."

Gota continued. "At this point, I believe your reasoning is sound, the timing fortuitous. Soriano's erratic behavior has raised eyebrows; even the heavy-lidded insiders are alarmed, including me. He has become Stalinesque, at least in terms of the body count and the paranoia. Men of rank have disappeared, likely held in underground cells to answer questions for having asked them. The faction supporting the general will listen. The question remains: Will they act? I believe they will so long as they feel less threatened from us than from the general and his overzealous thugs. As to actual charges against Soriano, at this time, I will defer to Antwain."

Ramirez looked to Fuqua. "Sir?"

Fuqua slapped the table with his meaty palm. "I wish we had more hard evidence on both the general and Heinrich. The problem is that we can't directly connect either of them to the drugs. We might be able to find a paper trail from the general linking them, but that could take a week. I could arrest Heinrich for placing a hazardous object on board an aircraft, essentially the same offense as phoning in a bomb threat, but that won't keep him in jail for more than an hour. However, the recording of the general may be enough to entice him to leave. As you say, hang himself with his own hideous words. Although a court of law may not find him guilty of conspiring to provide films of child rape, the entire military and most of the citizens will recognize his voice. Many of these men of power are cruel, and think nothing of rape and torture. But there is a line," said Fuqua, with a nod of his head. "Austin, I believe you are correct—no matter what, no one will want to stand on the general's side of that line."

"Other thoughts? Ideas?" asked Ramirez. "What else can we do?"

Fuqua gulped down half a cup of black coffee and then grinned. "Since Heinrich is the one sliced up and Cato is untouched, an assault charge against Heinrich is not likely to stick. By the way, I wish I had witnessed that little skirmish," he said, pulling on his cigar. "I heard she was wearing a sundress. I heard that she wears it extremely well. This Rita Sanchez must be some woman!"

"Yes, let your imagination soar. You would not be disappointed, if you were to meet her," said Ramirez.

"I should make a point of it. Anyway," continued Fuqua, flicking ash, "you have spoken of rumors, and I have heard them myself. Tales of Heinrich and his band of animal protectors committing acts of abomination. The fact that they were acting on your behalf, we will put that aside for now."

"You don't have to. I take full responsibility," said Ramirez.

Fuqua jammed the mangled tip of his double Panatela back into his mouth. "There is no one in this room who has not issued orders demanding results, without demanding to know the ways and means of execution. Heinrich's task was to stop the poaching. It is my understanding that he has entirely succeeded. Unless you have deceived us, everything else is speculation."

"If I had hard evidence, I'd submit it," said Ramirez.

"Let us continue," said Fuqua. "This changeover must coincide with the law, just as Esmerelda's temporary appointment does. Now, I can't issue a warrant and I can't send any men, but if it were possible to discover such evidence and remove it, I believe it would be admitted in our courts. If so, we could put Heinrich and his men away, permanently. Do you have anyone who can get into his castle, so to speak, gather incriminating material, and get out without getting himself killed? Or, more to the point, can you come up with someone stupid enough to try it, and clever enough to pull it off?"

Fuqua laughed out loud at his own quip and even Gota's dour lips turned upward. "In the meantime, Colonel Gota and I will discreetly start the downfall of General Soriano as best we can. We will make copies of the recording and distribute them to the other brass immediately. The rank and file will have access later this evening, and by tomorrow the world will know of it. But, by withholding the recording from the public until the new president is announced, much needed credibility will be created for the military. This will show the people that our commanders will do what is right and will cooperate with the new regime."

"Yes, and that is of the utmost importance," said Gota. "With the release of political prisoners and former freedoms restored, celebration, marches, and protests will follow. A certain amount of violence is inevitable. The people do not trust the army. However, our support for Esmerelda and rid-dance of Soriano will ease the transition. As promised we will use restraint to keep the peace."

"And hope Esmerelda's influence is strong enough to prevent rioting and destruction," added Fuqua.

Gota rose. Fuqua and Ramirez followed. "I have one more question, sir," stated Ramirez, addressing Fuqua. "If all goes as planned, do we encourage the general to leave, or do we hold him and prosecute him?"

"I have contemplated that question myself," said Fuqua, crushing out his cigar. "I believe that if General Soriano can find someone willing to take him in, on another continent, then we should be happy to provide the means of transportation. However, we must prove to the people that he goes with a minimal amount of money."

Ramirez looked to Gota. "Colonel?"

"I concur."

"If you will excuse me, gentlemen, I'm off to seek someone who is fool enough to break into Heinrich's castle and gather the evidence."

"And where will you find such a fool?" asked Fuqua.

Ramirez returned Fuqua's smile. "No further than in the mirror staring back at me. However, I know two men who are supposedly quite adept at portraying phantoms."

"And who are these ghosts?"

"Hector Cato, my associate, and Fox Revelstorm, the American flight attendant whose interview with the general will hopefully cause his demise."

Gota rubbed his chin. "Revelstorm certainly has guts and he did a professional job to elicit Soriano's intentions, but he is only a flight attendant. He would be a fool to tempt fate twice in less than twelve hours."

Ramirez shrugged. "Do not underestimate these Americans. They have proven to be quite resourceful. Heinrich has threatened the crew's relatives. I don't believe Revelstorm or any of them take kindly to threats. They will not hesitate to act. In fact, if this were ancient Rome, I think Revelstorm and Heinrich are at the outside of the Coliseum fighting their way to the center ring."

• • •

In a small apartment deep within the monstrous hillside structure Heinrich stood motionless in his bedroom, reality beginning to set in. It was a few minutes past nine in the evening. His icy-blue eyes stared into the mirror at the debacle that had corrupted his sculpted chest. He sported seven separate cuts: the longest fifteen inches, the shortest six. His once smooth Aryan skin looked like a jungle road, rutted and puckered with nearly four hundred stitches that held together antiseptic-tinged slabs of yellowish-blue flesh oozing drops of burnt-orange blood. All his wounds were superficial, except for the mental ones and he seethed with fury.

He fingered a stitch. That it had happened was unfathomable. That it was a woman who had done it was almost beyond comprehension. He allowed himself a moment to picture Rita Sanchez's horror stricken eyes and listen to her wretched screams, as he hacked her to pieces.

He had not held still while being sewn up and his personal on-site physician, Bauer, had threatened to sedate him. Heinrich threatened him back and Bauer shrugged, now knowing how it felt to stitch like Dr. Frankenstein.

Unclenching his jaw, Heinrich covered the mess with a dark red cotton shirt and flexed his body. Immediately, he felt a trickle of blood rush toward his waist. The healing would come later. He pushed the rage out of his head and into his body, for he knew he needed composure and strength. The last forty-eight hours had not gone well. His blood lust had clouded his judgment and challenging Ramirez had compounded it. The general's scheme to have Ramirez detained and jailed in Paisa de Rosada had seemed perfect until the fucking flight attendants ruined it. Worse, ten minutes ago he received a call from Seattle. The boy and the partner had disappeared, as well as his psychological advantage and leverage. Nevertheless, he left his bedroom and made his way downstairs, calm and focused. Men were on the move, plans in place, and if his capture squad didn't screw up, he would soon have all the flight attendants in his possession. But, even their impending deaths would not be enough to persuade Ramirez to sign over even an acre of his land. Ramirez would allow them to die. And, of course, Heinrich planned to kill them.

Heinrich had one card left to play: The one thing, he was certain, that was powerful enough to bring Ramirez to his knees.

"Where are they?" he asked, striding into the low-lit windowless war room. Blips from monitors darted across the ceiling.

"The crew heading toward the Forbidden Zone? Almost a quarter of the way," replied Emile, who stared at his screen and absentmindedly scratched his bandaged thumb.

"Let me know when they reach the scatter point. At that time I will give each of them their coordinate destinations. You will not monitor those coordinates, whether I give them from here or remotely."

"Yes, sir."

"Have you heard from the capture squad?"

"They are waiting to engage Ramirez's men. José, the dupe, is on the way."

"Jimenez is with him?"

"He just picked him up."

"Good," replied Heinrich, and headed for the stairs to the lower levels.

"What is so important about Jimenez?" asked Emile.

Heinrich stopped and turned. "Jimenez escorted the crew through security at the airstrip. They will recognize him and accept him. Emile, you have been efficient with your work, nearly invisible for one so large and, most importantly, have not asked questions. See to it that that pattern continues."

"Yes, sir."

"Excellent. Rondo is readying the Bell Huey for the night mission. Make sure Carlos is ready to dive with fresh film for the underwater camera."

"Yes, sir. After that, I'll be on my way," said Emile.

"We are a man short." Heinrich frowned. "I will need you in the 'copter."

Emile turned away from the board. "I would prefer not to, sir." Emile watched a spark of fury pass into Heinrich's eyes and freeze, until Heinrich blinked.

"Perhaps you can be accommodated. Let us see how the evening plays out."

"As you wish," replied Emile, with a slight smile.

• • •

Emile calculated the odds of killing Heinrich without a sound. Even odds, in his condition and armed. Unarmed, Emile knew his odds were poor. And Emile did not believe he could get outside undetected to warn Hector about Jimenez until Heinrich left. All he knew for sure was that Heinrich believed he had crossed him, which meant he was now a condemned man. It was only a question of when and how.

33

9:15 P.M. CST

Fox slung his black bag over his shoulder, nodded to Rita and Mike, stepped outside the door of his unit, and peered in both directions. In the distance, a torch-illuminated Ramirez stood at the far edge of the pathway waiting for Fox. Fox turned to Joey and watched the shadows dance across her face. They wound their arms around each other and squeezed. Joey hugged Fox as if she were trying to climb inside him.

"Look," Fox said, his voice barely above a whisper, "I'm going to be fine."

"It's not you I'm worried about," she replied, relaxing her arms. "It's Rita and Mike."

"What about you?" asked Fox.

"I'm prepared for whatever happens. In a perfect scenario, José picks us up, we wait out the night with Esmerelda, receive a call from Mary telling us Eduardo and Richie are safe, you gather evidence resulting in a successful manhunt and conviction of Heinrich, the general resigns, the country flips over, and we go home in the afternoon. Tell me that's the way this night goes down."

"You're right, that scenario is the least likely of any."

Joey nodded. "This is a war. Neither side will give up until it's over. I'm prepared to do what I have to do to keep Mike and Rita safe."

"What are you really saying?" asked Fox.

"The three of us are disappointed we're not going with you, but it's the right decision. In a war there are casualties. There may already have been casualties. We don't need any more caused by overzealous incompetents. Ramirez's men should have been here a half hour ago and Ramirez can't raise them. So, while you're headed for sure danger, I'm not sure we're out of danger. When I hug you I'm going to do it as if it's the last time, while I pray that it's not."

"Joey—"

She raised her hand. "No more words. I want to feel your arms around me," she whispered, wrapping her body around his. He could feel the strength of her fingers kneading the skin on his back, somehow penetrating his flesh and moving inward, the intensity so great he could feel the thumping of his heart and picture the oxygenated blood from his lungs gush into his atrium and out into his arteries. For a split second his mind blanked, and Joey vanished like a genie sucked back into his body. He felt her pressure lessen as she disengaged and stepped back. A chill ran through him. He gazed at her once again in astonishment.

Fox glanced over his shoulder. In the distance he barely saw Ramirez's nod. Reluctantly, Fox moved toward him.

"Take care of Hector," called Joey. "He and Rita have a lot to live for."

"We all do," he answered, with little conviction.

"Are you sure?"

"No."

"Neither am I."

Ramirez's van bounced along the dirt road. While the stars took center stage in the sky, the crescent-shaped moon was reduced to a bit player. Despite the grandeur overhead, to Fox they could have been zipping through a tunnel in Switzerland. The van's headlights obscured the glitter from above and the jungle, dense and opaque, loomed only a few feet on either side of them.

With a flashlight, Fox tried to concentrate on the drawings of Greta Heinrich's dark palace on his lap, but the thumping of his heart and the faint echo that followed distracted him. It was an echo that had never been there before. He switched off the flashlight, leaned back, and rubbed his forehead. *You don't believe in God, at least not the God that anyone else claims to know. You don't believe in psychics, yogis, gurus, or Betty Crocker. Hell, you don't even believe in UFOs but now you believe Joey Sabatini has done things you thought were impossible, and you wonder if she somehow inserted the beat of her heart into yours. Unbelievable.*

"Are you all right?" asked Ramirez, jarring him back to the task at hand.

Fox exhaled. "I guess most of us always teeter on the precipice of insanity."

Ramirez nodded. "I'm way past that. So are you." He turned up the palm of his right hand. "I mean, we're speeding through the jungle to go break into a blood-crazed lunatic's fortress. You call that sane?"

Fox laughed, shrugged his shoulders, and switched the flashlight back on.

One more thing you don't believe in: that what you believe and don't believe is going to matter if someone puts a bullet in your brain. He flipped through the drawings again.

"What do you think?" asked Ramirez.

"It's huge," said Fox.

"They call it the Hive. It's modeled after some Nazi fortress that was built into a cliff somewhere in Normandy. Not nearly as big, but the idea is the same, a vertical structure with a façade facing the water. It blends in with the land, but what's visible constitutes maybe twenty percent. The rest is built into the rock. Transylvanian in that there are supposed secret rooms, passages, torture chambers, and whatever else. It was one of those projects where no one said anything, the workers were housed on-site and didn't leave until they were no longer needed, and then gone."

"You mean you've never been inside?"

"I had washed my hands of it. I appropriated enough money to build it to resemble the original structure, which was my brother's intent. They blew through that money just blasting into the side of the hill. Greta had other plans, literally."

"Where did she get the money?"

"I don't know, but she slept with two men on a regular basis. They were General Soriano and a crooked casino owner, who happened to be Esmerelda's father. Enough said. Anyway, the plans in your hand are the first set, probably like looking at the first draft of a Dickens novel—practically worthless."

"Then, what you're saying is that we get in and see what we can find, not knowing where to look."

Fox could see Ramirez's teeth gleaming in the darkness of the car's interior. "I just gave Hector a huge raise. Let's see if he deserves it. He will have the plan and he will lead. Any problem with that?"

"No, if you trust—"

Fox was interrupted by Ramirez's ringing cell phone. Ramirez jerked it open. Ten seconds later the van was stopped, and the phone was crushed into Ramirez' right ear. Fox could not discern the words, but he knew the voice: Heinrich.

Ramirez jerked the set closed and smashed his right fist on the bench seat. A second later he was composed. He looked at Fox. "The worst possible thing has happened." He flipped the phone open again and pressed a button. "Hector? Listen. Have you heard from Emile? I need to know where Heinrich's men are." Ramirez listened for a moment. "Damn. I'll repeat back. Four are waiting to compromise the crew's protection at the Paraiso. And five are heading due east toward the Forbidden Zone boundary. No. We'll be at the rendezvous point in ten minutes."

Ramirez snapped the phone shut and jammed the van into gear. He turned to Fox and pointed to the cargo area. "On the side shelf behind me, middle one, there's a bulletproof vest and a red gel pack. I was going to have you wear it, but there's been a change of plan. I'm going to need it. I just hope Gustav plans to shoot me through the heart and not the head."

"Can you explain?"

"Yes, I have about two minutes left to respond to Heinrich. I need to talk this through. Stop me in one minute and thirty seconds."

Fox checked his watch and nodded.

"Heinrich has unearthed my one vulnerability. He doesn't know what it is, but that it exists. He has found a way to expose it and has threatened to do so. In order to stop him I must sign some land over to him. After I do, I feel he will make good on his promise to send his men back. If he thinks there's treasure, it's in his own best interest to keep it to himself. As soon as I do sign, he will shoot me. If this sounds like gibberish to you, so much the better. It's clear to me."

"You're meeting him alone?"

"Yes, and I'm probably closer to the meeting point, Heritage Lodge, than he is, although a time hasn't been set."

"Forty-five seconds. Of course, you can't shoot him until he calls his men off."

Ramirez shook his head. "Not even then. When I heard Heinrich's voice my hand moved to my holster. My empty holster. I left my gun on Esmerelda's desk four hours ago," he said, his voice sounding like the thud of a head hitting the floor.

Fox shined the light on his watch. "Make your call."

Ramirez ended his second conversation with Heinrich by conceding and immediately dialed the phone that had been left with the rest of the flight crew. "Damn! No one is answering, but it can be noisy in the bar area."

"Let's hope that José is almost there," said Fox.

Ramirez nodded and the van droned on through the darkness, the cab silent. Still stunned, he played the conversation back in his head. Ramirez wondered how Heinrich could know anything. Ramirez had gone to extraordinary means to prevent such a catastrophe.

"Greetings, uncle," Heinrich had said on the phone. "I would like to set up a meeting for this evening at the Heritage Lodge to finalize my separation from the company. Before you respond, hear me out. As I speak, I have five men making their way to the edge of the Forbidden Zone. All five are armed with high-definition video cameras capable of live broadcast, like any of our webcams."

"What is it that you want?" asked Ramirez.

"Hear me out," Heinrich repeated. "My men will be in strategic positions before daylight. I do not know what lies there. But whatever it is will be broadcast and recorded. I have a legal document in my possession. If you sign it, I will pull my men back; if you do not, the world will know the secret. Of course, if there is nothing there, then we will broadcast and film that as well."

"Entering the Forbidden Zone is a capital offense."

"Leave that to me."

"What am I signing?"

"A deed to the Pristine Peninsula, a mere 200,000 acres of the estate. With that in my possession you will hear no more from me, and I shall not oppose any actions you wish to take concerning the government of the country. Your decision in five minutes, please."

They reached a wide spot in the road and pulled over. Fox flipped on the cab light and unzipped his bag. He gently pulled out a cube the size of a pack of cigarettes. It looked like a petite jewelry box, sides lined with mother-of-pearl. Fox held it up. "This is a video camera with super wide-angle capabilities. If you get there first, put it in a discreet spot, someplace a knickknack might go, and push here," he said touching the ridge on the upper right corner, "and you're good for six hours. Push it again to stop it. At least when he shoots you, you can shoot him. One way or the other, we get him."

Ramirez nodded, and slipped the camera into his jacket pocket. Then he opened the phone and punched in another number.

"Who are you calling?" asked Fox.

"I'm arranging for someone to pick you up here. You're out of this."

Fox snatched the phone out of his hand and snapped it shut. He looked at Ramirez. "With all due respect, you have to pull yourself together."

"I am together."

"Good. This night is just getting started. So, you fucked up and forgot your gun."

"It's not just the gun."

Fox shrugged, and kept his voice light. "You just have to improvise. I never expected any protection other than what I can provide for myself. If I thought you were incompetent, I'd never be out here with you. Hell, one time, I forgot my passport and forgot I had a flask of vodka in my suitcase going into *Kuwait City*, for Christ sake. I could have been in jail for months. I got out of it."

"How?"

"With the redistribution of five thousand dollars cash. And, they let me keep the booze."

That elicited a soft chuckle. He sighed. "You're right. My transgression gave me pause to wonder if there are others, like involving you."

Fox cocked his head. "The program's been printed. The players are on the stage and they include me. While you're out getting yourself shot, Hector and I will gather what we can, and I'll fire away with these," he said, pulling a Nikon Digital SLR out of his bag. Fox pointed to his belt buckle.

"Like in the movies?" asked Ramirez.

"Better."

"What else do you have in the bag?"

"Around ninety-five hundred voices of persuasion," he said, holding up a wad of bills.

Headlights streamed around the corner and blazed toward them. "Thanks for the vote of confidence," said Ramirez.

"You're welcome."

The shrill sound of Ramirez's phone pierced the cab. A few seconds later, he set it back down on the seat and tapped his fingers on the leather. "That was José. He says your crew is in safe hands. He used the correct code words, but his voice sounded odd."

10:05 P.M. CST

For what seemed like the hundredth time Mike scanned the Paraiso lobby bar and read the body language of lovers and losers. He listened to the clink of glasses, the buzz of blenders, and the pop of corks. All of this sifted through a mélange of light that streamed from four different televisions and a 70s style strobe. He searched for anything that didn't seem right. So far, he had found nothing.

They had been sequestered behind a table along the far wall since 9:30, believing they were safer among a crowd. The view was optimal from that vantage point, and the number of bodies and the noise level had increased steadily. He glanced down at his nearly full ice tea, and wished it were straight bourbon, a little envious of the other patrons swirling their drinks and laughing like they hadn't a care in the world and probably didn't. Upon safe arrival at Esmerelda's place, he would have that drink—a large one.

Joey scribbled in her notebook with speed and intensity, and he still thought her mere presence was somehow miraculous. She could shrug it off, but as far as he was concerned, she had flat lined. Rita was writing letters to her son and family on hotel stationary. She had told Joey and Mike that she tried to sound casual, using lines like "Just in case anything happens to me…." But Mike watched her eyes moisten and thought that her heart must feel as if it were being wrenched from her chest at the mere idea of never seeing her son again.

Five minutes later the bellman, who had been cued to watch for José, strode through the room and nodded. "José is here and parked just in front of the porte cochère. Bring your bags and I will load them."

Relieved, they stood, swung their tote bags on top of their Rollaboards, and followed him out. Mike in front of Joey and Rita. He paused at the door to check the surroundings. The familiar black Lexus, glossy and luminous as if it were posing for an ad, was parked in front of the main lodge. Tiny jewel like lights backlighting a lush garden with a bench and a reflecting pond behind completed the picture.

Mike's relief was short-lived. José had said that if he were not alone, he had been compromised. The bright glare under the porte cochère leaked outward and a streetlight in front of the Lexus made it clear that someone occupied the front passenger seat. José sat motionless, apparently looking straight ahead. A man turned his head and gave a little wave. Mike recognized Jimenez as the friendly guy from Ramirez's airstrip. He had led them through security, showed them into the briefing room, and offered them something to drink.

Mike had a decision to make and a split second to make it. With a little flick of his wrist he motioned the women into the backseat. As soon as the rear hatch was closed, he pushed three dollars into the bellman's hand, thanked him, and watched him retreat to his station inside the main door. Mike sidled up to the front passenger door, swung it open, popped his head in, and offered his right hand to shake. He held it just under the rearview mirror, which forced Jimenez's attention forward. Mike's left hand slipped behind. Mike smiled. "Hey, man, great to see you."

It was all the words he needed. With his left hand clutching the thick neck, he rammed Jimenez's forehead into the dash four quick times, each with more force. José grabbed the gun that slipped out of Jimenez's left hand and deftly unbuckled the passenger seatbelt. Mike yanked the limp head back, satisfied with the unfocused eyes, and jerked him outside. He spun him onto the bench. He propped up his body and let Jimenez's head loll back and to the side. Mike looked around. No one. In three quick strides, he reached the rear hatch, popped it open, and grabbed a small flask out of his tote bag. He drizzled Jack Daniels over Jimenez's lips and onto his shirt.

Mike had just closed the hatch when a flash of light drew his attention. A blonde woman in her late twenties with a rock the size of a boulder on her ring finger, approached from the direction of the parking lot. She passed Jimenez with a disgusted look on her face and then turned her attention to Mike. "This guy looks like my husband did last night—drunk on his fat ass. He snored so loud that I rented another room. So what if it cost him an extra thousand? Where did this slob come from?"

"Over there," Mike pointed to the garden. "Passed out, face down. Maybe I should have thrown him into the pond."

She flashed him a wry smile and shook her head. "Either way, he's all wet."

Mike chuckled and climbed in, and sat in the space Jimenez had occupied less than a minute before. José eased the SUV forward into the darkness and said, "You were wise."

Mike nodded, for an instant conjuring up an image of the woman's husband—some rich guy in his fifties who couldn't see reach his shoes over his gut. "That lady wasn't."

Silence ensued for another minute as they left the sea and resort behind and climbed the switchbacks cut into the thick vegetation. Rita asked, "Am I the only one who feels like we should be screaming out of here, like at about a hundred miles-an-hour?"

"Yes, I had to stop myself from jamming the accelerator to the floorboard, but it happened so fast. No one was watched and we are not being followed," said José.

"My first impression was that it was good to have someone else on our side. He had been so nice," said Rita.

"That is what they were counting on," said José. "That is how I was compromised. However, there is sure to be trouble ahead. I don't believe Jimenez was working alone."

"Scenarios and options?" asked Joey.

Mike craned his neck to see the outline of Joey and Rita's heads. "What do you think about pulling over while we sort this out?"

The girls nodded. José stopped on the shoulder and switched on the dome light. Mike eyed him. "If Jimenez is with others, what are their numbers?" asked Mike.

"At least three or four. They would have needed that many to neutralize Ramirez's men. They're probably just outside of the resort's property. How do you wish to proceed?

We must assume they possess automatic weapons and it will be difficult to get past three or four men firing such weapons. The next four or five miles are curvy and will allow a top speed of only about forty-five. Let us say they have three, plus a lookout. Even if one man targets me, the driver, and another targets the tires, that's still ten rounds pumped into the passenger compartment by a third man. Someone other than me is likely to take a bullet."

"Unless Heinrich wants us alive and intact," said Rita.

"In that case, more rounds will be used to stop the vehicle," said José.

Joey spoke out, her faced shadowed and her voice low and even. "The scenario we can count on to happen is that if Heinrich gets us in his control, he will attempt to kill us and there is no one and no entity that can help us. Therefore, we must do everything to avoid capture."

"Okay," said Mike, "let's operate under that premise."

"Agreed," echoed Rita, who was draped over the backseat, removing the rapier which was strapped to her luggage.

"I see three options," said Joey. "We can run the gauntlet and hope their guns don't disable the vehicle, we can get out here and try to flee on foot using the cover of darkness, or we can find them, engage them, and eliminate them."

"You mean kill them?" asked Mike.

"We must disarm them. If we have to kill them to disarm them, so be it."

"And the third option would be your choice?"

"It would," Joey replied.

Again Mike looked to José. "Thoughts?"

José returned his gaze. "You did a quick and thorough job with Jimenez. But, are the women a help or hindrance?"

"Rita can handle blades. She disabled Heinrich and another man earlier today by herself."

"I'm no expert but I practiced firing a pistol at cans and targets on my grandfather's farm when I was a girl," said Joey.

The white glow overhead illuminated José's face enough to expose a slight smile. "Señor Ramirez entrusted me to deliver you safely to Esmerelda. Time will tell if I have made the right choice. We will engage," he said, and pulled the SUV back onto the road.

Five minutes later José guided the Lexus into a small lot at the top of the hill that provided parking next to the access for the asphalt trail that circumnavigated a large manmade lake. The first mile of the trail ran parallel to the road. Between the trail and the road stood a hedge of dwarf palms and banana plants standing eight to ten feet high and branches extending to a width of four to six feet. José thought it likely a lookout man would be stationed somewhere in this area; remote enough to observe without being seen by passing cars, but near enough to the hotel's main entrance that every vehicle must pass by. Rita questioned that notion, thinking that Jimenez himself would alert the others. "No matter," José had said, "We shall hunt for a lookout." José had also thought the most likely place the others were waiting would be a turnout a mile ahead at the end of the longest stretch of straight road in the next five.

In the confines of the Lexus they had changed into their darkest clothes, which were blue jeans and a dark blue nylon running shirt for Joey, jeans and a red tee for Rita and black jeans and a black long sleeved T-shirt for Mike. José removed his shirt and redonned his suit jacket over a bare torso. Mike asked him about his gun. "In my pocket without bullets. But I have another weapon, perhaps more valuable." He held up a plastic water bottle with a clear liquid inside and several handkerchiefs. "A fast-acting anesthetic. I am not such a good fighter and I do not like pain. I have observed that a man who is unconscious is less likely to inflict bodily damage. However, the trick is to apply the anesthetic to the opponent and not yourself."

Mike turned toward the backseat and saw in the dark, somehow, once again Joey's face glowing. To him, she exhibited the serenity of an angel. Meanwhile his stomach was tied in knots. "I know," said Mike, "You're not afraid, but you *are* concerned." Joey half smiled. Turning to Rita, he continued, "That's what she said to me a minute before the bomb was supposed to go off. I'm well trained in martial arts, but my MO is always to finish fights, not start them. I'm nervous as hell."

"So am I, but I know I can do what I have to do," said Rita.

They proceeded at a slow pace in silence, eyes intent, and soon adjusted to the wan emanation of the crescent moon and the glitter of starlight. Ears were attuned to every sound. After fifteen minutes and a half mile, José wondered if perhaps Rita was correct in thinking there was no lookout when they heard the beep of a two-way radio ahead on the road side of the hedge. They all froze and heard a voice, nearly too low to hear, filtered through the receiver. All they could understand was *"No, quince minutos."*

All four moved forward until Mike stopped and pointed. A light breeze rustled the leaves but through the hedge they could see the faint outline of a man. José nodded to Rita. They pushed and pulled leaves and branches apart, and the two of them entered the hedge. Rita's path would allow her to come out behind the man and José's path in front. When they were a step from emerging José held up his index finger. Rita nodded and stepped out as José rustled the branches. The short and stocky man dressed in fatigues leveled his rifle and peered in.

Right behind him, Rita pressed her blade into his lower back next to his spine. "Drop the rifle or I will sever your spinal cord," she said in Spanish. After a moment's hesitation the rifle rattled to the ground.

José stepped in front of the man, also speaking Spanish. "Where are the others?"

With no answer forthcoming Rita pushed the blade in enough to draw blood. A gasp and a nod of the head followed. "A half mile ahead."

"How many?" asked José.

"Three that I know. Maybe more."

"Weapons?"

"All I know of is one Glock, three rifles, and one Uzi."

"Positions?"

The man let out another gasp. "I was a last-minute guard. I don't know how they're set up. They might just be standing together next to the truck. We weren't expecting trouble."

"Or?" prompted José.

"They might be spread out."

"You have an appointment," said José. "The question is, will you wake up from it? I'm going to give you an anesthetic. If you struggle, my friend who is holding the tip of a nineteenth century English rapier against your back will fill you with holes, your blood will drain out, and you will not wake up. If you cooperate and breathe deeply, you will lose consciousness, but you will awaken. Which?"

"I will not struggle."

Five minutes later the four continued up the path with a rifle, pistol, and a throwing knife, courtesy of the man lying peaceably in the middle of the hedge, naked.

10:45 P.M. CST

The introductions had been brief. Fox's acceptance of Hector's leadership was briefer, yet he knew Hector Cato was not infallible. Nor was anyone, he thought, as he watched the taillights of Ramirez's van disappear. He wondered if he would ever see him again. To Fox's way of thinking, Ramirez possessed no gun and no collateral. If Heinrich were angry and ambitious enough to murder the closest thing he had to a father, why would he be content to shoot Ramirez in the chest and walk away? Fox shivered, and pictured a rabid Heinrich pumping an entire clip into every part of his uncle's body, including his head.

Fox shed his clothes while Hector rifled through the back of his Prius. He yanked out a duffel bag and tossed it at Fox's feet. "These fatigues are what most of Heinrich's men wear. They've been laundered several times with the same detergent used at the Hive for the proper scent."

Fox nodded and unzipped the bag. While he slipped on the fatigues, Fox replayed his "argument" with Ramirez moments before Hector had arrived.

"Maybe Hector is packing," Fox had said. "If he is, you should take it for your meeting with Heinrich."

Ramirez shook his head. "I doubt if Hector is carrying."

"It won't hurt to ask."

"No, we will not ask and I will not tell him what is to transpire," said Ramirez, as he adjusted the vest.

"If he's to be your right hand, you have to tell him. You have to tell him *something*."

"Leave that to me. You two are exposing yourselves to great danger. I want Hector totally focused on the task at hand, not distracted by what's going on with me." He caught Fox's eye. "Understood?"

"Understood."

While Fox buttoned his shirt, he asked Hector, "Do you have a gun with you?"

"No, I've never been interested in them. I don't know anything about them. Yesterday was the first time I ever pulled the trigger of one."

"Where?"

"In Ramirez's office—twice, on his order—the barrel against the side of my head. Afterward, I asked him if there were any bullets in the chamber. He told me I didn't want to know. I don't even know if he knew."

Fox whistled softly and tried to discern Hector's boyish face and bushy hair under the dim moonlight. "Wow."

Hector shot him a weak grin. "The first click wasn't so bad. The second time left me a little weak in the knees but I managed it without having to change my underwear. Anyway, I'm no tough guy, but I can fight a little. My forte is stealth. Yours as well, I've been told. Our objective is to get in and out of there without detection."

Fox finished dressing. They climbed in. "We're headed down the road a few more miles to a place where we can hide the car and proceed," said Hector. "I'll use this time to brief you. Once we're out of the car, we're rigged for silent running, with one exception; a man named Kurt, who should be alone in the kitchen when we arrive."

"Does he know we're coming?"

"No."

At the sound of a single beep, Hector flipped his phone open and studied the screen for a moment, then shut it with a sigh of relief. "My children are safe in L.A. and have just been put to bed."

"I'm happy for you." Fox lightly tapped Hector's shoulder.

"Thanks. Now, most of what I have comes from a man named Emile who works for Heinrich in the 'War Room,' but he is not privy to the rest of the palace. Assume they have listening devices throughout, although Emile has no idea who does the listening. But, he has heard the men call it the Ear instead of the Hive on many occasions. At least our timing is good. Most of Heinrich's men are gone. Getting to the Hive and getting in shouldn't be a problem. Two years ago, when Ramirez asked me to create a hidden path to reach Heinrich's place, I thought he was nuts, but little by little I did it, and periodically maintain it. As far as security goes, there shouldn't be any alarms. Emile enters through the kitchen. He's never encountered a locked door. He thinks they're so arrogant they actually hope someone breaks in and attacks them, so they can butcher the attackers.

"Emile has no proof. But he believes that every poacher caught was tortured and then dumped half alive from a Huey into what is known as Shark Alley. It is no secret that they have a filming cage submerged in the area and often film the marine activity. Emile believes that activity includes recording the poachers being shredded by sharks. In fact, Emile thinks they film most everything, including the torture sessions. Those films, in whatever form, will be our prime objective. With me, so far?"

"Let me guess," Fox interjected. "Emile doesn't know where the films are stored and the outside of the fortress is unguarded, but the film room and torture chambers may have alarms and codes to get in."

"Precisely. We do know that where we want to go is below the top three floors, but after that, nothing is firm. However, we may have an ally: the aforementioned Kurt, who according to Emile, hates Heinrich, but, right now, his fear of Heinrich is much stronger than his hatred."

"I might have a way to diminish his fear and increase his courage," said Fox, tapping his bag.

With night vision goggles, Fox and Hector threaded their way through the dense flora that blotted out any light from the sky. The pace was steady, yet they planted each footstep as if they were treading on the triggering device of a landmine. Any sounds they produced blended seamlessly with haphazard breaths of wind that rippled through the tangled foliage. The air was heavy with the scent of plumeria.

They emerged into a side yard. A ten foot wide band of cultivated trees and shrubs gave way to an expanse of lawn beginning thirty feet from the structure. They approached from the east, into the wind, the breeze masking their presence. From this viewpoint, the building looked like an oversized two-story stone house. They removed their goggles and started toward the southeast corner. Reaching it, they paused. The men then proceeded toward the northeast corner and the kitchen entrance. They hovered next to a massive granite wall that Fox figured was at least 250 feet long. Fox stood just to the left side of the door that led into the kitchen, while Hector crept past it, stopped under a window, rose, and peeked through. He stood, moved back to the door, twisted the knob, and pushed it open.

Across the oversized kitchen, an apron-clad Caucasian man was bent over a stainless steel sink rinsing a glass. When he shut off the water, Hector tapped his knuckle on a granite countertop. The man, in his mid-thirties with a light-brown flat-top, spun around. He gestured to Hector with a nod and untied his apron. His brown eyes registered only a hint of surprise. Hector bent his head to the out-of-doors. Kurt shuffled over, in no particular hurry, and followed Hector out. His eyes swept past Fox like he was no more than a post. Hector moved to the side of the house, but Kurt raised his arm and made a motion for them to follow. When they were on the other side of a thicket Kurt spoke in a low, lightly accented German voice. "What is it that you want?"

"My name is Hector Cato. I believe I met you once at a dinner."

"Yes, Mr. Cato. I was your waiter. What is it that you want?" he repeated, his voice still low.

"I know you agree with us that Heinrich is evil. We're here to seek evidence that will indict him. Will you help us retrieve it?" asked Hector.

"No."

Fox tried to get a read on Kurt in the filtered light that radiated from the kitchen window. The furrow between his brow indicated curiosity, but his rigid posture and clenched hands suggested Kurt was suppressing his emotions. "Do you like working for Heinrich?" Fox asked.

The furrow deepened, Kurt's eyes narrowed, and his thick lips pursed in rancor. He grunted. "I do not work for Herr Heinrich. I obey Herr Heinrich, like a slave obeys his master. Our life is a nightmare."

"Our?"

Kurt returned Fox's gaze, anger seeping from his eyes. "I had not seen a woman, not been with one in almost a year. I asked Herr Heinrich for a night to go into the town. He refused. A week later he brought a woman here with a minister. Herr Heinrich required a qualified nurse to assist his private physician and I, Kurt the houseboy, was in need of a woman. To Herr Heinrich, problem solved. To us, a nightmare," he repeated.

Sensing impatience from Hector, Fox placed the tip of his index finger on the end of his nose for a moment—a prearranged signal to pause. Fox believed Kurt knew *something* and his co-operation was crucial. Fox didn't believe Kurt was anywhere close to helping them. At this point, it would do no good to reveal the Butcher's pending demise or attempt to throw money at the man. Kurt's mental transformation would be a process, a slow step-by-step process. The first step was to keep Kurt talking. Fox ignored his body which was telling him to end this absurd conversation and get moving. He deliberately relaxed, widened his stance, and put his hands on his hips as if he had all night. "Why is it a nightmare for you and your, I assume, wife?"

"Yes, legally my wife," he said, his eyes cast down. "It is a nightmare for Rosanna. She is trapped with me, a man she loathes. She thinks I am an imbecile. It is a nightmare for me because, like a fool, I fell in love with her at first sight. Great beauty can bend a man's mind. If we were free of this accursed place, she would think different of me, much more for the better, I am sure."

Fox exhaled. Bingo.

"What does Heinrich have on her other than the usual threats?"

"*Ach*, she was the, as you say, the fall person for a medical clinic that ran an oxycodone scam. She was rotting in jail. The Butcher had her paroled. He gave her to Herr Heinrich and appointed him to be her parole officer. If she leaves, she would be thrown back into jail."

"Not a pretty vision is it?" said Fox.

"No, it is not."

"Well, then," said Fox, "try to picture this: It's a sunny day. The breeze is light and you don't have a care in the world. You're strolling the beach with Rosanna, her arm wrapped tight around your waist. Her hand creeps up your back and caresses it. When it reaches your neck, she pulls you to her.

She kisses you, tells you she loves you, and will always love you. Are you seeing it?"

"Impossible," said Kurt, who frowned and clenched his hands again.

"Very possible. You, my friend, can make that vision happen by helping us."

Kurt shook his head. "Herr Heinrich is mad, but brilliant. I do not wish to be tortured or endanger Rosanna. Maybe someday his luck will sour, like his smell, and Rosanna and I will be free of this."

"Does Heinrich have a media room? Where they watch movies or videos?" asked Hector.

"*Nein,* I will not tell you." He glared at both of them. "You two look at me and think, why does he not just leave? Disappear? I ask you, where does one go? Where does one disappear to and hide? Herr Heinrich is a hunter of men. Now there are none left to hunt and his rage has no limit and no outlet. He would welcome my disappearance. And, I will not leave Rosanna. If you find evidence, it is useless. The Butcher will protect him."

Finally Fox nodded to Hector to proceed; his patience finally rewarded.

"Not anymore," said Hector. "The general has indicted himself. He is resigning—tonight. Tomorrow at this time Esmerelda Castile will be the president and Soriano will either be under arrest or on his way to exile. Gota has the support of the army. Heinrich has no one to protect him and will have to answer for what he has done."

Kurt's eyes widened and he pushed his hand through his cropped hair.

Yes, Kurt's pilot light is finally lit. I just need to add fuel. Fox took advantage of his taller stature and took a step closer to Kurt. "There's a film room, isn't there?" He reached into his bag and pulled out a stack of bills with a rubber band holding them together and flipped the ends like a deck of cards. "Look," he continued, "just tell us where the room is and how to get into it, and I'll give you five thousand dollars to start out your new life with the woman who bends your mind."

"What Herr Cato says about the general is true?" asked Kurt. "How can you be sure?"

"Yes, he's finished. the Butcher wants into the child porn business. I posed as a distribution kingpin with a listening device planted on me. Soriano took it a step further and offered to provide footage of child rape. It was all recorded. Not even the general's inner circle will stand with him."

"Who are you? FBI?"

Fox shook his head. "Not even close. What's your last name?" asked Fox.

"I am Kurt Vogel." He stood even straighter.

"Hmm. Bird in German. Well, Mr. Vogel. You speak of luck? You can be the master of luck—yours and Heinrich's. It's time. It's time to spread your wings and fly from this cage. It's time you showed your wife the kind of husband you really are. Would she loathe the man who rescued her from this hellhole? What about it? Just give us the location and how to get in."

"Look," interjected Hector, "Fox here is an American flight attendant with no interest in this, except to help. You know the consequences if we're caught. Step up, give us a chance."

Something resembling a smile crossed Vogel's face as he spoke. "*Ja*, the question is, will Herr Heinrich be arrested or killed before he finds something is missing? If he finds something missing first, you will hear my screams halfway across the Pacific. Now, how much more money do you have in that bag?"

"Forty-five hundred."

"*Gut*. Give me the rest, and I will give you much more than just the location of the theater." He reached out his left hand for the money and his right to seal their arrangement.

11:15 P.M. CST

Fifteen minutes later Hector and Fox descended into the heart of the Hive through the back stairway. The steps were made of concrete and did not creak but the staircase was enclosed and sealed against fire, like those in a hotel, and even the rustling of clothing could echo with the volume of a bass drum. They made their way down five floors in near silence. They stopped at each exit door to listen. When they reached level E, Hector removed a tiny can of odorless lubricant from his bag and injected the liquid into the hinges. Kurt had indeed told all he knew, including that this particular door was prone to squeaking when opened.

They emerged into a long and narrow carpeted hallway. Soft light cast from recessed wall sconces provided adequate visibility and mingled with the muted, but ominous stench of Heinrich. Hector pointed forward, but before they moved, a door slammed shut and echoed somewhere in the interior. They scrambled back into the stairwell. They waited five minutes, ears pressed against the steel door. They detected only the sound of their own breathing. Fox and Hector moved back into the hall and continued.

Fox thought the Hive was an appropriate nickname for the stark, militaristic concrete tomb, yet some unexpected touches of feminine warmth emanated from the cushy bounce of short shag carpet and textured walls painted the rose color of a Mediterranean villa. Hector led. They moved quickly, but with deliberation, and paused periodically to listen. Fox noticed a scratching noise from the inseam of his shirt that rubbed against his side and raised his arm an inch to silence it.

Near their destination they froze at the sound of a whirring motor. The elevator. With a disregard for creating noise, they jumped into position on either side of the elevator door, and flattened their backs against the wall. But the car clunked to a stop a floor above them and all was still. Fox wiped a drop of sweat from his brow. They waited another minute then proceeded.

Forty seconds later they halted in front of a wide and richly varnished door. A mechanical lock was mounted next to the brass knob. Hector punched in *666#, twisted the little lever, pushed, and peered in. No people. They had found the media center that contained a theater-sized screen and about twenty club chairs.

Hector turned to Fox, nodded, and ducked inside. Fox proceeded down the hall and turned left until he came upon the first door on the right. Whereas the media room door had been wooden, this one was made of steel and its lock electronic with a keypad similar to a wall-mounted telephone. Kurt had been inside once, but only in the entrance.

He figured it was a small guest apartment and had noticed a great many books, videos, and DVDs. He did not know the code, but Kurt had overheard Heinrich tell one of his men that he was fond of using his mother's name for passwords.

Fox punched in "Greta." For a moment nothing happened, then the green glow of a small light appeared, and Fox was through the door. He was an inch away from closing it behind him when he spotted another keypad on the inside. He decided to leave the door ajar in case a different code was needed to get out.

Fox inspected the other rooms, which consisted of a stark bedroom, bathroom, an empty closet and no windows. Ten minutes later Hector joined him and ran a finger across his throat—an indication that he had found nothing. Fox pointed to the keypad and Hector raised a hand in acknowledgement. Fox resumed his inspection of the shelves of a built-in cabinet behind the half-open door.

Hector crossed to the other side of the room and pored through the contents of a free-standing bookcase. Hector found a cache of DVDs and popped open his miniature player. He scanned several and checking beginning, middle, and end. These were as titled: various scenes of sea life filmed from the underwater cage.

In the middle of the built-in were two drawers about ten inches tall. Fox examined both of them and came up empty. He checked again and noticed a different shadow cast in the one on the right. He felt along the bottom of the shelf above the drawer, inching his fingers back and across until at the very rear they ran into a small wooden garage. He pulled out an object, and held it up. An iPod with video. He pressed the power button. Names, dates, titles. He scrolled to one called

India Ike, and grimaced as he watched a man's leg torn off in one pass of a shark. As he turned toward Hector he experienced a subtle change in the light.

Hector must have noticed it as well. Fox watched Hector's legs flex, about to jump. Then the spit of a silencer shattered the still air. Hector spun around and flew back into the bookcase. He slumped to the carpet. Blood gushed through his shirt.

Fox stifled the impulse to scream and waited until the glint of gray metal and an outstretched arm slithered past the door's edge. Fox leapt. His body and the door crashed into the assailant's forearm. He heard a howl and the gun thudded onto the carpet. Fox kicked it away and turned. In a blur, he discerned a hulking man about to launch a roundhouse at his head. He ducked down and under, and, using the man's own momentum, propelled him over his back, headfirst into the bookcase, where he toppled and lay in a heap next to Hector. His eyes were unfocused, but open. Fox lurched forward, snatched up the gun, turned, and cracked the butt of it against the man's skull. His eyes closed.

Fox crept out into the hallway all the way to the corner and peered around it. Empty. He returned to Hector whose breathing came in uneven rasps. Fox knelt down next to him. "Can you get up?" he whispered.

Hector barely shook his head. "I'm done."

Fox pulled out the iPod. "I have it. What we need. It's all right here. Let's go."

"You go. I can't breathe. Bleeding to death. Fast. We discussed this," he wheezed. "You agreed. Leave. Now."

Fox opened his mouth to protest.

Hector rasped, "No."

Fox paused, and tried to quiet the screams in his head. *He* should be the one lying there dying, not a young man with two kids and a new love. Fox pressed his hand into Hector's, leaned forward, and kissed his forehead. "That's from Rita."

"Tell her it was all worth it. Everything. Even this, for our one night together."

"I'll tell her," Fox said, and gathered up Hector's bag and the gun. The original plan was to obtain the evidence and send Hector out with it, while Fox descended two levels lower to snap pictures of the torture chambers. Now, whatever the iPod contained must suffice. He could not let Hector die in vain by allowing himself to be captured. And, now that he had a gun, perhaps he could even up Ramirez's odds. He left and did not bother to wipe the tears which dripped out of his eyes.

A minute later a man in a bathrobe knelt over Hector and listened to the uneven breathing while he probed Hector's wound.

Hector opened his eyes. "Who are you?"

"A doctor."

"It's too late. I'm already dead," he panted, then closed his eyes.

"You're almost dead, young man, but not completely dead, unlike Hertz, the idiot steroid user lying next to you whose enlarged heart stopped. Yours still beats."

Sixty-two-year-old Doctor Henry Bauer, his stevedore arms bulging, gently picked up Hector and carried him to his infirmary one floor below. Bauer wondered whether for once, he could save someone worth saving. Bauer had never broken the Hippocratic oath or been sued for malpractice.

However, he was a medical pariah and banished from Essen, Germany, for performing experimental surgery on maimed factory workers. Heinrich had brought him over and provided him a lab for research in return for taking care of his men.

The fact that Bauer had met Hector once and liked him, only added to his urgency. He set Hector down and dialed Kurt and Rosanna's cottage, let it ring twice, and hung up. The couple would appear in a minute or less . He had known that at some point in time, when he had the opportunity, he would defy Heinrich. Now was that time. He had always pictured himself acting alone. But he needed Kurt and Rosanna; Kurt to clean up the mess and dispose of Hertz, Rosanna to assist in surgery. He needed them to keep Cato's presence a secret and he needed them to risk what he was risking: everything.

10:40 P.M. CST

Rita, marching ahead of Joey and Mike, followed José's footsteps through the bush with a quiet precision that masked the frayed state of her mind. Since she had seen the photos of Eduardo, the only time she didn't feel like her head was about to explode were the few moments when the tip of her rapier was stuck into the lookout's back. That focus had calmed her. Her emotions tumbled in a confused and continuous loop: from the fear of the what-if, to anger, and back to the what-if. Then the loop morphed to even more anger, directed toward everyone, including Fox for opening his big mouth and setting off Heinrich. And, finally, inward for thinking badly of Fox, as she remembered how much she had enjoyed Heinrich's embarrassment.

She glanced at her glowing Timex. By now whatever had happened to Eduardo and Sonya in the faraway Pacific Northwest was finished. Either her sister and son were safe, or in trouble. As for Fox and Hector, they were about to enter the lair of a psychopath. *How did things get so screwed up? We're supposed to be sitting on the beach sipping drinks topped with fruit and umbrellas. If Fox hadn't drop-kicked Heinrich's ego through the uprights, I wouldn't be slinking through the jungle next to this road with a pirate's rapier in my hand. And I wouldn't have experienced the best night of my entire life or met Hector. And now I'm frantic for him… Enough!* She refocused her attention on the dirt trail.

They continued eastward, until José slowed his pace, held up his hand, and stopped. He pointed ahead. Through the leaves the embers of three bobbing cigarettes glowed like fireflies then intensified whenever the smokers inhaled. They crept closer. Three men leaned against the back of a Hummer in an oval clearing— the place José had thought they would wait. Low voices were audible, but indecipherable, until one rose in obvious consternation. Joey raised Jimenez's pistol in question. José shook his head. After neutralizing the lookout they had discussed using the pistol and the rifle to disarm whomever lay ahead. But the uncertainty of numbers and the fact that they were up against at least one Uzi, made them wary of using those weapons.

A flicked cigarette butt streaked through the darkness like a shooting star. An American sounding voice doubled its volume. "Where the fuck are they? Back at the lodge sloshing down margaritas?" A small beam of light appeared. "I need to drain the monster." The man turned straight out from the road and moved toward the bushes.

José nodded to Mike. Mike tapped himself on the chest, and looped right, toward the light. A minute later, everyone heard a groan and a thud as a body hit the ground. Two more flashlights popped on and were pointed toward the noise.

José, Joey, and Rita sprinted in silence from the foliage, and scrambled to the side of the hulking Hummer for protection.

"You okay?" asked one of the men, who probed the foliage with his light. He moved to his left, while the other one flanked off to the right. José and Joey trailed the voice while Rita crept into position to intercept the other.

Mike used a tree for cover and waited until his man was a half step past him, the flashlight finally trained on his fallen companion. Using a quick compact jab, Mike buried his left fist into his target's gut. It was like hitting a concrete wall. Mike barely spun away from the barrel of a rifle but not before it grazed his chin. Following its arc, Mike grabbed the muzzle and tried to wrench it away, while he managed three kicks to his opponent's side. Suddenly the rifle was dropped, hands whirled and Mike staggered back, stung by a hard blow just under his eye. There was a slight pause as the two men sized each other up in the faint light. Mike was six feet, one-sixty, and figured out he was up against a guy at least six-three, two-twenty. It was a question of leverage. If he stayed inside, Mike could negate his foe's ability to extend his arms. He moved in close and engaged.

As soon as the fighting started, the man Rita had been trailing raised his rifle in that direction.

"Lower that weapon, unless you want to sit in a wheelchair the rest of your life," ordered Rita. She probed his spine with the tip of her rapier.

Startled, he attempted to whirl around, but more pressure stopped him.

"Lower it," she repeated.

"All right," he said, and let the rifle hang.

"What's your name?"

"Alvarez."

"Now, Alvarez," she ordered, "Hold your arms out to the side. Good. Reach back over your shoulders with both hands and grasp the rifle strap." She extended her arm, still keeping steady pressure and the tip of the rapier in his spine, took a step backward. "Lift your hands straight up, and toss the rifle away."

He jerked his hands up, fell into a crouch, grasped the rifle, and aimed. Rita was nowhere near his sights. She had anticipated the move and stepped to the side. In panic, he flung his body in the opposite direction. The blade of her rapier caught him on the side of the neck and across the trigger hand. The rifle dropped in front of him.

"I was hoping you were stupid enough to try that. Do you want me to finish you now?" she asked and kicked the rifle away, "or do you just want to bleed to death?"

Wild-eyed, he started to move his good hand. Rita smashed the hand guard of her weapon against his temple.

She straightened up, exhaled, and took a step in Mike's direction. She stopped at the sound of someone clapping and a man's voice. "Well done. You know, I told Alvarez and the others to expect the unexpected."

Rita whirled around.

A man dressed in tight pants, a blousy shirt, and sporting dark wavy hair adorned with a headband emerged from behind a swath of foliage. His body language told her he was quite relaxed.

"Who the hell are you? Johnny Depp? What do you want?" she asked, listening to the faint sounds of flesh pounding flesh in the distance.

"I'm so much better looking than Depp," he said, his voice sounding slightly British, then took on a harder tone. "Being a swordsman in this part of the world is a lonely profession. Actually, I'm more of a surgeon, removing limbs and exacting reminders on those who are unfaithful to General Soriano. Maiming or killing is so much more fun when the other person is fighting back. So, thank you for the opportunity. However, it's not what I want; it's what I'm going to do," he said, and brought his right hand from behind and raised a large two-edged sword.

"Spare me the Oscar speech, Johnny."

"First, you will listen, then I will cut you up very badly and have my way with you. Of course, I hope you're still alive when I'm doing it. But", he shrugged, "if you have succumbed, that's quite acceptable as well." He moved toward her.

"Wait!" Rita played for time. "Where are you from? How the hell do you fit into all of this?" She listened again for Mike and José.

"The Hamptons, New York." He pressed the flat side of the sword against his forehead and executed a slight bow. "Midgely, James Midgely, better known as Mighty Midgely, at your service. Oxford, class of 1998. Fencing master from 2001 to 2004. Heinrich's men alerted me to your presence and I was *so* hoping you would show up. I like the smell and the taste of blood. I am sure yours will run extra spicy. En garde," he said, and lashed out at her left shoulder.

"I'm sorry I asked, because I couldn't care less," said Rita, and parried the blow with a grunt.

Within thirty seconds he had nicked Rita twice and she steadily retreated. He wielded the longer and heavier weapon with the precision of her smaller rapier. She guessed it was some sort of cavalry weapon. She made a feint to her right. He pretended to react. She leapt forward and lunged. He sidestepped and she felt the flat edge of his sword smash into her ribs, almost knocking her down.

"I could have cut you in half, lady."

Rita knew it. He was stronger, quicker, swung a superior weapon, and had obviously been practicing. She could not beat him—conventionally. She jumped back into the deeper shadows to see what was behind her. The ground was flat, and a good-sized tree trunk had been downed and lay parallel to the direction of her retreat. *Desperate situations...* It had been part of her act at the Excalibur Hotel. Her opponent would think he had knocked the weapon from her hand when actually she had thrown it in a precise pattern to lay in wait for her.

Midgely was quickly upon her. She leveled a blow aimed at his right shoulder. As she had hoped, he was so quick that his blade met hers before she started her downward thrust. Her rapier flew out of her hand, making two arcs, the darkness masking its path. She pretended to stumble, went down, and somersaulted backward, coming to rest on her back next to the tree trunk, right arm jammed against it.

He was on top of her in an instant, the tip of his sword hovering above the base of her throat. He smiled at her, his teeth gleamed through the darkness. "I'm disappointed," he said, "after what you did to Heinrich, I had hoped you'd put up a better fight."

"I'm a single mother. I have an autistic child. I'm out of practice," she said.

"Why not kill the little bastard? Put him out of his misery. He's better off dead. However, don't think I'm totally unsympathetic. You let me take you without putting up a fuss, I'll finish your life quickly and without pain." He ran his free hand along the line of her jaw.

Rita gripped the hilt of her rapier and edged it out from under her leg. She widened her eyes to look fearful and met his gaze. "Why finish me?" she asked, and continued to maneuver the blade. Instantly she felt his sword tip prick her throat.

"Okay, okay," she said, her voice quivering.

"That's better." He straightened up, leveled his sword, and swung his left foot onto the tree trunk, straddling her. He dropped his eyes for only a second, left hand fumbling for his zipper. In one motion Rita thrust up her right arm, burying her rapier a hand-width into his crotch. He grimaced but did not cry out. She watched his sword hand start to react. She withdrew her blade. In the same instant, she rose up from the waist and ran him through just under the heart, her blade slipping through his ribs and out his back. He stared at her in disbelief then started to collapse.

She pushed him to the side so he wouldn't fall on her, then staggered to her feet. She gasped for air and stepped back, trembling. She steadied herself and yanked her weapon out of him and watched the dead man's blood streak down the blade and drip steadily into his gaping mouth. "Is that spicy enough for you, you dead bastard?"

With an untrained eye, Joey watched the two men trade blows. She resisted the urge to jump in, knowing her revolver was likely to find the wrong target, yet it seemed obvious that Mike needed help. His arms moved with windmill speed, but his opponent slipped most of his blows and countered with heavier punches.

José had just experienced what the man's muscles were capable of, having waded into the foray only to receive a backhand slap to the chin that knocked him down and nearly out. Joey had hauled José to his feet and steadied him while he teetered.

"Do you have the flashlight?" she asked.

With glassy eyes José nodded. "In my pocket."

"I'm going to move into the ten o'clock position relative to the hulk."

"What?"

"In front and to the left." She pulled off her shirt and unsnapped her bra. "When I yell 'now,' shine the light on my chest and make sure you don't shine it into Mike's eyes." José nodded again, and stared at her milk-white skin, his eyes now alert and focused.

Mike felt like a punching bag. They'd been at it for several minutes, an eternity for a fight. Most ended in mere seconds.

He backed up and created a gap between them. Out of the corner of his eye he saw motion on his right.

Joey moved into position then yelled, "Now"! The scream alone caused the man to turn his head, but what he saw froze him for a moment. Like a showgirl, Joey shook her breasts while José trained the flashlight on them.

Mike hopped forward and jumped, spinning his torso clockwise to generate power and lift. His legs rose above his body and with a quick one-two, his right, then his left foot connected with the side of his opponent's head. Mike fell back, hands behind to break his fall. He popped back up, delivering three quick kicks to the abdomen, finally staggering the larger man. A final single kick to the temple sent him to the ground. José ran up and rapped him hard on the side of the head with the butt of the gun.

Mike stood bent over, hands on his thighs, breathing deep. He turned to Joey. "Jesus," he panted.

"You probably had him right where you wanted him, but you looked a little beat up," she said.

Mike laughed. "Are you kidding me? I was getting pummeled." He stared at her a moment. "By the way, nice rack."

Joey knelt down and fetched her bra and shirt. "Nice enough to get his attention."

"And then some. Where's Rita?"

While José went to check on the Hummer's ignition system, Joey and Mike found Rita staggering across the open space, blood dripping from a nick on her shoulder, side and a gash just above her breast. "What happened?" asked Mike.

"I'm out here in the middle of the jungle and I happened to run into the best swordsman I've ever faced, who was also a psychopath."

"Was?" asked Mike.

"Yes, was. I was getting my ass kicked, but I killed him. I'll tell you about it later. Let's get out of here."

They watched José shut the driver's door to the Hummer the men had been leaning against less than ten minutes before. They jogged over. "Keyless ignition. Needs a code. We have to hike back."

José pointed to Alvarez moaning and still semiconscious. His blood seeped into the dirt. "What about him?"

"Not a problem He's dumping fuel big time," said Rita.

"Let's gather the rifles and leave everything else," said José.

"No. Wait. Something doesn't feel right," said Joey, cocking her head.

Engines roared to life. In seconds the clearing was flooded with light as three more Hummers rolled around the corner from the opposite direction flanked by nearly twenty sprinting foot soldiers.

"Put *down* the weapons," thundered a voice through a loud speaker.

10:55 P.M. CST

There was nowhere to run. Mike tossed the gun aside. Joey dropped the revolver. José slammed a rifle into the ground. Rita took aim at a beech tree and flung the rapier end-over-end, and buried the tip of the blade in the trunk as the hilt shimmered in the light at impact.

In the distance they heard the squeal of tires rounding the curve. A Lincoln Navigator bucked into the clearing, roiling up a cloud of dust. The driver's door jerked open. A soldier jumped out and raced around to the passenger door, opened it, and stood at salute. The Butcher clambered out, grinning with satisfaction, and flashed a dismissive wave to his driver. He peered at the two unconscious men who had just been dragged out of the woods and shook his head. He ambled over and pointed a flashlight on the one who was clutching his neck. "Gross incompetence. If you worked for me, I'd have you shot," he said in Spanish. Rita whispered the translation. Soriano pointed a finger at José, and two men escorted him into a Hummer.

"Gross would describe your stomach, general," said Mike, his right eye swollen nearly closed. "And if your definition of incompetence is lying on your back knocked out, well, I have a picture on my camera phone of you in the same position." Mike glanced around at the men who circled them, and nodded his head. "Any of you guys want to see it?"

Against the yellow-white glow of headlights, the general's face reddened. He pointed at Mike. "Put him in the back of my vehicle. I will question him myself."

"But sir," said the driver, "your—"

"I do not care. *Put him in.* If he tries to get out, shoot him."

A rifle waved Mike to the back of the general's vehicle. Mike flashed a look of confidence to Rita and Joey and climbed in.

The general continued and jabbed his finger into the chest of one man and then another. "You two take—"

"Sir!" yelled a voice. "It's Midgely. He's dead."

"What? What was he doing here?"

The circle parted and two men set Midgely's body and his sword in front of the general. Most of the men gasped in disbelief. Midgely had been the general's chief weapon of terror. Midgely's sword had relieved the general's opponents of arms, legs, and heads. Midgely, now bloodied and lifeless, was thought to be indestructible.

General Soriano gazed down at the body as if he had lost a puppy. "Who did this?"

Rita stepped forward. "I did."

"You? With what?"

"A pirate's rapier. There," she said, pointing to the tree.

A spotlight found the blade. There was a murmur of awe among the men and their eyes swept to the woman who had brought down the Mighty Midgely, which further infuriated the Butcher. He moved in front of her, stared at her and slapped her across the chin with the back of his hand.

Rita swung her arm to retaliate and two men restrained her. "You are filth," she blurted, "and he was vermin."

The Butcher raised his arm then lowered it and swept his gaze to the men he had fingered. "Take these two to the Hive. I'll let Gustav deal with them."

"You can't hold us," said Rita. "We're American citizens."

"Of course I can. You assaulted three soldiers and killed my personal aide. You will be questioned. The usual punishment for such a crime is death."

The general's glare swept over his men, and he sensed brashness and perhaps contempt, beneath their usual fear, which infuriated him. He fixated that fury on Joey's serenely defiant face. "You! Do you understand how much trouble you are in? Do you know that before this night has ended you will probably beg for death?"

Joey shrugged, but locked her eyes on his.

He drew his revolver and struck her across the cheek with his free hand. Her expression did not change "What are you thinking?" he demanded, unable to disengage from her.

"Oh, nothing much. Just that you are at the beginning of a very bad night."

"Oh no, this is the beginning of a very *good* night." He stepped forward again almost nose to nose.

Joey didn't flinch.

From across the road a soldier ran up to the general and saluted. "Sir, there is an urgent call from General Gota."

"Why didn't he call me on my personal phone?"

"I don't know, sir. He said it was an official summons from the president, and official summons come through channels. You can take it in the communications vehicle."

"The president is summoning *me*?" he muttered. *"I'm the one who does the summoning."*

The general turned and saw Joey's eyes still boring in on him. In a moment of uncertainty, he wondered if she knew something he didn't.

As Mike climbed into the rear seat of the general's Hummer, the dome light illuminated another occupant. She was a petite, doe-eyed woman in her twenties with long dark hair, not unlike Rita's, wearing what looked like a long, plain dress. He watched Rita and Joey stand up to the general and turned to the other occupant. "Sorry for the intrusion. I didn't have much choice."

"You're hurt."

"Not seriously, and who wants to know?"

"Are you the American flight attendant who knocked out my father?"

"*You* are General Soriano's daughter? You look nothing like him."

"So I'm told. All I know for sure is that I'm my mother's daughter. Are you the one?"

She seemed determined but reserved. Mike felt no hostility from her or revulsion toward her. "Yes, it was me. Does that make you angry?"

"Only that you didn't hit him harder."

Mike chuckled softly. "I'm Mike," he said, extending his battered hand.

"Caroline," she said, shaking it.

"Why are you here?" Mike asked.

"I'm a prisoner. He won't let me out of the compound, except to ride around. It's better than nothing." Mike noticed that her brow was furrowed.

"I'm sorry."

"I'm sorry you didn't kill him," she said, her voice icy cold. "It gets worse every day. He's evil. I wish he'd just die. He even used me to have someone shot, someone who was a brilliant engineer, who had never harmed anyone."

"Why was he shot?" Mike asked, noticing the look of disgust on her face even in the shadowy light.

"Because his mother leads the opposition."

Mike thought for a moment. He jammed his hand into his pocket and the sudden movement caused her to jump. He yanked it out. "Sorry. Look," he said, and shoved all six sugar packets into her hand. "These were given to me by someone who wanted your father dead. One package dissolved in a drink will take about two days, and supposedly the victim keels over from a heart attack. No trace of the drug. I was given the impression that more packages ingested closely together could significantly speed up the process."

She drew back in surprise. "Who was the—"

Mike shook his head. "We never had this conversation. No matter what happens I will never tell anyone, including my crew, that I gave these packets to you. Do you think you can do this? I need to know, now. Do you have a place you can hide them?"

She reached out her hand. "Only one," she said, and pulled up her dress and slipped them beneath her underwear.

Five seconds later the rear door flew open. Two arms grabbed Mike and jerked him out.

Soriano turned to his man. "Put him with the women. I return to the compound immediately. Tell Heinrich I want this one named Mike dissected. Tell him I want Mike to look like a disassembled automobile. Every part resting an inch from the one it was last attached to."

11 P.M. CST

Austin Ramirez had taken a vow to protect—with his life, if necessary—the integrity and anonymity of the indigenous people. Now, he was about to face that prospect. However, he felt certain Heinrich would comply and pull his men back. He had already sent the automated text and the code for Heinrich's demise to two of the four who shared the secret. He did not include Celeste Starr who was not up to speed with the group's agenda.

With Heinrich erased, the leak would be sealed. But there was the question of Heinrich's men. If they knew or suspected *anything*, they too, must be destroyed. He had only to push one button on his cell phone to communicate that verdict. Inwardly he smiled. The two things he hated the most were hubris and hypocrisy. He acknowledged that he was guilty of both.

Though he would not hesitate to make the ultimate sacrifice, it seemed like an especially inopportune time to die, just as his plans were coming to fruition. He allowed a rare moment of self-pity before squelching it. In addition to the Kevlar vest, he had only two things to help his cause: a kitchen knife that lay inside his sleeve and the recording of the general's interview with Fox's Wesley Thorpe. Armed with the knowledge that the Butcher could no longer protect him, Heinrich might give pause to committing murder when he would become the obvious suspect.

Ramirez stared up at the beamed ceiling of Heritage Lodge, and tried not to remember the past in this place he loved: his grandfather's warmth and his stories, making love for the first time with Esmerelda, and quiet afternoons on the pond with only the wildlife and his Nikon.

Now, he sat at the dining table under halogens turned bright while the rest of the lights remained off. This created a white halo in the center of the room while the perimeter remained dark. Fox's camera was placed inconspicuously in the shadows on a shelf next to the fireplace. Ramirez had waited for nearly a half hour, more than enough time to ponder his dilemma. He admitted that he had distanced himself from the boy he had partially raised and had turned a blind eye to the fact that Heinrich was often slighted and insulted.

Ramirez stroked his chin in thought. Heinrich was about to mimic the mentality of the ones he had so efficiently eliminated. The poachers, despite knowledge of the atrocities they would face if apprehended, could not resist the lure of the trophy. And now he, Ramirez, had become the trophy Heinrich could not resist.

Ramirez experienced a sudden urge to see himself, for he could not gauge his own emotions. He made his way into the bathroom, flipped on the light, and studied the image that stared back at him. What he saw pleased him—eyes clear, skin dry, and he detected no trace of fear, only a slight crease in his brow perhaps caused by anger. He opened his mouth and turned up his lips. He wanted to remember his face wearing a smile. When he had left Esmerelda, she had smiled at him for the first time in over twenty-five years and he had smiled back. A miracle. He switched off the light and returned to the dining table. Now he needed another one.

He listened to the sound of Heinrich's car as it approached, the crunch of gravel exploded like muted gunfire. Ramirez took a deep breath and exhaled.

Heinrich shuffled through the front door, pistol dangling in his right hand and a thin folder in the other. Parts of his shirt were glued to his chest with dried blood. "Greetings, uncle."

Ramirez did not buy Heinrich's nonchalance, but said nothing. He noted that the hunter's expression was neutral and composed.

Heinrich carefully slid his tattered body into a chair across and down from Ramirez. He left plenty of space between them, just as Ramirez thought he would. But Ramirez's place at the table had forced Heinrich to sit directly in line with the hidden camera, which was rolling.

He set down his gun to his right, opened the folder, and slid it across the smooth bare oak. "If you were armed you would have placed your weapon where I could see it," said Heinrich.

"Yes, I would have."

With a little wince Heinrich pointed to the papers. "Read it and sign, please," he said, and set a pen down in the middle of the table and pushed it toward Ramirez.

Ramirez studied the documents for nearly five minutes. "I will sign after you've pulled back your men. You have my word."

"Very well, uncle." Heinrich gripped his gun again. With his left hand he pulled out his phone. "Emile, send out code 317 to the men. When all have electronically and verbally confirmed, call me immediately." He gazed across at Ramirez. "This should take less than five minutes."

"Are your men in any way contaminated?"

Heinrich shook his head. "Each man was given a sealed pack with a combination lock on it. They have no idea what the combination is or what the packs contain or why they were sent out. It is not unusual for me to send them out with no mission, other than to obey me. My men are valuable assets. You are correct; if they had any inkling, I would be forced to eliminate them."

"What do you intend to do with the other piece of land, the one I'm signing over?"

Heinrich shrugged. "It is of no concern to you."

The phone rang. Heinrich flipped it open, pushed the speaker button, and turned it in Ramirez's direction. "Talk," ordered Heinrich.

"They are confirmed and are returning," said Emile.

"Thank you," said Heinrich and snapped the phone shut. "Sign, please."

"Does Emile have any idea where you are?"

"None. Uncle, sign it."

Ramirez snatched up the pen, scratched his signature on the line, and, flipped the folder back across the table as if it were a Frisbee. "The first order of business has been completed," said Ramirez. "The second is that you can stop calling me uncle. There's not a drop of Ramirez blood that flows through your body."

Heinrich's eyes narrowed.

"I had a DNA test done on you long ago to confirm it. I never bothered to have it cross referenced, but I strongly suspect your father is either Eddie Castle or General Soriano. Your mother entertained both men on a regular basis for financial and political considerations."

Heimlich straightened his back. "You are telling me my dear mother was paid for sex?"

"More or less, yes."

Heinrich attempted to jump out of his chair, but fell back, gasping in pain.

"Don't act so outraged. She sold her body like any other two-bit whore, only she had much more ambition and arrogance. It clouded her intelligence and judgment."

"Enough," said Heinrich through clenched teeth. He waved the gun at Ramirez, sweat and fresh blood beginning to saturate his shirt.

Ramirez leaned forward. "How else do you explain your mother forcing her way into the cage of an agitated jaguar when a professional trainer had just fled? Why do you think you hate everything and everyone, and lust after destruction? You're killing your mother over and over, and I don't blame you. She was evil, just like you."

Heinrich snatched up the gun. A shot rang out; a bullet thumped into the underside of a stair step.

Unfazed, Ramirez sat back in his chair and continued on, his voice terse. "I've been asked by everyone I know, including my parents and grandparents, why I didn't toss you and your mother out with the rest of the trash. I'll tell you why. Because, on his death bed, my brother asked me not to. You and Ramon had one thing in common: bad karma. From the time he was born until the day he died, everything went against him and he suffered. Here you were, raised by a monster, a mother who cared nothing for you, but used you to get to my family. She broke you like a horse for her own amusement. You were fathered by one of the two most heinous men I have ever known. I gave you every chance to overcome the odds. You failed."

"You used me!"

"To get rid of the poachers, yes. It was your decision as to how to do it."

Heinrich bowed his head for a moment and fought for composure. "Are you done?"

"Am I? I suspect there's a third order of business."

"There is," said Heinrich.

"What is it?"

"Your death."

"There's one thing you should know." Ramirez opened the palm of his hand and laid a mini MP3 player on the table. "It's a recording of Soriano attempting to do business with the world's leading child pornographer. The general took it a step further. He offered to supply a steady stream of kiddy rape. The man he met with was a plant with a recording device. The general will step down any minute now. The president will resign and Esmerelda Castile will take over with the army's blessing. The Butcher can no longer protect you."

Heinrich shrugged. "Congratulations. You finally have what you want. It is a pity for you that you won't be present to enjoy your efforts."

"If you kill me, you will be the only suspect."

Heinrich sat back. "Not if it looks like an accident." He gestured with the gun for Ramirez to stand. Then Heinrich slowly rose; the halogens illuminating the anticipation in his eyes. "You are on your way to a midnight swim."

Fox retraced his steps from the core of the Hive and emerged having seen no one. He darted across the lawn, past the cultivated trees. He donned his night vision goggles and crept into the protection of Hector's hidden corridor. Headlights appeared in the distance filtered through bushes that paralleled the path. Despite the floral density, Fox flattened himself on the ground. He listened as the vehicle slowed. He wondered if it could be Heinrich. *I'm still close to the parking area. I now possess a gun. I could surprise Heinrich and end this thing. No, you have the evidence. Deliver it.* Fox scrambled forward.

He felt his phone vibrate, pulled it out of his pocket, and checked the screen. *Mission complete. All are safe in Bliss.* He exhaled in relief, and forwarded the message to the phone Mike had been given. He did not know that Mike, Joey, and Rita were in the backseat of the Hummer that had just passed him by.

Ramirez kept his eyes fastened to Heinrich and shook his head in refusal.

Heinrich made an exaggerated shrug and popped open his phone. "Emile."

"Where am I going swimming? The ocean?" asked Ramirez in resignation.

"Nothing," Heinrich said, into the phone and hung up. He met Ramirez's gaze. "Heritage Pond, of course."

"What assurances do I have that you won't turn them around as soon as I'm in the water?" he asked. He noticed that Heinrich fidgeted, his body betrayed the calmness of his voice.

"None. I am sure you have this figured out. I will find out for myself at a later date what lies out there. I have no desire at this time to reveal anything, but if you do not cooperate, I will not hesitate."

"We have established the fact that killing me makes no sense for you," said Ramirez. "So, you want to show me you're stronger, tougher, and superior? Why don't we fight, man-to-man, no weapons? Or are you afraid?"

"*Enough*," Heinrich rasped, his anger gushed to the surface. He made a fist. "I am injured; otherwise I would rip you apart with my bare hands." He leveled the gun at Ramirez. "Let us be absolutely clear. *I* am in charge now. Of *everything*," he shouted. "If for any reason you do not end up in the pond, my men will make an about-face. Now *move*."

Ramirez calculated the odds. Heinrich had kept his distance. He had no chance to physically engage him. Could he survive a swim in the pond? I wouldn't bet on it, he thought and started toward the French doors that led out the rear of the manor to the pathway and pond below. A gust of wind rippled the grass and Ramirez breathed deep the sweet air and listened to the hum of a million crickets.

Heinrich, drenched in sweat and blood, but more composed, waved him over to the small pier. A ramp led down to a float. Tied to it were two boats with oars, a small dinghy, and a larger flat-bottomed vessel shaped like a block letter I.

Ramirez started toward the dinghy. Heinrich's gun flashed under the starlight as he pointed to the larger craft. "It would take four or five men to overturn the barge, perhaps only one to capsize the dingy. Get into the rower's box. Take us across to the north end, about fifty meters from shore, into the lily pads. The new caiman mother will not take kindly to the intrusion."

Ramirez rowed at a steady pace while Heinrich sat near the stern, in an anchored chair. He was out of reach of arms and oars. Ramirez studied the oar ends, droplets that slid into water after each stroke, their lifelike phosphorescence. He listened to their tinkle as it grew in volume until it sounded as loud as Niagara Falls. He brought his focus back to the pond, but could not remove the buzz from his brain.

Five minutes later, after several promptings, Ramirez had positioned the boat where Heinrich seemed to want it.

Heinrich ordered Ramirez to his feet. "A splash, please. You may swim in any direction you wish, but do not come nearer than ten meters to this boat."

"You are a fool to do this," said Ramirez, as he stood on the edge of the barge.

"And you are a fool to think that you could handle me like a pet. Dispose of me when I became inconvenient. You are about to pay for your betrayal."

Ramirez turned to him and smiled, and shook his head. "Ignorance and arrogance have always been a bad combination. Adios," he said, and jumped over the side.

He hit the water feet first, penetrated the blackness, kicked aside lily vines and surfaced. He swam toward shallower water. The buzz in his mind had been replaced by a series of thumps. He turned his head in mid-stroke to see

Heinrich slapping the surface of the water with the oars. Ramirez didn't know Heinrich had practiced this procedure for months, a signal that fresh meat was arriving. The community of caimans had developed a taste for human flesh, although frozen and in smaller pieces.

Ramirez saw movement on the shore. One set of jaws snapped at another and an eight-foot spectacled caiman slipped into the water. Ramirez stopped all movement. A minute later the calm current churned beneath him and in an instant two jaws had clamped themselves to his midsection. The Kevlar vest stopped their penetration into his flesh, but the air had been sucked out of him as the beast pulled him under.

Heinrich's entire body vibrated as Ramirez's head bobbed up once then disappeared. He stood, held out his arm, and pointed his finger at the roiling water. "Who's the smart one now? You have fucked with me for the last time, uncle. I wish I could hear you scream. *Guten appetit*, my reptilian friends."

He took hold of the oars and rowed back in haste, his pain masked by a surge of adrenaline. He secured the boat, untied the dinghy, and pushed it out toward the middle of the pond. He returned to the lodge, did a quick scan to make sure he had left nothing behind, picked up the MP3 player, and climbed into his car. When he reached the main road, he turned north instead of south, which would have been the most direct way to the Hive. He would turn west, and then south to appear to have arrived from Quintana City. A mile up the road he made a sweeping left turn and just missed the headlights in his rearview mirror of a car that turned onto the manor road, the car Fox Revelstorm drove.

As soon as the caiman clamped down, it began to thrash in an effort to crush Ramirez's midsection, while rear claws shredded the flesh on Ramirez' lower legs. But that was superficial to the real trouble. Ramirez felt the downward pull toward the bottom and went under. Caimans swallow whole anything they can. Larger prey, they drown, and then rip off large chunks for dining. With an already depleted air supply, Ramirez had little time to escape. However, his arms were free and he had repeatedly smacked the caiman between the eyes with the heel of his hand, with no result. He ceased resisting for a moment and concentrated on freeing the kitchen knife under his right sleeve. His first attempt to grasp it with his left hand resulted in a gash to his middle finger. Nevertheless, he grabbed it by the blade and yanked it out nearly losing his grip. He managed to position his fingers around the handle, and gripped it tight. He swung the blade up and into the unarmored flesh of the caiman's lower jaw. The initial thrust seemed unnoticed, but the ripping action produced the desired result. The caiman disengaged, and with the vest's buoyancy, Ramirez popped to the surface, his lungs sucking air for life, while his ribs screamed in agony. He spun around in the water and searched for the reptile. Twenty feet away two eyes surfaced and stared, turned toward the shore, then disappeared.

Though Ramirez wanted out of the water, he was on the wrong side of the pond. He had no choice but to swim across. He began to stroke—as smoothly and quietly as possible.

During the rainy season, when the river occasionally overflowed into the pond, certain river dwellers arrived and did not make it back. Ramirez was worried about piranha. He knew they didn't usually feed at night, but have an attraction to blood. He was sure he bled. He heard a splash, but was unable to discern its direction. He assumed it was a caiman and, despite the pain, took deeper breaths to prepare for another trip under.

After spotting only Ramirez's van, Fox decided to forgo stealth, as he pictured Ramirez face down in a pool of blood. He jumped out of his car, banged open the front door to the lodge and stepped in. It took him less than five minutes to decide that the interior was deserted. He bolted out the front door and circled the house. When he reached the rear, his ears were drawn to a noise that rippled from the pond. He waded through the long grass, found the trail, and ran toward the pier, shouting Ramirez's name. Down the ramp onto the float he saw the unmoored dinghy bumping against the barge. He considered the small craft. It would move much faster, but the difficulty of hauling someone out of the water was greater. He untied the flat boat and splashed the oars into the water.

"Ramirez," he shouted.

"Here, can you see my hand?" rasped Ramirez.

Fox spotted it in the distance. "Yes, I see you."

Five minutes later Ramirez, lay on the barge's deck, panting, every breath a knife to his sides. He suspected cracked, if not broken, ribs. Fox made a quick initial exam and determined that while Ramirez's legs had sustained deep gashes, no arteries or veins had been nicked. Without a word

Fox jumped back into the rower's box and propelled them back to the float.

Inside the manor, Fox helped Ramirez out of his clothes and into the shower. It was only when Ramirez was dry and Fox had begun to wrap his legs with gauze from a medical kit did they converse.

"Where's Hector?" Ramirez asked in a whispered voice. His back was supported against the headboard of the bed, his legs in front of him.

Fox finished wrapping Ramirez's leg and looked at him in the bright light. "He was shot. I don't think he made it. But I have the evidence you need. An iPod full of images."

Ramirez closed his eyes for a moment and shook his head, then opened them and swung himself off the bed and onto his feet. "I must get that evidence to Attorney General Fuqua and rendezvous with General Gota," he said, and yanked spare clothes out of the bedroom dresser. "There's even more on your camera. If we can obtain a search warrant immediately we might be able to surprise Heinrich. Have you heard from the rest of your crew?"

"No, I can't raise them. I'm worried, and Heinrich is loose."

Ramirez finished dressing. "Let's go."

"Are you capable of making the drive by yourself?" asked Fox.

"Yes, I can make it. What about you?"

"I have a bad feeling about my crew. If they're in harm's way, I believe I have the means to get them back," said Fox.

"What means is that?"

"Laying my head on a chopping block and betting Heinrich would relish the opportunity to remove it."

11:15 P.M. CST

Kurt Vogel deleted the Word document from his computer in the pantry, backed his chair away from the small desk, and rose. He snatched the printed sheet, left the kitchen, and strode across the driveway to the cottage where he and Rosanna lived. He opened the bedroom door. His wife was in bed with a romance novel propped across her chest.

"You agreed only to enter at the designated times," she said.

Without a word, Kurt dropped the paper on the bed, turned, and left the room.

She picked it up and read.

Dearest Rosanna,

While you read this, two men—Hector Cato, who works for Austin Ramirez, and Fox Revelstorm, who claims he is an American flight attendant here on a layover—are searching the interior of the Hive for evidence that will put Herr Heinrich away forever. Revelstorm also claims that he playacted as a child pornographer and induced General Soriano to incriminate himself. Revelstorm wore a wire and recorded the conversation. Cato says the general will resign tonight. Esmerelda Castile will become president with the army's support. Herr Heinrich will have the general's protection no longer. Perhaps I am crazy, but I believe them. Why else would they be fool enough to break into a madman's castle?

I told them where to look for evidence, gave them codes to rooms, and how to get in and out to avoid detection. For this they paid me $9,500. In the grease pit under the prep table in the kitchen are two sealed packages. One has $4,500 and a thicker one has $5,000. If Herr Heinrich finds out someone has broken in, anyone here at the time will be questioned and/or tortured until they talk. Then they will be killed. That, I think, includes you. If I am questioned, I will talk immediately, then I will face the consequences. You will know where the money is hidden. Retrieve it and flee.

If I escape that fate and Herr Heinrich is arrested, I hope that you will allow me to court you in a traditional manner and show you the real me. Of course, we can immediately have the marriage annulled if that is your wish. I want us to continue in any way that pleases you. If you want never to see me again, take the package of $5,000, and leave the other package for me. I will not contact you. If it is your desire to be rid of me, you will be rid of me.

In either case, alone or together be ready to leave in a moment's notice. Anything can happen tonight. If nothing does, I am still committed to freeing us from this nightmare we are living. When you have finished reading, rip this into small pieces and flush it down the toilet. Kurt

Kurt was slumped on the sofa in the darkened living room when he heard the toilet flush. The bedroom door opened. Roseanna stepped into the room, the light from the bedroom creating a silhouette of her shape. Her index finger rested on her lower lip. Kurt levitated. The phone from Bauer's office buzzed twice and turned silent.

"That means he needs us both, right now," she said, with a small smile. "We will talk later."

Kurt thought he would melt.

Heinrich replayed the last hour several times in his head, and came to the conclusion that his performance had been flawless. He allowed himself to smile. Then a chuckle escaped his mouth, followed by outright laughter. A minute later he stopped the car and gingerly climbed out. His cackling had turned convulsive and he was literally tearing himself apart. He leaned against the car, gathered control, and managed to calm himself by concentrating on his one regret: not seeing fear in Ramirez's face. There was none during their conversation, nor as he marched out the door of the lodge, nor when he rowed the barge, and nor when he jumped. *No matter. He's dead and in pieces.*

He climbed back in, put the car in gear, and eyed the MP3 player Ramirez had left with him for a moment. In his resolve to let nothing deter him, he had barely listened to Ramirez's ramblings about the general being in trouble. And, despite his initial anger, he had suppressed the revelations of his birth and his mother's tawdriness. He had stashed it into a mental container he would open at a later time. For now, if

Soriano was in trouble, there would be trouble for those who believed they could fuck with the Butcher.

He took his eyes off the road and pushed the play button. Within three minutes, he started to unravel right along with the general. When it finished, he pounded the dash until his fist was bruised and bloody. Killing, maiming, and rape were all perfectly acceptable, but the general had forced the army's hand by crossing the only line that could not be crossed. He listened again, and noticed something familiar in Thorp's voice and word choice. How he had maneuvered the general and got him to talk? Who was this Thorp? *And to think I had him in the cab.*

A wave of nausea swept over him as he pushed the speed dial. Emile answered. "Put Rondo on," Heinrich ordered.

"Rondo, here, sir."

"Has the cleanup been completed?"

"Yes, sir."

"Trophies?"

"All removed to the remote location."

"We are clean?"

"As a whistle," said Rondo.

"Good. We may have visitors soon."

"Sir, the package arrived, courtesy of General Soriano, nearly an hour ago."

"How many?" asked Heinrich.

"Only three. The one named Revelstorm was not with them. Orders?"

"Commence the drop and filming as soon as possible. Then have the film taken to the remote location. Stay low and be quick. Take Emile."

"We don't really need him."

"I need to know whether he can be trusted. If he does not show the appropriate enthusiasm for this, add him to the count."

There was a short pause. "Yes, sir."

Heinrich flipped the phone shut and exhaled, somewhat relieved. As the tension had built up with Ramirez over the last two weeks he had decided to eliminate anything incriminating. It had been a wise decision. He only needed to remove one additional small item which he would do immediately upon arrival.

He returned his attention to the idiocy of the Butcher and to the weasely Wesley Thorp. This stranger's sharp tongue was beginning to remind him of the impertinent Fox Revelstorm, who should be dead from multiple knife wounds.

A moment later, Heinrich slammed on the brakes as another wave of fierce nausea surged through him. He stopped the car, shouldered open the door, and retched his guts out. Bitter bile upchucked with the realization that Revelstorm had played the part of Thorp. He raised his sickened head and followed the beacon of his headlights splitting open the darkness. When his eyes came to light's end he swore he saw Fox and Joey staring back at him, mocking him.

Bauer nodded them through the half-open door while he scrubbed his hands. "Close it," he said to Kurt. He directed his attention to Rosanna. "Mr. Cato has a single bullet wound to the chest. I suspect a major vessel has been compromised and his lung has collapsed. We need to work fast." He turned to Kurt. "One floor up in the apartment that I believe is called the Coral room is Hertz. Punch in G-R-E-T-A to get in and out. He's dead. He was hit on the head, but I am quite certain he died of heart failure. At any rate you need to get him out of there. Put him in the walk-in or bring him down here. He's not going to be easy to maneuver, but I have to oper—"

"*Ja*, I will take care of it and clean what needs cleaning. Did you see Cato's companion?"

"Just the back of him as he left. He should be gone."

Kurt nodded.

Bauer was already barking orders at Rosanna.

Kurt had a better idea. He also believed for the first time in two years, that he had a future. It was risky. But, if undetected, he would answer the inevitable question of: Where is, and what happened to, Hertz?

Kurt entered the room expecting a smelly mess, but apparently Hertz had not eaten in some time. He propped the body against the wall and draped it over his shoulder. He took one step and almost collapsed, but managed to stagger forward. Carrying nearly two hundred pounds of dead weight, he headed for the stairwell and four more floors down. Kurt had made it his business to keep his ears open to idle talk between the men. He had learned that surveillance monitoring was spotty but, as of three days ago, the stairwell cameras were not working.

Outside, one main pathway led down to the water with two alternates. He would employ the seldom used north alternate, steep with rock steps and switchbacks. And he knew the overgrown trees would block any surveillance. A tree trimming crew was due tomorrow. Yet the same trees blocking the cameras also blocked the lights. He considered dragging Hertz down the path but decided against it, not sure if he could cover the marks in the dark. Instead, Kurt picked his way along the path one tortuous step at a time. He pictured himself tumbling down the hill, head over ass, tangled up with a dead man, ending up maimed or, worse, brain dead.

With sweat pouring off his face, he got Hertz about halfway to the ocean and picked out a wide step. He unburdened the body from his back, held him up upright under the arms, then turned him around as if Hertz had been climbing upward. He bent the torso a little to the right and let go, allowing him to collapse naturally as if he had had a heart attack during the climb. If Bauer was correct, an autopsy would show that he had indeed died of heart failure and the blow to the right side of his head was caused by the fall on the rock steps.

Satisfied, Kurt waited a minute to catch his breath, then retraced his steps to the apartment's front room. The bookcase was askew from Hector and Hertz banging into it. Kurt straightened it out and then replaced scattered books and magazines. He found two drops of blood on the carpet which he daubed with Kleenex and spot remover. Using a can of Lysol he sprayed knobs and handles and wiped them clean, backed out, and rearmed the door. He made his way to the cottage, showered and waited for Rosanna, concerned for Hector Cato, and nervous as a schoolboy over Rosanna's decision.

Bauer had just closed Hector's wound when the telephone rang. The sound startled him for an instant and a bead of sweat glistened on his forehead. "It's Heinrich," Bauer said to Rosanna. "Finish for me, but stay quiet."

Bauer picked up. "I want you to do something for me," said Heinrich.

"You sound fatigued. Do you require additional pain medication?"

"No. I want you to leave the premises as soon as possible. You have two days off. I will contact you. The same for Kurt and Rosanna. Inform them. Take the minivan. The keys are on the keyboard. I am still thirty to thirty-five minutes away."

"Understood," said Bauer, as he set down the receiver.

"I heard," said Rosanna. "What do you think?"

"I think Heinrich is expecting company."

"What do we do?"

"Have Kurt ready the minivan. Tell him to fold down the right-hand back and middle seats to accommodate the stretcher, and then send him down to help me carry Cato up the stairs. No elevator. I'll finish here, while you grab what you need."

"Do you think it's safe for him?" she asked, looking at the still unconscious Hector.

"Safer than leaving him."

Kurt was waiting outside the front door. Rosanna approached him and stopped. She peered into his eyes.

He waited, barely able to breathe.

"We are leaving. Now. But I will say that, at first, I did not believe you were not in on this with Heinrich, that you two had picked me out as a sex toy. A month ago I realized that you were innocent. But, I have had a hard time believing in the notion that you've been making love to me instead of fucking me. I am starting to believe. You did not have to do what you did. A woman thinks twice about leaving a man who is willing to do so much to set her free. We will have the annulment and start over. I will not abandon you." She leaned forward and kissed him softly on the lips. "We are leaving," she repeated, and whispered the details.

Kurt could not keep a smile off his face.

Kurt and Bauer moved into the stairwell with Hector on a stretcher. But even through the thick concrete walls they heard the rotors of the Huey accelerate and the big helicopter liftoff its pad. "It's been a while, but that means one thing," said Bauer, in a low voice. "A drop."

"I hope it's the last one," replied Kurt.

11:30 P.M. CST

The Hummer carrying Rita, Joey, and Mike came to an abrupt stop in the driveway in front of the Hive. Its rear doors were yanked open and the three were waved out by four men toting rifles. No talk occurred. The driver handed a folded piece of paper to one of Heinrich's men. As soon as the doors slammed shut, the Hummer U-turned and sped back down the lane into the night, as if the men inside feared exposure to a deadly disease.

The flight crew was led to a side door and into a hallway. "Are we getting the grand tour?" asked Mike, in an attempt to regain his mental agility after the crushing disappointment in the jungle.

"Not exactly," said a wiry young man with a cockney accent. "But where you're going I can assure you the view will be unobstructed."

"Shut up, Bingham," said the biggest one, who made the man Mike had just fought look small.

They were escorted into an elevator and descended from level eight to level one. Through a maze of passages they marched, seemingly in a circle. Mike tried to remember every turn. He counted the number of his steps and the lights they passed under. He didn't know if these men were aware of his fighting skills, but they seemed wary and gave him no opportunity to engage. "Anyone bring bread crumbs? A ball of string?" asked Mike.

His comments were met with silence.

Finally they stood in front of a steel door which was opened by Bingham. He flipped on the light switch, motioned them inside, withdrew, and locked the door from the outside.

Joey looked around in the dim light of a single bulb and took inventory. Concrete walls—ceiling and floor—painted a pale yellow-green. Three rickety, hard chairs sat next to a small wooden table with a toilet and a sink in the corner. Bare bolts jutted out of the walls in various places suggesting equipment had once been attached to them. Four threaded holes in the floor forming a rectangular pattern and led her to believe that a much larger table, one which was immovable, had once sat in the middle of the room. The remnants of industrial strength cleanser permeated the air. Her instinct told her much suffering had occurred in this room.

"How do we get out of whatever is about to happen?" asked Rita.

"I don't know, but if you two were thinking of using your feminine charms, forget it," Mike replied.

"What do mean?"

"Mike means they were checking him out, not us," said Joey.

"I don't know what these guys are into, but I'm pretty sure they aren't interested in sex with women," said Mike.

Rita sighed and shook her head. "I bled Heinrich pretty good. He's probably going to want to return the favor."

Joey listened to the two of them conjecture and narrowed her focus. She slowed down her breathing, then her heart rate, and finally her mind. It was simple; she would do what was necessary—*anything* that was necessary. As the minutes ticked by, she watched the strain on their faces, and admired their control. She assumed the three of them were being made to wait, to heighten their fear. But fear was irrelevant. Rita and Mike had already proved that, no matter how afraid, fear would not debilitate them. As for Joey, one side of her was totally engaged with the task at hand, the other coolly detached.

Almost an hour later the door opened. The three with rifles stood outside. A fourth man, who looked like an action hero, entered. He was tan with shoulder-length dark hair, and day-old bristle on his face.

"Have a chair, please," he said, with a slight Spanish accent.

They sat.

"Thank you. My name is Rondo."

"Where's Heinrich?" asked Rita.

"He won't be attending. But he wanted me to tell you the plan. We will embark on a helicopter ride, out over the ocean, not too far. We will hover in a certain area and then you will jump out. Most likely you will be eaten by sharks and the feeding will be captured on film from a cage suspended below the surface."

"How humane," said Mike.

"As to that, I would disagree and agree," said Rondo, who scratched the stubble on his face. "Forcing you to jump is, of course, quite inhumane, but then that's the way most of us here are programmed. We like wild animals much better than people. On the other hand," he said, fishing a note from his pocket, "it seems that General Soriano is a bit put out with you. I have been instructed to quote, 'disassemble you' before dropping you, which is actually standard procedure. But I have neither the time nor the inclination. In fact, you will be the first to hit the water. Completely intact, I might add."

"Thank you for being forthright," said Mike.

"Why shouldn't I be? You will be dead inside an hour—"

"Aren't we a part of the animal kingdom?" interrupted Rita.

Rondo sighed. "If it makes you feel any better, if it were up to me, I would send you back to your hotel. But it is *not* up to me. Heinrich is clever and strong. Here, no one trusts anyone. We do what we are told and we survive. Anyone can openly challenge Heinrich, any time. Three have and three have died. Parts of their bodies have been preserved as a reminder of such foolish fantasies. Heinrich calls them trophies. I have no desire to end up as a trophy. *Comprende?*"

"Which parts?" asked Rita.

"Their heads."

Rita shook her head in disgust. "Heinrich is an idiot and he's overrated. Your cronies look so 'roided up, their balls must have shrunk to the size of peanuts. No wonder you bow down."

"You had him at a considerable disadvantage when you sliced him up."

"Isn't that the point? Excuse the pun," Rita replied.

Rondo ran his hand through his thick mane. "I'm beginning to understand Heinrich's dislike. You are quite irritating," said Rondo.

"Midgely didn't think much of me, either," Rita said.

Rondo stared at her. "Midgely? *You* fought Midgely?"

"Yes, I fought Midgely, and when I was through with him, he was ball-less and dead as well." Rita's anger bubbled into her vocal cords. "The way I see it, you are going to allow the cold-blooded killing of three innocent people, who have done nothing except piss off a total whack job, because you don't have the guts to tell him to fuck off or fight us himself. You're nothing but a half-assed, pretty boy coward."

Rondo leaned against the table and smiled at her. "Coward to you; pragmatist to me."

"Why the film?" asked Mike, afraid Rondo might pull a gun and shoot Rita.

Rondo turned his attention to Mike. "Heinrich has discovered a small but extremely lucrative market for such footage. There exist a few very wealthy men and one woman who salivate at the opportunity to watch our intruders get torn apart and eaten by sharks. Since nothing new has been produced in some time the demand should be immense." Rondo glanced at Joey and Rita. "You two will have the honor of being the first females." He paused. "I apologize. I do not mean to make light of this, but you will jump. Or if you prefer, we will shoot you through the heart as you stand in the doorway.

But if you leap, at least you have a chance. It is rare, but on occasion, no matter what is available, some sharks will not feed. You only need to swim a mile-and-a-half to reach shore."

"You said you always follow orders. You have chosen not to disassemble me. Why not choose to let us go?" asked Mike.

"As far as your destruction, that was a request from Soriano, not an order from Heinrich."

"Will you permit me to ask you a hypothetical question?" asked Joey, her body languidly draped in the rigid chair, as if she were lazing on the lounge deck of a cruise ship.

Rondo studied her for a moment. "You really have no idea what's in store for you, do you? Perhaps you are in denial, Señorita."

"You made yourself clear enough. By the time this short conversation is over, you will be the one in denial. May I ask the question, please?"

Rondo shrugged. "Ask."

"What would happen to Heinrich if Soriano is forced to resign and arrested, or exiled? Take it a step further. What would happen to you?"

"Such a thing is nearly impossible."

"Answer the question," said Joey, with some bite in her voice, rising to meet his gaze.

"I don't know," said Rondo.

"Yes, you *do* know. You would have to hope you could escape the country before you were arrested."

"Enough of this. You are leaving in five minutes."

"The fact is," said Joey. "Soriano has already stepped down, or will shortly. If he can find refuge on another continent he will be allowed to leave. If not, he will be arrested."

Rondo shot her a dismissive smile.

"Oh, yes, Mr. Rondo," she said, moving toward him. "Be assured, you have become a trapeze artist in the middle of a triple somersault a hundred feet in the air. Heinrich's hands have been coated with grease and your net has been removed. The one thing you can count on is the authorities arriving here, most likely before the sun rises. You do not want the blood of three dead Americans staining your hands." She held his eyes with hers. "It is obvious you are not crude or pigheaded. I only ask you to check out my story before we go."

Her words sent a chill through Rondo's body, along with his recollection of Heinrich's questions only a few minutes earlier concerning the removal of trophies and the possibility of visitors. He hadn't really thought of the crew as people, only enemies Heinrich wanted eliminated. The money for the film was also a factor. Heinrich had guaranteed him at least $200,000.

Five minutes later Rondo stood alone outside and dialed Heinrich. He asked about Soriano. Heinrich's answer stunned him. Screw the money, he thought. It's too risky.

Rondo overcame the sick feeling in his gut and plowed ahead into uncharted waters. "Sir, we should rethink dropping the Americans, considering the recent circumstances."

"Rondo, are you questioning my orders?"

He gulped. "Yes sir, I am. If you recall, you gave me that privilege, as well as the order to invoke it if I thought necessary. I think it's necessary."

"Very well, Mr. Rondo, what is your recommendation?"

"We tell them it was a mistake, my mistake, and return them to their hotel. Perhaps pay them to remain quiet. And then, I believe we should make preparations to leave."

Heinrich's end became silent, as if he were contemplating. Finally he answered. "Your concern and your suggestions have been considered and noted, but you will continue with the drop, and the Americans will disappear forever. Understood?"

"Yes, sir."

Rondo returned to the holding cell and studied the prisoners for a moment. "Escort them to the 'copter, and proceed with the operation."

JANUARY 25, 12:55 A.M. CST

At gunpoint, they shuffled down the trail to the pad, the Huey silhouetted like a giant insect above the water. Mike experienced the same fluttering in his stomach as he had a mere thirty-one hours ago when the bomb in Ramirez's jet was supposed to detonate. Despite another countdown to his probable demise he was grateful to escape the confines of the concrete box. It not only had held his body, but his thoughts as well, which seemed to ricochet off the walls and crash back into his brain, twisted and distorted. Time slowed as he took a deep breath and raised his arms above his head, exhaled, and let his mind expand. He listened to the drone of crickets and the soft cooing of night birds. He wondered why his vision was so acute in the darkness, why he could see past the spotlights illuminating the pad and capture every detail in the phosphorescent waves breaking below.

It was clear to Mike that at some point he would make his stand, as futile as that seemed. He would not leave the helicopter without a fight. As they reached the end of the trail, he smiled to himself and thought that what they really needed was a deal with the shark gods—a mutual nonaggression pact, starting immediately. No barbecued shark steaks from the supermarket, in exchange for no human loin from the sea.

The Huey's starboard sliding door was open and revealed its interior, made larger with the removal of several seats which allowed a ceiling-high cubicle labeled Special Ops Equipment. They marched up the boarding ramp and were met by a middle-aged man with deeply stained reddish-brown teeth. He grabbed each of their right hands and slapped a cuff around their wrists. The opposite cuffs were snapped shut around a horizontal rail attached to the cabin's low ceiling. They stood facing the open door, forward to aft: Joey, Rita, and Mike, who had to turn his head sideways to fit under the low ceiling.

Rita looked around. The Hispanic man who had cuffed them sat back down in an aft- facing seat directly behind the copilot on the starboard side. He spat betel leaf juice into a small bucket. Another larger man was located starboard aft, in the gunner's seat which faced starboard. His head was obscured in the shadows until he stood to adjust his seat. It was Emile. Rita stifled her initial outrage that he could be a part of something so awful. She remembered his attraction to her and his playful humor even after she had sliced him up like a Sunday roast, as he put it. Perhaps he was not present by choice. Maybe he would become an ally. She kept her eyes on him until he finally looked her way. His expression remained neutral and he said nothing.

Joey had also spotted Emile as she climbed the ramp. Remembering Rita's description of him and his bandaged arm and thumb made it obvious. She watched his face closely. Outwardly, his expression remained passive, but his was a face prone to much expression she decided, and sensed that he was suppressing it. She also sensed his discomfort. She had vowed to find a way. Perhaps Emile was part of the answer.

Rondo sat in the captain's seat next to the pockmarked behemoth Vargas, the copilot. They read their checklist and started flipping switches. The turbines whined, the engines roared, and the forty-eight-foot rotor picked up speed, sounding like a giant eggbeater. Mike had a moment of disbelief, as if the whole thing was a sick joke, until he glanced at the three cuffed hands that dangled from the bar. He caught Rita's eyes. He saw anger and resolve, and not a bit of fear. He willed his mind to find a way out.

Five minutes later they lifted off, rose to three hundred feet, rotated, and flew south.

In the distance Joey spotted the lights of a vessel and a stream of illumination that glowed from under the surface of the sea. She caught the attention of the man sitting in front of her, Taser gun on his lap, and some sort of holstered pistol attached to his belt. He smiled as he chewed and spit, the blood lust obvious in his dark eyes. "What's your name?" she yelled, above the thumping noise.

"Belize," he yelled back, making it sound like palaeeeze. "I am from Peru."

She smiled. "Well, Mr. Belize," she said, mimicking him. "What do you think? Clothes or no clothes?"

His grin vanished. "This is no beach party. They have not told you?"

"Oh, yes, we are very aware of what is *supposed* to happen. What will *actually* happen might be something entirely different—like, who actually goes swimming. So, clothes or no clothes?"

He frowned, as if astounded she was making light about when her panties should be soiled. "We have always thrown them in naked. It makes for better film. No one said anything to me," he said, squirting the bucket. "I think the clothes would just tangle you up when you hit the water."

The Huey cruised into position in line with the light of the filming cage and hovered.

Vargas removed his headset, and swiveled around to face Belize. "I have the boss on the line. He wants this done—now."

"Wait," yelled Joey. "Tell Heinrich I'll make a deal with him. No one will have to shove me or shoot me. In exchange, he will order you to return and release the others."

"Joey, no, we're all going in together," shouted Rita.

Joey ignored her and refocused on Vargas. "If he does, *I* will release *him*."

"What in the hell are you talking about? You're all going down," said Vargas.

"Just tell him, he'll know what I mean. Tell him!"

She watched Vargas slip his headset over his ears and speak into the microphone. A minute later he rotated again, his mouth slack as if he could hardly believe what he was about to say. "He agreed to your terms."

"Tell him that if he reneges, he will not be released and will not likely survive the night."

The message was relayed, the nod given to Belize, whose eyes blazed with surprise.

"How high are we?" asked Joey, deaf to Rita's and Mike's continued protests.

Belize took a step forward and peered at the altimeter. "One hundred feet," he shouted over the noise.

"Request fifty."

She watched Rondo in the captain's chair shrug as he took the craft down.

"Fifty feet," yelled Rondo.

"Joey, this makes no sense," Mike yelled. "Heinrich will never go for it. As soon as you're in, we're next. If the three of us go together and stay together, maybe we'll look more formidable to whatever's in the water."

"Please," begged Rita, her voice nearly lost in the din.

Joey shook her head. "I'm going swimming and you're going home."

She held up her cuffed hand to Belize. "Take this off."

From his pocket he pulled out a key chain which was attached to his belt loop.

Joey said to him, "A quick hug for them. Then, I'm out of my clothes and in. Don't shove me. Tell them to shine the spotlight on the exact place they want me to land."

Belize nodded and turned the key. Joey looped her arms around a frantic Rita and pulled her close. "You must survive. *Live.* Promise me." She felt Rita's head nodding, though she was still saying, "No," between sobs.

Then she hugged Mike. He said, "Joey, don't. I know you're only concerned, but I'm afraid for you."

"I'll be fine. It's only a leap of faith."

She released him and turned to Emile, found his eyes, and held them until he blinked.

She stripped out of her clothes. Without looking back she poised herself on the edge, bent her knees, and catapulted herself into the white light.

• • •

When Rondo had informed Emile that he was to participate in the drop, Emile had said nothing. He guessed his loyalty was to be tested, but also surmised that if he did nothing to interfere, that would be good enough for Rondo. Emile and Rondo had two things in common: unlike the others, they liked women and did not like the extracurricular activities of the rest of their band. Emile was sure that Rondo had a conscience, however deeply buried. But Rondo was also fanatically devoted to Heinrich. There had to be a reason, but Emile had not figured it out.

For the last two hours Emile had pondered what could be done to save the crew. He calculated the odds, then measured his own conscience against those odds. It came down to this: as the night unfolded, if at any time he figured he had a better than ten-percent chance of freeing them, he would take it. If less than ten percent he still might try, but if he didn't, he could live with himself. That is until Joey Sabatini laid her eyes on his.

He had first seen her eye him as she climbed up the ramp. He felt as naked as a newborn, as if she had downloaded his entire essence in one glance. He did not believe in telepathy or anything of the sort, and attempted to dismiss those thoughts, but had little success.

As they moved toward the target area, he had tried to come up with a way to get close to Belize without arousing his suspicion, but Belize had always hated him, and would likely shoot him at the first sign of any movement. He had no opening.

Joey is shouting something back and forth with Vargas. I can barely hear over the roar of the engines. She has made some kind of deal. Seconds later Belize releases her wrist, she hugs Rita and Mike, and strips out of her clothes. But all the time, her eyes are on me. She turns, stands on the edge like an Olympic diver and is gone. It is as if she had a death wish; as if she had told me, I have done my part, now do yours. But, what do I do?

Heart pounding, Emile shook the vision from his head and peered over the edge. With the spotlight turned off he saw only the glow emanate from the cage. Moments later a fast-moving, mammoth-sized shadow appeared in the stream of light, almost blotting it out. He flinched as the shadow and light collided. The beam skewed upward like an out-of-control gyroscope. Seconds later it abruptly ceased. Belize yelled to Vargas to contact Carlos in the filming cage.

Emile watched Rondo and Vargas speak with growing animation, arms raised to emphasize their points. Emile guessed that Carlos did not respond and that Heinrich had ordered the drop to continue.

Finally, Vargas turned to Belize and pointed at Rita and Mike. He emphatically pointed out the door. Emile moved forward just far enough to partially expose himself. "No," he shouted and glanced quickly at Mike, before he ducked down. Emile felt the sting of Belize's Taser glance off his shoulder and retreated. The cubicle provided enough cover to force Belize to move toward Mike and Rita. Belize yanked his pistol out of the holster and crept aft. Emile inched further behind the cubicle.

Emile made eye contact with Mike, thinking: Belize, just take one more step.

"If you touch them, I'll rip your ugly head off your shoulders," Emile shouted, luring Belize to him.

"You are a dead man, Emile." Eyes bulging, Belize lunged.

Mike grabbed the bar with both hands, thrust his right foot out and up, and knocked the gun from Belize's hand. His torso and left leg followed, rising up. From the ceiling his foot shot downward, his heel buried itself in the middle of the Peruvian's back. Stunned, Belize landed in a heap in front of Emile along with the weapon. But instead of grabbing it, Emile yanked the key chain from Belize's pocket, which severed the belt loop. He tossed it to Rita, as he fell backward. Belize spotted the gun and wiggled toward it. Rita, flipped through the key chain, grasped the smallest key, inserted it, and shook off her cuff. She dived over Belize, snatched the pistol, held it under her stomach, and skidded into Emile's seat, head first.

Vargas craned his head and peered aft. He did not see Belize, but saw Emile rise and start to move forward. Instinctively he jerked the yoke and turned the Huey nearly on its starboard side. Like a released bomb, Belize dropped into space, screaming.

Rita, pinned momentarily under the seat, was tossed against the fuselage wall aft of the open door. In a blur she saw Emile slide head first out the opening. She threw her arm forward, grabbed his right leg and held on. Mike, still tentacled to the rail, clung with both hands, and hung straight down.

The Huey pitched and nearly stalled as Rondo fought for control. He finally stabilized the aircraft in an upright position.

Using her legs for leverage Rita managed to haul Emile in, inch by inch, until his other foot appeared far enough inside so he could grasp the edge and heave himself aboard. Gasping, they both leaned against the bulkhead for a moment. "Good God, woman," Emile said into her ear, "you were hanging on to two hundred and thirty pounds. Why didn't you just let go?"

Between pants she said, "I was afraid for the fish."

They scrambled to their feet and Emile grabbed the gun. Rita retrieved the key chain lodged under Emile's chair. Vargas rose, climbed out, and turned around. Emile had the gun on him and motioned him back into his seat.

"Fly this thing while I chat with Rondo," he yelled.

Rita freed Mike and they yanked the door closed and made their way forward. "Thank goodness, I can hear again." The closed door muffled some of the roar of the engines. "All the noise has scrambled my brain," said Mike.

Emile stood behind Rondo and held the weapon. "If you please, I will now give the orders. This ship will set down on Ramirez's strip."

"Negative," said Rondo. "Either I put us into the sea or we head back to the pad."

Rita jumped forward. "I've had it with this shit. Shoot both of them," she screamed.

"And who will fly?" asked Rondo.

"I can handle this bucket of bolts. Get out. Emile, blast him now, and yank his ass out of there. Then fry the other one."

"You can operate this contraption?" asked Emile above the din.

"As well as I operate a sword. You witnessed that. Go on."

"That I did. Painfully did," he said, holding out his arm.

"Wait," said Rondo, craning his neck toward them. "Give me thirty seconds. I won't try anything."

Emile nodded.

"What's he doing?" asked Rita.

"Calculating the outcome of his trial."

Rondo turned around and faced Emile. "I never tortured anyone. Will you testify for me?"

"I will testify that you repeatedly told me you were not involved with the torture. I will testify that I believed you and still do. And I will testify that you did not want to make this drop."

Rondo nodded and looked over at Vargas. "It's over."

Vargas violently shook his head. "No way."

"Head north," ordered Emile. "Maintain altitude for another minute." He stared at Vargas. "We're clear of Shark Alley. You can leave whenever you like."

Without a word, Vargas rose, shucked off his boots, checked his sheaf for his knife, and gave the nod to Rondo. Vargas opened the door, stepped out and disappeared.

Once the door had been reclosed, Emile resumed giving orders. "Return to the drop point and search the water for any sign of her. You will know better than I the proper procedures. Call search and rescue. As soon as they arrive on scene, we land at Ramirez's. Radio ahead for a greeting party."

Mike looked over at Rita's ashen face and put his arms around her. She collapsed into him and he held her while she shuddered. When her breathing steadied, he guided her into the seat Emile had occupied. Mike plopped down next to her on the floor. "It's weird how everything happened," he said. "How somehow Joey orchestrated this. I mean, when Emile yelled 'no' he caught my eye, barely gave me a nod, but I knew exactly what he was doing and exactly what I had to do."

Rita nodded, her mind numb, her body limp with exhaustion.

"Have you really flown a helicopter before?" he asked.

"No."

"Have you flown *anything, ever?*"

"A crop duster. Once."

"Remind me never to play poker with you."

"I wasn't bluffing," she said. "I snapped. I wanted in that seat. I would have figured it out." She started to cry. "I just can't believe she's gone and we're here."

They both leaned back in silence, reality overwhelming them.

Mike fought his body's desire to shut down and straightened his torso. He rocked up on his knees and. gently placed his hands on Rita's shoulders. "If anyone can survive, it's Joey," he said, trying to put some optimism into his voice.

He did not tell her that he had doubts as to her desire to survive.

1:15 A.M. CST

Joey had taken one previous leap of faith—into an escape slide while held in the arms of Fox Revelstorm. In that leap she believed she had found something akin to perfection, if not the essence of God. From the door of the burning airplane to the bottom of the slide had taken less than three seconds, but to her it felt much longer, almost eternal. This leap would be no different, she told herself. She dived outward and a wave of joy washed over her. Toward the beam of light she streaked, until it became the same white light she had dreamed of earlier in the day, with Fox's arms, once again, wrapped tightly around her.

    She knifed into the water, momentum propelling her down until she nearly reached the end of the spotlight's penetration. She ascended into the lower edge of the light which emanated from the camera cage, spun her body around, and gathered her bearings. With the filming cage at her back, fifty yards away, she gazed ahead. A huge black obstacle, which looked like a submarine, sped toward her and engulfed the streaming light as if it were a propellant. But, soon enough, she could discern the gaping mouth and rows of jagged teeth. This was no boat. She waited almost passively, with curiosity, but the shark remained a few feet above her depth. He sped over her so fast, his wake sent her body end over end. A moment later she felt a strong concussion as the rogue shark rammed into the cage, shattered the bars, and ripped off the head and one shoulder of the cameraman in a single bite. For a moment the camera light tipped on its side and spewed straight up, then extinguished. In an instant the sea was a roil with sharks flashing past her to join the frenzy. She was ignored.

With long languid strokes she surfaced, took in air, and watched the Huey hover above. It began to move forward and climb, then lurched on its side and nearly stalled. The engines whined and labored.

Another five minutes came and went, and the righted Huey turned around and began to search for her. Emile had somehow managed it, she thought. Several times the light shone right on her and she waved her arms. It was as if she were invisible. Twenty minutes later a fleet of copters buzzed into position and took over the hunt. Joey treaded water for a moment and watched the Huey break off and head north toward Ramirez's strip. She kicked her legs and swam toward shore.

She attempted to make herself more visible whenever she heard a chopper above, and had turned over on her back. But while floating, an incessant urge had come to her while she surveyed the universe above. She was to enter the jungle and follow her instincts and the jungle's compelling voice.

She checked the position of the moon, kicked toward shore, and began to swim. She wondered if she had a decision to make.

1:30 A.M. CST

Racked with pain, Heinrich lurched into his empty castle, and made inquiries through a central P.A. With no response, he made his way to the war room and checked the board. The men he had sent out toward the Forbidden Zone were still an hour away. That was understandable. But where were Beattie and Blanco? *And where in the fuck is Hertz?* He grasped the microphone again and put out an all-call. Once again his request was met with silence.

He contacted the helicopter. "Where are Beattie and Blanco?" he demanded.

"No idea, sir," answered Rondo. "A couple of Soriano's men dropped off the flight attendants. They said nothing and did not get out of their vehicle."

"What about Hertz?"

"I haven't seen him."

"You should be back on the pad by now. I told you I wanted it done quickly."

"Yes, you did. But Emile now has control of the aircraft. We will be landing shortly at the Ramirez strip."

"Are you telling me Braun and Sanchez are still with you?"

"Affirmative."

Heinrich slammed his sore fist on the desk. "This is mutiny, Rondo."

"Emile possesses the weapons. I'm sorry. Our existence, as we knew it, is over. I would leave ASAP, sir. Sir?"

Heinrich was already in the elevator on his way to the Coral Room. Despite stitches that popped out of his chest like the Titanic's rivets, he bounded out and down the hall. Through the door, he yanked open the cabinet and jammed his sweat-drenched hand into the hidden compartment that had held the iPod. His bellows echoed throughout the eight floors of the Hive, but there was no one present to hear them.

1:45 A.M. CST

Joey kept stroking, long and steady, scarcely aware of anything except for her hands cupping the water, pulling it past her, and the constant kick of her legs pushing it behind her. She had lost track of time and her ears were deaf to the drone above. She kept her direction constant by her westward angle with the moonlight. She stopped only once, when she became aware of deep shadows in front of her. She was close. Five minutes later she touched the sand and gathered her legs under her and stood up in waist-deep water. A wave from behind knocked her down, the strength that had brought her ashore suddenly spent. Her head barely above the surface, she crawled onto the beach and gasped for air, her heart pounded in her chest. A few minutes later her breathing eased. She ignored the coolness that had consumed her body, and once again focused on the intense pull from the jungle.

She managed to stand. She wobbled in the sand and willed herself not to fall down. A few minutes later she regained most of her balance, stumbled up the beach and stopped one step shy of the jungle. She moved two steps ahead and everything changed. Her chill and fatigue vanished, replaced by warmth that soothed body and spirit. She could hear millions of whispers, feel the caress of the wind funneled through the vast, overhead canopy, and see the tiniest web built into every leaf. She sniffed and smelled the lushness of vegetation and the rot of plant and animal waste. The intense cacophony startled her, but soon it all made sense, like walking through a forest mildly aware of chirping birds and the rustle of branches magnified a hundredfold.

She pinched the skin on her forearm. She felt nothing. She retreated to where she had stood prior to entering. Her heightened senses disappeared. She pinched herself again and felt pain.

Without hesitation she reentered the jungle and lurched forward, driven by an undefined purpose, yet sure she would find it. She was acutely aware of the smallest of details and awed by the perfect harmony, as if every living thing moved in an arc, and the arcs intersected in a precise symphonic balance. Even the screaming discord of creatures being devoured by other creatures was part of the intricate rhythm.

She glanced down. A wide parade of army ants advanced toward their destination as one. She placed her foot just above them and they scurried to either side, the column splitting in two. Then she placed her foot on the ground. They continued to flow around her, but did not touch her.

She continued and penetrated deeper into the jungle, gaining elevation. The terrain became more rugged with rock formations that jutted out of the flora. Her heart beat rapidly. Surely she was close to her purpose. For an instant she experienced the same sense of fierce protection as when Heinrich had invaded her room at the Paraiso. She stopped and gazed up. Fifteen feet above her loomed a ledge that fronted a cave. It beckoned. She climbed. Once she reached the ledge, she peered into the blackness, her eyes wide, and ears attuned. Two jaguar kittens lay asleep in the lair, alone and vulnerable. A jolt of adrenaline coursed through her. She backed up to scan her surroundings ready to do battle with anything that would harm them. The maternal instinct again. She would wait here like a sentry for the mother's return and repel any predators just as the kittens' real mother would do. Sure of her purpose, Joey plopped down on the ledge and leaned back against the rock. She pondered the nature of motherhood.

2:00 A.M. CST

Heinrich had stuffed his pockets with cash snatched from two safes. He clutched a bag of jewels and was out the door when his phone rang. "Finally," he mouthed before answering.

"Heinrich," he said.

"Fox Revelstorm, here. How's your evening going, Gus?"

"You!" shouted Heinrich.

"Yeah, it's me."

"Where are you?"

"Where would you like me to be?" asked Fox.

"Somewhere where I can end your miserable existence."

"Perfect. That's why I called, to provide you with that opportunity."

"I have no time for games," said Heinrich.

"I played a game with the general. He lost. Maybe you think you can do better."

That silenced Heinrich for a moment. "If we were to meet, the authorities will be waiting for me."

"No, they won't. But there are requirements. I'm at the home of Celeste Starr. I believe you have visited her studio before and her unique art conclave. You will visit the conclave again for a new experience. After you're finished, we'll have a short conversation. Then you can proceed as desired."

"You said 'requirements.' Plural."

"Yes, there is one other. Our conversation will be frank. We can talk as long as you want. At a minimum, I will ask you five questions and I will be allowed up to ten. You will answer with complete honesty and total candor. You may ask me anything and I, too, will respond in kind."

Heinrich hesitated. "Are you armed?"

"No, and I won't be."

"I will take a minute to think this over," said Heinrich. *What does he want? Why would the lamb invite the wolf into the sheep's den? He must still be out of contact with his crew, which would account for his motivation.* Heinrich drummed his fingers against the wall. *If I were to tell Revelstorm what happened, that motivation would disappear and so would my opportunity to kill him. But what if Revelstorm were to find out their safe outcome while I am en route? Would he back out? No, Revelstorm would not go back on his word.* "What about a wire?"

"I can assure you the conversation will be heard by no one else and will not be recorded. If we're both alive and you're arrested, I will not reveal any of our conversation to the authorities."

"You actually believe you will still be alive after I depart?"

"I don't know. I think I have a chance. I guess I'm betting my life on it, aren't I? Do we have an agreement?"

"I will arrive in forty minutes. You have *no* chance." He snapped the phone shut so hard it cracked.

2:20 A.M. CST

Celeste's hand started to cramp and wisps of blonde hair had escaped her ponytail, their ends now coated with samples from her paint palette. She had been at work all evening, preparing for Janelle's portrait by sketching her in watercolor from several different angles. The drugged cat had cooperated by rolling over several times in her sleep. Celeste had recorded almost every square inch of the magnificent beast. She also had photos, but the lens was no match for her interpretive eye. She had completed over a dozen, knowing she wouldn't have the opportunity for long.

Fox was due any minute and she wasn't sure how they would greet each other given the pressure he'd been under all day and night. A minute later she sensed his presence and whirled around. His sudden appearance forced a gasp from her. He covered the distance between them and wrapped his arms around her back, pulled her to him, and kissed her passionately.

"What was that for?" she asked, surprised but pleased.

"For me. I deserve a second of bliss. You look beautiful in orange. And black," he said, playfully, examining the other side of her face.

"And you look tired and fatigued."

"How about worried sick?"

"That too, but everything here is ready. Are you sure you want to do this?"

"I need to know where and what's happening with my crew. Heinrich will be here in less than half an hour. It's time for you to leave."

She shook her head. "I'm staying. I've been thinking about this. When Heinrich walks in the studio, I'll be the one to greet him. When he comes out of the conclave, you'll be waiting there. I like your chances much better if he sees the footage before he sees you. In fact, despite any curiosity he may have for the conclave, his freedom is at stake and his time is limited. At the first sight of you, he'll pull the trigger."

Fox rubbed his chin and nodded. "You're right. That makes more sense."

They gathered up Celeste's materials and flipped off the portables which lit Janelle's temporary enclosure.

Celeste's landline rang as they entered the studio.

"Fox, it's Mike," said Celeste, handing over the receiver.

Fox spent the next fifteen minutes with the phone pressed to his ear. His emotions soared with relief. But they plummeted at the news of Joey. When he listened to his heart, he detected her echo. He didn't know if that meant she was alive or if the echo was all that was left of her.

As soon as Fox hung up the landline, Ramirez rang his cell phone. It was official. Soriano was out and Esmerelda was in. And Hector was alive. Fox flipped his phone shut, snapped a paper towel off the roll, and wiped the sweat from his forehead.

Celeste took his hands in hers. "What do we do now? We know Mike and Rita are safe. There's no need to put yourself in jeopardy."

Fox paused. "I see what you mean, but we stay with the plan. I need to know exactly what happened in Joey's room. I mean I *have* to know. And, Heinrich is going to tell me."

2:35 A.M. CST

One at a time Heinrich slid his clammy hands off the steering wheel and wiped them on his pants. His tired eyes blinked like strobes and he could barely focus on the road ahead. He was beginning to experience second thoughts and a vague sense of discomfort. Reality was sinking in. He had to leave the country. Surely the authorities possessed the iPod and, if Soriano wasn't already deposed, he would be soon. He involuntarily shook his head and any self-doubt vanished. *I will have plenty of time to dispose of Revelstorm before they figure out where I am going, the bumbling idiots.*

Five minutes later he followed his shadow through the open door into Celeste's studio, pistol drawn. Celeste sat in a folding chair just inside.

"Where is he?" demanded Heinrich, with the wave of his gun. "Leaving you alive was not included in the negotiations."

"No, it wasn't, but experiencing the conclave was. When you are finished in there, Fox will be sitting in this chair."

Heinrich strode over and put the barrel against her head. "Where *is* he?"

"Right behind you. Get the gun away from her. She is not the one you want to hurt," said Fox.

Heinrich's mouth twitched, but he lowered the gun and faced Fox. "For once, you are right." He turned back to Celeste. "You have always treated me with dignity. You deserve my respect."

She nodded and Heinrich took a step toward Fox, brandishing the weapon. "As I told you before, I don't have time to play your games. I need to be quick and thorough, just as I was with Ramirez."

"You weren't thorough enough. I plucked him from the pond. He's fine."

Stunned, Heinrich stared at him with eyes wide. "You lie. I saw the caiman pull him under, its jaws around his chest."

"Its jaws were clamped around a Kevlar vest. Call Ramirez. He'll answer. Go ahead."

Heinrich tried to block out the rising din in his head, but could not. Instead, he raised the gun again.

"Put it down," said Fox, his voice a whip. "Be a man. Honor your commitment and go into the conclave. Or are you a coward? You think you're tough? You say you can handle pain? Go inside. You will feel the worst kind of pain, yet your body will not be touched. Now, move, and leave the gun on the table. I don't want you shooting up the exhibit. Don't worry, it'll be sitting there—untouched—when you come out." With that Fox spun around and stepped out through the door which Heinrich had entered.

An image of Joey Sabatini laughing at Heinrich flashed through his head. In a daze, Heinrich stared at his gun, barely held in a limp hand. He shook his head to clear the cobwebs, and said to Celeste, "I will go in."

"Would you care for a briefing of what you'll experience in there? Or would you like to enter with no preconceived notions?"

"I will enter."

"Very well," said Celeste. "Walk in and shut the door. Make sure you hear the latch engage. Stand in the middle, and face the amber light. I'll dim the other lights and start the program."

Heinrich nodded and made it halfway across the room before the doubt crept in again. Why would he allow himself to be led into a closed compartment that could probably be barred from the outside or have poisonous gas pumped in? He craned his neck around. "No tricks?"

"No tricks."

He paused and stared at her a moment, then entered and closed the door behind him. It was like standing on the inside of a globe, near the South Pole with the rest of the inner world above him. The arced surfaces were finished in a smooth neutral color, perfect for reflecting filmed images. The lights dimmed. In an instant the room came alive, around and above him. Totally disoriented with sensory overload he gasped for air while his eyes adjusted to the brightness of a spring morning.

He was back at the Hive, and stood in a large clearing. All around him birds chirped, monkeys chattered, flies buzzed, and a sweet morning breeze tousled his hair. Straight ahead, he gazed at the cat's enclosure and listened to the escalating frustration of Lucerne, the trainer who kept backpedaling from the agitated young jaguar.

In the distance, he heard a shout, and the panorama expanded. His mother. "She has you," Heinrich heard her say. "Don't give in to her, Lucerne. You are the boss. Make her understand."

Lucerne let himself out and trotted over to her. "I will try one other tactic. If this fails, I am finished."

As soon as Lucerne had left, Janelle hunkered down and the camera point of view was narrowed to Greta and Hess, Greta's elderly thinned-lipped confidante and aide. Heinrich had always hated him. They sat on a bench facing each other.

"Your son is late again, Frau."

"My son is perpetually late."

"Return him to the mine. That will end his tardiness."

Greta shook her golden mane. "His tardiness is the least of my concerns."

Heinrich watched her tilt her head a degree or two, a habit that signified a decision was to be made.

"What are your concerns, Frau?" asked Hess.

"I acquired the infant to mold him into a great warrior, a man of steel, a giant who would help me forge an empire and lead with an iron fist. As you are aware, Gustav is an abject failure. He is ruthless enough, but imagination and discipline are nowhere to be found in his addled brain."

"Perhaps it was a mistake for me to arrange the switch at birth," said Hess.

"It should have worked. His mother was brilliant and his father an Adonis with brains, while my son was fathered by a cute puppy dog, only less smart. But, what was done is done. I no longer have the ability or patience to pour money into a useless investment. If he were exceptional, I might overlook his fatal flaw, but he is nowhere close. He is a homosexual and he stinks of fear. I will no longer tolerate it."

Heinrich jammed his hand into his pocket, seeking his gun to shoot her in the head, forgetting that it was lying on a table outside the conclave.

Greta swatted at a fly and returned her gaze to Hess. She nodded her head. "Perhaps you are right," she continued. "The mine will serve our purposes. Send him there and arrange an accident. I am scheduled to turn over part of my estate to him in the near future. He is twenty-five. See to it he does not reach twenty-six."

"As you wish, Frau."

Heinrich almost stopped breathing. His maimed chest felt like an anvil rested upon it.

The camera moved back to the training pen. Lucerne reentered with a longer whip in hand. Janelle batted her paws at him and growled, then leaped forward. Her jaws snapped and she hissed.

Lucerne carefully retreated, popped back out through the gate, and strode toward Greta and Hess, who had both risen from the bench.

"Madam," he said, sweat pouring off his face, "this is a wild animal who does not like the notion of being trained. Here," he said, thrusting a pile of bills at her, "This is all the money you have paid me. Keep it, I am not going back in there."

"You will do as I say," she screamed, spraying his face with spittle.

"No, I am through."

"You are yellow," she bellowed and snatched the whip from his hand. "This is how you tame a beast," she said, and cracked the whip across his face, drawing blood.

Lucerne ran.

"Come back here, you weakling. I will show you," she said, and almost ran toward the enclosure.

Fury intensifying, she undid the latch, smashed her shoulder into the door, flung it closed and latched it behind her. She stared at the cat and raised her arm. In one leap Janelle had Greta's head in her mouth, jaws crunched down from the top of her forehead and up from under her jaw removing one eye and half of Greta's face. The image jiggled for a moment, probably from the shock of the cameraman. Shouting voices could be heard in the distance.

Heinrich had always imagined her screams, and they had given him nightmares. After she died, he had vowed to kill the cat. But now, as he heard the wails, their echoes rang even more hideously, but he felt nothing but the steady disintegration of his body and mind.

Just as they had done over and over in their training, one of Ramirez's men scampered into view with a tranquilizer gun and shot Janelle while the standby ambulance rolled into view. A minute later the shooter gave a nod and the EMTs burst in and administered to her. Two minutes later they carried a moaning Greta out. Her face was a grotesque mask, but Heinrich did not look away. She was slipped into the ambulance, the camera faded out, and the lights went up.

Heinrich swayed as if he were drunk, all the muscles that held him upright almost at the breaking point. He breathed hard and choked down rising bile, steadied himself then reeled out the door into the studio. As promised, Fox Revelstorm sat in the chair Celeste had vacated, and an empty one sat opposite him.

Heinrich's shaking hand finally grasped the gun from the table and he lurched forward in half steps. He tried to aim the pistol but could barely get it passed his knee. In a sudden surge of strength, he managed to extend his arm waist-high. An instant later a blast thundered through the room. Heinrich staggered back. A second shot drove him into the conclave wall where he slumped to the floor. Heinrich raised his head up and to the left. He stared at Celeste who still had her gun pointed at him. "Thank you," he wheezed.

Fox was dumbfounded, the shot momentarily paralyzing him. When the second one was fired, he leaped forward and knelt in front of Heinrich. "Stay with me," pleaded Fox.

Heinrich shook his head. "No."

"What about Joey? Did you try to kill her, but couldn't?"

Blood seeped out his mouth, but Heinrich made a barely perceptible nod.

"With what?"

Heinrich managed to make a fist, as if he were holding a knife, then fell back, eyes closed. They did not open again.

"No," groaned Fox.

On his knees, his back to her, Fox slowly swung his head around and found Celeste's eyes. They were neither defiant nor apologetic. She spoke. But he did not hear the words until much later.

• • •

Celeste discovered the alert a few minutes after Fox had arrived. She kept hearing a noise that came from the cottage, and finally entered to investigate when the distinctive beep of the special phone went off again. She had listened three times and rechecked the code. The conclusion had sickened her but her resolve was steadfast.

She had hidden behind her work bench and waited for Heinrich to emerge from the conclave. She hoped he would make it easier for her by charging out, resolute in his intent to kill Fox. The crushed look on Heinrich's face told her Fox had been right: the film had all but destroyed him. She hesitated as he raised his gun, then exhaled, fired and fired again. She watched the ensuing seconds unfold like an inescapable nightmare.

Still on his knees, backlight creating a halo around his hair, Fox slowly swung his body around and found her eyes with his. She nearly crumpled to the ground. She lowered her head and spoke. "The world and I have already lost one great man, because of the evil of others. I could not risk another such tragedy. If I am to lose you, so be it, but you remain among the living and the world is better off for it." She did not tell him that less than thirty miles away an indigenous people were once again safe from the stain of the outside world.

After only one night with Fox she had instinctively understood his life had been shaped by a series of betrayals. She vowed to herself she would break that cycle. Whether as a friend or lover, *she* would be the one he could always trust. She raised her head. He stared at her, his eyes bleared with disbelief and sadness. She could almost visualize the inevitable rebuilding of the steel shell she had penetrated. She had lost him.

45

5:40 A.M. CST

Caroline Soriano strode briskly through the long hallway that led from her bedroom to her father's study, her pattering pumps echoing off the marble walls. Her silk dress swooshed and rubbed against her body producing sparks of static electricity that sounded like thunder to her. Her mind was made up, yet her head pounded. Her father, the general, had finally called for her.

It had been a surrealistic evening. Since they had returned to the compound she had not been to bed and had not changed clothes. Earlier, summoned to the great hall, she had listened with sick fascination to the broadcast of her father's sordid conversation with Fox, then witnessed Gota's stunning dismissal of the general. She shuddered at her father's outrage and subsequent refusal to accept his ouster. She heard his pathetic plea to his inner circle of men answered by silence. Then they fell in behind Gota to show their new allegiance. With the tyrant stripped of his power, the feeble president stepped forward. In his most forceful speech ever, he promised a new era of freedom, resigned from office, and named Esmerelda Castile to lead as interim president.

Since his ouster at 2:30 a.m., the general had been given until 8 a.m. to find a country on another continent to provide him sanctuary.

Caroline paused for a moment then knocked on the door and listened as he grunted the order to enter. Red-faced and scowling, he glanced at her briefly, then continued his assault on a document with his fountain pen until the point buckled. He slammed it into a wastebasket.

With a semblance of composure, he swiveled in his chair, plucked up a telescopic pointer, and tapped it against a world map mounted on the wall. "We have a new home, my dear. Myanmar. Our plane leaves at 8:30, in less than three hours," he said, glancing at his watch. "Pack two bags. The rest will follow."

"But father, this is my home. I'm twenty-three. I would like to stay."

"Your job will be to establish a household for me while I settle into *my* job, which will be to rid a sensitive area of pesky renegades. These rebels have no idea what they face. In a matter of months I will prove myself indispensable to the generals who run the country. I will *do* my job. If you have done yours, perhaps in a year we can discuss your future."

With the bob of his head, he dismissed her. She knew it was the end of the discussion. She smiled and nodded demurely. "Very well, father. Would you care for a coffee drink? A latte to keep you awake?"

"Splendid. Make it extra sweet to counteract the bitter taste in my mouth."

"Of course, father."

She quickly made her way to the empty kitchen, knowing the pantry help and chefs were soon to arrive. Before flipping on the lights she hiked up her dress and recovered the packets Mike had given her. She emptied all six into a mug she then pressed into the back of a deep cabinet. She retreated into the hallway restroom, tossed the empty packets into the toilet, and then flushed. She returned to the kitchen, retrieved the mug, flipped on the lights, and started the espresso machine. Two minutes later she listened to the steady drip, drip, drip, praying that each plop was but a minute of time before her father departed the earth. Perhaps she would face eternal hell for his murder, but no one else would have to face hell on earth because of him.

6 A.M. CST

Esmerelda and Ramirez sipped chamomile tea in her home office while she finished signing a stack of papers. A single lamp illuminated her desk, leaving the rest of the room in shadows. "There is much to celebrate, but it is empty without the return of the American woman," said Esmerelda. Ramirez barely nodded his head, seemingly lost in his own thoughts. She guessed Ramirez felt personally responsible for the young woman dropped in shark-infested waters and was probably at war with his conscience.

Esmerelda's view was different. After hearing the story of the crew's remarkable evening, she recalled her own image of Joey, an image she was determined to burn into her memory to draw on for the future. When the crew had been brought to her office, the room had crackled with tension and rancor, her own included. While Rita and Mike expressed their outrage, Joey looked right at her and studied her. Joey was calm, serene, curious, and showed not a hint of fear. As acting president, she would do well to project such a persona.

Yet as she and Ramirez entered her house and passed by the hall mirror, she was shocked by her own likeness, a smiling woman, youthful in appearance, age lines formed from years of bitterness, gone—sloughed away like the peel of an orange, revealing a fresh face that could not contain the giddiness of love regained.

"You should get some rest," she said, raising her eyes and studying him in the dim light.

He shook his head. Even that small action activated his ribs and he let out a muffled gasp. "If I could. I had hoped to get through this night with not a drop of blood spilled, except mine," he said, lightly touching his slacks which covered his bandaged legs. "Now this, one possible casualty—an innocent American."

"And if Joey Sabatini is indeed a casualty, she must never be forgotten. Ever."

Ramirez nodded his head. "I agree."

She eyed him. "Though it's been many years, I still know you. I can tell by the way you look at me, something else occupies your mind besides the state of the government and Joey Sabatini."

"Not really."

"Yes, most certainly."

Ramirez chuckled and threw out his hands. "Very well. But this is, as the Americans say, from out of left field."

"Well?" she prompted.

He exhaled with slow deliberation. "I want to be a father. I've possessed a strong desire for some time and feel a sense of urgency. I want the mother to be someone I love or could love. Do you think it's possible, I mean do you think maybe you would want another?" His voice trailed off and he cocked his head as if he acknowledged the verbal butchering of his own thoughts.

She grinned in amusement as a drop of sweat appeared on his forehead. But she did nothing to alleviate his discomfort. "Another what?" she asked.

He gulped. "Child. I mean, are you even capable of bearing another—?"

"There's only one way to find out," she interrupted. She reached for him, took his hand, and led him out of the office toward her bedroom. "After all, it worked pretty well the last time we tried it."

He had told her the truth about what he knew—and what he didn't know—and suddenly, she loved him even more for it. She decided right then and there that, if elected, she would serve one term, then retire to raise their second child—together.

7 A.M. C.S.T

General Soriano was found by an aide, slumped over his desk, dead of an apparent heart attack.

6:00 A.M. CST

Alone on the beach, Fox sat hunched on a towel, arms draped over raised knees, and eyes focused straight ahead at the waves breaking on the sand. Behind him the first streaks of red light cleared the jungle's canopy and seeped color into the gray ocean. A lone raptor screeched overhead intent on the sea below, as if it too, were searching for Joey. Numbness had settled into Fox, his brain sluggish and his body aching. He had mostly compartmentalized Heinrich's death. Celeste, for the moment, was expunged, but remained like a blinking light on a message machine. At some point he would have to deal with the agony of her deception. For now, he focused on Joey and tried to ignore the random thoughts that streaked like meteors and bombarded his fatigued mind.

Other than the obvious, he didn't even know what he wished for, or what *to* wish for. Maybe the obvious wasn't so obvious after all. *What does Joey want? She desperately wants to feel the magic or the peace, or whatever the hell it was, that* she did with me on that slide. What if she's found it, for eternity? If she has what she wants, why would she come back? And if she has what she wants, would I wish her to come back? Should I wish her to come back? Or is she now just a pile of bones lying on the ocean floor? Fox had carved out a life for himself by relying on what he knew to be real and let go of everything else he couldn't comprehend. Now, only the incomprehensible and the unknown seemed important.

He took a deep breath, leaned back, stretched his legs, and wiggled his toes in the sand. He half expected Joey to emerge from the sea as if she'd returned from a leisurely swim, wondering what all the fuss was about. He wanted to tell her the fucking fuss was about a woman's obsession with him. *Now I'm the one obsessed. She came out of nowhere like a whirlwind, tantalized me with her beauty, her otherworldliness, and a hint of something elusive, something important, something I need to know. And now she's gone? Disappeared forever, without telling me? It's as if Moses had decided the Ten Commandments weren't that important and simply left them on the mountaintop to crumble into dust.*

Fox took the heel of his hand and tapped the side of his head. "Stop it," he said aloud. His head heavy, he lay back on the towel, and burrowed his body into the sand until he was overcome with exhaustion.

6:00 A.M. C.S.T

With every breath Joey seemed to soak up the essence of a million new life forms. The sensory overload continued to stagger her, but the speed at which she caught up and her capacity to engage had fully integrated her mind with the living jungle. She understood the perfection in the imperfection of species as they mutated and adapted to every changing influence to accomplish one thing: survival. The revelations intoxicated her and the pull of the universe was strong, but still, this time, it was different. No waffling. She was determined to return to the beach, her former self, and ultimately the arms of Fox. But it wasn't only the jungle beckoning her to stay. There was a new voice, one borne on the breeze, vaguely familiar, that implored her to return, insistent and relentless. *Return to where?*

Just before dawn, like the thump of a bass note, Joey sensed the mother Jaguar's presence nearby. It was time to leave. She attempted to rise, but could not move. She tried again, but her muscles did not obey. Only her mind rose and, now detached from her body, ascended into space. From the stars she saw herself cradled into a natural impression in the rock, head back as if sleeping. *Where am I?* Though she had soared into the light before, she had never felt separated from her body. She told herself it was not fear she felt, only a vague discomfort.

Then she watched her flesh dissolve into a stream of light which drew her inside. In a blur of speed she traveled backward through her entire life until the day of the crash. She witnessed a young girl slumped over in a burning airplane. She was led right through the girl's chest and into her heart, which had stopped beating, to spare her the pain of burning up. But the child resisted. A moment later Fox appeared and she restarted her heart.

As Joey made the voyage back to the present she learned that her heart had stopped many times. With each incident, she had reveled in the bliss but felt impelled to return to earth for some purpose. Although upon awakening, she never had retained a memory of the journey. But with each occurrence her heart weakened.

From space, she floated back into her body and blinked her eyes open, totally awake. Her chest heaved and her breathing became shallow. She was also aware, once again, of voices from the past that called to her and for her. One of them called her "mother." A montage of still images sped through her head and, for an instant, she saw a blonde woman behind the wheel of a car, speeding toward the voice of a frightened child, a child who needed her. *Mother? Yes, I was a mother. I had children. I was to protect them, but I did not. Where are they?* She gazed at the fading stars and was rewarded with one clear image. Joey was on the bed in her room at the Paraiso staring at Fox on the carpet searching for evidence of Heinrich. She wanted to kiss the top of his head and tell him the danger was past and everything would be okay.

But now, it wasn't okay for Joey. Once again she tried to rise, but lacked the strength. *No, I'm not ready.* She smelled the mustiness of rotting vegetation and listened to the crickets harmonize with the wind. The moon seemed to disappear and, though dawn was imminent, the shadows closed in on her. *You've been arrogant. You never considered not having a choice. You may be part of God, but you are not God.* She could not understand it. It had always been agonizing to return, but now a sadness so profound gripped her like an anchor, pulled her under, and forced the breath from her lungs. *My life is over.* Tears streamed down her cheeks.

She sensed a shift in the wind, closed her eyes, and breathed. More oxygen made its way through her arteries, calming her a bit. She thought of Rita and Mike, and dared to believe that they were now safe. She relished their escape for a moment, picturing the two of them hugging each other in relief.

But the call from beyond was too strong and becoming more familiar. Joey heeded it, but she could not shake her sorrow and discontent. She wanted Fox's arms around her and prayed for one more chance, despite knowing that this time, when her heart stopped, it would not restart. Her eyes bore in on a dangling leaf high up in the canopy, a leaf that had spent the last six months converting sunlight into nourishment for its host, but its time was finished.

Joey's last beats were in progress. She willed a hundred more, and finally her body responded. On her stomach, she crawled into the cave between the two kittens. She rested her hands on their necks, closed her eyes, and let the light consume her.

The sonic boom of a howler monkey permeated the jungle. The breeze picked up strength and a crop of leaves desperate to hang onto life and separated from their branches, fluttered to earth and became part of it once again.

6:30 A.M. CST

Fox bolted to his feet totally disoriented, but unconsciously placed his hand over his heart. The echo had disappeared.

"No, Joey, no. Don't go. Please don't go," he cried aloud. But, he knew she was gone. He sank to his knees and covered his face with his hands. When he removed them, Joey's image shimmered on the horizon for an instant, as if she stood on the water. Her lips were parted in a knowing smile and her eyes were calm and they comforted him. Somehow her expression reminded him of his mother.

10: 40 A.M. CST

Alone, his short hair mussed in the mid-morning breeze, Fox leaned over the rail of his hotel room deck and stared out at the horizon. He lifted his head and scanned the heavens, sunbeams unhindered in a clear sky. But as he returned his gaze to the sea he wondered why it had turned gray, as if all the color had evaporated into the black depths.

He thought back to the blur of the morning. By 7:30 he had made it back to the Paraiso. He had only been in his room for fifteen minutes when his phone rang. It was Ramirez. Joey had been found at 6:40 by his men tracking Janelle. The cat had been picked up from Celeste's temporary enclosure and released at 5:30. A helicopter found a clearing to set down and Joey was with the medical examiner by 7:30. Ramirez himself identified her.

Fox hadn't known until that moment he still held out hope for her survival. More hope than he should have allowed, given the crushing pain that had forced the air from his lungs.

He spun around then leaned back. He looked at the remains of a room service tray he had shared with Mike who had eaten heartily while recounting his night with Joey and Rita. It had only been the two of them because Rita was at the hospital with Hector. Fox stared down at a piece of dry toast, intact except for one corner he had bitten off. It was all he could swallow.

It wasn't that he couldn't remember what Mike had said, but for the moment he was fixated on the image of Joey, swan-diving out of a helicopter into the sea, wearing only a smile. It was a smile Fox could not let go of. Mike had described it as an "I know something that you don't" smile. Fox knew that look from Joey. It was alluring, calming, and now haunting.

Their conversation had ended with Mike offering to gather up Joey's belongings. Fox shook his head. No, he would do it. He exhaled. Now was the time.

Fox strode back through the slider, kicked off his shoes, and, after hesitating, entered her adjoining unit on tiptoes as if he were trying not to wake her. He surveyed the sitting room and then the bedroom where he froze for a moment. Her presence was strong and the sweet scent of her lingered.

Joey's suitcase was empty. Her clothes rested in bamboo dresser drawers or hung in the closet. Undergarments from the dresser he tucked into the suitcase exactly as they lay in the drawer. Her uniform and a long sleeved T-shirt hung on wooden hangers. A pair of jeans draped over a hook. *How does she fold these things?* He inspected the shirt and jeans and searched for creases. He didn't find any and delicately handled the garments like biblical shrouds. He folded them until they looked like they had just come out of a package. When he was finished, he placed them in her luggage, but the order didn't seem proper. *Would she put jeans on top of underwear?* He didn't know why, but he wanted to make it perfect. After the fourth try he gave up and let it be.

The fifteen handwritten pages she had left for him to read the day before were still on the nightstand. He had read only two before she had entered the room. He picked them up and held them in front of him. There was so much more he wanted from her, yet he could barely look at them, let alone read. Nevertheless, he placed them in his own tote.

With all her belongings finally assembled and ready, he retreated to his bedroom. But sleep was elusive. He was quite surprised when he awoke in her bed.

11 A.M. CST

Rita's eyes swept over the hospital room where Hector rested. He remained unconscious, his hair tousled and yet somehow perfect. She had been with him for an hour. Tubes to feed and monitor tethered him to his bed. The single room was bright with natural light from a large window overlooking an intricate knot garden. Cool air drifted downward from the ceiling vent and Rita wondered if it were somehow scented, for it smelled fresh. She was surprised and grateful the newly opened hospital, perched on a bluff south of Quintana City, was so modern and well equipped. The bright colors and muted accents created an atmosphere of healing. She scanned the blinking lights and instruments. Hector's pulse and heart rate remained steady. *Will my heart ever slow down?*

The doctor had told her that Hector was going to recover and she was relieved, but couldn't escape the feeling that she was about to explode. She rose and went into the small bathroom and splashed cold water on her face. Her insides felt shaken. She gazed into the mirror and watched her mouth start to move. "You have to speak. You must," she said aloud.

She settled into her chair at Hector's side and once again took his hand in hers. "I have to talk about what happened and what will happen. If I don't, I'll explode So, here it comes. One thing I know is that I will never be the same." Rita hesitated, and swallowed hard. "There was no expectation implied or stated from Joey, only one directive. To live. That's all Joey wants from me, so that is what she will receive. I will live with passion. I will recognize my fears, but not bow to them. I will strive for pure thoughts and bold actions." Her breath caught and she brushed a tear from her eye. "And for every day I live, at the end of it I will thank God and Joey Sabatini."

Rita reached for a tissue from the Kleenex box and blew her nose. Hector's eyelids twitched a millimeter. His face looked serene as if he were enjoying a pleasant dream, and she silently swore that more color had seeped into his cheeks. She picked up his hand again. "I have spoken with your grandmother. She is very much shaken, but she and the children will arrive from Los Angeles at about the time I leave. But, I will be back within a week with my son. I'm taking a leave from Consolidated. Emile will find a place for me and my boy close to yours for us to spend the nights.

During the days, I will help you heal and help your grandmother with all the children." She squeezed his hand a little tighter. "When you are well, we will decide our future. I have set no limitations as to what or where that future lies. But, no matter what, I will be here until you are totally recovered."

Rita stood and went to the window. She watched two green birds take flight and then soar until they were mere specks against the blue sky. She forced herself to take three deep breaths. She exhaled, stretched her arms over her head, then sat back in her chair. "It feels much better to talk, so I'll start at the beginning, the very beginning...."

12:05 P.M. CST

From under the porte cochère, Mike observed an almost inert Fox until the black limo pulled up to them. Fox appeared almost translucent, as if half the molecules that made up his body were missing. In conversation earlier that morning, Fox had barely spoken and when he did it was in monosyllables. Mike had known him for nearly ten years and not only liked him, but greatly admired him. His wit and guile were legendary, but to Mike, that was exaggerated. To him, Fox was the poster child for proper choices and was always willing to help anyone. And now he wished *he* could be the one to help. But he sensed, right now, doing nothing was the right thing to do.

Mike breathed in the salt air and savored its scent, but noted his lack of tears and sadness. He was embarrassed at how much he had eaten earlier while Fox ate nothing. But Mike could not stop himself. His experience and training had told him that he would shed plenty of tears later. For now, although his body ached and his head hurt, he had never felt so *alive*. Joey had given him a gift and he would accept it. He had used focus and discipline to become a martial artist of exceptional skill, but that discipline had not carried over to other parts of his life. He knew he was guilty of demanding too much instant gratification, racking up too much debt, and partying like he was still in his twenties. But, from the time José had picked them up some fifty hours earlier he had reviewed his behavior. He had done the right things and acted with courage and conviction. There was no reason he couldn't, and shouldn't, continue. Next week, he would return to Quintana with Richie and they would discuss their future with Ramirez.

Mike heard his name called and turned to see a diminutive man in a black suit and red tie hop out of the driver's seat of the limo. He practically jumped onto Mike to hug him. Mike, sporting a black eye and bruises up and down his bare arms, turned to Fox. "Allow me to introduce you to José. A couple of days ago he pulled a gun on me. Now, he's an old friend."

Fox took a step forward. "I'm Fox."

José pumped Fox's hand with both of his. "It is a great honor to meet you. Please," he said, opening the rear door. Fox hesitated for a moment, and scanned the sea, before he climbed in.

They followed the army escort truck up the twisting road, the same road that Mike had travelled nineteen hours before with Rita, Joey, and José. Mike reflected upon how everything seemed so different. They passed the small lake where José had parked the SUV—the gleaming water bright blue instead of inky black. Next they drove by the spot on the road where they had neutralized the lookout. The flora was lush, but not nearly as dense as Mike remembered. Finally, they drove toward the small pullout next to the road that had seemed immense during the night, abuzz with vehicles, harsh lamps, and a squad of soldiers. José stopped the limo.

"It was right there," said Mike, his voice barely louder than the hum of the limo's air conditioning. "I saw it all through the window of Soriano's Hummer. He yelled at Joey, then threatened and slapped her. She stood tall and stared him down like he was a schoolyard bully." Mike took a deep breath. "I didn't see an ounce of fear in her. And when the general turned away *he* looked frightened."

Fox looked at him and nodded, listening.

Mike continued. "It was the same thing when she challenged Rondo. But now, as I play it back in my mind, her face is always glowing. I'm still here because of her—on two counts." He shook his head. "It boggles my mind."

José swung the limo back onto the main road. There was a long silence in the car.

"Thanks for calling the crew desk and arranging the deadhead tickets," said Fox, in a dull voice.

"Sure. Did you get the other seat?" asked Mike

Fox nodded. "I got it."

"Buying a last-minute first class seat had to lighten your wallet."

"It did, but right now, twelve hundred dollars seems like a bargain."

"I'm glad you got what you wanted. By the way, Ramirez called a few minutes ago, just before I left my room. Esmerelda addressed the country. It went well. He said the airport will be a mob scene. Lots of media. He's arranged for us to drive past it all, straight to the plane. Unless you *want* to talk to them."

Fox frowned in surprise. "Media for us? *Can* we talk to them?"

"I think so. What happened has nothing to do with NTSB."

Fox shook his head. "Not me. I've said enough for a lifetime."

They drove on in silence, each lost in thought. Finally Mike asked, "Did you break it to Joey's folks?"

Fox nodded, then rubbed his forehead and closed his eyes.

"I personally know the hell of hearing someone close has died, but it had to be tough for you to tell her parents their only child was gone," said Mike.

"It was hard. They both knew who I was. They both knew that I was the reason she joined Consolidated. Her mother's name is Ashley. She totally lost it. Jeff, her father, didn't believe me at first. Then he got mad. He said he had warned her that reuniting with me was a bad idea. Then he apologized, profusely. Thanked me for giving her sixteen more years and allowing him to see her grow up. An hour later he called and said they were both flying to Seattle to meet the plane."

As they neared the airport they saw crowds of colorfully dressed people lining both sides of the drab road. Some were chanting U-S-A, some shouting their names. The limo slowed. José craned his head around for a moment to the backseat and made eye contact. "It would mean a lot to the people if you rolled down your windows so they can see you. You might even wave."

"Really?" asked Mike.

"Yes, really. Please? Señor Mike, look at the sign coming up ahead on the right."

Mike's window went down and he stuck his head out. What he saw dumbfounded him. On a 4-by-8-foot piece of cardboard was a cartoon drawing of Mike with his fist, the size of a bowling ball, crushing the general's face.

"Jesus," said Mike.

José chuckled. "See, you are already legends. You knocked out the Butcher and Rita slew the Mighty Midgely."

Fox had his finger on the window button but removed it. He found José's narrowed eyes in the rearview mirror. "I'm sorry," said Fox. "I mean no disrespect. I just can't."

José's expression softened. "It is okay. For you, it is a sad day. But, for us, the people, it is the happiest day in years. All civil liberties have been restored. It means we can walk the streets without fear. When you are ready, come back. No one will forget how you risked your life for us."

Mike raised a tentative hand and the crowd applauded as they rolled past.

• • •

The introductions with the Los Angeles crew working the flight to Seattle were solemn and short, the four women flight attendants teary-eyed. When Rita stepped onto the aircraft and embraced Fox, the finality of it all rolled over him like a tsunami. A moment later he took strength from Rita. Her makeup was smeared and skin puffy, but her brown eyes blazed with a feral ferocity. She straightened up, lowered her shoulders, and pushed out her chest.

"Joey told me to survive," Rita told him. "She told me to *live*, and that's what I intend to do. To the max."

The general boarding began and they took their seats. Rita in 3A, and Mike next to her on the aisle in 3B. Fox fingered the two boarding stubs in his hand. 3C and 3D. He wasn't exactly sure why he purchased 3D, perhaps because it just didn't seem right for Joey to merely ride in the cargo hold. Her body may be in there, but he pictured her sitting next to him.

Ramirez entered the jet bridge wheezing and limping, eyes squinting in the dim light. With a downcast head Celeste plodded behind him as if she were tied to him with a rope. His euphoria had been tempered by Joey's death and Celeste's sacrifice; yet as he sifted through it all, the picture took on a sharper focus.

At the Heritage House, when he had sent out the alarm and instructions regarding Heinrich's breech of the Forbidden Zone, he had not contacted Celeste, believing it was too much to put on her so soon. But after he delivered the iPod full of evidence to Attorney General Fuqua, and the events of the night continued to unfold, the idea trickled back into his mind. Upon further examination, he had told himself, it all adds up: Revelstorm was attempting to lure Heinrich to him. Janelle, who Heinrich had vowed to kill, was sequestered at Celeste's cottage. Fox and Celeste were connected. Heinrich *had* to be eliminated. There was a decent chance they would all intersect at the cottage sometime before dawn. Celeste might have the opportunity to eliminate Heinrich before he or the other two confidants could get to him. Ramirez sent the code to Celeste at 2:30 a.m.

As Ramirez hobbled toward the brighter light inside the aircraft he asked himself a simple question: *Was the cost of the new government acceptable, including the death of an innocent woman? Yes, but onlybecause I know, I too, was willing to make the ultimate sacrifice. And when faced with death, I never considered backing off, because* this *was the* time.

He glanced back at Celeste's stoic face. *Yes, it all added up, but you knew beforehand the consequence of her being the one to literally pull the trigger and to commit murder. Ultimately, that is why you sent her the code: to bring her fully into the family, to bind her to you and the ancestors, and to insure the preservation of the estate for as long as she lives.* Ramirez took a deep breath and held it, reeling with pain and holding on to it until he saw white, before finally expelling it. *I can live with it. And I will.*

There was no way for Ramirez to know that whatever bond Celeste and Fox had created with each other would be another casualty in his one-night revolution. She had told Ramirez that Fox would not even look at her while the authorities questioned them. But Fox had backed up her story of self-defense. She had also told Ramirez that she was certain Fox would never want to see her again. When he asked her to elaborate, she had shaken her head and said, "I took away the thing he wants the most. He trusted me. I betrayed that trust." Nevertheless, under the guise of meeting some important people, including Bill and Melinda Gates, he prevailed upon her to travel to Seattle with him.

Ramirez fingered his mustache. Celeste had passed the ultimate test, and was already paying a steep price. She would keep her silence and he would not interfere with her relationship with Fox. But at least he had fixed it so that they would both be breathing the same air for the next six hours. He shrugged his shoulders and allowed himself a small grin. Perhaps their close proximity would allow animal magnetism to do its work.

Ramirez gripped the edge of the door for support and stepped into the cabin. He turned left to first class while Celeste turned right into economy. He shook Fox and Mike's hands, then presented a handwritten note to Rita from the new president. While Rita opened it, Ramirez whispered to Fox that Celeste was sitting on the aisle at row thirteen.

Fox barely acknowledged him with an almost imperceptible nod.

Rita read the note and passed it to Mike, who passed it across the aisle to Fox.

Dear Rita, Mike, and Fox, I cannot express my sorrow over the loss of your brave flying partner. Nor can I ever adequately express the depth of my gratitude and the gratitude of the entire country for what you all accomplished. But, I can promise you that Joey Sabatini will live on in the hearts of our countrymen and she will never, ever be forgotten, nor will you. With gratitude and sincerity, Esmerelda Castile, President of Quintana.

As Fox finished reading, he sensed a presence leaning over him. He looked up and saw a vaguely familiar face and a flight officer badge dangling from a shirt pocket.

The man stuck out his hand. "Harry Bristol. I think we've flown together. Do you mind if I slip in there? I've been trying to get out of here for two days. The cockpit is full," he said, inching his way in toward the open window seat.

"Harry, I'm really sorry, but no."

"But it's the only seat."

"I'm—"

Mike tapped Harry on the shoulder. Harry turned and followed Mike forward to the galley. A minute later Harry returned and stuck out his hand again. "I'm the one who's sorry. I didn't know it was yours. I didn't know anything. Best of luck."

"Thanks for understanding," replied Fox, making eye contact.

Bristol left and Fox nodded his thanks to Mike. Then he said, "Joey was a shooting star in my life, a brilliant effervescence, and she's gone." Fox rubbed his brow. "It's like being in a dark place, but one full of promise, maybe a sort of treasure room. A light goes on for a split second. You see things but you can't quite make them out, yet you know it's good, and important. The light will never go on again."

The door to the 757 closed and, after the safety video ended, Mike reached into his tote bag and with gentle deliberation eased out a spiral notebook. He turned to Fox and held it up. "Joey said I was to give this to you if she didn't make it. At a time I deemed appropriate." He turned his palms upward. "I don't know if this is the appropriate time or not, but maybe somehow these pages might provide some illumination and comfort."

Fox set the notebook on this lap, unopened. He listened to the engines whine and let his body sink back into the seat as the jet hurtled down the runway and shot into the air. He took a deep breath, exhaled, and began to read.

Dear Fox,

You're only reading this because I am no longer with you, at least not in the flesh. As I write, so does Rita. Mike continues to scan the bar area. While part of me is totally calm, another part is disjointed and scatterbrained. I have never considered myself any kind of prognosticator or seer, yet I am being bombarded with certain visions—not literal visions, more like strong feelings that I cannot let go of. I'm not sure how to say what I want to say but, through this gibberish scrawl, I hope it somehow comes through.

Fox stopped for a moment. The irony of the word "scrawl" tripped him. Though she had crossed out words and entire sentences, the shape of the letters were beautifully drawn. He traced a graceful line with one finger, then continued to read as if he could pull her calm essence off the page and absorb it.

I believe two things: With my mind, I stopped Heinrich from killing us and I can stop my heart any time I want to. And yes, this morning in my room at Ramirez's compound, I came close to letting myself expire as I reveled in the bliss. But I tell you this: I have no death wish. In fact, my desire to live has never been stronger. That is first and foremost.

Second, is the notion...no, more like the certainty, that, above all else, Rita must survive, and if necessary I must ensure it. Why? I can't say. Maybe it's the maternal instinct that's been buried deep within me suddenly rising forth. She is the mother of a son who needs her. Perhaps it's no more than that. But I also have the crazy feeling that maybe this is what I'm supposed to do, why I'm here. Nutcase thinking, I know. I don't believe God is talking to me, sending me divine instructions or any of that. I'm trying to make this clear, while I'm confused, too.

The next paragraph was scratched out. Fox made out something about highs not possible without lows.

It's no use. I'll just say this; I believe our night is just beginning and we are facing great danger. Right or wrong, crazy or not crazy, I am committed to Mike and Rita, especially Rita. I will do whatever I believe necessary to ensure her survival.

Fox had to pause to wipe the teary blur from his eyes.

Next: I have certain advantages. I cannot be intimidated by the prospect of pain or death. But, at this moment, I am afraid of only one thing: that I will never feel your lips on mine again. And that is why I am writing to you. All these years, my life has been centered on the few seconds of divine bliss I felt in the slide the day you rescued me. I had been longing and aching to experience the immortality of it while still alive. And, because of you, I did. But now, I feel emotions that I can barely remember as a child. And I savor them. I can still feel your body pressed up against mine, your fingers on my neck, our legs intertwined. I curse the timing of Ramirez's arrival, that we didn't complete our journey. I didn't know I could experience such pleasure. Mind and body were fully connected. I watched it happen to Rita and Hector. Such deep emotion. I experienced it for the first and last time, with you.

This leads me to the final thing: Celeste. She is the other comet that keeps streaking through my mind's eye. It's crazy, but I can't ignore it. When I spoke with her on the plane I remember thinking that I had somehow seen right into her core. She exuded pure goodness even though she had been damaged by the loss of her husband (she told me that). It seemed her intellect was sky-high but her spirit was sweet and grounded. I have no idea what will become of your relationship, but you are connected. She will become precious to you.

We'll always be joined together, and I am grateful for our brief reunion, and our even briefer physical union. I came to you seeking the perfection I had felt as a child. Instead I found something even better: the human elixir. I think it's called love. It's only possible because we are imperfect. Now, I would gladly trade the bliss I've been chasing all these years, and finally found, for the exhilaration of love and the certainty of great pain when it ends. Though it was short, it was worth the price I have paid. Yours for eternity, Joey.

Gently, Fox began to shut the notebook as he focused on the last line. *Yours for eternity, Joey.* He closed his eyes. He did not sleep, but he allowed Celeste into his head. She appeared to him just as she had after he exited her enclave awaiting his verdict. These were the questioning eyes, trembling hands, and the stark vulnerability. The scene changed as he watched her pull the trigger for the second time. He saw the grim determination and the execution of it. Yet now there was something else, a sadness that radiated from her.

He shook the vision away and refocused on the notebook. Joey was reaching out to him, pulling him to her, bidding him to rise. His breath quickened. He leaned out into the aisle and looked to the rear of the plane. The beverage cart was moving forward to the front of the economy section. He rose and, feeling a touch lightheaded, staggered aft but managed to step behind the cart as it reached the open area between first class and economy.

Celeste sat on the aisle in 13C. Her blonde hair pushed behind her ears, hands folded in front of her, and eyes closed as if she were meditating. Fox placed his index finger on hers. Celeste opened her eyes a slit, then wide in surprise. "Would you care to take a walk?" he asked.

She nodded and rose, and followed him to the aft galley. He noticed the familiar jagged metal on the countertop and the foam insert that dangled from the ceiling panel. "Same airplane as the one that flew us down here," he remarked.

"It seems like so long ago, like eons have passed since then," said Celeste, in a soft voice.

Fox shivered for a moment, struck by the way Celeste looked—almost exactly as she appeared to him in his vision, once again open and vulnerable. "Well," said Fox, conjuring a half smile, "you're going to be stuck with me for a while longer—at least another twenty minutes until that cart makes it back here."

Celeste's face brightened. "Is that a promise?"

He gazed at her for a moment before he replied, allowing her aura to seep into his. "With a little prodding, I've thought about what happened in your studio and what didn't happen. I don't want or need to know any more than I already know. This is the way I'll think of it from now on: you shot Heinrich because you had to. It had nothing to do with me. I know what your arms say when they're wrapped around me. They say, 'You can trust me.' I do trust you, but I want to hear you say it out loud."

"You can trust me," she said, reaching for his hand.

"Can I trust you to tell me you care about me, until you don't?" He took her other hand in his.

"Yes."

"Can I trust you to tell me if it's not working for you?" he asked, pulling her gently to him.

"Yes."

"Now, I want to feel that trust."

He gathered her in and held her close. A minute later they let go of each other.

"Now what?" she asked.

"We wait," he said taking her hand again.

They stood holding hands until the cart returned to the galley, then wove their way back up the aisle. When Celeste reached her row, she touched his hand and began to sit down. Instead Fox gripped her fingers and with a light tug eased her into the first class cabin. He beckoned her into the window seat next to his.

Celeste cocked her head, waiting for an explanation.

"I thought I purchased this seat for Joey. She told me I was mistaken. It was for you all along."

THE END

Made in the USA
Charleston, SC
02 August 2013